Dancing with
Mao and Miguel

Dancing with Mao and Miguel

Kitty Kroger

DIVISION STREET BOOKS
LOS ANGELES

Division Street Books
Los Angeles, CA 90065
For information about permission to reproduce selections from this
book, email divisionstreetbooks@gmail.com.

Printed in the United States of America

Cover photo by the author.
Book design by Jack Lanning in collaboration with the author.
Visit the author's website at kittykroger.com.

ISBN 978-0-9849288-0-4
Library of Congress Control Number: 2012933038

This is a work of fiction. Any references to historical events; to real
people, living or dead; or to real locales are either the product of the
author's imagination or are used fictitiously. Any reference to actual
persons is entirely coincidental. Various aspects of the cities of Jersey
City and New York City have likewise been altered.

For Dad and Mom and Chuck and Jeremy
and
for the Occupy Movement
so they can see how it was for some of us
back then

Thanks to...

Thanks to the Pasadena II Writing Group for the many hours you spent critiquing my novel week after week. I'm so grateful!

Alyson Ross	Roger Scott
Paul Krehbiel	Stephanie Barshefski
Ray Elisondo	

Thanks also to the following individuals for their support and critiques:

Robert Felker	Christine Matchett
Carol Crouse	Jay Hadley
Kaarisa Karley	Peter Hodes
Joe Cutter	Rich Dawson
Francie Frías	

Thanks to my reading group:

Adele Wallace	Joan Kramer
Harriet Aronow	Joan Hoffman
Linda Facher	Nancy Berlin

Two other writing groups provided invaluable support:

Pasadena Fiction Writers Salon
Barnes & Noble Writers Circle

If I can't dance I don't want to be
a part of your revolution.

EMMA GOLDMAN

PART 1

1. Jenny

BECAUSE I SUSPECT THAT MY CO-WORKER Juan at the next furnace is an informant, I wait until he turns his back, then extract a stack of leaflets from between the pages of the *Daily News*, which I always bring in with me to work. I slide the leaflets underneath my blue work shirt where they nestle snugly against my ribs over my thermal underwear.

Heading down the shed for my 2 a.m. break, I shiver from the icy gusts that shoot through the open ends of the long building. The chill seeps into the marrow of my bones and holds fast there, like a visitor who's outworn her welcome and shows no sign of leaving.

I'm working in a copper refinery in Central New Jersey on the graveyard shift. Perfect name for it. Buried alive.

Solitary figures in silver asbestos jackets huddle next to far-flung furnaces that glow like tiny havens in a frigid, post-nuclear wasteland. On the way to the break room I hand out leaflets to a few trusted co-workers, urging them to attend a meeting next week at a local bar: *we're organizing a caucus to run in the union election, to oppose the incumbents, who are selling us down the river.*

As I enter the break room, at first I notice nothing different. The clock on the wall behind the cracked plastic tells me there are *only* five-and-a-half more hours to go. Common wisdom in the plant: ignore the clock.

Harsh fluorescent lights illuminate the dingy space. A heater in the corner sputters, straining to deliver each wisp of lukewarm air. The radio on the cigarette machine plays John Lennon's latest: "Whatever Gets You Through the Night." Mm-hmm.

Then I see him—a worker I've never seen before—sitting at a table staring into his coffee. The first thing I notice is his skin. A dark shade of brown. He appears about my age—in his late twenties or early thirties. Like most workers he's probably an immigrant from the Caribbean, but he could be Afro-American.

Seeing a new man or woman in the break room always animates me. A fresh worker to scope out. Will he or she turn out to be *advanced,* a person who grasps intuitively that bosses and workers have nothing in common? Discovering an advanced worker is like winning the lottery. Or will he be a *middle worker,* satisfied to have a union job that "pays a decent wage." He doesn't look as if he'll be *backwards*—those are the racist workers, anti-communists, sometimes in league with the bosses, sometimes anti-union.

Unlike most men I run across in the plant, something about this one sends a thrill through me, a frisson of apprehension and anticipation, an impulse to flee offset by a curiosity that nails me to the spot.

What will unfold—*or unravel?*

The man glances up from his musing. I pretend not to notice him and make my way to the row of dented machines, scrutinizing them even though they are as familiar as *The Feminine Mystique* and *The Autobiography of Malcolm X,* books that I cut my radical teeth on. The machines offer sodas, Cheez-Its, Oreo cookies. Black water masquerading as coffee. Although I'm wide awake now, just a moment ago my heavy eyelids craved caffeine so I slip a quarter into the slot and watch liquid drizzle into a paper cup. Removing my asbestos gloves, I press the cream and sugar button a few times with the butt of my hand, hoping to camouflage the taste.

"*El café está mal.*" The man holds aloft his paper cup and smiles, his teeth flashing. The coffee stinks. His voice is deep and measured. Masculine.

I drop my helmet on the table with a clunk and slide onto a wooden bench across from him. Eye to eye and so close—that's scary, but it would seem awkward—even rude—to sit at another table in this small and otherwise deserted break room. I drop my eyes and gain time by studying the etchings in the surface of the Formica table. Pornographic slogans in English and Spanish. Crude stick figures. Remnants of the not-so-distant days when the plant was an all-male domain, before Title VII of the Civil Rights Act kicked in. The graffiti irritated me when I first started working here, but now I scarcely notice. Except at times like this.

"*Ya sé. Pero estoy enganchada,*" I say. Probably a fractured way to say, "I'm hooked on the caffeine."

"*Me llamo Miguel,*" he says. It's an accent I recognize as Dominican. And I recognize the name too.

"¿Miguel Cimarrón? *El amigo de Felicia?*" He nods.

Felicia, my downstairs neighbor and best friend, who works here at Dynamic Metals on the afternoon shift, has mentioned Miguel. "He was in the civil war in my country," Felicia said. "He's a revolutionary, Yenny, but"—she rolled her eyes—"he's trouble with a...how do you say? With a capital T."

"Trouble? What do you mean?" I asked.

Felicia shook her head and said, "Woman problems."

"With you, Felicia?"

She hesitated—I'm sure of it—before responding. "*¡Pero que no!* Of course not!" Then she added, with a little laugh, "He's living with someone but if you ever see him at work, run the other way." Fat chance of that! As soon as she let slip that he was a revolutionary, I was captivated.

Miguel extends both hands across the table, capturing my chilled fingers in his warm palms, holding them too long. "*Y tú eres* Yenny. Yenny *Manzana.* Yenny Apple. *Mucho gusto!*" Glad to meet you!

"Igualmente," I say. Same here. I pull my hands away. Why, after all these years, am I so uneasy with physical contact from men? An uncomfortable pause ensues; quickly I break it. "So. What are you doing in this department? Felicia said you worked in the smelter." I gesture in the direction of the department across the yard. I've switched to English now, curious to know how much he understands.

"They just transfer me for tonight over here to Tough Peach," he answers in English. Tough Pitch. That quirky name. It took me a while to find out that it refers to how efficiently the copper conducts electricity.

Miguel pulls out a pack of Marlboros and extends it.

"Cigarrillo?"

"Thanks. I don't smoke. Not anymore."

"You do before?"

"I made a bet with a guy here to see which of us could quit first."

One very thick black eyebrow slowly rises. "Are you gambler then, Yenny?"

The way he says it makes my cheeks feel warm on the inside. "Do you like working in the smelter?" I ask. "Pretty rough, isn't it? I mean, it's hot over there. And dangerous. I've heard they have more accidents and—"

He holds up his hand. "What I like," he says, teasing out each word, "is people who take *riesgos.*" Risks. He adds, *"Riesgos* make life exciting, you no believe?" I smile uneasily; Felicia's warning is starting to make sense.

Taking risks is not one of my strong suits, although some folks would point out that my political work requires sneaking in leaflets, challenging union bureaucrats, making split decisions about whom to trust. And over the years I've met these challenges. But as for my personal life, it's dull dull dull! And I can't seem to break out of that. Right this moment I'd love to appear as gritty and seasoned as he must be.

He lights a Marlboro and exhales, leans back against the wall, stretches his legs out on the bench. A curve dances about his soft full lips. His dimples fascinate me, but I lower my eyes and busy myself disengaging the waxed paper from my ham sandwich. When I steal another glance at him, *he's still watching me.*

"What Felicia tell you about me?" he asks, cocking his head.

"That…that you were involved in the uprising in the Dominican Republic." *He fought in the streets, Yenny!*

"How long you work here?" he asks.

"Almost three months." I take a bite and force myself to chew.

"You like?"

"I guess." That's a question that's been getting harder to answer—even to myself. What skepticism, what ugly doubts, have wormed their way into my consciousness lately. "I mean, it's hard, heavy, dirty, but…."

"But the money is good."

"It's not *that*!" He looks puzzled. I lower my voice. "It's not that."

"Of course not. You no work here just for the money, right, Yenny?"

Another difficult question that's usually edged with hostility: *you're a subversive, aren't you?* But his face displays only curiosity.

"No, I'm not working here just for the money."

"Then why? Why you work here?"

Voices intrude in my thoughts: *what's a nice, middle-class girl like you doing in a hellhole like this? You've worked in one plant after another for four whole years? Why haven't you recruited more workers? What can you possibly hope to accomplish?*

"Felicia must have told you about our collective," I say.

"A little." There's something about the way he listens so closely, as if what I say matters. No one—except maybe for Charlie and Felicia—pays attention to me like that.

I could tell him things. That our organization has the goal of remolding unions into fighting bodies again like in the Thirties and Forties, when rank-and-file workers occupied auto plants in Flint, Michigan, when longshoremen shut down the West Coast, when rubber workers struck in Akron. How often I've wondered what it would be like to live back then, when the working class was militant, when workers had pride and solidarity. I could tell him that we believe in the workers' ability to make revolution once they become aware of their history and their power. I could quote Mao: "Learn from the masses, and then teach them."

But I won't tell him all that. Not here, anyway, in this grimy break room with the scratchy heater and the poor excuse for coffee. Not now, when my break is almost over.

"You no have to work in a place like this. You are educate, *verdad?* Why you do it?"

Haven't I asked myself that a million times lately?

"I believe in the political work." I could stop here; that summarizes it. But I feel the passion welling up in me. Is it his presence? So I add, "And I like the feeling that I'm part of something beyond myself."

I peer at him suspiciously. If I see even a glimmer of ridicule, even a slight crinkle around the eyes, hear even a polite cough, I'll cut this off faster than you can say *Mao Tse-tung.* But he's waiting, studying me, as silent as a cauldron of copper. I continue. "I'm part of the struggle of workers all over the world for a better life."

Do I still believe that?

The heater in the corner hisses. Miguel's coffee sits untouched, growing cold. Unlike his eyes, which glow like embers; unlike my face, which burns.

"Does that sound sappy?" I ask.

As if in a trance he doesn't reply at first. Then he says, "Soppy?"

"Sentimental." I say it in English, but it's the same word in Spanish.

He shakes his head. "No. No. It no sound *sentimental.*" He says the word in Spanish, with the accent on the last syllable.

What's come over me? I never talk this way to strangers. It's not only silly, it's reckless. But, no! That's paranoia. How could he be an agent? He's Felicia's friend; he's a revolutionary.

I stand and peer through the break room's pitted plastic window that faces into the plant. Seeing no one, I extract the leaflets, warm from the heat of my body, and set them on the coffee machine. I peel off the top one. "We're trying to get a progressive slate elected to the union," I say, relieved to slip back into my brisk, efficient manner, as if pulling on an old sweater.

Yes, I've recovered my senses. A vision flashes through my mind of recruiting Miguel. I can hear the accolades. Even Cindy, the cell leader, who scarcely approves of me, will finally be proud. *Way to go, Jenny! An advanced worker!*

Advanced. I think back with a touch of nostalgia to the days before I was political when I would meet new folks and think: *he's a little weird,* or *she's nice.* But now it's always: *are they advanced, middle, or backwards?*

"Maybe you'd like to attend the next meeting?" I ask Miguel. I hand him a leaflet.

He looks past the leaflet directly at me, and I stand with my arm awkwardly extended. "We go together?" he asks.

I pull my hand in and sit back down. I expected the usual *I'll try* or even the *Sure, I'll be there* that I get from folks who never show up.

Warning bells again. I mustn't forget: he lives with someone. Felicia told me so. It's against my moral code to take up with another woman's boyfriend. Before I even heard of the collective, I was crystal clear about *that*; after all, I don't come out of the women's movement for nothing.

But Felicia also said, *Maybe they're going to break up. All the time they fight.*

Through the window I see Juan Toledo, my co-worker, approaching with another man. I stand up and knock over my half-full cup of coffee, which sloshes onto the table top. Miguel mops it up with a handful of napkins. I thrust the leaflet into my pocket.

Juan bursts through the door, stomping his feet as if ridding them of snow. The other man, with grease-smeared coveralls and wrenches poking from the pockets of his coveralls, follows Juan and leers at me. Juan casts a suspicious glance at Miguel, then at me, and smirks as if to say, *What have you been up to with this guy?* Then his eyes land on the leaflets on top of the coffee machine. Now another look creeps into his eyes, but all he says is, "Are you planning on staying here all night?"

I sigh. Whenever I work with Juan Toledo, the graveyard shift drags more than usual. His every pore oozes disapproval. He's accused me of things: *I don't pull my weight.* Definitely not true! *I take too long at breaks.* Well, maybe, once in a while, but for good reason: I'm the shop steward. *I trash the union.* Wrong again! It's not the union that I loathe but the current leadership. They drop grievances that are winnable—like when a guy was fired last month for talking back to a foreman who'd told him to go to hell. The union officers sit in the cushy union hall while we workers toil in the icy New Jersey cold or the blazing New Jersey heat. In the last contract they surrendered a day of our vacation time—for no good reason! And they root out communists and other radicals who do the work *they* should be doing.

I crumple my empty paper cup and jam it into the overflowing trash can, along with the remainder of my sandwich; the garbage will probably attract rats by night's end. I snatch up my helmet and gloves from the table. Miguel hastily assembles his gear and follows me from the break room. Just outside, he places his hand on my jacket sleeve and leans in so close it makes me dizzy. "Yenny, you make me a favor?" he says, almost in a whisper.

The urgent quality of his voice draws me toward him like a moth to light. We must look like co-conspirators. "What is it?" I whisper back.

"Tomorrow at the station in Jersey City you pick me up?" When I hesitate, he adds, "My car is in the shop, and the *guagua* take forever. Tonight a friend give me a ride." *Guagua.* Slang for *bus* in the Dominican Republic, Felicia told me. How can I deny that simple request, a favor for a fellow worker in need? Anyone would say yes. And I can use the opportunity to find out about his role in the rebellion in Santo Domingo in 1965.

I find myself nodding. Before he takes off in the other direction, he reaches for my hand and squeezes it three times. Like a code. But what does it mean? All the way back to my station I feel the imprint of his hand. I scan the length of the shed. How different the workplace seems a mere 20 minutes later. The chill and tedium have become a distant memory. What looked like a wasteland now looks like a vast heaven of glowing stars.

I lower the shield on my hard hat and fling a shovelful of coal into the furnace. Sparks fly at me and flames warm my face through the mesh screen. I secure the furnace door, force a lever in place with my shovel, and turn to heat up the backs of my legs. At another furnace I see liquid copper flowing like honey out of a spigot and into cement molds, settling in abstract swirls before it cools and hardens.

Such beauty in the midst of bleakness.

2. Jenny
OCTOBER 1974

I ARRIVE HOME FROM WORK AT DAWN and eat breakfast at Felicia's, who lives downstairs from me. It's my job to bring lox or pan dulce (sweet rolls) that I pick up on the way home from work, or even Kahlua, when I'm in a celebratory mood. Which isn't often these days, but this morning is different so I stop off at my apartment to grab the half-full bottle of Kahlua from the kitchen shelf.

Felicia cooks with such panache and joy that I feel no guilt letting her do it. Today I avoid mentioning Miguel. It feels disloyal, but something constrains me. Or maybe I want to get Charlie's reaction first; I'll be seeing him in a few hours.

After leaving Felicia's, I flip on the TV and watch President Ford attempting to justify to Congress why he's pardoned Tricky Dick Nixon. I finally fall asleep on my too soft sofa-bed mattress and dream of fighting on the barricades—do barricades still exist?—next to a revolutionary who looks just like Miguel. In the dream I'm wearing a green Mao cap with a red star on the brim, and my long curly hair waves and my silky white blouse billows in the wind. I wake up four hours later, and remind myself that my hair is as straight as the line between points A and B, and way too short to blow in the wind.

But at least I didn't dream about Duncan again.

It's almost mid-afternoon. I throw a load of t-shirts and jeans into the little washing machine next to my stove. While the clothes are churning, I steep a cup of tea, position my Olivetti on the kitchen table, and whip up a leaflet about the bus drivers' strike, which I painstakingly translate into Spanish, my bilingual dictionary open in front of me. Later I take clothes out of the washer, open

12

the kitchen window, perch on the sill, and lean out into the bitter wind. A clothesline stretches across the courtyard and I crank it as I pin up the damp garments. The shirts form silhouettes against the gray backdrop of the sky. I mix a meatloaf. While it's baking I take notes on John Gerassi's *The Great Fear in Latin America,* which will be discussed at the next collective meeting. When the timer buzzes, I scoop the meatloaf into Tupperware containers for "lunches."

It's time to go so I hastily zip the freshly typed leaflet into a plastic folder, bundle myself up, and leave the apartment. The pasty sun has dropped low in the sky by now; the air has acquired a raw chill. I scurry down Jersey Avenue to Grove Street, then turn left to the printer's.

Emerging with a backpack of yellow leaflets, I hotfoot it down Grove Street, carefully sidestepping patches of ice. The city has shoveled the snow to the edges of the sidewalk, where it lies in mounds the color of granite. I pass Mac's Bakery; Mac waves at me from behind the counter and flashes a toothy grin. I pass the shoemaker's, the post office, and Dotty's Café. People bustle along on their way home from work, in a hurry to beat the descending darkness and night chill. I keep an eye out for Charlie.

When I finally arrive at the Grove Street PATH station at five after five, there he is! I have a moment to observe him before he sees me. It's hard to explain what Charlie means to me. Along with Bonnie, he initiated me into the ways of the collective. As a friend I can talk to him about almost anything.

He's huddled on a bench, his parka pulled tightly around his body, his wool stocking cap slightly askew. His face glows with the golden hues of the bleached sunset. I hug him through his parka—it's like hugging a pillow.

"Sorry I'm late," I say, my rapid breaths forming puffs against the sky.

"So what else is new?" The skin around his gray-blue eyes crinkles.

I explain even though I know he's kidding that I had to wait in line at the printer's. His gloved hands reach out for a stack of leaflets; he scans them. "Oh, they turned out beautiful," he says, and then he adds, "Like you, babe!" and brushes the tip of my nose with his glove.

"You're looking fab yourself," I say, grinning. We've been leafleting twice a month for—how long has it been? Over two years?

As usual he challenges me. "Let's see who can lose these the fastest. Get ready...get set...."

"You're on," I say, as I always do. But this time I've tricked him—handed him more than his share. It's only fair. More people take leaflets from Charlie than from me. Is it his boyish innocence, his stubbly face, the rakish tilt of his cap? What is it that draws *me* to him?

Some people have a certain charisma, I think. For a moment I resent him, but that soon passes. It's hard to hold anything against Charlie.

"Brrr. Hot chocolate afterward?" he asks.

"What a novel idea," I say, loving him again, laughing because he doesn't have to ask. It's our routine, our treat for work well done. A hot chocolate or coffee in winter, a milkshake or iced tea in summer, at Dotty's Café.

As usual we flank the double doors to the station. Charlie extends a leaflet to a man in a hooded windbreaker. "Have you heard about the bus drivers' strike?"

The man grunts, waves his arm, and moves on, head bent against the wind. A man wearing a cap with earflaps asks, "What's this all about?"

Charlie hands him a leaflet. "The bus drivers are on strike, and we're having a meeting Monday night to figure out how the community can support them."

"Like what?"

"Food drives, picket lines, rallies—things like that."

"Sure hope the strike don't last long," the man says, skimming the leaflet. "My brother-in-law's been giving me a ride to work these days." He rolls his eyes. "Believe me, that ain't no picnic." Charlie rolls his eyes too. His look says, *How awful for you.*

Sometimes I try to emulate that sympathetic look that Charlie gets. It must be fun when strangers confide in you. But I always revert back to my analytical ways: too rational, too in my head.

I'm impatient to tell Charlie about Miguel, but just then three boys exit the station; I hand them leaflets. "What grade you guys in?" I ask.

"Sixth," they chime eagerly, almost in unison.

"Do you know about the bus drivers' strike?"

"My uncle's a bus driver," says the boy with "The Exorcist" written across the front of his jacket. He looks at the leaflet. "What's this about?"

I refrain from suggesting he read it himself. I summarize the content.

The boy with braces on his teeth asks, "Can we help?" I furnish them with a hefty stack of leaflets and they race across the street to the supermarket, the gruesome image of a crazed Linda Blair on the back of the one boy's jacket. They thrust leaflets at people emerging with grocery bags. Charlie and I grin.

Engaging with the masses buoys my spirits. I relish the street life of Downtown Jersey City, its vitality and diversity. And being with Charlie sweetens everything.

A woman with a long woolen coat and a cane takes a leaflet. "Thank you, dearie," she says in a crackly voice. A Greek accent? I stretch out a leaflet to three Anglo men who sweep past and avert their eyes as if I were panhandling.

Someone in the collective has told me that out of every 40 leaflets distributed, one person will actually attend an event. That statistic has stayed with me. I study people's faces. Which one will it be? Often it's the one you least expect.

In addition to the one person that will show up, approximately another dozen will actually read the information on the leaflet. Thirteen out of 40 isn't so bad. If we just keep at it, we'll eventually build an organization, even a movement, although lately with increasing layoffs and plant closures, doubts keep dogging me.

The crowd ebbs. The sunset's refracted radiance through the clouds has faded to gray; twilight lingers a few more minutes. Charlie and I seize the opportunity to talk. Before I mention Miguel it will be wiser to make small talk. For once I pay attention to my intuition. "Any word yet from General Motors?" I ask.

"Nothing so far, but any day now. Meanwhile, I'll just keep grinding away at Pearson's." He chuckles. "Literally."

I chuckle too. Pearson Rivets is the small shop in Hoboken where Charlie operates a grinding machine. Three months ago he was laid off from a steel mill and is now applying for jobs in other *strategic* plants like auto or metal. Strategic for a revolution, that is, because of their size and the relatively high level of consciousness of workers there.

I finally bring myself to say it. "Guess who I met last night at work?"

"Beats me."

"A guy who actually participated in the rebellion in Santo Domingo in 1965."

A man spins around. "Santo Domingo? I am there. 1965!"

"*Andale!*" I say with excitement. Right on! I pass him a leaflet. He turns it over to the Spanish side. The man is tall, with dark skin and soulful eyes like Miguel's, which seem to penetrate mine as if the two of us were all alone at the station. What *is* it about Dominican men? I'll have to ask Felicia.

We talk for a moment in Spanish and he takes a generous handful of leaflets. As he dissolves into the crowd I follow him with my eyes.

"Go on," Charlie says. Is he frowning, or is it just the harsh station light in his eyes?

Still flushed from the encounter with the Dominican man, I give him a blank look. "Where was I?"

"This cat you met at work."

"Oh yeah, his name's Miguel. A friend of Felicia's." My voice quickens. "He transferred to my department last night."

"What kind of friend?"

16

"Not that kind of friend."

"What about him?"

The abrupt tone of Charlie's voice prompts me to subdue my exuberance and say calmly, as if commenting on the weather, "He seems *advanced.*"

"What's he doing in the U.S. if he's a revolutionary?" Charlie asks, and yes, there's a definite edge to his voice. "Why isn't he back home fighting Balaguer's regime, helping his people?"

His sharp tone annoys me. "How should I know?" I snap. "Maybe he had to flee. Did that ever occur to you?"

Three men reach for leaflets, and I pivot away from Charlie. The white guy says, "We're bus drivers."

"You're strikers?" I ask. Such encounters often occur when we're in the streets, yet they still take me by surprise.

Their laughter booms. The black guy says, "Well, we sure as hell ain't scabs."

The guy with the Puerto Rican accent adds, "*Gracias!* Right on! We'll be there for sure."

As they fade away, I think, *This* is why I show up here week after week! I turn back to Charlie. "Sorry," I say.

"Hey, I was just curious. Is something going on?"

My cheeks feel warm. "Not at *all.* He's living with someone," I say. "It's just exciting to meet an advanced worker." I can't wait to change the subject, even though I need to talk to someone about Miguel and I thought Charlie would understand. We've been close friends for a while now and supported each other through personal crises. The time that his kitten got run over—the black one with white paws that he'd rescued on the midnight shift just as some fellow workers—"drunk as skunks," he said—were about to toss it into the microwave oven. Or the time I had strep throat and he came over to my apartment and made chicken soup for me and read me poems by Pablo Neruda and played Nina Simone on my stereo. He'd wiped my face with a damp towel while I lay in bed underneath three blankets, alternately shivering and sweating.

Charlie attended two years of college at CUNY and then dropped out to work with the movement. Unlike me, he's a *red diaper baby*, which means that his parents were in the Communist Party. During McCarthyism his father was forced out of his job as a free-lance journalist because no newspaper would accept his copy. He worked at a series of blue-collar jobs. That was before the Party sold out and became *revisionist*, which means that it's no longer revolutionary as it used to be but wastes its time on reforms and electoral politics. Basically, the collective's position is that the Communist Party, despite its glorious past, is now like a left branch of the Democratic party.

Once I asked Charlie, "What's it like to be at odds with your parents? I mean, you both call yourselves communists. It must be weird."

"We can't talk about these things," he said. He looked down at the menu and asked rhetorically, "So what *do* we talk about?" He paused. "Nothing meaningful, that's for sure."

I reached across the table and placed my hand on his. "My parents won't talk to me about politics, either. They're Republicans."

There are dark things about myself, though, that I haven't divulged to Charlie or Felicia: that I've never had a long-term relationship, not once in my entire 28 years, that I fear intimacy and that I mistrust men. That I'm *broken*.

"Hello, anyone in there?" Charlie asks. He taps my forehead with his index finger. I realize I've been distributing leaflets like a robot. It's started to snow. Large flakes cling to Charlie's cap and gloves and nose. "I asked you if they're hiring at the refinery yet." The annoyance in his voice again surprises me.

"Not now," I say, "but it wouldn't hurt to put your application in anyway."

"I did. Months ago." He looks at me with resentment. "*Remember?*"

"Oh, yeah," I say. (But I don't.)

"Maybe I should withdraw my application; there's probably enough of you without me: Roger, Felicia, you, and now Miguel." He looks away. "I don't guess you need me."

My eyes widen. "Of course we need *you*, Charlie." What's eating him? He acts almost jealous. It's obvious that Charlie is way too young for me. 25 to my 28. As for Charlie, he must feel the same way since he kids me about being "the older woman in his life." As though the idea of anything between us is ridiculous. And he's never shown any of *that* kind of attraction toward me.

Has he?

I gaze briefly at Charlie, who's looking away from me. I need to thrust these thoughts aside or they'll jeopardize our friendship. I force a light, playful tone. "Hey, Charlie, it's still ten years before the revolution. I guess we'll need you."

"*Ten years?*" he says smiling, and I note with relief that he's himself again. "What a pessimist! I'll give you five-and-a-half, and not a day more." Although we're kidding, we know it's a serious question. The national board of the Anna Louise Strong League (the name of the collective) has presented the branches with documents arguing that conditions are ripening: the socialist revolution will most likely occur sometime within the decade if we recruit the proletariat (industrial workers) and build a strong party.

I'm relieved that Charlie has dropped the subject of Miguel. What is this thing I have for Miguel anyway? Am I still having schoolgirl crushes at age 28? And I keep forgetting there's another woman in his life; perhaps I should tape reminders to my refrigerator and my bathroom mirror: "DON'T EVEN THINK ABOUT IT!"

We duck under an overhang. A flurry of people bursts from the station into the cold, streetlights illuminating their faces. I hand out leaflets as fast as possible. My fingertips feel numb; I've cut the tips off the fingers of my gloves so I can separate leaflets.

Suddenly a fortyish man in work boots and coveralls materializes in front of me. He snatches up a leaflet and waves it in my face. Caught off-guard, I step back, then instantly regret appearing weak. "What's this?" he barks. "More of that commie shit?" Several passers-by turn to gawk at us. A woman grips her husband's arm as they hurry past, casting worried glances backwards. Mr. Coveralls crumples the leaflet and hurls it at my feet.

Such street incidents used to shock me, wound me, but I've gotten used to them. If anything, hostility adds spice to the leafleting. As Mao says, "All reactionaries are paper tigers." (If only I could be so blasé about *personal* rejections.)

"But surely you want to support the bus drivers?" I say sweetly.

Livid now, he shakes his fist at me. "They earn too much as it is!" he yells. "You know what they get in benefits?" As he turns away, he delivers the coup de grace: "That's why the city has no money to fix potholes."

Somewhat sheepishly I pick up the crushed leaflet and stuff it into a trash can. Bully for me; I just drove the man further into the enemy camp. This is another example of how I ignore my better judgment, my intuition, who someday may just slink away and throw herself in front of a car. I look sidelong at Charlie, who shrugs. "I like your spunk," he says.

That's Charlie for you.

We're almost out of leaflets. I hand one to a little girl with blond pigtails. She's clasping the hand of a man in a ski jacket. "Thank you very much," the little girl chirps, holding the leaflet away from her by its corner, as if uncertain what manner of species it is.

A plump, grandmotherly type with both hands full of grocery bags, says cheerily, "Just shove it in the bag, honey." I do, and then pass a leaflet to a young man with earphones attached to a transistor radio. A swarm of people suddenly swooshes from the station; my frozen fingers can't separate leaflets fast enough.

A bevy of high school girls emerges and flutters around Charlie like colorful birds. Their giggles tinkle in the crisp night air. They promise to take leaflets to their school and bring people to the meeting.

A three-quarter moon almost masked by a cloud emerges from between two high-rise apartment buildings. Charlie relinquishes his remaining leaflets to a group of workers with metal lunch pails and steel-toed boots, and he holds up empty hands. "I win." We head across the street to Dotty's Café. Charlie's tension seems to have melted. No matter how many problems we arrive with, leafleting usually cheers us up.

He flings his arm across my shoulders. The snow is coming down thicker now, and it will be another cold night at work, although not as cold as when there's no cloud cover and you can see all the way to Orion's Belt—see the whole Milky Way almost. On those nights whenever possible I sneak out of the shed at work to peer up at the sky. Such panoramas make me realize what I'm struggling for. It's more than just basic needs; it's for the opportunity to appreciate this beautiful Earth. "We want bread, but we want roses too," as the chant goes.

The thought of riding to work with Miguel in just a few short hours makes me tingle with anticipation. Perhaps he'll jolt me out of my funk.

Charlie's arm rests snugly on my shoulders. It feels comforting, even through the padding of our jackets. We push through the door into Dotty's, where warmth and the aroma of fresh coffee embrace us. Dionne Warwick's "I Say a Little Prayer" emerges from the jukebox.

"Are you going to the party Saturday night?" Charlie asks me as we look for a booth.

The party, at Cindy's. I'd forgotten. "Oh yeah, sure," I say.

But my thoughts have already turned back to Miguel.

3. Miguel

OCTOBER 1974

I TAKE THE A-TRAIN FROM EL BRONX to 33rd Street, where I pick up a dozen donuts. Then I wait at the PATH station for half an hour. I buy a *Diario* but soon give up trying to read it and just pace the station. What does it mean that she's agreed to give me a ride?

I haven't said anything to Angélica, the girl I live with, about Yenny. Angélica's jealous—and temperamental too.

It's precisely 10 p.m. and here she is! She pulls her Rambler to the curb and I get in. It's strange and exciting to sit next to this *gringa* with eyes as blue as the Ozama River under the midday sun. Felicia said she was political; is that why she's so serious? Not flirtatious like most of the Dominican and Puerto Rican *chicas* I know. She throws me slightly off my game. And yet…the day before, in the break room, there was something in her eyes. She wasn't exactly flirting but…what *was* it?

She looks at me, a brief smile—that gap-toothed grin that probably drives guys around the bend—and turns her glance back to the road. I offer her a donut. *Another storm blowing in,* she says. She asks what kind of car I drive.

But when she asks me about my country, that's when she really lights up. "Miguel, I'm curious about what it was like—the civil war," she says. "I mean, you must have been in high school then."

"How much you know about my country?" I answer after a brief hesitation.

"A little."

Being careful. It's become a habit. But it would be stupid to suspect her of spying or working for *la migra*. I relax. Hey, she's curious, that's all. I should be glad that someone shows interest in

22

that period. People today seem to have amnesia about the civil war. Only interested in their own narrow lives. Even *los Quisqueyanos* (Dominicans) themselves, rarely mention it. Sometimes I wonder, was it all a dream? Could we really have come so close to victory? It blows my mind to think about those days again after all these years of fighting to forget them.

"What you like to hear?"

"Not the facts," she tells me. "What I want to know is what happened to *you* during that time." In the dark her eyes burn like my cat Suerte's, back home in Santo Domingo. "Were you scared?"

"Is a long story," I say, hoping that will put an end to her questions. And to my relief she doesn't press me. But the gleam fades from her eyes. I put a hand on her shoulder; she reacts with a flinch. She's got me all confused. I remove my hand and say, "Maybe we get together sometime and I tell you about it."

"That's probably not a wise idea," she says right away, looking away from me and out the driver's side window. "I mean, your girlfriend and all...."

I frown. Felicia probably already spilled the *frijoles* about Angélica so I figure it's no use hiding it. Felicia and Yenny probably tell each other everything. That's how women are. Especially *Señorita Cotorra.* Miss Blabbermouth.

"Yeah, I live with someone."

She looks a little sad about that, I can see. A good sign; no reason to give up yet. I try again to get the conversation back on track. "What more you like beside the politic?" It's hard to tell in the dark, but I'm pretty sure she blushes at this. She seems so naive about flirting that this should be a cinch. "You like dance?"

There's a slight pause. "Yeah. But I'm not so good at it."

"I show you. You ever dance *merengue?*"

She shakes her head diagonally. Does she or doesn't she? "I'll make you a deal," she says. "You tell me about the Dominican civil war and then I'll have breakfast with you after work tomorrow morning and tell you about me."

23

Mierda (shit), this is tougher than I thought. I consider her offer. I try to recall that look that came over her face yesterday in the break room when she mentioned the civil war. Admiration? Awe? In the past I've noted the way some women get around revolutionary men. Revolution is an aphrodisiac for them. Perhaps it will be worth it to tell her just a little bit. But then again, how can I hope to explain it in my bare-bones English?

"Is a deal," I say, but I'll probably regret it. "Already you know about Trujillo and Juan Bosch?"

"I know about the dictatorship under Trujillo. *Brutal*."

"Sí. For over 30 years."

"And then he was assassinated?"

"'*Ajusticiamiento*'. We no call it assassination. We call it '*ajusticiamiento*.' You know this word?" But I know she doesn't. None of the *gringos* do.

"*A-jus-ti-ci-a-mien-to?*" She stumbles over the syllables.

"Sí. It mean 'bring to justice.'"

"That works!" She looks delighted. "It's like an *adjustment*, like bringing things back into *balance*." She seems to get off on words.

"But the people still get no break," I say. "The son of Trujillo, he take over after his dad is kill, and he continue torture people." I dig my fingers into my neck and shoulders; the muscles are clenching again. After all these years I'm about to unearth these monsters. But her enthusiasm goads me on.

"A couple years later, after the people elect Juan Bosch, things get better. *Much* more better. Democracy come and the unions are legal again. The *papá* of my best friend Nico get a big raise. The people, we go to bed at night with no *bam bam bam*"—I bang my fist on the dashboard three times—"on the door."

We're on the turnpike now. I continue. "But after only seven months Bosch is—how you say? Depose. In a *golpe de estado*."

"Coup d'etat," Yenny says. "Go on."

My story is going to impress her, I can see that. I feel myself growing hard in anticipation, but the thought of the rebellion fills my veins with the heebie-jeebies.

"Sí, a coup d'etat. *Presidente* Juan Bosch escape to Cuba. *El pueblo* demand his return. But not my father. He jump up and down so happy when Bosch go. But my father no count; he is policeman."

"And when the rebellion started, where were you then?"

Taillights on the turnpike begin to blur. I feel myself sucked like a guppy down a drain into the midst of the events of April 1965. I shiver. I struggle back up into the present.

She looks at me. "Go on," she prompts, her voice sounding breathless. The way it might sound in bed?

Reluctantly, I give in. "It start one afternoon after school we go to the house of Nico."

"Your best friend."

"Sí. In reality we are four best friends: me, Nico, Marco, and Julio. We call ourselves Los Muchachos (The Boys). We are *inseparables.*"

"Always together."

"Sí. For a few months we—how you say—*smell* something in the air. But also we have a contact in the army who tell us things."

"Who?"

"*Capitán* Mendoza, the father of my friend Julio."

"Why would he do that?"

"He is army captain, and he tell us that some soldiers are planning a...a contragolpe."

"A counter-coup? Are you saying that some of the soldiers wanted Bosch to return?"

"Sí. Julio's father is one of the rebel section of the military that want to bring Juan Bosch back to the power. Everybody love Bosch. We four Muchachos want Juan Bosch return too."

"So you're all at your friend Nico's house," Yenny prompts.

"Nico live in the Barrios Altos near the Duarte Bridge."

"Barrios Altos?"

"The poor neighborhood where the most of the people in Santo Domingo live. Is not like barrios here. All houses are connect with one wall, a tin roof, many doors. The house of Nico is one room, with a big patio in the courtyard where all neighbor womans cook and wash clothes and the mans play cards."

My mind drifts back....

La hermana de Nico está allá...Nico's sister Serena is there, wearing a touch of bright red lipstick—as much as her papá will allow— and a yellow sundress. Ice cold guava smoothies pressed into our hands, the glasses sweating. Serena sitting next to me, the white sleeve of my school uniform brushing her bare shoulder. I take a deep breath, inhaling her odor of guava and magnolia.

Lights crisscross Yenny's face.

"We listen to the radio. Suddenly a voice interrupt the music. 'The government fall. Everyone, to the streets—peacefully. Go to the Palacio Presidencial.'"

"I can't imagine a radio station calling people to a demonstration," Yenny says, her eyes wide.

"When we hear the news on the radio, we all head for the *Palacio*," I say. "Is *maravilloso*. Crazy. Full of joy. Everyone in the streets. Cars honking. People shouting the name of Bosch."

Entrelazamos los dedos, Serena y yo...Serena and I interlace fingers as we push through the crowd.

"The *Palacio Presidencial* is surround," I say. "Look like huge wedding cake decorate with people hanging from windows, waving banners that say, *'QUÉ VIVA LA REVOLUCIÓN!'"* I pause to relive that moment. "But the police come and break us up. They make a curfew." Yenny's face falls. "The rebel soldiers—the ones on our side—never appear. We are crazy disappointed. We think, the rebellion fail. I go to home. My papi is member of the *Policía Nacional*. Before, many days, almost he kick me out of the house for talk pro-Bosch. I learn to shut up when he is there."

I narrow my eyes. I'll never forgive my father for his role in enforcing the brutality under Trujillo!

Llego a la casa esa noche…I arrive home that night. Eight empty bottles of Presidente lined up like sentinels on the floor next to my dad's armchair. "Where the hell have you been?" he scowls. Words thick on his tongue.

I'm prepared. "I got caught up in the crowds and the roads were blocked. I hung out with Julio for a couple hours. We listened to the radio."

He nods. Leaning back in his chair. Julio. Julio is OK, the son of a military man.

Then he says, "If I ever catch you out there with that rabble…." His words hanging feebly in the air. Beer bottle waving. "Law and order," he says, raising the bottle. "Never forget that we are a nation of laws. Without law we are barbarians."

He's drunk—drunk enough. My shoulders relax. "What about you, Papá? Were you out there?"

"They sent me to the Barrios Altos!" Shaking his head. Furious. "Those animals!"

"What happened?"

"Everyone was in the streets throwing things. A rock hit me— here!" Pointing to his chest. "I tell you, I'm glad I got out in one piece." Another swig of beer.

The traffic on the turnpike slows. An accident up ahead? I keep talking. "Mamá want Papá to leave the city until everything is finish," I say. "My Tío Pepe live in Baní, about 20 *kilómetros*. The brother of my papi."

"Did your dad leave?"

"Sí." I frown.

Papi tiene amantes en Baní...Papi has lovers in Baní. Three years earlier he and I visit Uncle Pepe there. Mamá stays behind in the city with the younger kids. One morning I stroll down to the beach before breakfast. Clumps of fishermen, surfers, clam diggers. I spread a towel, watch the girls.

Then I see him. My papi. Off to the south, near the bay. That cocky step, that barrel chest. Even though he's far away, I know it's him.

She's young—much younger than my mother. Long hair flowing down her back almost to her waist, leg muscles taut, bronze skin glowing. Exuding something I don't understand then: sex appeal. Papi lifts her in his arms, racing into the water. The girl shrieking. A tightening in my groin.

"And the next day?" Yenny's question yanks me back.

"We find new hope." A relieved smile makes her face so soft I could kiss it. "In the night everything turn again," I say.

"What happened?" The question sounds urgent. For just a minute the image of her wanting sex as bad as she wants this information electrifies me. I shake my head and continue.

"First, I meet Los Muchachos at the fruit market. The rebels take the city again, take back the radio station. Big crowds demand that Bosch return. The next morning the radio call people to come together at the Duarte Bridge and block it so that the enemy tanks—the *Loyalistas*—no can cross the Ozama River and enter the city."

"Block it? With what?"

"That is the problem. The people no have weapons. The rebel soldiers still no let people have guns." I smile. "But *we* get them."

"You got *guns?*" Her lips part, her nostrils flare. The Rambler swerves across the yellow line into the neighboring lane. The guy in the Thunderbird next to us lays on the horn. Yenny jerks the wheel and the Rambler lurches back into our lane. I look at her curiously. This is what she's wanted to hear all along, isn't it? About the weapons. This is what fascinates her. Well, she's a revolutionary. And it *is* pretty amazing that we got ahold of guns.

"Julio's father, he help us get them."

Nos alineamos a la estación…We line up at the 16th of August Army Base, controlled by the rebel soldiers. Hundreds of people. Waiting for over an hour, the line stagnant, people grumbling. Julio, saying, "Wait right here." Cutting to the front of the line and disappearing among the people. The door of the office opening. Julio's father, Capt. Mendoza, tall, in uniform, trim mustache, air of importance, appearing at the top of the steps. Julio beside him, signaling us. We bypass the long line of citizens, enter the office.

Blinking in the dim light. A room with metal desk and folding chairs. A handful of officers standing around awkwardly. Rifles in a heap in one corner. Captain Mendoza handing each of us a rifle. Providing Julio with several rounds of ammo. Looking him severely in the face.

"Show your amigos how to use these, mijo; otherwise they are useless—maybe worse. You hear me?" Embracing Julio, warmly shaking hands with each one of us. "Don't tell people where you got these!" Ushering us out a back door onto a service road that leads past other white stucco buildings. "Take care, son." Snapping an order to a guard. We exit through a chain-link gate into the street.

A couple of kilómetros to Parque Enriquillo. Marco cradling his rifle across his chest as if it were a baby. Nico cocking the trigger, aiming at imaginary enemies in doorways.

"It's not a toy," I snap, holding my rifle stiffly at my side. Coño, what have we done? My dad's disapproval. My mother's worry.

The park almost deserted. Julio, teaching us the basics. Keep fingers off the trigger, safety on, load chamber, position ourselves, grip weapon, sight target, squeeze trigger, follow through. We line up soda bottles, taking aim. Bottles shatter. Young boys watch, whispering, nudging.

*No one can believe that I'm the best shot. "A natural," Julio laughs.
"A sharpshooter!"*

The Muchachos socking my arm. "Oye, Fidel! Oye, Che!"

*"I can't believe I'm doing this," Marco says, his chest expanding.
He, who always shies away from mechanical things, he, who always
embraces ideas. Beaming, peering over his glasses, which have slipped
down his nose. Quoting: "'To revolt is a natural tendency of life.'"
Raising his rifle over his head with both hands. We stare at him, open-
mouthed. "Bakunin," he explains. Marco, so fond of anarchists.*

"We take our guns to the Duarte Bridge," I tell Yenny. "Just a
few blocks away. We pass a gas station. People occupy the pumps
and fill glasses and vases with gasoline for cocktails Molotov. We
follow instructions from Radio Santo Domingo.

"The gasoline get on the pants and shoes of the people. We go
around puddles of gasoline."

*Una estudiante de secundaria tiene un frasco…A high school girl
holds a jar, her legs splattered with fuel. "Ándale, muchacha!" I say. She
grins, raising the jar as if toasting a grand enterprise.*

Yenny pulls up at a toll booth and sprinkles a handful of coins
into the metal basket. Traffic is seriously backed up, I note with
surprise.

"The radio told people how to make *bombs*?" Yenny asks,
incredulous.

"Sí, sí, *Radio Santo Domingo*. The rebels take control of it early
and never let go."

"But how could you hear the radio?"

"Transistors. All the kids have them. "

I pause and gaze into the night. What happened next changed
everything. "The rebel soldiers decide to give to everybody the
weapons," I say.

She slows the car to a crawl. An accident. The right two lanes are cordoned off. My gaze takes in a couple of bodies on gurneys, and vehicles with flashing lights. I glance at the clock on the dashboard. We're almost an hour late. Great! If only the traffic stays slow and the snow continues. With luck we'll get stuck in a snow bank when we exit the turnpike. I'm playing for time, time to work through this. My urge to get this story out astounds me. Maybe it's the way Yenny hangs on my words. Yes, she's making me do this, despite the warning pulse in my forehead, the voice in my head that shrieks at me, *Don't open these old wounds!*

"Every house on Nico's street have a rifle or machine gun," I tell Yenny, ignoring the voice. "*Los Tigres* patrol the streets."

"Los Tigres?"

"Bands of teenage boys. All have rifles."

Mucha gente se reune a la estación de la policía…A crowd gathers at the police station. We Muchachos move closer. Two men are surrounded—a policeman and a man in his thirties, who holds a pistol to the cop's temple. "Justicia! Justicia!" chants the crowd. A third man, stepping out of the circle behind the cop, hitting him over the head with an iron bar. The cop, sinking to his knees, toppling to the ground. A murmur issuing from the crowd, which moves on as one body.

I lean against a pole, bracing myself, throwing up in the gutter. Thank God Papi is out of the city….

Turning back to Nico's house. His papá bartering with a deserter with haunted eyes and trembling hands. Three rifles for Nico's papá in exchange for civvies for the deserter: two pairs of pants, a couple of work shirts.

Staying at Nico's that night, sleeping on the floor on straw mats. Serena sandwiching herself between me and Nico. Laying her head on my chest. I put my arm around her and feel myself grow hard. All night, sniper fire disturbs my fitful sleep.

Traffic on the turnpike has picked up so I speak faster. "The third day the *Loyalistas* bomb the *Barrios Altos.*"

Yenny sucks in her breath. "Oh, my God! Were you there?"

Now I'm getting to stuff I don't want to recall. But momentum propels me. "It happen in the middle of a bad dream about my papá."

Finalmente me duermo…Finally I fall asleep. A nightmare. Papi strung up to the ceiling fan of the police station. An old woman, her face etched with deep lines, brandishing a carving knife. With one swift motion slitting open my father's belly. A river of tortured and mangled bodies flowing out….

I'm jolted awake to the harsh sound of wood splintering, of screams and gunfire.

"I wake up, look out, see people running," I say. "Blood on legs, on heads. We rush outside. Shake our fists at the planes. The *papá* of Nico aim a little mirror at the planes.

"Nowhere to hide. On the radio of Nico we hear the voice of a woman. She sound hysterical. She say, *Everybody into the streets— with clubs, stones, weapons, even barehanded. Fight. Fight for your country.* The voice make my heart beat *hard* and so proud for my country.

"I join arms with Julio and Nico and Marco. We shout slogans like, *"Viva la Constitución."* A minister wave a cross in my face and shout, 'Jesús, Jesús, be with us now.' I no believe in that stuff, but I make the cross anyway."

Niños gritan, lloran…Little kids screaming and crying out and clutching the legs of their mamás. Bodies lying in the streets; wounded and dazed neighbors staggering around them. A Red Cross ambulance pulls up to the curb. Marco and I help roll a man with crushed legs onto a stretcher. We heave the stretcher into the van. An explosion throws me to the ground. Dirt scraping my cheek. I look up and see Julio writhing in pain, a piece of shrapnel protruding from his thigh. Blood running down his leg and mixing with the dirt in the road. Marco sprains his ankle while ducking for cover. Everyone with cuts on hands, legs from broken glass.

"I see a phone booth," I tell Yenny. "A slogan is painted on it: "'*Morir para la constitución!*'"

"Die for the Constitution," she translates.

"Sí. I step inside. I dial Mamá, and she answer fast. I no can stop crying. Do I ever see her again?

"She explode with tears like a *bomba*. '*Por favor, mijo,*' she tell me, and I feel her terror that go through the wire. 'Come home.'

"'Sí, sí, Mamá,' I promise her. 'I go, I go.' But I know is not true.

"At nightfall, the bombing stop. We return to the house of Nico. His front door is smash. We see a bullet hole in the picture of Jesús that hang on the living room wall." I pause. "Guess where is the hole."

"Where?"

"In the chest, exactly where the heart is."

"My God, Miguel! That's so *poetic!*" I stare at her. Poetic?

"The half of the houses on the block of Nico are hit. Julio no can walk good. Me and Nico wash his leg, pull shrapnel, and cover it with clean rags and medicine that the sister of Nico bring from her work at *Hospital Morgan*. The mamá of Nico make stew of goat meat, plantains, yucca, cilantro. Is the best I eat in my life! I never forget! We eat and no talk. We drink coffee. *Now* we talk."

Serena se para y se sienta, se para y se sienta… Serena keeps standing up and sitting down, restless, beside herself. "You can't imagine the nightmare it was at the hospital," she says, wiping sweat from her forehead. "No water, no electricity, no blood for transfusions. The Red Cross kept bringing in more wounded." Pausing, putting her hands on her forehead, breathing hard. Her eyes deep in their sockets in the candlelight.

"The next day, Tuesday, the bombing of the poor barrios start up again."

"Oh, no!" Yenny says. "How could people stand any more, Miguel?"

I feel a lump in my throat. "We no choose," I say. "But then the most important battle of all take place—the one that turn everything in our direction."

"Tell me!"

"The enemy tanks—the *Loyalistas*—from San Isidro come across the Duarte Bridge to invade Santo Domingo, to invade *us*."

"Did they get into the city?"

"Yes," I say. "But they are shock when they see thousands of citizens there to welcome them—*con armas!*" With weapons!

Llegamos a la Puente. We arrive at the bridge. Civilians have already erected huge barricades of overturned cars and downed electrical wires. The people bombarding the Loyalistas from San Isidro with machine gun fire, rifle fire, and Molotov cocktails. We join the fray, squeezed with the crowds against the ramshackle houses. Watching the tanks painfully proceeding through the narrow streets, backtracking, trying again.

Following the tanks, jumping over bodies, children, rubble. The tanks muscling a path southwest, centimeter by centimeter, into the inner city. I peer into the hatch of a tank and see crazed eyes looking back at me. Wondering how that poor slob feels mowing down his fellow citizens. Wanting to tear him limb from limb, and yet, strangely, wanting to comfort him: things will be all right, compa!

Snowflakes are falling on the windshield now. The wipers beat out a rhythm. One two one two.

"After five blocks into the rebel zone, the tanks can go no more," I say. "Too many people with arms, too many rebel soldiers."

"They retreated?" Yenny sounds skeptical.

My own voice is husky. "The tanks turn around and return over the bridge, return to San Isidro. Is a *milagro* (miracle)! A great victory!"

"So the people actually won? But I thought—"

"This seem to be the turn point."

Yenny looks at me as if, like *Jesucristo*, I walk on water. Just thinking about the battle of Duarte Bridge again makes me want to cry, but to have this *chica* hanging on my words? It feels good—*damn* good.

Then I sigh. "But the victory cost a lot. Everywhere are bodies, rocks, glass. A little girl lie on the body of her dead brother. I pull her. She crying. I carry her and look for her family. I cannot find. She cry loud now. She hold me." I close my eyes for a moment. "I finally give her to the Red Cross truck."

I don't mention the death toll—over a thousand from that one afternoon alone.

"A man in a jeep give me and Julio a ride. The face of Julio is white. He look like he not going to make it. We leave him at his house. I go to my house. My mamá hold me so tight that I no can breathe. One of my neighbors who desert the military tell me that the soldiers are demoralize, no more want to fight."

Yenny exits the turnpike. I stop talking and pay attention to the road. We're getting close to work now, driving past the trailer park, the Methodist Church, the Chastity Saloon. I'm almost through with my story. I look at her, fascinated by the mixture of emotions on her face.

But now comes the worst part. "500 U.S. Marines come on shore the next day," I say.

The indignation in Yenny's face reminds me for a moment of Serena.

"LBJ say he don't want 'another Cuba in Latin America.'" Whenever I think about LBJ, I feel as if a rat is gnawing on my insides. "No one believe that about communism. Everyone have signs. 'YANQUIS GO HOME!'" I squeeze my eyes tight, remembering those final weeks. The start of the long siege. The beginning of the end.

"What was it like after the marines invaded?" Yenny asks.

"*Los Yanquis* surround the rebels with tanks and howitzers. They interrogate Marco, then let him go with warning. Julio is still at his house with a hole in the thigh. Only Nico and me remain." *And Serena.* "The Barrios Altos are cut off from food, water, and weapons.

"For a week me and Nico smuggle weapons and grenades into the barrio through the sewers. A rat bite Nico on the ankle. The skin turn ugly purple and red. We fight a battle with the Green Berets in the sewers. Women smuggle handguns into the barrio under their dresses." *Including Serena.* I shudder, remembering the desperation and the ferocious—but futile—courage of my *compañeros.*

"I feel so ashamed of my country," Yenny says. "How can you endure being here, Miguel, after all that?"

I shrug. I sure as hell don't want to get into *that.* "Anyway, after two weeks of this, *Operación Limpieza* begin. May 14. A day I never forget."

"Operation Mop-up?"

"Sí. House to house. Dominican military and Yankee marines. It take about a week."

"Was that the end of it then?" Yenny asks.

"Mostly. Nico and I bury our guns in my patio and run."

There's a silence and then she asks, "How did you deal with the disappointment? The anger? The grief?"

I let the question hang. I can already see smoke from the refinery's smelter up ahead. I want to reach over and touch her hair, but after the way she flinched earlier, I'm afraid to. Yenny Apple. *Yenny Manzana.* Never have I met any *gringa* like this.

I haven't told her about the aftermath of the revolution, about the wave of terror carried out by the military against the rebels. Talking about the rebellion has shaken me down to my work boots. I can't be left alone now with all these emotions spinning in my head. At work I won't have any chance to talk to her—except maybe in the lunch room. And that's too public.

"*Stop*! Don't drive in there, Yenny."

She starts. "What's the matter?"

"Let's deash tonight."

Her face flushes and she says, "Ditch?"

"*Deash,* yeah. A place is up the road—Los Globos. You go there one time? We drink a beer and talk more."

"I'm sorry, Miguel, I can't." She enters the parking lot, looking for a spot, but every place is taken. She circles the lot twice; it's kind of silly. I'm glad she can't find anything.

Finally a fucking station wagon pulls out and Yenny slides the car into the space, cuts the motor. She turns to face me. "See you on the ride home?" Is it a question? What's the matter with her? Couldn't she handle my story? I knew I shouldn't have gone into all that. But she was the one who insisted! It's her own fault.

Slipping the hood of her jacket over her head, she grabs her sack lunch and steps out into the cold. Her neck bends against the wind and the swirling snowflakes as she heads toward the locker room. I struggle to keep up with her. Just as we get to the entrance, she turns and leans into me. The wind almost whisks her words away.

"I can't tell you what this has meant to me. Thank you." I watch her hurry off down the hall toward the women's locker room. She's thanking me? Then why didn't she come with me to Los Globos? She's weirder than I thought.

In the locker room I rest my head against my locker and shut my eyes. Perhaps I should forget her, hitch a ride home with someone else after the shift. Is she annoyed at my asking her to ditch? Well, that's her problem. She could always say no. Which she did!

I twirl the combination on my locker and sit on the bench to pull off my shoes. I didn't mean we should have sex, if that's what she thought! OK, it did cross my mind when I first climbed into her car. And yesterday, when she agreed to give me a ride...I *had* wondered if anything more would develop. But now I just need to talk, to wind this up.

It's strange, but now that I've told her my story, I feel as if a heavy rock has rolled off or me. For years I've kept this to myself. Will I have fewer nightmares now? *Or will I have more?* A warm surge flows through me as I recall how she listened to me, encouraged me, almost begged me to continue. I open my locker and pull out my asbestos jacket. And suddenly I chuckle, anticipating the ride home.

An image of Angélica appears before my eyes. *Jesús y María.* I brush that image aside.

As I enter Tough Pitch, a foreman approaches. "You're working back in the smelter tonight, Cimarrón," he barks, and passes on. Shit. My upbeat mood is already shrinking. The smelter is dirty and dangerous and reeks like sulfur. Worst of all, I won't get to see Yenny the whole night. I look down the shed; she's nowhere to be seen.

All I know about her is the little that Felicia has told me. Yenny is such an enigma. So politically savvy yet cagey, guarded.

Later this morning over breakfast, I'll try to figure her out. I hope she won't change her mind; I hope she won't let me down.

4. Jenny
OCTOBER 1974

IN THE LOCKER ROOM I STRIP OFF my t-shirt and jeans, and pull on coveralls and a faded blue work shirt. The shard of mirror on the wall shows my face pale despite the cold. Even though I'm late, I sit on a bench, staring numbly at the locker in front of me.

Why did I resist ditching work? Yes, I'm still on my first year's probation so it's important to give management no excuse to fire me. But a few hours at Los Globos? What harm could that do? Is my need to show up every night just another desperate stab for approval? It's so safe, sticking to the tried and true. And it's so tedious, always playing the good girl.

I rarely miss a day. I can recall each one of my absences since I went blue collar four years ago. One time I sprained my ankle bowling at a fundraiser for the United Farm Workers. Another time my car blew a head gasket. And then there was that entire week when I had strep throat. I was working at the time in a small shop making Venetian blinds. When I returned from sick leave, the foreman called me into the office and threatened to dismiss me even though I'd presented a doctor's note. The injustice of that threat rankled me for days, especially since I had a perfect work record. And never mind my own health, was it really in the company's interest for me to spread a contagious disease throughout the plant?

I sigh and set out across the yard to Tough Pitch where I peer up and down the shed for a glimpse of Miguel. He's nowhere to be seen. I hurry on to my work station.

My partner for the night, Alexis Alanis, a bear of a man with a bushy beard and a hearty laugh, has already been working alone for over an hour but he doesn't seem resentful. "Figured you weren't gonna make it," he says in his deep voice.

"Sorry, Lexy. Big accident on the turnpike. Gruesome."

"Everything OK?"

"Oh, yeah. We…I…wasn't involved."

I open the furnace door to check the fuel level. Should be good for another twenty minutes. I shiver. It's another of those bitterly cold October nights in central New Jersey.

"Anything happening?" I ask Lexy.

"Exciting night. The president of Dynamic Metals paid a visit and ordered a raise and an extra week of vacation for everyone. Oh, and a 30-hour week."

I chuckle. I like working with Alexis. He's funny but his jokes aren't off-color. And he treats me like an equal. Many male workers here at the refinery resent the women hired under Title VII. Why on earth would you want to work with all these men, they say. Why not work in a factory with other women?

The men who don't seem to begrudge our presence treat us just the opposite, rushing forward to snatch bricks or buckets from our hands. "You'll hurt yourself," they say, edging us firmly aside. Perhaps we should be grateful, but such favors lead to resentment: *the girls can't pull their weight.*

Over my nine months here, I've developed the muscles to prove I can pull my weight. So what if I can't lift as much as most men? I can work with another man—or woman—to lift any weight at all. And those macho men that lift 100-pound bags of cement by themselves—is that really wise?

Anyway, as Chairman Mao says, "Women hold up half the sky."

I open the door of my furnace and check the flames. Someone approaches from the side—Inca Chocano, an immigrant from Peru. He's one of the many South and Central Americans working here. He lowers his voice and pulls off his helmet, freeing his charcoal black hair.

"Can I talk to you a minute, Yenny?" We move to the other side of the furnace. Inca shifts from foot to foot, both hands holding his helmet. "What I come by for," he says, clearing his throat, "is that Tony's making me work overtime again." His eyes smolder. "It ain't my turn. I just done it two nights ago."

I nod in sympathy. It's only been a month since I became shop steward on this shift. As shop steward, I'm privy to things: I know that Inca's wife is going through a difficult pregnancy. Inca probably has to cook and take care of the kids after putting in a full night's work here at the refinery. Chances are he's not getting much sleep.

"Hey, I'll talk to Tony," I say to him. "See if I can get this straightened out." Then I touch his shirt sleeve with my gloved hand. "By the way, how's your wife doing?"

"She's holding up."

"And you?"

"Oh, I'm all right," he says, reddening. He turns to leave. "Thanks for your help."

"No problem. That's my job." (After all, I'm glad to have *something* to do besides stand around the furnace and think about Miguel Cimarrón all evening.)

As a union rep, I find that I'm treated *like a man*. In other words, they respect me. When the former steward retired, I was the only candidate who ran for his position. I'd only been here two months, which meant I had little job protection, but we in the collective decided it would be safe for me to run. If I were elected, I should assume a low-key and respectful attitude so as not to raise any *red flags*. Double-entendre intended.

I shovel more coal into the furnace, secure the door, and head over to where a forklift has dumped 100-pound bags of cement. Another woman and I quickly heave them onto a cart before some well-meaning man can rush over and shunt us aside. Then I haul the cart over to furnace Number 6, which is being rebuilt, and convince a man that I'm capable of helping him unload the bags. He probably fears being tagged a sissy for accepting my help. I return to my area and my thoughts revert to you know who.

Miguel Cimarrón. Where's he working tonight? A few hours ago when I saw him waiting for me at the PATH station, I felt jittery. The first thing he did when he got in the car was to offer me a jelly donut from a white paper bag. "You like?" I accepted the donut and turned the Rambler up Newark Avenue toward the turnpike. As he thanked me for picking him up, he placed his hand on my shoulder. I felt a current run through my body, alarming me with its intensity. Everything seemed suddenly more vivid: taillights twinkled, neon lights glowed in Technicolor.

I wanted to rush through the small talk and on to the real thing, but for some reason he seemed reluctant to get into the civil war. Was I too pushy? Perhaps he feared reprisals. Perhaps he's undocumented....

Tony Mickles, the foreman, approaches. He wears metal-rimmed glasses and a pressed work shirt and tie. He looks formal, strait-laced, and has an aura of superiority. Tony's a stern, no-nonsense type, with not a hint of the solidarity I sometimes sense from black workers—the ones who give me that *look* that says, *You as a woman and me as a black man, we both been through struggles for our rights. I can relate to you.*

At least, that's what I imagine the look says, but probably it just means, *You're hot, mama. Let's get it on.*

"You wanted to see me?" Tony Mickles asks. His forehead wrinkles. With annoyance? Does it get under his skin, dealing with a female?

"It's about Inca."

"Wait," he says. "Let me guess. He's bellyaching about overtime again."

"It's not his turn, Tony."

"That's bullshit." He taps the roster he carries under his arm. "It's all right here. I can't be doing him no special favors."

"Let me see the roster," I say. "Please."

I immediately regret saying please. *Please* is polite, weak. It sounds like a request. I have a *right* to review the roster and I should have reminded him of that. Matter of fact. Authoritative.

Rolling his eyes, he surrenders the clipboard. I scroll down the meticulously handwritten list of names, dates, and times. Everything appears on the up and up. I feel disappointed; it *is* Inca's turn. I hand back the clipboard.

"Tony," I say, pitching my voice a little lower. "Inca needs the time off more than he needs the money. You know about his wife's condition, don't you?"

"Hey," Tony steps back, holding up a hand and shaking his head as if I'm about to ask him to declare a holiday. "I'm just doing my job."

"Well, Tony, I heard that Jimmy O'Malley is looking for more overtime."

Tony hesitates, screws up his mouth, and finally says, "I'll get back to you." He spins around and takes off. A forklift with chunks of copper arrives at my furnace. I open the door and guide the copper into the furnace, then slam the door shut. As the forklift backs away, I sit on a bench and my thoughts return to Miguel.

Flowing along in that steady stream of traffic, "Midnight Train to Georgia" on the radio, Miguel's deep voice telling his story, I found myself swept back in time to the Santo Domingo of the 1960s. I was in the street beside him, the heat braising my skin, dirt mingling with sweat on my face, thirst swelling my throat. I could see children blocking intersections, mothers descending in droves on tanks and spreading out around them like a colorful human web, demonstrators spilling into the streets, holding aloft red banners and rifles.

I get up from the bench and tell Lexy I'm going on break. Twenty minutes, that's all I allow myself! Lexy's patience can only be stretched so far. When one of us leaves on break, the other has to cover both furnaces. So far he hasn't reproached me—the way my other co-worker Juan Toledo does—for the minutes I tack on to my breaks, which I only do because I'm forced to handle union business at that time. The contract provides a relief person only when there's a formal grievance. All the preliminary investigation of a case, all my attempts to resolve a problem before it comes to a grievance, these I have to do during my breaks. Which means that I often skip meals or eat standing around my furnace.

I take a detour to the break room to give Inca an update when a woman waves at me. Bettina Solís, a single mom with three kids. She's cleaning out molds with an air hose, and the dust settles around her. Loose coveralls don't quite conceal her curvaceousness, but her curves don't mean she's weak; I've watched her shovel sand like a man. *Like a man!* It seems that's the highest compliment around here!

"That idiot Fulgencio is out of control," Bettina says.

"Fulgencio Cruz?"

"Yep."

Uh-oh. "A contradiction among the people," as Mao calls it. In other words, two of the *good guys* in conflict.

"What do you mean, out of control?"

"He can't keep his hands off me."

"Like what?"

"Every time he sees me, he pinches my ass or touches me *here.*" She pokes her breast, and for a fleeting second I envy the way her finger sinks into it like into a pillow. I grit my teeth. Thank God the union doesn't bring grievances against fellow workers because I'd have a hard time defending Fulgencio on this one.

"He'd better watch it or I'll jam my shovel up his ass," Bettina adds, narrowing her eyes. "I've had it with that loser."

"I'll talk to him," I say, admiring her militancy. If only she'd get so worked up about the bosses! "Sounds like Fulgencio needs a lesson."

Someone has seen Fulgencio in the repair shop. As I head over that way, I wonder again why I didn't go to the bar with Miguel.

My college roommate Amber pops into my mind, and the thought of her fills me with a sense of inadequacy. Amber would have gone off with Miguel in a flash. I can hear her regaling me with tales of her latest liaison, leaning back on the bed in our dorm room in her black satin pajamas, smoking a Virginia Slim.

But I'm not Amber. I'm a *good girl.* Not the good girl of my mother's generation, of course. Even today society would label me a rebel, a radical, a lefty, or any one of a dozen other epithets better left unsaid. But at my core, no matter how confident I appear, I feel like a child trying to please the grown-ups.

I find Fulgencio in a pit, applying a wrench to the underside of a forklift. I recognize him as Juan Toledo's friend, the guy who ogled me in the break room last night. His coveralls are streaked with grease; his dark hair is slicked straight back, giving him a Fonzie look. As I bend over to talk to him, he whistles through a gap in his teeth. He can't be whistling at my cleavage because it doesn't exist. Mmm, I guess he's an *equal opportunity* sexist.

"Hey, Fulgencio, how you doing?" I say cheerfully. He smirks and pops his Juicy Fruit. Before he can respond with anything he might regret, I add, "I'm Jenny, the shop steward over in Tough Pitch."

"I know who you are, baby." The smirk still clings to his lips; perhaps they're frozen in that position.

"I'm here about Bettina."

"Bettina who?"

"Bettina *Solís*, Fulgencio."

"What about her?"

"Are you aware she's plenty pissed?"

"Union business is confidential," he says. "Didn't anyone tell you that yet?"

"This concerns *you*, Fulgencio."

"Ain't you out of your turf? This here is Jimmy's territory."

"Unfortunately for you, Fulgencio, Bettina is on my turf."

"What I got to do with that broad?"

"Apparently, you've been getting too—how shall I say it—too *familiar*."

"Says her."

"So you deny it?"

"Ain't no crime against being friendly," he responds, turning back to the forklift, applying his wrench.

"You call it *friendly*, others might call it *aggressive*. Touching someone against their will is against the contract," I lie, knowing that the contract sadly says nothing about this.

"Well, I ain't done nothing," he says.

"That's not what Bettina says."

His jaw clenches. "Well, she's a little *confused.*"

I sigh and change tack. "Anyway, Fulgencio, that's not why I came over. I just wanted to do you a little favor." He blinks. "Are you aware that Bettina's boyfriend is a professional wrestler?" His face darkens and the smirk finally fades. "Apparently her boyfriend has an evil temper; he's like a rabid dog when he gets mad." *And fire shoots from his mouth and he grows fangs too.*

A touch of something creeps into Fulgencio's eyes. I sincerely hope it's fear. "Aw, you're pulling my leg," he says.

"I asked Bettina not to say anything to him until I talked to you. I told her you seemed like a reasonable man." Sometimes I'm so good at lying that I belong in "Psycho."

Fulgencio narrows his eyes. "Why don't you mind your own friggin' business?"

"This *is* my business," I say sweetly. "Don't say I didn't warn you." I grin to myself as I saunter away. I can't wait to tell Charlie about *this.*

Will Miguel be in the break room? Just thinking about him perks me up like a few sips of strong coffee. How inspiring the Dominican rebellion was! Yes, it was crushed, but the sheer audacity of it thrills me—the people rising up and shaking off their oppression.

Mao has said, "Political power grows out of the barrel of a gun." How thrilling it is to talk about armed struggle. But when the day arrives here in the U.S., will I be ready? Or will I cower under a bed? Take that accident tonight on the turnpike: chunks of metal and fragments of glass glittering in the grisly light. One car had crashed into a divider; another was flattened like a beer can. A body, covered with a blanket, lay on a gurney. It was like a war zone! As we drove slowly by, I felt the blood drain from my face. Talk is one thing, but how sobering to confront such wreckage casually strewn along the highway like Snickers wrappers.

I push open the break room door. Two workers in their early twenties play checkers.

Spike, the cute one with the long hair and acne, raises his hand in a salute. "Hey, Jenny," he says.

Has anyone seen Miguel Cimarrón?

"They buried him back in the smelter."

Slumping into a chair, I contemplate this news while digging around in my backpack for a container of meatloaf. The smelter. It means I won't see him for three more hours, which seems like a cruelly long time to wait before finding out if he's so disgusted that he hitches a ride with someone else. Please let him ride home with me.

Juan Toledo, my work partner from yesterday, bursts into the break room and looms over me, his arms crossed. "Jesus, aren't you ever at your station?" I keep chewing on my meat loaf and don't look up. "I suppose you're badmouthing the union again." He's so close he's almost touching me.

I give in. "Not the union, Juan," I say, focusing on my coffee cup. "I love the union."

"It sure don't sound like it."

"If I was to badmouth anyone, it would be your friends, the union bureaucrats, who exchange our well-being for a few crumbs from the bosses."

"Says you."

I sit up tall. The top of my head comes only to his mid-chest. I crane my neck, lock eyes with him, and glower. "Why do I scare you so much, Juan?"

He takes a step back. "I…I ain't afraid of you," he stutters, scowling.

I let out a breath. "Well, if your union friends are doing what they're supposed to, then who cares what I say?"

"Humph." He turns abruptly and stamps out of the lunch room. I give a half-shrug, chomp on a carrot stick, look at the clock, and sink back into my thoughts.

Why *did* Miguel show so little emotion at the pileup on the turnpike? Maybe he's seen so much already that he's immune to blood and death? Is it different when you're in the middle of a revolution? Do you get caught up in it and slough off your fears?

Or maybe when you've been oppressed for so long, something just snaps?

Mao Tse-tung has said, "A revolution is not a dinner party, or writing an essay, or painting a picture, or doing embroidery." And I know this much: when the revolution occurs, Cindy and others in the collective will embrace it. Will I?

I've lost my appetite; I stuff the half-eaten meatloaf back into its container. I reassure myself that the revolution won't start for at least five years, probably ten. Plenty of time to prepare—if I only knew how.

I leave the break room and hurry back to relieve Lexy. "Take an extra-long break," I say. "I owe you big time." He waves his hand, an *it's-nothing-forget-it* gesture. My throat constricts; I'm going to bake him some chocolate chip cookies. With extra chocolate.

I finish stoking the furnace with more coal and check the status of the molten copper. Tony Mickles, the foreman, approaches again.

"Jimmy will work the overtime," he says. His tone is less edgy; he meets my eyes this time.

"Thanks, Tony," I say. As he leaves, he salutes me. I get a kick out of people saluting me now that I'm a shop steward. R-E-S-P-E-C-T! It does feel good.

At 5 a.m. when my afternoon break finally arrives, I promise myself to be gone just a few minutes. I have to pee but I'm pretty sure I can hold it until seven. Instead, I'll utilize the time to get back to Bettina. I find her sitting on a bag of sand, polishing off a sandwich. Two male workers keep her company. "Can't Get Enough of Your Love, Babe" plays on a small radio.

"Fulgencio won't bother you for a while," I say. "I told him your boyfriend was a professional wrestler." I chuckle as I recall the alarm in his eyes.

Bettina chortles. "Why don't I think of things like that?"

"Tell me if he even looks at you again." God, I sound tough.

This time I do indeed head straight back to my station, and miraculously no one waylays me. I pass Tony's office; his head is hunched over his desk.

Back at my furnace, I think about how our ride ended. After the wreck on the turnpike, we rode in silence for a minute. The snowfall made the roads slippery and demanded my close attention, but images of the rebellion floated across my vision like slides. Cocooned in the car with him, sharing his story—it felt so intimate, but as we approached Dynamic Metals, I glanced at the car clock and my euphoria evaporated. A whole hour late!

Then Miguel shouted, "Stop! Don't drive in there, Yenny!" At first I thought I was about to hit something, but then I realized he'd only meant, *Keep going!*

How conflicted I felt. But while I was agonizing, the car steered itself into the parking lot. Once there, I couldn't find a space and had to circle three times, staring straight ahead, my ears burning, feeling his eyes boring into my cheek. Was he hoping I wouldn't find a spot? And if that station wagon hadn't pulled out right then, to my relief—and to my disappointment—I might have driven right out of the lot with him into a new adventure.

Chances like this don't occur twice. You have to take advantage of them. Life pitched me one of those home-run balls, and I let it sail right past me. The problem is that life plods along on its humdrum way for months, so when something like this occurs, I'm not expecting it. If only I could receive a little advance notice: *Attention! Something momentous and life-changing is about to happen! Don't blow it!*

I curse the hesitation—the fear—that keeps me from plunging full throttle into life.

5. Jenny

IT SEEMS MY AGONIZING WAS IN VAIN: Miguel does want to ride home with me. We locate a café off the expressway in Elizabeth—a safe enough distance from the plant to avoid fellow workers. From the café's phone booth I call Felicia. *Don't prepare breakfast for me; I'm eating with Miguel.* I hear a sharp intake of breath before she says "OK" in a voice that suggests it may or may not be OK. Does she think I can't handle myself? I return to the table. When I see the back of his neck and how it curves into his spine, it strikes me that maybe she's right.

I slide into the booth. Our waitress is petite and brisk, like so many breakfast waitresses, and wears a red bow around her waist, tied in the front. Her "good morning" sounds Puerto Rican. She brings us menus, water, coffee.

Miguel adds two spoonfuls of sugar and a dollop of half and half to his coffee. I take mine black.

"So tell me about yourself, Yenny Apple," he says in Spanish. I wonder why his flirtatiousness has vanished.

I hesitate—not because of the Spanish; I can hold my own there. I hesitate because his request ("Tell me about yourself") is so sweeping. "What do you want to know?" I ask.

"How about starting with where you were born," he says.

"In a small Colorado town named Mountainview."

"Pretty name. What was it like, this *Vista de las Montañas?*"

A sense of well-being, followed closely by unease, comes over me whenever I talk about Mountainview. I filter out the unease. "The town was wonderful," I say. "It was surrounded by mountains. The bus ride to school took me alongside thick pine forests.

Sometimes I'd see deer or even a bear from the window. I lived there until I was thirteen."

"It sounds pretty. I visited a small town like that in Wyoming once."

The waitress interrupts to take our orders: eggs and bacon for him, oatmeal and a bowl of melon slices for me. I study his dark-brown skin and watch his lips caress the rim of his coffee cup. Then he looks expectantly at me.

"When I was thirteen we moved to Southern California," I continue. "My dad was transferred there. He's an engineer."

"To Los Angeles?"

"To Pomona, which is near L.A."

"Pomona? The goddess of fruit?"

I reflect. "I never once thought about the origin of the name. How strange."

"We learned Roman mythology in grade school."

"I guess we didn't."

"Did you like Pomona? The city, that is?"

"I hated all that asphalt." I don't know the word for *asphalt* in Spanish, so I say it in English, hoping he'll understand.

"Didn't *Vista de las Montañas* have asphalt?"

"Yes, of course, but the whole city of Pomona seemed to be asphalt-gray. No mountains, no forests, no snow. At least not outside my front door. I missed my childhood hikes in the woods, the wildlife, the ice that formed little patterns like doilies on the storm windows. And let's not forget the most important thing," I add, smiling. "Who wants to ice skate on a rink? How boring!" Miguel laughs—a deep and throaty laugh that makes me feel like laughing too.

The only good thing about the move to California was that my nasty cousin Duncan, who married a farm girl and became a snowplow driver, was left far behind. I'd never have to see him again.

"How did you like school?" Miguel asks. But I don't want to talk about that. It was in junior high where I first became aware of a paralyzing fear.

My eighth-grade English teacher, Mrs. Underwood, assigns me a partner on a debate team. His name is Ricky O'Malley. I've overheard other girls talk about him: He's so cute! When Mrs. Underwood gives us class time to work together, he shoves his desk over until it clanks against mine. My hands sweat, my heart thumps, not from excitement but from terror. All I can think of is my cousin Duncan taking those two giant strides across the room until he sat by my side on the playhouse cot.

My great ideas about the topic—"The U.S. Should Ban the Death Penalty"—dissipate. I try to focus as Ricky lays out a strategy and begins recording ideas, but all I hear is the quill of his pen scratching across rough paper.

"Hey, what do you think about all this?" he finally asks, looking at me. I blush, stammer, then go silent. He's too close! "The cat got your tongue?" he asks. He gives me time to respond, then his upper lip curls. "Aw, heck." He stands and crumples the paper. "I can't work like this." To my horror, he stomps across the room, the paper gripped in his hand, to Mrs. Underwood's desk and exclaims, "Can I work with someone else? She won't talk. She's a stick." Thirty-two heads turn toward him, then swivel in my direction. Mrs. Underwood assigns him to work with another student. With an index finger she summons me to her desk. My every step is full of trepidation.

"What's the problem, Jenny?" Mrs. Underwood asks, her voice not quite suppressing her annoyance. Her lipstick is bubblegum pink; cracks appear in it as she purses her lips.

"I...I...."

"Don't you like debate, then?"

"Yes, but...could I work with a girl, please, Mrs. Underwood?"

Mrs. Underwood's nostrils flare. She taps the tapered pink nail of her index finger on the desktop and raises her ice-blue eyes to the ceiling. "There's no one available now, Jenny, so this is what we'll do. I want you to study the issue and write an essay on it. I nod and return to my seat.

I don't understand the potency of my fear, but I suspect that it's not Ricky himself but any boy that would fill me with terror. It isn't that I never had male friends. In Colorado there was Sammy Griffin. We collected insects and climbed trees. But that was all innocence and fun. Nothing like the way Ricky and other boys look at us girls now. They stand around in pimply groups, smirking, their voices cracking, their giggles so high-pitched that they sound like girls.

"I was shy," I tell Miguel. "It was difficult to make new friends."

"You don't seem so shy now," he says. If he only knew.

The waitress sets our food before us. "The plates are hot," she warns. Miguel squeezes a plastic dispenser, smothering his hash browns in spirals of catsup.

"Then we moved to Riverside, another suburb, even further from L.A."

"Was that better?"

"Prettier but more of the same. I detested the freeways and the tidy grids of suburban streets with quaint but misleading labels: *lanes, courts, ways, terraces.* Those weren't *lanes,"* I say indignantly. "I yearned for a downtown with real lanes and with cozy shops where I knew everyone. Riverside's downtown was dying a painful death; its only reason for existence was a beautiful old Spanish-style hotel called the Mission Inn. But that was mainly for tourists. Even the downtown movie theaters closed. Everyone shopped and hung out at a giant new shopping mall that glittered like Las Vegas." Miguel nods and forces honey out of a plastic bear onto his toast.

I don't outgrow my fear of boys, despite my mother's reassurances: You will, dear, don't worry. *I daydream about them, though. Not about individual boys but about some amorphous and faceless Boy-Man, who will sweep me off my feet, as in the pictures on the covers of the romance novels I've seen on dime-store book racks. With actual boys, though, I avoid all contact. As if one-half of the human race are aliens.*

"And I didn't relate to most of the girls either," I continue. "They seemed so superficial—always gossiping, always talking about boys. I walked home alone."

Trudging along, my eyes cast downward toward the cracks in the sidewalk ("break your mother's back"), mulling over the humiliations of the day: that snide remark about my shoes, the last one to be chosen for the basketball team, odd girl out when we paired up in home economics class. My mother would probe: Have you met any nice boys yet?... Which boys sit near you?... Do any of them like you?

"I felt like a glass ornament," I say, "pretty enough, but hollow, easily shattered." Miguel looks concerned and I tell myself to abandon this self-pity before he gets sick of it.

"How could you have so much and not be happy?" he asks.

"I'm not sure."

"Maybe Americans have *too* much," he says.

I don't respond. Ask me a question about the class struggle and I'll talk for hours, but ask me why people aren't *happy* and I don't know what to say.

"Anyway, sorry, go on," he says. "This is interesting." He looks as if he means it.

"When I arrived home from school every day, I'd mumble hello to my mom, grab a root beer from the refrigerator, and hurry off to my bedroom to read. It was the female protagonists who saved me." *Nancy Drew and Jane Eyre, Elizabeth Bennet and Scarlet O'Hara.*

"Saved you?"

"From killing myself." Miguel looks startled, and I smile reassuringly. "Just kidding. But the books gave me *solace*. I could lose myself in them. You know what I mean?"

He nods uncertainly. Has he ever lost himself in a book?

"No girls phoned me to exchange homework or dissect high school romances." For some reason I'm telling him things I've kept locked up until now. "When the phone rang, it was for my mother, the chatterbox, who chirped away to neighbors and friends. Their conversations seemed superficial, yet I longed to be able to talk so easily myself."

"So you're not a talker? That's hard to believe. Look at you now."

"Not really. Not in social settings. Small talk, chit-chat, that stuff scares me."

The café is slowly filling up with groggy working folks catching a quick bite before heading out to their jobs. Others, like us, are enjoying a more leisurely breakfast after a night on graveyard.

"With politics it's different," I say. "I can talk about the war and Nixon until the furnaces run cold."

Miguel raises his empty cup and catches the waitress's eye. I notice the muscles in his arms. What would they feel like around my shoulders?

"Anyway," I continue, "in my later years of high school, things improved. I formed an uneasy bond with a clique of girls. But their fascination with boys and school dances didn't interest me. Schoolwork also separated us; if I received a grade as low as a B, my mood sank, whereas they were quite content with Cs and Ds."

"You didn't like boys?" he asks, sounding even more skeptical.

When did I let that slip?

Perhaps he senses my embarrassment because he changes the subject. "But you got good grades, you were smart."

"Smart? No smarter than lots of people. It's just that I'd long since figured out how to play the system. I knew what teachers wanted and I knew how to take tests. Besides, I came from college-educated parents; I was on a college track." How different our experiences are. Can he relate to what I'm saying? "In fact, by my eighteenth birthday—that was 1964—I couldn't wait to get to college."

My daydreams about males continue, but in these new dreams the callow high school boy is replaced by a dark-haired college man, suave, sophisticated, who sits next to me over espresso in the college coffee shop, discussing Plato while holding my hand under the table.

"Why were you so eager to get to college?" Miguel asks.

I drain my coffee. "To escape my dreary life. To find kindred spirits. College would throw me among people who shared my passion to discover *the meaning of life.*" (And in such an environment, I hoped my shyness would melt away and romance would blossom.) "I chose a small liberal arts college in Oregon. I was lucky; unlike most kids, my parents paid for tuition, room and board, transportation, expenses. And they even bought me a Volkswagen Beetle."

Miguel whistles. "You had it all, Yenny Apple."

"At college, all of Western civilization lay before me like a feast. I was nourished by Greek and Roman classics, by Kant and Hegel and Shakespeare and Verdi." Who needed any other men?

Miguel seems familiar with these names. Is he self-educated or did he attend college, I wonder.

"In those two years—from 1964 to 1966—the thick walls of the liberal arts curriculum cloistered me. But there was a downside."

"What was that?"

"I was oblivious to the turmoil occurring outside those walls: the Civil Rights Movement, the Free Speech Movement." The murders of Schwerner, Goodman, and Chaney in Mississippi. SNCC. So-called "race riots" in Harlem. The assassination of Malcolm X. Anti-war demonstrations. SDS. "Have you heard about those?" I ask. "You must have come to the U.S. about that time."

"I know about them," he says. He leans across the table and points his fork at me. "Sorry to interrupt, but can you tell me why Americans are so out of it?"

Americans. Is he including me? "Out of it?"

"So unaware of the rest of the world. Can you explain it to me?"

"I don't understand it either," I say uneasily.

"Maybe it's because the country is so big. It's easier to isolate yourself."

"I guess so," I say.

"It's remarkable," he says. "Everyone in the Dominican Republic knows exactly what's going on in the U.S. A few years ago your whole country was aflame. Or so it seemed. Then I arrive here and find out that most people are just watching events on TV, if they're aware of them at all." He shakes his head. "Their own country!"

I feel ashamed. Once again I resent my conservative upbringing that made it so easy to ignore history in the making. "It's a complex question," I say, mirroring what he said on the way to work to avoid telling me his story.

He doesn't look appeased. He pushes his plate aside. "Does it bother you if I smoke?" I shake my head and he taps a cigarette on the table. "Anyway, go on," he sighs.

"After two years of college my roommate and I took a road trip across country. *To broaden our horizons*, we said. Once in Manhattan, I sold my car to my roommate, found a room at the YWCA, and transferred to Columbia."

"Just like that?" He lights his cigarette; I feel the tickle of nicotine craving.

"Manhattan opened up a new world to me. Diversity, sophistication."

"What happened to your roommate? Wasn't she turned on by Manhattan?"

"No."

"Why you and not she?"

"She was a farm girl. The city was too chaotic for her, she said."

"You weren't political yet, were you?"

"Not yet. But one day soon after I arrived—it was the summer of 1966—I was meandering up Broadway when I heard a roar over by Times Square. A line of marchers stretched from one side of the street to the other." *Shouting, voices bouncing off buildings, energy exploding into the street.* "They were chanting 'Hey hey LBJ/ How many kids did you kill today?' and 'Ho Ho/ Ho Chi Minh/ the NLF is gonna win.'

"Some of their banners read, 'U.S. OUT OF VIETNAM.' Demonstrators wore t-shirts and hats with provocative slogans like 'Imperialism Sucks,' 'Fuck this War' and 'LBJ=Hitler.' I stood there gaping. Who were these people? Radicals? Anarchists? *Communists?* They seemed to have such power. I was scared but strangely attracted." The way I feel about you, I think. I regard the sheen of his knuckle as he holds his coffee cup.

"Attracted?" he asks. "What attracted you?"

"You know what really got to me, I think, was the *passion!* I envied them their *passion.* As if their lives had some meaning outside of their own skin."

"Go on," he says. I marvel at how his eyes switch from curiosity to bewilderment to comprehension to approval.

"Someone handed me a leaflet, an invitation to an anti-war meeting. I folded it and buried it in my backpack. In my room at the Y, I removed it, smoothed it out on the table, and read and re-read it. I taped it to the bathroom mirror and pondered it while I brushed my teeth. I was uneasy. These were the people the media had warned against. *Violent* people. But even more alarming to me was the tedium of my life, the lack of fervor, the way my youth was slipping away."

And once it was gone, what would follow?

I ponder what to wear to the meeting; anti-war t-shirts and caps and buttons aren't part of my wardrobe. I settle for jeans and a pastel blue blouse with ruffles down the front.

The subway carries me downtown. I'm keyed up, restless, on edge; I sense that something pivotal is about to happen. At the community center, I hunker down on a bench at the rear, hoping no one will notice me. Phrases like "U.S. imperialism," "freedom fighters," and "ruling class" fly back and forth. One speaker wears shades, a camouflage outfit, and combat boots. His hair is teased out around his face like a huge bubble. He calls for unity between Afro-Americans and Vietnamese against "our common enemy." Another speaker with shoulder-length hair, a beard, and a Mao button condemns U.S. incursions into other countries. I have only a vague idea what they're referring to.

"I attended that meeting," I tell Miguel. "Certain books on history and politics were mentioned. I dutifully jotted them down on a notepad and went straight from the meeting to an alternative bookstore in the Village, where I bought some of those books, then spent the next three days reading them, hardly eating or sleeping. Even though history had always bored me, these books were different. They were written about ordinary people, poor people, oppressed people. Not just 'dead white men,' as we say. The first book I read was the *Autobiography of Malcolm X*." Miguel nods. "You know it?"

"I read it." He scratches his head absent-mindedly and I notice how thick his hair is, dense with tight curls. "It's a good book," he says.

I force myself to forget about his hair. "I kept reading and a new world unfolded. Or rather, the same world but turned upside down."

"I bet that was a shock." He adds, "For someone as unaware as you were."

"First I was shocked, then miserable. Kindly Uncle Sam was turning out to be a pretender, hiding behind the flag like some Wizard of Oz." Now Miguel's eyes seem spellbound.

What is this effect he has on me?

"My misery gradually turned to anger. At Columbia I changed my major from English literature to history and threw myself into the women's movement and the anti-war movement."

"What an about-face!"

I laugh. "I even pierced my ears."

"Oh, my God. Not that!" He reaches across the table. "Let me see." He touches my earlobe.

I feel myself blush and quickly get back to my story. "I'd always felt this…this *humiliation* as a woman. And this resentment at the way we were portrayed on TV and in the news—and by men whenever they thought we weren't listening."

Miguel nods. It's about 9 a.m. The dull roar of the breakfast crowd has subsided so I lower my voice.

"After graduation, I took a part-time job—as a saleswoman in a dress shop on 14th Street—and moved into a third-story walkup in Chinatown The bathtub was in the kitchen, and on the landing between floors was a shared toilet. The cockroaches were as big as mice and would scatter when I'd turn on the lights."

"Wow," says Miguel. "You lived *there?*"

"For two years—until 1970," I say. "In the winter it was freezing and in the summer sweltering. All my free time was spent in the movement: anti-war, feminism, anti-racism, prisoners' rights. It was exhilarating at first."

"At first?"

"After a while the exhilaration faded but it was still satisfying. And fun! Sometimes, though, I wondered if we were treading water. Would we be fighting the same issues 50 years from now?"

I'm active in everything, friendly with everyone, but loneliness is wearing me down, impossible to ignore any longer. Why is it so hard to make close friends?

It's then that I come up with a solution. I'll adopt a baby! Someone to take care of, someone to keep me company, someone who will love me.

I visit an agency, fill out endless forms. The receptionist in her matched sweater set and her meticulous makeup, is congenial. But her warmth quickly fades when she peruses my paperwork.

"You're not married?" Shock edges its way through her words. "And you want to adopt?"

"Yes," I say meekly, feeling like a naughty child.

"Uh, well"—she struggles to regain her composure—"we'll call you, then, when it's time for the interview."

But I know I'll hear nothing more from that quarter.

Miguel says, "I see where this is going. You wanted something more than just activism."

"And I got it! Through a woman named Bonnie. Her t-shirt read 'I Love Lenin.'"

"John?"

"Vladimir."

At an antiwar meeting, a petite but solid woman wearing construction boots sits down next to me. I'm intrigued by her self-assurance.

"Hi, I'm Bonnie. How do you like that book?" she asks, indicating Soledad Brother, *the paperback in my hands.*

"It's fascinating."

"Have you read The Wretched of the Earth?

"Not yet," I say. (But I think I've heard of it.)

"It deals with the psychology of colonization. You'll like it," she says with certitude.

"Bonnie was an intellectual. I was flattered that she even talked to me."

"You're too modest," he says.

"Maybe. Anyway, under her guidance, I began reading Marxist texts. I remember starting with the *Communist Manifesto* and then *The Origins of the Family* by Engels and *What Is To Be Done?* by Lenin. I had so many questions: why is the U.S. always bogged down in a war? Why are people in the projects barely surviving—and in such a rich country? Why don't poor countries ever catch up to us? And why are women so oppressed all over the globe?"

"It's refreshing to see an American concerned about these things," Miguel says.

"From then on when I read the news, it got easier to see the underlying causes of current events. You know what I mean?" He nods and his eyes have that admiring look again. I squirm and quickly add, "From what you said last night, I'm assuming you're a Marxist yourself?"

"It doesn't have the stigma over there that it does here," he says. "Lots of us are communists."

I take that as a yes and move on. "After studying more, I no longer wanted to read analyses by *Newsweek* or the *New York Times.* Even the *Guardian*—the one in New York City—didn't provide the depth I was craving. But Marxism did."

"For example?"

"Like how the wealthy became wealthy, how workers are exploited. And it offered solutions too."

"It sounds exciting, but aren't you maybe a little idealistic?"

"I'm not blinded by Marxism," I assure him. "I quickly learned that not everything fits neatly into a mold. Life is messy. Even among socialists there are sharp differences about how to interpret things and what to do."

"It's the same in my country. There are so many different groups: Trotskyist, Leninist, Maoist."

"But regardless," I say, "Marxism is still the only interpretation of world politics that makes sense to me."

"Me too," he agrees, staring into space. A long column of ash falls off the tip of his cigarette and onto the table. His index finger is crooked, as if it were once broken. "So how did you get from there to actually joining an organization?" he asks. "That's a leap, isn't it?"

"Not so much. Bonnie began inviting me to leaflet at factory gates. Her friends respected my opinions and made me feel welcome. I was invited to other events and slowly absorbed into their work."

"What were these people like?"

"Friendly. Dedicated. Passionate. Gutsy. Schooled in socialist theory."

"It sounds like you were ready to take things a step further."

"That's it! After years of working in those other groups, I wanted to get at root causes—and root solutions."

A few noisy teenagers enter the café. Probably ditching. They order Dr. Peppers and fries to go. They'll die young.

"How did you feel when you found out these people were communists?" he asked.

"I wasn't even shocked; I was delighted."

"Which organization was it?"

"It's called the Anna Louise Strong League."

"Who's she?"

"She was an activist who supported the revolution in the Soviet Union when it was still revolutionary, and then she raised doubts about the Soviet Union and turned to China, where she lived until she died four years ago." Someone puts a dime into the little jukebox on the wall of their booth and a country song makes its way over to where we're sitting. I explain. "The League is a national organization, trying to build a revolutionary party. After I worked for a few months with Bonnie and her friends, they asked me to join."

"And you did?" Miguel says.

"I thought it over. What would joining mean? The League believes in working in factories to develop the proletariat as the *vanguard* of a future revolution. I'd have to quit my part-time job in the clothing shop on 14th Street and take on full-time work that was totally unfamiliar to me." The waitress clears away our plates and tops off our coffee.

"Quite a life change," Miguel says. "Especially for a middle-class American like you."

"But I didn't care! I was bursting with anticipation. I'd read about the role of the proletariat. I couldn't wait to meet them. They were like an exotic species to me."

"Did your parents object?"

"They were a continent away, weren't they? And anyway, no one was to know that I joined the collective because its members— except for a few leaders—are secret."

"Why is that?"

"To protect it. From agents."

"So you joined," he says again.

"I joined."

"Have you ever regretted it?"

I can hear the whir of the milkshake machine. So early in the day? "No, I never regretted it." (I hope I'm not lying, that my current doubts are just an aberration.) "The collective provided me with a purpose for my life, a vehicle for changing the world. And"—I pause, thinking it over—"I gained a new family as well."

For a long time after I joined, the camaraderie satisfied my need for friends. We were all best friends. Two members in particular became my special friends: Charlie and—after I recruited her—Felicia. It's only recently that I've grown so dissatisfied; something isn't right anymore.

"After you joined, what changed?"

"Under the collective's guidance, I quickly found a job in an auto plant here in Jersey and was thrust abruptly into the blue collar world. I moved out of the walk-up in Chinatown and into an apartment in Jersey City."

"You worked in auto?"

"Yes, but I was fired for organizing."

"Can they do that?"

"Not officially. They make up some excuse or other. But that's what it was."

"How long have you been working in industry?" Miguel asks.

"About four years now."

His look of unabashed admiration feels good now. Real good. That little crescent scar next to his left eye is so beautiful, I want to touch it. I decide not to worry so much, to just let myself be friends with him.

I can handle that.

6. Jenny
OCTOBER 1974

THAT SAME NIGHT I'M ON THE SOFA in Cindy's railroad apartment, listening to Leonard Cohen's "First We Take Manhattan," sipping a Cuba Libre, and watching the dancing. Delicate rice-paper globes from the arched floor lamps cast disks on the ceiling of the darkened living room. It's past 1 a.m. already; only a few diehards remain. Felicia slipped away an hour ago.

I haven't kept track of how many beers I've drunk; a while ago when Nick produced a bottle of Bacardi, I switched to rum and Coke. I haven't counted those, either.

My thoughts drift to Miguel Cimarrón. How close I felt to him last night and this morning, and how bereft when the ride ended and he disappeared into the PATH station. All afternoon I've teetered between excitement and anxiety about what this strange attraction on my part will lead to. When Charlie phoned to remind me of the party tonight—which I'd again forgotten—I jumped at the opportunity to get my mind off Miguel.

Couples are slow-dancing. Charlie is dancing with Kate, a member of the collective and a college student at Rutgers. Charlie's face is dwarfed by her Afro. Cindy, the head of the collective, is dancing with her testy husband Matt. Not a hair on her platinum blond pageboy is out of place. He's holding her just a little stiffly. Nothing too passionate. *They're* not tipsy, oh no.

Just to my right, two working-class contacts from Cindy's factory are stapled together. You can't really call that dancing. I take note of the woman's mini-skirt and black eye shadow.

Sergio and Esme, a Puerto Rican couple, who lead our strike support work and will soon become members, we hope, are ballroom dancing. She slides off his arm, then he catches her and reels her in. Nick and June, the laid-back leaders of the Brooklyn collective, make up the final couple.

I tap my foot to the music. The room tilts like a ship in rough water. The dancing has burnt up some of my blood alcohol but I'm far beyond sober. Charlie, my number one partner tonight, has, like me, danced fast and guzzled even faster. My eyes follow him and Kate now. He winks at me over her shoulder, and I raise a wobbly glass to him.

The song ends. Kate unpeels herself from Charlie and wanders over to the hi-fi. Charlie tumbles into the lumpy sofa and slings his arm around my shoulders. Kate puts a record on the turntable and begins dancing with Nick. "What a Wonderful World." The song is like hot chocolate at Dotty's Café on a snowy day.

"Let's do it," Charlie says, standing and pulling me up with him. Charlie smells like beer and peppermint. I imagine how Miguel would smell. Like gunpowder? Like Caribbean beaches? Like revolution?

Despite my vertigo, I relax into Charlie's arms, enjoying the certainty that he won't let me fall. Such trust is a wonderful thing. What a pity that I have to get drunk to experience it.

I've danced with Charlie at many parties but never for so long, so close, so intoxicated. I'm surprised by something hard until I realize it's his erection. I'm embarrassed—for myself and for him. Charlie's my buddy, my partner, my confidant.

Keeping time to the music, he steers me through the doorway into the next room, the study, where our weekly cell meetings occur. It's dark and quiet in here except for light and music drifting in from the living room. He backs me to a desk and presses himself against me. His hand migrates down my thigh to my crotch, probing me through my jeans. Insistent.

Bingo. A shock of pleasure. My knees go soft and I cling to him. He pulls me closer and presses his lips against mine. Then his tongue is in my mouth, exploring. And so easily I find that my tongue is in *his* mouth too.

What's happening? What if someone walks in on us? I lean back on the edge of the desk, crushing some papers, and envision Cindy the next morning, puckering her lips in disapproval when she discovers her crumpled report to the leadership in Chicago. Charlie's warm hand slides under my t-shirt and along my abdomen.

In the living room I hear Nick say, "God, it's so late and I've got a committee meeting at eight this morning. Can you believe it?"

Charlie extracts his hand and steps to the side. Nick and June enter the study. "Hey, you guys," June says. "Great party, huh?"

I nod. "Yeah. Great."

Charlie echoes, "Great party."

Did they notice anything? They pass through the study to the bedroom.

"Wanna get out of here?" Charlie whispers into my ear, sending a tickle shooting all the way down to my ankles.

"Yeah," I whisper, gripping his arm to steady myself.

Almost immediately, however, panic seizes me. I know the recurring pattern. A swift turn-on and an even swifter turn-off. Will tonight be any different? I've never done it with a friend. But that's part of the problem: I don't feel sexually attracted to friends.

The intervening moments don't help, either. The time it takes to say thank you to Cindy, to locate my jacket and knit cap in the tumbled heap of coats on the bed without waking Sergio and Esme's sleeping daughter, to pull on my boots, to collect my bowl of sour cream-onion dip, to descend three flights of stairs, to climb into his Ford pickup and head for his apartment.

As we drive the ten blocks, I'm sitting tongue-tied next to him, thinking: I'm scared. I'm numb. I don't know the rules. I'll be terrible. He'll be disgusted. The radio plays "Tonight's the Night." My anxiety builds. I glance at Charlie, and he reaches for my hand. "I'm glad we're doing this," he says, smiling. He begins to sing along with the music.

Sure you are, I think. You've probably lost all respect for me by now. And you're probably congratulating yourself for scoring. I look at him with resentment but he doesn't notice because he's re-directed his eyes onto the icy road.

Having sex means trusting. And I do trust Charlie. I trust him to listen to me, to keep my secrets, to be my friend. But can I trust him or any guy not to judge my too-small breasts or bony elbows, my inexperience, my lack of expertise? And can I trust that he isn't using me? In spite of the many feminist workshops I've attended on female sexuality, I've yet to derive any joy from sex.

Charlie drives down the icy street in the slow, methodical manner of someone who knows his brain is foggy. Please, Mr. Cop, please, Mr. Pig, *pull us over.*

At a stop sign Charlie squeezes the brakes to avoid skidding on the icy road; then he squeezes the back of my neck. He traces a line on my cheek with his forefinger. I pull away slightly; did he notice? I'm completely numb; my eyes won't focus. All those rum and cokes! But it's too late to back out now. Suddenly, a playhouse floats before my eyes and I want to scream. But nothing comes out.

He leaves the pickup at the curb in front of his apartment. Mitten in glove, we lurch across the snowy patches and bleak, dead brown grass and enter a large wooden house with an ample front porch. I follow him up two flights of creaky stairs to his apartment. He unlocks the door. Inside, it's as cold as Dynamic Metals in January. I shiver and he switches on the wall heater. "It should warm up right away," he assures me, pulling me tight and kissing me. His body heat would have felt good under other circumstances, but all I'm aware of now is a sense of foreboding.

"You want a drink?"

"I've had enough, I think."

"Me too." He wiggles out of his jacket. "Excuse me," he says, "I'll be right back." He heads toward the rear of the apartment and calls out, "Make yourself at home."

Gingerly I sit down on the sofa, avoiding the spot where the vinyl has curled back from the stuffing. I imagine him in his bedroom picking up underwear, throwing it into the closet, putting on fresh sheets. (I hope.) I look around the apartment. In spite of our close friendship, I've never been here before. It looks sparse. On the coffee table there's an ashtray, a pack of Marlboros, and a black mug with half a cup of cold coffee and curdled milk. On the sofa, there's a *Playboy* open at the centerfold next to Lenin's *What Is To Be Done?*, an electricity bill, and a variety of colorful leaflets announcing events and rallies. On an aluminum TV tray, there's a jar of Skippy's peanut butter. I glance toward the kitchen. The counter's bare except for a bag of Frito Lays and a jar of Smucker's orange marmalade.

Charlie appears, leans over, and kisses me on the lips.

"Come on," he whispers, and leads me down the hall. I feel as if I'm on the way to an execution. *My* execution.

In the bedroom a banker's lamp casts an emerald glow on the walls. The asparagus-green paint is flaking.

"Nice pink walls," I say.

"You're so funny," Charlie says, and kisses me on the forehead. "Actually, they look like puke, don't you think?" He moves down to my nose, my chin, my neck.

"Will the landlord let you repaint them?"

"Maybe," he murmurs. He pulls up my t-shirt and nuzzles me between the breasts. I wiggle away from him. Now that he knows how small my breasts are—something that has shamed me all my life—will he want to call the whole thing off? *(Oh mother of God, she's flat as a leaflet!)* At this moment I would prefer to be anywhere else in time or space, but I don't want *that* to be the reason.

Charlie shivers. Is he repelled? Or is he cold? He bounces from foot to foot. Maybe he has to pee.

With one quick motion he unzips my plaid jacket. "Oh," I say. He pulls off my cap and mittens.

"I always wondered what this would be like, Jenny Apple," he says. "Did you?"

Never! Charlie is my buddy, that's *it!*

71

"Sometimes," I say. "Sort of."

"I thought so. At least...I was hoping." He yanks off his boots.

The bed has been hastily made. Charlie pulls back a quilt and two thermal blankets. The sheets look as if they've been jammed into a closet, but at least no odors emerge, thank God. Charlie guides me onto the bed, bends over, and struggles to pull off my boots.

"Oof," he says. I find myself all the way undressed but am not sure how it happened. "You're so beautiful," he says.

Now that's a lie. It's probably one of the things men say to beguile women. I lie on my back, pull the covers up, and grip them to my naked breasts as if they're a life buoy and I can't swim. He slides in beside me. "Are you comfortable?" he says. I'd laugh if I weren't so terrified.

"Um-hmm," I say, my lips clenched.

With one hand he massages my left breast, and with the other he rubs me *down there*. I'm suddenly reminded of Duncan and it's all I can do not to hurl aside the covers, spring out of bed, and flee into the cold. No longer do I experience pleasure at Charlie's touch; I'm dead down there. As I knew I would be.

"Can we turn out the lights?" I ask.

"Sure." He snaps off the lamp. "How's that?" His hands resume their work.

"Umm."

He props himself over me. He's thrown back the covers; I'm freezing. "Are you warm enough?" he asks.

"Yeah."

I thrust my legs out, bend my knees, arch my lower back. Isn't that what you're supposed to do? Then I hold that position, letting him do all the *heavy lifting*. I hope it's over soon.

Moonlight drifts in through the window. He watches me and starts moving, rhythmically, gently at first, then picking up speed.

I squeeze my eyes shut. Should I moan and squirm as I've seen in the movies? He moves above me, more intensely. It doesn't seem to faze him that he's fucking a non-moving object. Is he even aware that this is a one-man show?

Up down up down. He propels my body on the mattress above the squeaky bedsprings. We ride out the tempest like a ship on a turbulent sea. "Oh, *yes!*" he calls out. "Oh, *babe!*"

With a loud groan he collapses on top of me, his penis inside. How long will he leave it there?

He seems oblivious to my...my *frigidity*. (What a horrible word, *frigidity*. I looked it up once: "persistently averse to sexual intercourse." *Persistently averse?* That implies recalcitrance, willfulness, like a naughty child refusing to eat her Brussels sprouts.)

He kisses me. "Thank you," he says, breathing heavily.

Thank you? As if I've serviced him? Like a prostitute? Now I'm getting irritated. What have *I* gotten from all this? Why is all the fun on his side?

But perhaps he hasn't enjoyed it either. How can it be any fun to screw a mannequin? Should I fake an orgasm next time? How *do* you fake an orgasm?

"I want to come again," he whispers. *Oh, no, not again!*

"OK," I whisper back.

Did he use a condom? I can't tell and am sure as hell not going to expose my ignorance by asking. He begins to move up and down on me again, more slowly this time. This time I feel like a log, mounted and propelled by a lumberjack. Will he finally notice that I'm not present?

How can a man enjoy sex when the woman is emotionally *missing in action?* Charlie climaxes, then rolls off me and lies there, breathing hard. He kisses me and pulls up the sheet, covering us both. "How was it for you?" he asks. *Is he kidding?*

"Fine," I say. I've completely renounced any semblance of honesty. If I had the nerve to speak honestly, I'd say, *I'm totally freaked out!* But could he possibly understand?

"What would you like?" *Like?* Oh my God, I'd like to be out of here!

"Nothing," I say.

He holds me tight. I lie there, my eyes stuck open, trapped in his embrace. After a while his arms relax around me. He kisses my neck, releases me, and closes his eyes, his arm flung across my waist. He begins to snore softly.

I carefully remove his arm and consider getting dressed and leaving. But my car is ten blocks away at Cindy's, and it's dark and icy outside—not to mention, the middle of the night. I turn away from Charlie and try to fall asleep, but my mind keeps replaying the encounter. Charlie's uneven snoring jangles my nerves. I turn back and watch him sleeping in the dim moonlight. I study his boyishness, the caramel-brown lock of hair falling across his face. Is this really happening?

Morning light pokes through the blinds, and I regard the naked back of this strange man next to me, trying to recognize my friend Charlie. Will things ever again be the same easy way between us? As bad as last night was, it would be even worse to lose his friendship.

I slip out from beneath the sheets and search for my underwear. On the floor I find my panties and pull them on, glancing anxiously at Charlie to make sure he's still asleep. I don't want him to see me naked, which is ironic since just a few hours earlier, I had sex with him. My padded bra is nowhere to be found. Clutching a pillow to my chest, I look under the bed and peek under the sheets.

"What's up?" Charlie says, stretching and yawning.

"My bra," I mumble, my face burning. "I can't find it."

He feels around the bed and fishes it out from beneath the sheets. "Here," he says.

"Thanks." I blush and turn away from him while fastening the hooks. Charlie watches me.

"Why are you getting dressed?" he asks.

"I have to leave."

He fumbles for the bedside clock, holds it to his face and peers at it, one eye closed. "It's only 7:30, babe." He reaches for the table, misses it, and the clock clatters to the floor. He ignores it. "Have some breakfast first," he coaxes.

"I can't."

"Why not?"

"Um…" I sit on the edge of the bed and put my head in my hands.

Charlie sits up in bed. "Look," he says, gingerly touching my shoulder. "I don't remember much of what happened at the party…what led to this…it just seemed to happen…." He removes his hand. "But I hope it doesn't change things between us, babe."

I twist a corner of the sheet around my fingers and say nothing. What more is there to say? Everything has *already* changed.

He persists. "I mean the friendship we have. Maybe we shouldn't have mixed sex with it."

"I'm sorry too," I say.

"Don't get me wrong, it was great! It's just that I don't want to jeopardize things between us."

"So why did we do it?" I ask.

"We were horny, I guess. At least I was." He scrutinizes me. "And you seemed to be too." I look at the corner of the sheet. It's unraveling. I should ask him if he has a needle and thread. "Say something," he says.

I squirm. "I'm really embarrassed. I'm not sure what to say."

"Yeah, I'm embarrassed too."

"You are?"

"And I'm getting the feeling maybe you didn't enjoy it much…."

"Yes, I did…I mean, no, I didn't." There! It's a relief to be genuine for a change, but now he'll know the truth—that something's horribly wrong with me. He looks so worried that I say, "It's not your fault. I have some hang-ups, that's all." I tie my shoelaces. *Hang-ups.* Just in the nick of time I came up with that word. A kinder word than *frigid.* This is more like the Charlie I know. It's coming back to me, what it's like to be his friend. We can *talk* about things.

Of course, being dressed helps too.

Charlie gets out of bed, seemingly unabashed at his nakedness. "Hold that thought," he says, and strides into the bathroom. I avert my eyes but not before I see his penis hanging down in full view. I hear him urinate, flush the toilet, brush his teeth. He reenters the bedroom, a towel wrapped around his waist, and rummages through the closet.

"What kind of hang-ups?" he asks.

"Couldn't you tell?"

He casts me a sheepish look. "I was so drunk I hardly noticed anything, I'm sorry to say. That's probably why it wasn't so good for you." He pulls on a faded t-shirt, then turns his back and lets the towel drop. I sneak a look at the crack in his butt.

So he really doesn't care that I wasn't involved. That's good. It means that I don't have to worry so much in the future about performing.

But it's also bad! Selfish! Unfair! My thoughts are in knots; later, when I'm alone, I'll have to untangle them.

Charlie tousles my hair. "Come on, I'll make us an omelet," he says. "And some strong coffee. Black OK? The milk's gone bad."

"Just tell me this," I say, following him into the kitchen. "Did you use protection?"

"Absolutely," Charlie says. "A Trojan Magnum XL."

"XL?"

He wiggles his eyebrows. "Extra large."

7. Jenny
NOVEMBER 1974

MIGUEL IS REASSIGNED TO THE SMELTER so we seldom see each other but decide to eat together whenever possible in Tough Pitch. I rearrange my lunch breaks to coincide with his. Never have I felt such a strong attraction to anyone, and I look forward to our lunches more than I should—sharing leftover pizza and *sancocho*, comparing idioms and slang in Spanish and English (*Ni fú ni fá:* you're stuck. *Lo que va, viene:* what goes around comes around). We play chess: he shows me the basic moves on a magnetic board he brings into work. He teases me: *Great move! Bobby Fischer, step aside!* Or he'll say—gleefully— *"Ni fú ni fá."* He helps me take care of union business, delivering messages to workers at their stations, discussing job conflicts with me. At first I'll speak English and he'll speak Spanish, but we usually end up *both* speaking Spanish.

He's taken, I remind myself. But I find myself hoping that things between him and his girlfriend don't work out. Ashamed of such uncharitable thoughts, I decide that the only thing to do is stop eating lunch with him. The best solution would be to quit cold, but I can't bear the thought of that. So I make up my mind to eliminate one lunch a week, then two, etc.

On Monday I tell him, "Sorry, but tomorrow the foreman wants me to take a late lunch; I'll eat with you again on Wednesday." The disappointment on his face prompts me to say, "I'll talk to the foreman and see if he'll change his mind." After that single feeble attempt, we continue eating together as if nothing has been said. From now on it's a steady diet of Miguel for lunch.

It's already been four weeks since that disastrous party at Cindy's. I reflect on it with humiliation, despite the conversation Charlie and I had over breakfast the next morning. We haven't leafleted together since. He keeps making brief phone calls with his excuses: he has to fly home to Chicago for the Christmas holidays. He sprained his ankle ice skating. He has to attend a funeral for a cousin in Tupper Lake, who consumed six shots of Jack Daniels and drove his car into an icy river.

I myself have a few (less dramatic) excuses: the flu, a house guest, a demonstration to attend. Now another Thursday afternoon has rolled around. Unfortunately, we've both used up all our excuses.

Arriving ahead of Charlie, I sit on a low concrete wall. The sun casts long shadows in front of the PATH station, and snow melts in the gutters. Faded grass pokes through dirty heaps of snow. I glance up Grove Street; no sign of him yet. I'm determined to act natural when I see him. For a week now I've been rehearsing it: *acting natural.* The problem is that I can't get a grip on what *natural* means. As I see him approach, I try to remember which of the two of us usually initiates our hug.

We sidestep the hug and make our way to the entrance of the station. It was his turn to bring leaflets and he passes me my portion of them.

"Not so cold today," he says.

"No, it's nice."

The weather? Is that all we have to talk about? What did we used to talk about? These days it's Miguel that crowds everything out of my mind, but I can't talk to Charlie about *him.* Silence settles over us as we pass out leaflets. I'm glad to have something to keep me busy. Give it time, I tell myself.

Afterward, Charlie comes up with some reason not to stop at Rosie's for hot chocolate; I add my own thin excuse. We head home in different directions.

One day Miguel and I are sitting in the break room. No one else is there. It's 3:30 a.m. and my eyelids are drooping. Miguel says morosely, "My girlfriend and me, we no understand us." His words jolt me awake. He changes the subject before I can come up with an appropriate response.

A few days later during his break, I'm tamping the dirt around my furnace with a shovel when he stops by my station and says, "I move out today."

My breath feels trapped in my lungs. "From your girlfriend's?" I ask, continuing to tamp the dirt.

"She is too bossy."

I keep on tamping.

He pulls off his helmet and lets it swing by the strap over his arm. There's a ring of sweat and soot on his forehead, and he wipes it away with a rag.

"She want that I stay home all the time." Domineering.

"She is young," he continues. Immature.

"She no political," he says. *Like you are, Yenny.*

"How did you two meet?" I finally ask.

"Our parents, they are friends for much time. They want that we marry."

"Do you love her?" None of your business, Jenny Apple.

"I never really desire her but I have *obligación.*"

Not a good basis for a relationship.

"She scold much," Miguel says. "Scold, scold, scold, all the time." A nag. I shudder and vow never to be that kind of woman.

"Where are you staying?" I ask.

"In El Bronx. At my cousin's. Pablo and his wife Yesenia. On the *sofá.*"

"I'm sorry you're having these problems," I say. Liar, liar, pants on fire.

Miguel's shoulder barely moves. "That is the life."

Shouldn't he appear more distressed?

⋘ ⋘ ⋘ ⋘ ⋘

At first, Miguel's breakup with Angélica makes no difference to our friendship. We still talk shop. It's *Miguel's* opinions about the organizing work that I rely on most, even though the collective holds weekly meetings where we examine shop matters and turn them inside out like laundry about to go into the wash. But when someone is actually working in your plant and on your same shift, he has an edge.

By early February he drives his car from the Bronx to my place every morning; then we take turns driving to the plant in Central Jersey. For some reason he decides to move out of his cousin Pablo's apartment and in with some friends—Julio and his wife Hermalinda.

"Julio? The guy whose father was a rebel in the military?" Anticipation flows through me like hot copper.

Julio is studying to be a registered nurse at CUNY, and his wife Hermalinda is a social worker. To my delight, she too was involved in the civil war in Santo Domingo. We all meet at a Dominican restaurant on the Upper West Side, where they introduce me to *sancocho de gallina* (chicken stew) and *pecao* (fish). As they reminisce about Santo Domingo, they throw in tidbits about the rebellion: *Remember, Miguel, when you taught Serena to shoot a rifle?* (Who's Serena?) *Remember when Nico's mother confronted that soldier and offered him some* pan dulce?

I feel like a dog panting for table scraps.

After we part with Julio and Hermalinda, Miguel and I stroll downtown and take in a triple feature at an all-night theater on 42nd Street: "The Towering Inferno," "Stepford Wives," and "French Connection II." We eat breakfast at a diner in Lower Manhattan before he escorts me to the PATH station. I watch him from the window as my train pulls away, his face full of longing.

The next weekend Miguel has something to show me in Manhattan. We take the train to the Upper West Side and he leads me a few blocks to a large brick building near Columbia. A red banner hangs from a second-story window, declaring in English and Spanish, "ALL POWER TO THE PEOPLE." He tells me that Marco Marquez and his *compañeros* are squatting in the building.

"Marco Marquez?"

"The Muchacho. Remember? Our anarchist."

Suddenly I recall that Felicia's former anarchist boyfriend was also named Marco. "He was Felicia's boyfriend, wasn't he? That's how you met her."

Miguel nods. He ushers me inside. Clusters of people are busy cleaning or painting or sitting cross-legged on the floor in a circle—apparently having a meeting. A smell of garlic and onions comes from a kitchen somewhere. A class of primary school kids is touring the building, led by their pony-tailed teacher. We locate Marco on a rickety ladder, applying chili pepper-red paint to one wall of a spacious room. His long hair is tangled; his graying white T-shirt is spattered.

He climbs down the ladder and kisses me on both cheeks.

"*Bienvenida*," he says, beaming. "*Fulano* (So and so) here finally brings you by. It's about time!" Putting an arm around me, he whisks me away, abandoning Miguel to the company of a muscular man in a sleeveless t-shirt, who's hanging a poster of Mother Jones on the wall. "MOURN THE DEAD BUT FIGHT LIKE HELL FOR THE LIVING," it reads in English and Spanish.

Marco's eyes glisten as he guides me through the former apartment building, showing me the future day care center, clinic, and food co-op, in large rooms created from ripped-out walls. He raises an index finger. "We've occupied this building because it belongs to the city and we are the city," he says. "This community needs day care, health care. We're going to provide it.

"Never forget this: 'Government is an association of men who do violence to the rest of us.'" As I'm pondering the quote, he adds,

"Leo Tolstoy said that."

On the subway home Miguel tells me that he visits Marco from time to time "to keep in touch." Miguel and his friends have been forced to forsake their homeland, sometimes for political reasons, other times for economic ones. Miguel himself had to leave after he was arrested for organizing a union at a tortilla plant. His father's connections got him out of prison that time, but things were too dangerous for him to stay in his country. Many of his friends have joined struggles here on the East Coast for housing, equal pay, or immigrants' rights, while others just try to make a living—like his best friend Nico, an auto mechanic in the Bronx with a new baby.

Miguel sighs. "Everything back home is shit. That fascist Balaguer is entrenched as president. The secret police are still active."

After these two visits to his friends, Miguel and I go out on a regular basis. We love dinners in Chinatown, jazz in the Village, snowball fights in Central Park. And he teaches me to dance the *merengue*.

"Left right, left right. As if you're marching," he coaches me. We've gravitated to a corner of the small dance floor at a club in Jersey City. The music of Charlie Palmieri is playing. I'm the only non-Latino there. Puerto Rican and Dominican couples fill the dance floor, moving rapidly, squeezed together. Even though I've been watching them over a Cuba Libre ever since we arrived, I haven't been able to figure out their moves; it's all too fast. I step tentatively to the left and bring my right foot together. "That's good." Miguel smiles encouragingly. "Step together, step together."

"This is not so hard after all," I say, surprised.

"Just keep up the *left right*," he repeats. "Just keep marching to the beat."

When I'm confident that my feet have mastered the steps, he adds, "Now the secret of *merengue* is to keep the upper body straight but move your hips with each step." He illustrates, swinging his hips. (I knew there must be more to it than just *left right, left right.*) I try the hip action, feeling self-conscious. "Keep up the *left right* but add the swing of the hips." After I practice for a while, it feels more natural.

"That's *it!*" he finally says, beaming. He grabs me and pulls me into the center of the crowd. One woman's hips look as if they're disconnected from the rest of her body. Her long hair waves from side to side. No one pays any attention to me; I cast off my inhibition and give myself over to the music.

⋖ ⋖ ⋖ ⋖ ⋖

A friendly foreman agrees to rework my schedule so Miguel and I can have the same weekends off. Requesting a favor from a boss gives me pause; favoritism is one of the many offenses I hold against the union *misleadership*. And as a shop steward, I need to set an impeccable example. But Danny Sugar is not your typical foreman. He would never demand payback. He's as close to salt of the earth as a foreman can get. He doesn't look down on us workers; he doesn't flaunt his authority. You won't find him loafing in an air-conditioned office while we sweat away on the shop floor; he jokes around with us and even takes his turn working a jackhammer or mixing cement. He cooperates with me as shop steward to deflect problems before they balloon into grievances. His tinkering with my schedule doesn't seem like a favor at all; after all, he does it for everyone, doesn't he?

8. Jenny

ONE SATURDAY AFTERNOON A MONTH AFTER my bedroom romp with Charlie, I've just finished taking a bath when the phone rings. Wrapping myself in a towel, I pad across the living room, my bare feet leaving wet footprints on the linoleum.

"Is this Jenny Apple?" a male voice asks.

I stand there shivering. "Yes. Who's this?"

"This is Andy Mack, Jane's brother."

"Jane?"

"Janie. Your high school friend. From back home in Riverside."

"Janie? Janie Mack?" I plop down on the sofa. I haven't seen my best friend from high school in years. I rarely even think about her except when I receive her hastily scribbled note at the bottom of a mimeographed Christmas letter that brags about their three children, her husband's job in aerospace, her work for the Republican Party and the Baptist church. Everything that I detest—except for the three kids.

But when I hear her brother's voice, nostalgia for Janie flows through me. She's one of the girls that befriended me back in my sophomore year of high school when I was, once again, the new kid in a new school in a new city. Everyone had long since chosen their circle of friends, and breaking into those entrenched spheres was a formidable task, especially for a shy girl like me who'd never learned the art of chitchat nor the complex rules of adolescent friendship.

Enter Janie Mack, who not only introduced me to her friends but who spent a solid year trying to introduce me to Jesus Christ, "our Lord and Savior." I'll always remember church camp with Janie in the San Bernardino Mountains north of Riverside because it offered me my first palatable experience with a boy—sweet, because I was able to surrender my panic, but bitter too, because of its abrupt ending.

Bobby Jones is shy and ungainly. Two reasons, perhaps, that I feel safe with him. We spend all our time at camp together—swimming, harmonizing to hymns like "What a Friend We Have in Jesus," playing ping pong and tic-tac-toe and War, singing "Kookaburra." One night during a clandestine, candle-lit game on the rough-hewn floor of one of the cabins, Bobby spins a bottle. Candlelight reflects off the bottle and onto our faces. The bottle slowly fades comes to a halt—aiming right at me. There's a pause, then Bobby rises and approaches me. His t-shirt smells freshly laundered as he kneels next to me; his lips are as soft as the marshmallows we made s'mores out of earlier that night.

When the week of camp is over, Bobby and I stand outside in the chill morning air behind the camp kitchen. His hands are in his jeans pockets; he shifts from foot to foot. Should I ask for his phone number? But girls don't do that. Why isn't he asking me for mine?

"Well, I sure had fun," he says, scuffing the dust with the heel of his sneaker.

"Me too."

Bobby looks over at his dad, who's leaning against a panel station wagon, smoking a cigarette. The engine is idling. His dad's body is stiff with impatience, and he reaches through the front window, honks the horn, and gestures at Bobby.

Bobby looks back at me. "Well...see you, I guess," he says. He reaches out and pats my shoulder, before drifting out of my life. As he drives off he waves at me—my final view of him. Mixed with my fond memories are hurt and resentment that he hasn't liked me enough to ask for my phone number. Years later, one sleepless night, I suddenly shoot up in bed; it occurs to me that Bobby did like me. It was just that he was as shy as I was.

Andy Mack's laugh charms me. "I think I met you back when you were in high school, but you probably don't remember. I picked up Jane and some of her friends at a pizza place one day and gave you all rides home. You were the one with the ponytail, weren't you?"

Of course I recall that night and I recall Janie's older brother. How handsome he was, how mature. His smile made me blush—it was directed at me, I was sure, and I promptly developed a crush on him, which lasted for weeks. But to my disappointment our paths never crossed again.

"I'm in the city for a convention," he says.

"What kind of convention?" I ask. *What does he want?*

"Plastics," he says.

I recall "The Graduate," one of my favorite movies, and laugh.

"'Plastics,'" I say, my voice imitating Mr. Robinson from the movie. Andy Mack laughs too. I ask, "So you're an executive or something?"

"Well, the title is Assistant Sales Manager to the Vice-President. So yes, I guess I am, in a way. Nothing important, though. Just another cog."

"Sounds impressive to me," I say. "Does that make you a member of the ruling class?" I try to sound as if I'm kidding, but I'm not.

He chuckles. "Sorry for the late notice, but Janie suggested I look you up. I don't know anyone in town and wondered if you'd like to meet me in Manhattan for dinner."

Absolutely no sound comes from my mouth.

"Hello?" Andy says.

"Um, can I call you right back?" I ask.

I hang up after getting his number. In the bathroom I pull on my jeans and t-shirt. Does accepting him mean I'm agreeing to have sex with him? Especially after he's paid for an expensive meal? On the other hand, wouldn't it be *impolite* to refuse his invitation?

And maybe a little *mean* to not offer him some company when he's all alone in the city? The brother of my former best friend?

I'm at one of those frat parties in my freshman year of college where the booze flows freely, the lighting almost isn't, and everyone is high on weed. All evening I drink beer, then wine, then tequila. Someone passes me a joint—a boy from the state college, a "party school," they say. Then he flitters around me like a humming bird. The encounter takes place on dirty sheets in a back bedroom. The next day, to my chagrin, I can't recall his name; did we even bother to introduce ourselves? I obliterate all memory of the experience by joining the ski team and training for hours every afternoon.

In my sophomore year one day at a downtown intersection, my tire goes flat. A sexy red convertible happens along. A man in a suit steps out. "Dave Smibbons, at your service," he says, a bubble of laughter in his throat. His crookedly appealing grin and his smell of caramel aftershave lotion bewitch me. He installs the spare tire and treats me to lunch at a nearby Italian restaurant. He's a Ford showroom salesman, he tells me. At some point during the linguini with squid and basil sauce, a fine Chardonnay, and the tête-à-tête, an irresistible sexual attraction grips me. After lunch Dave Smibbons invites me to his apartment, and I accept.

It's the beginning of a tawdry ritual. Every Wednesday I meet him for lunch in an upscale Italian or French restaurant. After a glass of wine, the conversation turns to sex. "You turn me on so much," he says in a low, sultry voice. "I'm so hot for you." Or, "I could do things to you that you can't imagine." I listen, blushing, alcohol-impaired, feeling moistness between my legs and a warm tingling in my genitals that make me want to press my body tight against him.

We return to his spare apartment. On his coffee table is a brass alarm clock, which I set for 2:30 p.m. We proceed to make out. By now, however, I'm dry, no longer desiring him, but I carry on with it because I've allowed him to pay for the foie gras at Pierre's. He fondles me—fully clothed, I insist—as we half lie, half hang off his velveteen sofa.

"This is so difficult for me," he says panting, as he said the last time and the time before that. "I get so frustrated."

The alarm clock rings. I slide out from under him and rush off to my Renaissance lit class. Shame accompanies me but also the conundrum as to why sitting with him in the restaurant turns me on so much more than the real stuff afterward in his dim bachelor apartment. It's unsavory, but I can't deny that being wanted like that gives me a certain satisfaction. Even though I'm sure he only wants my body.

Driving back to campus, a verse from the literature assignment for that day runs through my head.

> *Had we but world enough, and time,*
> *This coyness, Lady, were no crime....*

Finally one afternoon out of boredom I yield to him, my panties around my ankles, my collegiate corduroy skirt bunched around my waist. When it's over, I arise from the sofa, tug my panties up, yank my skirt down, run my fingers through my hair, and flee.

It's over.

Dave Smibbons calls me that night and for several days afterward, but I tell my roommate I'm "out." The phone calls become a trickle, then dry up like a summer creek. I sit with my hands in my chin and ponder the silent phone.

Why don't I know what I want?

I accept Andy Mack's invitation. Is it the looming prospect of yet another dateless Saturday night? Is it the novelty? Am I lulled by the matter-of-fact sound of his voice and the knowledge that he's the brother of an old friend?

As soon as I see him in the Plaza Hotel lobby, wearing an Armani wool suit, his polished black shoes reflecting the chandeliers, I want to turn and flee. As a rising star at a corporate firm, he'll be way too sophisticated for me. What will we talk about? What will I do if he comes on to me? And if he knew who I really was, what would he think? Besides, he's the epitome of everything I despise.

Why am I consorting with the enemy?

Andy Mack doesn't seem at all bothered by my lack of sophistication. As he wines and dines me in the Oak Room, it's one of those times in my life when I'm able to let go of the tension that so often clings to me in a social setting. His descriptions of the stodgy speakers at the convention are hilarious, as are his stories of growing up in Riverside. He tells me about Janie: "She's still deep into this religious thing and she's much more conservative than I am, but she's the same sweet little sister she always was. She wants me to tell her all about you. She was so excited when I agreed to call you."

How seldom I laugh with complete abandon like this, laugh until my ribs ache. By the time we get to the crème brûlée and Kahlua, I've sunk deep into the delightful decadence of this one weekend evening amidst the thousands that I spend reading or watching reruns of "I Love Lucy."

After dinner, although I know better, I accompany Andy up to his twentieth-floor suite. "Just to see the view," I promise myself. Room service delivers Swiss chocolate and brandy, and we curl up facing each other on the brocade sofa, surrounded by overstuffed pillows.

Our easy communication over dinner has taken me by surprise—he seems almost like *my* big brother too. He's down-to-earth, cordial, intelligent. He's even a liberal.

And a future CEO.

Of course I know that CEOs aren't the enemy. In fact, many of them are probably wonderful parents, husbands, even contributors to charity. It's the capitalist system that presses people like Andy Mack into carrying out its dirty work. It's what he represents and the type of work he does. "A cog in the machine"—those were his own words. My thoughts, benumbed, swirl like the burnt orange cognac in my snifter.

Somehow we stray onto the topic of the Sexual Revolution. "Everyone in my generation seems to relish it," I tell Andy Mack. "They love being free to thumb their noses at bourgeois morality and its double standards." He's listening, his elbow on the back of the sofa, his chin in his hand. "But what's liberating to everyone else feels like unbearable pressure to me."

Several years after I arrived in New York City, I first heard the word orgasm. A friend in a women's group gave me a pamphlet to read by someone named Anne Koedt. "The Myth of the Vaginal Orgasm."

The vaginal *what?*

The modern women's movement was gaining steam and I attended a sexuality workshop at the Women's Center in Manhattan. I participated in group discussions of Anne Koedt's pamphlet. One time we sat in a circle on the floor and explored our vulvae with mirrors.

But knowledge of the facts of female sociology and physiology was insufficient. I still couldn't masturbate my way to orgasm—although my clitoris chafed from the attempts. Nor did my recent enlightenment come to my aid when confronted with the pressing urgency of a sweaty, aroused male—the groping, the hot breath, the engorged penis. And nothing—neither workshops nor a brief trial with therapy—kept Duncan's harrowing image from accosting me over and over again.

Once I arrived in New York I fell into a few sexual situations. When I found myself alone with a man in his or my apartment, I couldn't figure out how to extricate myself; I didn't want to hurt his feelings. And I wanted to be *normal like everyone else.* Maybe this time it would work.

But it never did. I made sure those encounters remained one-night stands. Over time I became ever more skilled at keeping things impersonal. Friendly but never flirtatious, polite but aloof. My activism enabled this. And although I was excited about my political activities, there was a sharp edge of loneliness on Saturday nights and an unsettled feeling that something was off-balance.

"I've never even had an orgasm—" I stop, horrified. How did we get onto this subject? Perhaps Andy's easy-going nature and charm have disarmed me. And that can lead me into a jam; Dave Smibbons flashes through my head. I squeeze my eyes shut and wince. "I can't believe I said that."

Andy Mack looks as if he's considering something. "You're not alone," he says.

What does *that* mean? Oh my God, he'll think I want to go to bed with him. My best friend's brother!

"I may have something that will interest you," he says. He walks to the dresser, retrieves a gray briefcase, and returns to the sofa with it. He pops the latch. In the case are rows of plastic objects. He pulls a small white one out of its clamp in the felt-lined case.

"My company sells these," Andy Mack says. "They're called mini-massagers." The object is shaped like a tube of lipstick and about the same size. "They're used for sore muscles. But they also serve as"—he looks at me as if unsure whether to continue—"they serve as vibrators."

It's 1969. I'm standing in line in the New York Public Library in Manhattan to check out yet another book in my endless quest to unlock the enigma of my sexuality. I pray that the grandfatherly library clerk won't smirk or, even worse, comment on the title. I twist my head a quarter-turn to eye the man in line behind me: is he peeping over my shoulder? After the clerk stamps the book and pushes it toward me, I turn it upside down and exit, imagining eyes trained on my back. At home I pore through the book and see pictures of various kinds of vibrators used for over a hundred years. "In the past century," I read, "vibrators were used to treat 'hysteria' in women, a 'disease' caused, among other things, by lack of satisfaction during intercourse."

Andy Mack continues. "After being fairly popular in the teens and twenties—even to the extent of being advertised in *Ladies Home Journal*, if you can believe that, everything changed when porn movies started featuring them. Respectable magazines refused to run their ads anymore, and vibrators went under the radar for *forty years*." He hands the massager to me and I turn it around in my hand. "But lately they're getting respectable again, thanks to the women's movement. Have you heard of Eve's Garden?"

I shake my head.

"It's a kind of sex toy shop just for women. It opened this year over on 57th Street, not far from here. They're one of our best buyers now."

"So *that's* what you meant by plastics."

"Among other things. Don't take this wrong; we're a legitimate company."

"I can't wait to visit Eve's Garden."

"You can have that one." He gestures to the vibrator. "Take it home; try it out."

I put my hands together in prayer position. "I'm eternally indebted to you."

He laughs. "By the way, there's a huge interest these days in women's sexuality. Last month in Manhattan there was even a conference on the subject. It's been a boon for our business, that's for sure."

The collective would regard such conferences as *petit-bourgeois* (middle-class) diversions because they don't speak directly to working class women's issues such as equal pay for equal work and the double duty of women workers in the factory and the home.

"I wish I'd known about the conference," I say. And I mean it.

"One of the women that works at Eve's Garden told me it was a huge success, especially the workshop by Betty Dodson."

"Betty Dodson?"

"She's a Ph.D. who's written a book in the field."

"What on earth was her workshop about?"

"It was called 'Masturbation and Orgasm.' And she discussed vibrators and how women can achieve sexual satisfaction. Many women—and men—know nothing about any of this. You're hardly the only one."

Andy Mack presented me with a wonderful gift. One remarkable little apparatus, so small you can carry it around in your pocket, has the potential to create such pleasure. Just when I'm suffering agony over what happened with Charlie—dismay that once again my body has padlocked the door and hung out the "GONE FISHING" sign—there's a shock of delight that steals my breath away. The orgasm feels so monumental that my shame crumbles in its presence.

But I use it alone. I still don't trust men—not in bed, not naked, not intimate. Whenever I think about having joyful sex with a real person—with a *man*—an image of Duncan invades my mind and pushes out the thought.

9. Jenny

FEBRUARY 1975

ONE MORNING I ASK MIGUEL IF HE'D LIKE to stop off at Felicia's for breakfast.

"I don't think so," he says. I stare at him, tilting my head. He explains. "I don't want to disturb her."

"Oh, is that all," I say, shedding my gloves and work jacket. "Don't worry about *that*; she'll be glad to see you. I'll call to let her know you're coming."

I arrive ahead of him at my apartment building. (We haven't carpooled today because I came to work directly from a meeting in Newark.) The door to Felicia's apartment stands ajar, and the smell of fried bacon and *tortillas de huevos* floats into the hallway. Felicia's tomcat Perdido sniffs my shoes as I enter. "*Hola, preciosa,*" says Felicia. She's barefoot, her toenails painted a carroty orange. I admire her miniskirt and scoop-neck top that bares ample cleavage. I arrange the *pan dulce* on a platter. Felicia hands me a mug of coffee, then scoops up Perdido and strokes him.

A year and a half ago, before we became best friends, I was curious about the tall slender woman who lived on the floor beneath me and who ran, not walked, up and down the stairs of our building. Her skin was the color of toffee; her untamed curls were thick as tangled yarn. She usually carried a canvas bag slung over her shoulder. One day she was sitting on the stoop, absorbed in a book—*History Will Absolve Me* by Fidel Castro—when I invited her up for coffee.

I brew espresso, Felicia sits on the windowsill at the open window. Then we climb out onto the fire escape and perch on the iron steps, gazing down through the railing and sipping coffee. Kids play on a jungle gym in the park across the street.

I ask her how she likes the Castro book. "It's fascinating," she says. "A boyfriend told me about it."

Her boyfriend turned out to be Marco, Miguel's friend. (That's how Miguel met Felicia.) Marco initiated Felicia into the readings of anarchists like Mikhail Bakunin and Emma Goldman. When she broke up with Marco, she continued her education, reading Franz Fanon, Kwame Nkrumah, Karl Marx.

"Have you been in the U.S. long?" I ask her.

"Five years." Her glance drifts across the park to a little boy on a teeter-totter; her eyes seem to grow distant. "I left my son with my mom. I haven't seen him for two years."

I can't imagine it—leaving your son behind. Not me! Never! But how little I know about the exigencies of survival.

"What's his name?"

"Guillermo." She turns back to me. "He's seven now."

Later she pulls a wallet from her backpack and extracts a black and white photo from a cloudy plastic sleeve. In the picture, a boy stands in front of a short older woman, whose arms are on his shoulders. They're both smiling. The boy has two missing teeth; the woman more than that. In the background is a little house and tidy garden with two trees.

"That's him and my mom in front of our house."

"He's cute!" I say.

"He's the apple of my eye."

She tells me she put money down on the house last year. "Each month I send payments."

"How can you afford to buy a house?"

"Houses don't cost so much over there. And I worked two jobs when I first got here."

"Doing what?"

"Housekeeper, garment worker, waitress—you name it. I also lived with my cousin so I didn't pay rent."

In 1973, when the copper refinery in central New Jersey grudgingly opened its doors to female workers, Felicia was one of the first women to apply. The money was the best she'd made on any job. By the time I met her, she'd been on the afternoon shift there for over a year. I'd just been laid off at the Ford plant in Mahwah, New Jersey, so I jumped at the chance to apply there. I was hired immediately.

Miguel arrives shortly and joins us in the kitchen. Felicia kisses him on both cheeks. "How you doing, Cimarrón?" she asks. She allows him no time to respond. "By the way, what happened with you and Angélica?"

A flash of annoyance crosses his face. "We broke up," he says curtly, in Spanish.

In English Felicia says, "I know *that*. But how come?" Felicia speaks English whenever possible. It's a matter of pride with her. *After all, I live in America now*, she'll say.

"*Es complicado*," Miguel replies in Spanish.

"So what else is new?" she says in English. "Things are always complicated."

"*Eso es*," he says. That's how it is.

"Oh, Miguel, you can tell *me*," she says. In English again.

"*Sí, pero no quiero.*" Yes, but I don't want to.

There's a tense silence. Felicia pours Miguel's coffee into a big yellow mug that says: "IT'S A BEAUTIFUL DAY IN THE NEIGHBORHOOD." From the other side of the cup a placid Mr. Rogers stares out at me. Felicia motions for Miguel to take a seat.

"But *querido*," she says, "I thought you two were trying to work it." Can't she see that he doesn't want to talk about it? On the other hand, his irritation does seem a bit excessive.

He glares at Felicia and the words burst from his lips. "She kicked me out!"

I blink and pour too much half and half into his coffee. That isn't what he told me.

"She did? How come?" Felicia asks.

"I don't want to talk about it! OK? *If* that's all right with you."

I bite my thumbnail. What's this about? Felicia's admonition about Miguel and his "woman problems" suddenly returns to me; I thrust it into a back pocket of my mind.

People do change, I want to tell Felicia. I sympathize with Miguel's resentment. I myself have once or twice been the focus of her *meddling*, although that may be too harsh a word. She'd probably call it *offering support* or *being a good friend.*

Felicia pouts. "Well, it's a free country," she says. She raises her shoulders and holds them there as if they're stuck. "I guess."

Miguel pushes back his chair. It scrapes across the linoleum floor. "Gotta go," he says. He throws his denim jacket over his shoulder.

Felicia grabs a sleeve of the jacket and yanks it off his shoulder. She tosses the jacket through the bedroom door, where it lands on the floor and Perdido sniffs at it. Felicia pushes Miguel into a chair. "No, no, no, don't go! You stay! Eat! What's your hurry? Have some coffee! Some *pan* and *huevos! Please!*" She glances at me, a worried look on her face. I wait in suspense. Miguel's back is stiff. Then Felicia says,

"Miguel, what's new at work?"

There's a pause. His back relaxes slightly. He casts a resentful glance at Felicia. "I would have told you sooner if you'd let me. It's been a terrible night."

Felicia looks contrite. "What happened, Miguel?"

Miguel pulls a pack of Marlboros from his shirt pocket and lights up a cancer stick. "Couple of guys got burnt," he says.

"In the smelter?"

"Yeah. Danilo De Luca and Roberto Santiago. You know them?"

"I've heard of them," Felicia says.

"What happened?" I ask.

Miguel clenches his jaw as if he'd like to beat the crap out of someone. "The foreman ordered them to spray down a furnace before it cooled! The damned thing blew up on them just before the end of the shift."

"Are they OK?"

"Berto didn't look that bad to me but Danilo was burnt all over. It was awful. They were both carried away by an ambulance."

"*¡Que horror!*" I say, my fork suspended. The smelter is the dirtiest, hottest department in the plant. The vision of Danilo, burnt and clinging to life, sickens me. And what if that should happen to Miguel?

Felicia succumbs to Spanish. "*Ay, diós mío!*" she says.

Silence descends upon us. Then Felicia, her eyes flashing, says, "It's all that *pinche* foreman's fault; he made them clean out the furnaces too soon."

"The guys in the smelter are up in arms," Miguel says.

"And the union?" I ask.

"No word yet when I left," Miguel says. "But it just happened."

Felicia snorts. "The union leaders will make noises, try to sound militant, but they won't do anything. Trust me."

"The guys in the smelter say they want a union meeting right away."

"Good idea!" Felicia says. "I'll spread the word on night shift."

"Yenny, you can organize Tough Pitch on graveyard," Miguel says.

"And I'll ask the union to call an emergency meeting," I say. "If this doesn't move them, nothing will."

We lean toward each other, all talking at once. We drink coffee and discuss strategy. I jot things down on a pink notepad that Felicia pulls out of a crammed kitchen drawer. Miguel lights up another cigarette. Felicia paces the room, tossing out ideas. I munch on a *pan dulce* and keep writing. We drink more coffee.

"Every morning we eat breakfast together," I tell Miguel. "Maybe you should join us." A brief frown appears on Felicia's face. Did Miguel see it? Damn, I should have asked her first. Too impulsive—*again!*

Back in my apartment by 10 a.m., I can't sleep; my head is awhirl with ideas. The light that sneaks in around the blinds irritates me. Finally I get up and mix a batter of brownies. I'll bake them later and take them to work for some of the guys. Then I boil some water for tea, pour the tea into a glass with rum and lemon juice and honey. Propped up in bed, I sip it until I feel drowsy, then sink into a deep sleep.

◅━ ◅━ ◅━ ◅━ ◅━

A pall hangs over the plant. Portable radios are silent. No "Stairway to Heaven" or "Maggie May." No "Sha la la la—la la la." No groups of young guys lounging near the vending machines and telling dirty jokes. Foremen hunker down in their offices. Everyone seems vigilant, like loved ones around a deathbed.

When I arrive at my station, three workers linger there. "Hi, guys. What's up?" I ask. I deposit my metal lunchbox and my newspaper behind a bench and pull an asbestos jacket from a hook.

Joe Lamb paces, his hands in the pockets of his coveralls. "Explosion in the smelter. It don't look good for Danilo De Luca," he tells me, nervous energy behind his gruff voice. "He's in the ICU with 90% burns." He pulls at his beard. "The priest came, delivered the last rites."

"Them mother-fuckers!" Jerome Rivers explodes. He wipes the sweat from his dark face with a rag. The scar on his jaw quivers.

"*Pendejos!*" Eric Corzo says, spitting onto the dirt floor. Then he looks at me. "*Disculpe.*" Sorry. His wiry body is tense.

"And how's Roberto?" I ask.

"He was released, thank God," says Joe Lamb.

My thoughts are racing. This outrage requires action. And who's in a better position to organize it than me? After all, for several months I've listened to details of workers' personal lives. I've filed grievances, urged them to take stands—even for the right to be issued clean coveralls on every shift.

Hey, Joe, I'll say, wiping the sweat from my forehead, *can you stop by the union this afternoon? They're going to discuss the new contract.* And Joe will hem and haw. *Yeah, I'll try, Jenny, but it ain't easy right now, you know. The old lady's folks are visiting from Tallahassee.*

Unlike most shop stewards, I flat-out take their side. *You need to leave early, Hector? Sure, let me talk to the foreman.* And Hector will throw me a look of gratitude: *I just can't talk to that...that guy, Jenny.*

I've pressed leaflets into their often indifferent hands: *Here, read this. It explains how the war is robbing us of resources.* I've shown them the connection between job conditions and capitalism: *For every extra bar of copper they squeeze out of us, Maria, the more profit they make; that's why all the speed-up.* I've cajoled them to attend meetings, rallies, and fund-raisers: *This is why it's important. Do you need a ride?*

It's obvious to everyone that I'm different. They may not know about my framed diploma tucked away in a bottom dresser drawer under some college compositions that I aced, but I can't hide the fact that I'm petit bourgeois. I've worked hard to fit in, to prove that someone from the middle-class can survive in this plant and that a woman can carry her weight in a man's world. I know they respect me even if they don't embrace all of my weird notions.

Perhaps my hard work will pay off now. What's important is to focus their rage. I spring into action. "There'll be a meeting at the union hall right after work," I say. "Pass it on."

My co-worker, Andre Boucher, covers for me as I lope across the plant to the phone booth in the break room. Almost ripping the accordion doors off their hinges, I stick a dime in the phone and dial a number.

It rings seven long times. "Yeah?" answers a gruff and groggy voice, that of Mitch Talabante, the union VP.

"Mitch! It's Jenny from the plant."

"Jenny who?"

"Jenny Apple," I say impatiently. "From Tough Pitch. The shop steward." He knows very well who I am.

"Oh." Pause. "Yeah." Pause. "What's up?"

"We've got a situation here. It looks like Danilo De Luca ain't going to make it. The guys are ready to blow. I've called a meeting at the union hall right after work this morning. We may need to plan a job action."

"Whoa, Nelly," Mitch says, no longer sounding groggy. In fact, he sounds as if he's been doused with ice water. "Slow down. Slow *waaaay* down. Let's not get hysterical here."

"Don't call me *hysterical!*"

"It's your job to cool them down, Jenny, not let them run amuck."

Amuck! "Why should they cool it? The situation is outrageous!"

Mitch Talabante's voice rises a few decibels, and he sounds like a geyser about to erupt. "Now *outrageous* is going too far, young lady. You need to think before you shoot off your mouth. The situation's bad, yes, but let's not fan the flames!"

"Look, Mitch." My voice rises to match his. "Just to save a few bucks, the company orders the furnace cleaned before it's cold? This sort of thing happens over and over. Why do you downplay it?"

"This is a time to act responsibly, Jenny," Mitch says in that condescending voice of his that makes me feel like shoving him off the roof of the union hall.

"*Responsibly?*" I clench my fist. "What does that shit mean? Are you even listening? A life has probably been lost, all because the company put profit over safety!"

"There you go again with that rant about profit." *Rant?* I close my eyes and take a deep breath. Mitch carefully articulates his words. "If Dynamic Metals didn't make money, Jenny, none of us would have a job, would we? It's your duty to get the men to see reason and to wait for something to be worked out between the company and the union leadership. The union leaders are the ones who were elected to do this. You forget you're just a shop steward." *Lowly* shop steward, he means.

I'm sweating. I put my head against the smeared window of the claustrophobic booth, close my eyes, and wait for Mitch's voice in my ear to stop. He's still blathering. "The union will take care of this in an orderly and efficient manner. If the men are upset, I'm sorry. Tell them to come by the union hall when it opens at nine." He pauses. "That's the best I can do."

"Wait, wait, don't hang up," I say. "These men and women get off at seven-thirty, Mitch. They ain't going to stand around and wait ninety minutes for you to open the hall." Silence. "Listen. It's our union hall." My voice is harsh. "Our dues pay the goddamned rent. Today after work we're having a meeting. Either you open the fucking doors, or we'll meet in the parking lot."

I hope I can pull that one off. Sweat trickles down my forehead to my eyebrows. The line is still silent. Then Mitch says stiffly, "I'll pass your message along to Wayne," and punctuates it with a sharp click.

Is this a minor victory? Wayne Dooley, the president of the local, will probably drag himself out of his beauty sleep to unlock the union hall; he'll want to keep control over things.

But even if he doesn't show up, we *can* have a meeting in the parking lot, can't we? I burst out of the lunchroom and move rapidly from station to station, advising people of the meeting. Back at my own workplace, I inform Andre Boucher. Miguel comes by and I tell him to call Felicia: *Wake her up, Miguel.*

Workers keep coming by my station to talk. Never have I seen them so fired up. There's talk of a wildcat, of confronting the smelter foreman, Bernie Doogle, who's been placed on leave. Miguel returns: *Felicia will be at the meeting.* She'll call some of her co-workers on the evening shift and tell them to spread the word.

During break, people crowd into the lunch room. Joe Lamb stands on a chair; his goggles hang around his neck. The room grows hushed. He informs us that he's just called the hospital. Danilo De Luca is still hanging on. By a thread.

"We got to walk out," Sami Lopez says. He pulls off his helmet, revealing his wavy hair. "We ain't got no choice."

"Walkin' out ain't going to get us nowhere," Morgan Amchuk argues. "We just lose pay." His Slavic accent is drowned out in yelling and booing.

Sami Lopez pushes his helmet at someone and scrambles onto a table. "What you want? Lose pay or lose life?" People cheer.

"Let 'em dock our pay! We'll sue 'em!" yells stocky Domingo Velez.

"Yenny, what do you think?" asks Elvira Escobar, her hair coming loose from her bun and hanging halfway down her cheek.

"Jen-*ny!* Yen-*ny!*" Workers thump the tabletops and chant my name. Joe Lamb and Sami Lopez grab me under the arms and half-lift, half-boost me up and onto the table before I know what's happening.

Sami Lopez waves his arms. "Shut up! Show some respect here. Our shop steward is going to speak."

His words bring a film of tears to my eyes. I survey their faces. There's Lexy in the back, his arms crossed, leaning against the wall, looking like a proud father. There's Bettina Solís, angry and determined, her eyes flashing. There's Juan Toledo, his arms at his sides, fists clenched. The vein in his forehead pulses. Even Fulgencio Cruz is standing on the side, a dull, watchful look on his face.

Everyone looks up at me. The mood is expectant, hushed. If I'm careless, the momentum could dissipate.

I survey them, then speak. "The company has gone too far," I say, searching for the right words—the crucial words—that will channel this emotion and transform it into action.

"Right on, sister!"

"You tell it, baby!"

"Andale!"

"It's time to let the bosses know we have limits!" All eyes are on me, waiting. "We need to demand a meeting. We need new work rules for cleaning out the furnaces." I can feel my fervor growing. "Not next year, not next week, not tomorrow. *Immediately!*"

There's a hush. Everyone is staring at me. No one speaks. Did I get it wrong? Did I go too far? Why are they so silent?

Then the room explodes in cheers.

"No standards, no work!" I yell, raising my fist. Picking up the chant, they yell, "No standards, no work!"

"We demand a union meeting after work *this morning*," I continue. I hesitate just the right amount of time to create suspense. "And no is not an answer!"

"*No is not an answer!*" The crowded room seems united. Voices swell. "*No standards, no work!*" They climb onto tables and chairs, eyes on fire, fists pumping the air.

"And we demand compensation for the families of Danilo and Roberto!" I shout over the din.

"Right on!" they yell.

I'm exhilarated; the workers are waking up to their power. Moments like these are why the collective has spent so many sleepless nights, so many exhausting days, organizing the proletariat.

As workers hurry back to their stations, their voices echo. "*No standards, no work!*" and "*No is not an answer!*"

Thirty minutes before the shift ends, Tough Pitch gets word of Danilo De Luca's death. The news flows into the yard and the adjoining departments like a river spilling its banks. Workers drop tools and strip off protective garments as they make their way to the locker rooms. Still no foremen in sight. Outside the main entrance, the midnight shift intercepts the dayshift, urging workers not to enter the plant. Miguel and I join the crowd, then drive six blocks to the union hall.

The shades are drawn, the doors padlocked. The parking lot in front is jammed with double-parked cars. Workers mill about, tension reflected on their faces. Suddenly Wayne Dooley's silver Eldorado careens through the lot, zigzagging around vehicles, and comes to a screeching halt in the no-parking zone in front of the entrance. From the driver's side emerges Wayne, his stocky torso in a too-tight down jacket. Mitch Talabante unfolds his lanky body from the passenger side. He's wearing jeans and a black leather jacket.

Wayne and Mitch march to the front door, their gazes fixed straight ahead. The mass of men and women who fill the lot make way for them. With a large set of keys on a ring, Mitch unlocks a padlock, a deadbolt, and two other locks. Wayne and Mitch enter. Workers press forward and squeeze through the double doors into the large, chilly hall with its high windows, wooden floors, and raised podium. They grab folding chairs from the sides of the room and arrange them in hasty rows. Wayne and Mitch stand on the platform at the podium, talking to a cluster of guys who surround them like bodyguards. Occasionally they glance over at me; I pretend not to notice. I'm sitting with Miguel on the aisle near the rear, in order to better observe the entire room. I scan the crowd for Felicia.

Wayne Dooley steps to the podium and speaks into the mike. "Brothers and sisters, thank you for coming," he says. He waits while the room quiets down and workers scramble for seats. "It's a damn shame what happened to Brothers Danilo and Roberto." His voice changes cadence, sounding more upbeat and reassuring. "You'll be relieved to know, however, that even as we speak, we're engaging in talks with the company about compensation for their families."

Workers shift uneasily in their folding chairs. "What about the work rules?" Jerome Rivers' voice breaks in. There's a grumbling of assent. Wayne Dooley's eyes shift from side to side, as if checking out the exits. "Don't worry about work rules," he says. "I can assure you we've got everything covered. The company will be setting new standards."

"When?" shouts a voice from the rear.

"Right away...as soon as possible."

"Fuck that! We want standards *now!*" shouts Eric Corzo. "We don't want another worker to die while we're waiting on some bureaucratic bullshit."

"We ain't going to clean no more furnaces while they're hot," yells Gary Radulovic, a smelter worker. Rumbling turns into a growl.

Suddenly the double doors at the rear open wide, letting daylight into the gloomy hall. Everyone turns in their folding chairs to see Felicia, her arm linked with that of a short man with thinning gray hair, a leathery face, and a scar that runs down his left cheek. He has to be Mr. DeLuca. The two progress somberly down the center of the room, followed, like a funeral procession, by dozens of dayshift workers—perhaps half of the entire shift.

I'm stunned. They've shut the mother down!

Everyone stands and watches as Mr. De Luca and Felicia proceed to the front of the room and take seats on two hastily vacated folding chairs. The dayshift workers bunch together around the edges of the room. The crowd has swelled to over a hundred!

Wayne Dooley looks grim. Is it because of Danilo's death or because the meeting has gotten out of control? I approach the front of the room, calling out, "Brother Wayne, may I have the floor?"

Wayne opens his mouth but whatever he was about to say is drowned out by a burst of cheers. As I sweep past him to the podium, I feel his resentful breath on my neck.

I welcome Mr. De Luca and express sorrow for his son's death on behalf of all the workers. Felicia gives me a thumbs-up. She's wearing work gear and a long-sleeved, black shirt. Tears appear on workers' faces as they stand and applaud Mr. De Luca. After they sit down, I relate what I've just learned from Miguel on the ride to the union hall: that when Mr. De Luca, senior, retired a couple of years ago, he'd worked at Dynamic Metals for 34 years; that his son

Danilo was earning an engineering degree in night school at Union County College; that Danilo and his wife have two children.

Would Mr. De Luca like to say a few words?

The crowd applauds long and loud as Mr. De Luca advances slowly toward the podium, where he puts his fist to his chest and waits for the applause to die down. I lower the mike for him.

"My heart thanks you for being here," he says. "You honor me, you are my brothers."

"And sisters," calls out a woman from the rear. "We're with you too, honey."

"And sisters," agrees Mr. DeLuca. He holds out his arms. "And I hope you will all honor my son by doing something about these working conditions. This should never have happened. How...how long—" His voice breaks. The crowd stands and applauds. Mr. De Luca swallows. "How long do we have to put up with this?" he says, with dignified fury.

As he returns to his seat, I thank him and say that something *will* be done, that the men and women of the plant demand compensation for Danilo's and Roberto's families, as well as an immediate work rule dealing with the furnaces.

"Did I get that right?" I ask the crowd. "Is that what you want?"

The room rocks with howls of affirmation. I yell, "And you want the union to *fight* for that. Is that right?" More shouts. "And until there's an agreement, until the plant is *safe,* you won't go back. *Is that right?"* The workers stomp their feet until the floor thunders. As the roar subsides, my voice resonates. "Let's make this official by a show of hands. How many want to stay home until regulations are established?"

It's about as unanimous as it can get. I look at Wayne. "How soon can you get a meeting with the company?"

"I'll call them right after we adjourn," he says. His well-muscled body seems to have shrunk. I'd pity him if he weren't such a weasel.

"We surely do appreciate that," I say.

Before leaving the union hall, some of us draft a leaflet calling for support of a job action. We mimeograph it on the machine in the union workroom. Wayne Dooley and Mitch Talabante hang around, getting in the way, trying to pretend they're still in charge. The rest of the workers hightail it back to the refinery, where they picket the entrance. We rush the leaflets over to the plant and hang around with workers there.

An emergency meeting with the company is called. The rank and file demands to be there too; Wayne and Mitch raise only weak objections. Probably they know we won't be denied. A volunteer group of male and female workers, including Miguel, Felicia, and me, attends the meeting. Prior to the onset of the afternoon shift, the company has already accepted our demands: from now on, before cleaning commences, furnaces will be allowed to cool to 120 degrees. Furthermore, Danilo's and Roberto's families will receive compensation. A temporary agreement is drawn up. By afternoon shift, work has resumed.

Under our pressure, the union soon files a complaint with the feds, and Dynamic Metals does institute safer work rules. In my opinion, the company doesn't care much about the death of Danilo and the near-death of Roberto. Even if individual bosses might have a heart, the executives out there in St. Louis focus on profits. The deaths are calculated in dollars and cents. Waiting a few more hours before cleaning out furnaces is probably worth a short-term loss of profit in order to forestall a lawsuit or a fine or a strike.

It's a small but significant victory. Even secondary victories these days are few and far between so the collective savors it and hopes to build more successes on top of it.

10. Jenny

DANILO'S FUNERAL IS HELD A WEEK LATER at the Methodist Church. Roberto and many other workers speak. Standing there holding a hymnal, I wonder how many workers have died because of the callousness of the bosses, their cold-blooded drive for profits and ever more profits.

I look at the grim demeanors of the other workers, some with tear-streaked faces, and feel a great pride in them. This is why they're the vanguard—they know that an injury to one is an injury to all.

Although I didn't know Danilo personally, I send him a silent message that his death wasn't in vain. It resulted in work rules being changed, and who knows how many lives in the future will be saved because of that?

It's Miguel's turn to drive to work. There's something about the intimacy of being confined together in a small space while zipping 60 miles an hour down a turnpike that I find comforting. One night on the way to work—Miguel is driving—I ask him whether he agrees with the collective's position on monogamy.

"Which is?"

"That men and women should have exclusive relationships," I explain. The collective believes that infidelity leads to divisiveness. It's considered anti-proletarian.

"I support that," he says.

"You do?" No hesitation? No wavering?

He's told me about his family in Santo Domingo, and I always assumed some of his dad's chauvinist behavior would have rubbed off on him. His father strayed from time to time; according to Miguel, his mother repeatedly forgave him. Miguel has eight siblings, all younger than him, some of whom are the fruits of his father's romantic forays. His mother even raised some of those babies when his dad's mistresses couldn't.

"It's the only way to build trust," Miguel replies matter-of-factly, as if saying, *Yes, I'll have another cup of coffee.*

A sudden warmth comes over me and I gently touch his thigh. As he reaches for my hand; my body tingles.

"I'm a feminist," he says.

"You are?"

"Absolutamente."

He tells me that as a teenager he resented being forced to lie to his mother about his father's behavior. Sometimes Miguel would flee the house and seek refuge shooting pool at the local bar or hanging out in the plaza with his friends.

"So you believe in being faithful to your girlfriends, then?" I ask, still feeling skeptical. After all, feminism could mean free love to him.

"Men assume it's their right to sample what's out there," he says, steering his Plymouth Valiant into the refinery parking lot, "but I don't agree."

I'm impressed with his words but I'm still not convinced. "You'd never run around on a girlfriend then?"

He finds a parking space and backs the car in, cuts the ignition, and turns to face me. Our shift starts in a few minutes, but neither of us makes a move to get out.

"I have to be honest" he says. "I've enjoyed my little *coqueterías* in the past. But I'm beyond all that now."

Coqueterías? Flirtations? What does he mean? Putting the moves on someone? Cheating? One thing is for sure, he didn't betray Angélica. At least not with me. (That counts for something.) And he just said he's "beyond all that" now. But….

But I can't get *"coqueterías"* out of my mind. I'm 28 years old and still not sure what flirting consists of? Is it teasing? Joking around? Or is it explicitly sexual? Once when I asked Felicia, she said anything could be considered flirting but that it might not *really* be flirting; it depended on the context. Context? Which context?

"How about you? Would you fool around?" Miguel asks, smoothing back a lock of hair from my forehead. *"Equal rights for womans* and all that?"

"Oh, no! Never!" I respond. "I believe in being faithful, in building trust between two people."

He looks impatient and waves his hand. "But haven't you ever been tempted?"

That's a question that I'm not able to answer without giving too much away. To be *tempted y*ou have to be in a relationship. So I reply, "Not exactly." His eyes narrow, but he says nothing. I open the car door and get out. I walk slowly into the plant, my mind in a whirl.

But I feel myself drawing ever closer to him. It's not only because he fought in the revolution. There are other qualities too: the fun we have, his ability to listen, the comfort I feel around him. For the first time in my life I'm getting emotionally involved with a man. But tension lies under the surface. I know that our friendship can't remain platonic forever; I dread the inevitable changes. It reminds me of knowing as a child that I'm going to get a spanking but not knowing when.

⋙⋙⋙⋙⋙⋙⋙⋙⋙⋙

One balmy Thursday afternoon as we're leafleting, Charlie says, "You're a kind of hero."

I look at him with surprise. In the past he wouldn't have put it that way. He would have teased me: *What have we here? Another Mother Jones?*

"It wasn't *me*," I say, embarrassed. "It was the situation in the plant. I just helped move things along."

"Oh, give me a break," he says. His eyebrows slant inward. "You underestimate the role of the vanguard."

The hint of irritation in his voice stings. "It's kind of tough trying to live up to all this fuss, that's all," I say.

Now he grants me a reassuring grin. "You don't have to live up to anything," he says. "Just relax and bask in the sunshine."

Before we say goodbye, I'm determined to get Charlie's advice on something: how would he define flirting?

"It's when a person looks or talks a certain way to signal that they're interested. Why?"

I shrug. "No reason." But what is that "certain way"? I'm still in the dark but realize that I'm not comfortable pursuing this with Charlie. Upon parting, we do manage to hug each other, but is the hug a little more tentative than usual? Does the hesitation come from him or from me or from both of us?

More proof that mixing sex with friendship confuses everything.

❮❮❮ ❮❮❮ ❮❮❮ ❮❮❮ ❮❮❮

One day Miguel pulls into the refinery parking lot and kills the ignition. He slides across the plastic seat toward me and strokes my hand. His touch arouses that feeling in the pit of my stomach as if something has come unmoored.

"It's time that we go more far, Yenny Apple," he says in English, continuing to stroke my hand with a light touch. "You want that we be more close?" His breath warms my cheek; my heart races. He continues, "You experience *la Revolución Sexual*. You are *feminista*. Why this is such a large deal? I no understand." He searches my eyes.

I scoot to the right a few inches until the handle of the car door digs into my ribs. My face burns. The dashboard acquires a sudden fascination.

Miguel sighs, slides back to the driver's side, and opens the door. How long will he put up with this, I wonder. After breakfast at Felicia's that morning, I invite him upstairs with me for the first time. We make out on the lumpy sofa.

"Let's open the bed so we'll be more comfortable," he murmurs, nuzzling my neck. Of course, even I'm not so naïve that I don't know what "opening the bed" means, so I awkwardly decline. It's not that I don't enjoy the touching, but I'm all too aware of the numbness that always accompanies "going more far."

One sunny day after a fresh snow the night before, Miguel and I are sitting on a bench in Central Park. I ask him if he's ever considered joining the collective. After all, his politics seem to match ours.

"What that mean?" he asks. Snow plops from a branch onto the ground.

I switch to Spanish and explain the word *join*.

He switches to Spanish too. "No, I mean, what would joining mean concretely?"

"It means you'd be part of the strategy meetings that occur weekly. You'd be a part of the inner workings instead of just a *contact*." I pull my mitten off and pull it on again. There's a knot in my stomach, but I try to look nonchalant. If he'd only join, it would open up so many things that I can't talk to him about now. It would bring us closer, as close as we could get almost (short of being lovers). And, I have to say it: I'd look good in the eyes of the collective. In fact, they've been pressuring me for some time to ask him, but I've put off their request. I'm afraid he'll say no.

Miguel is thoughtful. "I only have a green card," he says.

I figured as much. "If it makes you feel better, Miguel, you'd be one of the secret members—like me. Like most of us. Of course there's no guarantee that we won't be infiltrated, but that's unlikely. No one should know you're a member except the other members of the cell and the leadership."

He considers. "I think it might work," he says.

"Then you'll join us?" My heart beats like a hammer.

"Yes."

I'm thrilled. But is he joining because he's committed to the collective's political line or because he wants to impress me? There's no way to know so I decide to assume the former. And after he's a member, he'll get closer to our work and learn to love it.

After Miguel joins the collective, our conversations take on a new layer. We dissect meetings: *Whose point of view do you think was correct—Bonnie's or Esme's?... Do you think that what Matt said about that worker at his shop harbored bourgeois tendencies?* We talk shop: *Is Jaime a vanguard worker, and how can we get him out to the next union meeting?... How do we neutralize that die-hard Frank?... How do we win over Jill?* We hash out current events: Watergate, Vietnam, nuclear testing in Nevada.

And we tease each other:

Mao made mistakes, too, you know.

Better not let the collective hear you say that.

One night after leafleting on the way back to my apartment in the cold and dark, the snow crunching under my boots, I recall what Charlie said the morning after our *romp in the sack:* that he feared things would change between us. An image appears before my eyes, unbidden, unwelcome. Charlie hovering over me, the moonlight on his face, a lock of hair hanging down. I shake my head and focus on a brightly lit display window. A black sequined evening gown adorns the headless torso of a mannequin.

Crossing the street, I turn up Jersey Avenue.

I've given Miguel a key to my apartment; it makes things more convenient. Will he have let himself in by the time I get home? I shiver and pull up the hood of my duffle coat. In the record store window, Paul Simon's latest, "Still Crazy After All These Years," is featured.

How long can I get away with dodging Miguel? These days, you have to *put out*. The expression itself sounds like something offered without joy, almost like a duty. Some people I know say they *do it* on the first date. Others wait until the second or third. To me, that's way too soon. Sex is not a casual undertaking. Sex is momentous! Like a moon landing!

A few people still wait until marriage, but even to me that seems too long. Wouldn't it be terrible to find out on your wedding night that the two of you were *sexually incompatible?* (Whatever that means.)

When I arrive at the corner, I look up at my apartment window. The lights are on. Anticipation and a touch of anxiety make me shiver again as I climb the stairs. Before I can turn the key, the door opens. I smell fresh-brewed coffee. Miguel kisses me on the cheek, then pulls me to him and presses his lips to mine. I blush and glance down the hallway.

He pulls me inside, closes the door, and kisses me on the eyes, the nose, the neck. My body, chilled from the walk home, is suddenly shot through with warmth and I feel my insides go spongy. Why not take a leap into a new experience? But that familiar grip of panic seizes me and excuses flood my mind: we have to go to work tonight! What if I turn him off? I'm not ready yet!

I slide out from his embrace and enter the kitchen. "Oooh, coffee," I chirp. "It smells heavenly."

An hour later at a Puerto Rican café on Grove Street we're sitting next to each other in a booth, shoulders touching, and sharing an order of *arroz con pollo.* Miguel says, in Spanish as usual, "Tomorrow morning after work why don't I stay over with you?"

Over.

I could say, "Oh, I'll be so exhausted." But that's the threadbare excuse I used last time. "I have a meeting bright and early," I could say. But I don't. And I'm not eager to lie to him so early in our relationship...no, what am I thinking? I don't *ever* want to lie to him.

He finally says, "Don't you like me that way, Yenny?"

"Of course I do," I say, although if I were honest I'd say that I'm confused about what I feel. I place my hand over his. "I like you a lot…it's just…." My voice trails off. "I'm just scared." There! I've said it!

"Scared of what?" he asks.

"I…I'm not sure," I say. "For one thing, I might not be any good—"

"You'll be good," he assures me. When I look unconvinced, he adds, "I can't believe you're worried about whether you'll be good or not."

"But I am."

"I'll love having sex with you no matter what. Really!" He squeezes my hand and kisses me on the cheek.

"No, wait. I need to tell you this. I need you to know." I pull my hand away.

He looks startled. "Go on," he says gravely.

"I…I sometimes shut down at a crucial point."

He looks puzzled. "Shut down?"

"I mean, first I want it. Then"—I turn my palms up—"I don't."

"You mean you change your mind?"

"It's like my *body* changes its mind."

He looks at me with skepticism in his eyes. He switches to English. "I want to be with you," he says. "No important if you have errors. I no am sure how much time I can go on so. For a man is difficult. And I like you much, Yenny."

I feel uneasy. Over the years a number of guys have explained to me that for men, once they're aroused, it's frustrating—"*unbearably* frustrating," they've said urgently—not to have intercourse. In fact, sometimes they can't control themselves, they say. Maybe I should just let him do it. My gift to him because I love him. *Put out.*

Perhaps Miguel reads the pain and ambivalence in my face, because he backs off—as he's done before. "*Está bién*, Yenny, I can wait. Until you are ready. So long it take. Sorry." He switches to Spanish. "I just get carried away. I know some women want to go slow. Don't worry." He looks at me with such concern that big tears spill from my eyes and splash onto the vinyl tablecloth with its purple flowers.

One night in my apartment Miguel settles himself into the armchair on the other side of the room and crosses his legs. It's clear that something's on his mind and he's determined not to be distracted. I hope this isn't the night he's decided that the effort of waiting isn't worth it.

"Let's talk about sex one more time," he says in Spanish.

Oh no!

"All right," I say reluctantly. I curl up on the sofa and try to appear as if my insides aren't shriveling.

"I can't figure this out. Maybe it's your parents. Were they up-tight about sex?" he asks, looking as if he's struggling with a difficult math problem.

Is that all he wants to know? I can talk about my parents. "No, not at all, Dr. Freud," I assure him. "As far as I can tell, Mom and Dad are well-adjusted in that area." My mother once confided to me that when she looked out the window and saw my father's car pulling up the driveway at the end of the day, her heart went "pitter-patter." *Even after all these years,* she said. Of course, I can't be sure about my parents' sex life; they don't talk openly about it. But it's the *looks* they give each other, their frequent casual kisses.

"Are you a virgin, then?" Miguel asks.

"No." My hand gravitates to my mouth, ready to chew on a thumbnail, but I force it down to my lap. This feels like "20 Questions" and he's getting warm. I stand up. "Want to go to a movie?"

He ignores me and remains seated, musing. "Didn't you enjoy sex in the past?"

I sink back onto the sofa. This question has hit the target, and the target is me. I want to tell him: *None of it was enjoyable.* I take a deep breath and speak in a barely perceptible voice.

"All...all bad."

"*Caramba!*" He leans forward in the armchair. "Did someone abuse you?"

The space behind my eyes turns velvety black. I hug my body and rock, sobbing soundlessly. Miguel reaches for a box of tissues and hands it over, then waits while I straighten up and blow my nose.

"Something happened," I say, scarcely breathing.

"What happened?"

"Something...something bad." He waits. "I've never...never told anyone."

"Do you want to tell me?" he invites, his voice low, almost a whisper.

The wind rattles the window. I stand up, pull a blanket from a cupboard, throw it around my shoulders, and sit back down. Despite the wrap, I'm trembling. My body is coming apart.

I swallow. "I was eight years old...."

Miguel nods encouragingly.

"I...I was by myself...in the back yard...."

He nods again.

"My father had painted a shed and converted it into a play-house. Sometimes I slept overnight out there with a girlfriend." I'm breathing hard. "It was a beautiful summer day...the best Colorado weather...warm and peaceful. I was lying on the cot reading a book, totally absorbed in my story. So safe, so content...."

"And then?" Miguel prompts.

I twist my hands nervously. "I suddenly became aware of...of a presence. You know how you suddenly realize you're not alone?"

The room is so quiet that Miguel must be holding his breath.

"I looked up. My cousin Duncan was standing in the doorway."

My lungs constrict, making speech difficult. But I manage to tell him the story.

Even before a big shadow falls across my book, i know someone is present. I'm lying on my stomach on the cot, reading The Bobbsey Twins, *in the playhouse my daddy made that year for my eighth birthday. My sandals are on the floor beside the cot; my feet are raised, ankles crossed. I look up. Duncan, my 15-year-old cousin, stands silhouetted in the doorway of the playhouse.*

"Hi," he says. His eyes sweep the room. He directs his gaze to the open window across from me.

"Hi," I say, trying to be nice, as my parents have taught me, even though I don't feel it. In fact, I'm unable to summon, even from deep inside of my eight-year-old self, a teensy weensy bit of warmth for Duncan. I don't like the way his squinty eyes pierce my body like a barbecue stick. I don't like how he never looks at my face when he talks to me. And his legs below his shorts are thick with hair.

But I don't want to hurt his feelings.

"When did you get here, Dunny?"

"A few minutes ago," he says. He closes the playhouse door and comes a step closer. "Just wanted to say hi. We're going to leave in a minute."

I roll over and sit up. "Hi."

Duncan takes two steps to the window and closes it.

"Hey!" I protest. "I want it open."

"No, you don't. Didn't anyone tell you that too much fresh air will kill you?" His grin seems fake, like Mommy's glass diamond earrings. In three more steps he moves to the cot and sits down right next to me, his thigh squeezing mine. My own thigh is like a pencil next to his. The smell of pepperoni and onions comes from his mouth as he presses closer. The way he runs his eyes over my body is yucky. He sits there for a moment, not moving, just studying me. Then his face takes on a look as if he was daydreaming and his eyes start to frost over.

I try to stand, want to open the window again. But his big hand clamps down on my thigh, right over the scar where I gashed myself on the swing set when I was five. My leg is pinned to the bed.

"Stop it," I say, yipping like the neighbor's puppy when you step on its tail.

"Shhh," he says.

It's so unfair. It's against the rules. This is my playhouse. It's my place to go to forget about my problems. To get away from my parents for a while. To find solitude.

But now he's spoiling it for me.

Quicker than you can say Jack Robinson, he wiggles his hand down down down, right inside my shorts, and grabs me—hard!

"Dunny, stop!" Panic races through me. "What are you doing?"

"Getting to know you better," he says.

I twist away from him. With a grunt he seizes my shoulders and pushes me down on the cot, flat on my back, knocking the breath out of me. He yanks at my shorts and panties. I hear a rip. They are down around my knees. I open my mouth to scream, but he says, "Don't you dare or I'll sock you so hard you'll end up on the moon!" His voice is thick with danger; I lie there, immobile. He wrenches my shorts and panties down over my ankles and tosses them into a heap on the floor. Throwing his body on top of mine, robbing me of breath, he grinds himself on my stomach. I can hardly breathe; his body feels like a dinosaur.

I open my eyes wide in horror and bite my lip so I won't scream. I don't understand what's happening but I know it's nasty. Between my legs I feel his hand rubbing me hard, and then his fingers are inside me. It burns like fire. I squirm, I can't help it, but it only makes the pain worse.

He's silent, breathing hard, and lifts himself a little above me, removes his fingers. Now I can breathe better. His hand seems to be busy down below with his own body. Then a warm liquid spurts onto my bare stomach. He collapses on top of me and lies still. Is he dead?

I want him off of me more than anything in the world. My chest feels like ropes are wrapped around it. I want to complain—You hurt me!—but suddenly his slimy fingers press my mouth shut. They smell; it's a sickening sweetness that makes me want to puke.

Rage wells up in me and I snarl at him like the neighbor dog snarls at me. Look what he's done. How dare he? I'll never feel safe here again. I want to burst out of my skin, but his body pins me like the butterflies on the bulletin board at school.

He stands up and hisses, "Don't you dare tell anyone or you'll be sorry." Why is he so furious? He shakes his fist in my face until my nose is squished, and snaps, "It's all your fault, you little tease!"

My fault! Tease! Now my anger turns to confusion and tears spring to my eyes. Did I tease him? What did I say? Is that why he's mad at me? Did I hurt his feelings? The way mine are hurt?

"Dunny, where are you? We're leaving," Aunt Elvira's voice shrills. Mean, blabbermouth Aunt Elvira. But for once it's a relief to hear her voice.

Duncan hastily zips his pants and passes a hand across his hair, then squeezes my upper arm so tight I wince in pain. As he disappears through the playhouse door, his eyes shoot flames at me.

I place two exploratory fingers on my midriff, then jerk my hand away from the sticky mess. Grabbing my shorts from the floor, I wipe myself dry, averting my eyes from my stomach. Afraid to make a peep, I lie there listening to my cousin Duncan and Aunty Elvira say goodbye to my parents, listening to the car doors slam and the engine start. Then I pull on my panties and wet shorts. I lie back on the cot, shaking and trying to quiet my sobs.

My confusion turns to shame. I know I've done something bad. My parents will notice and demand to know what happened. Perhaps they'll scold me; my dad might spank me. After what just happened, I don't think I could stand that.

Minutes later I duck into the house through the backdoor and sneak up the stairs; in the bathroom I lock the door. Between my legs it feels like a bee sting. I scrub myself with a washcloth until my skin turns red as a beet.

All these years I've kept silent about Duncan, first out of fear and later out of shame. Have I just made a horrible mistake?

Miguel paces the room. He doesn't look at me. Then he sits down beside me and takes my hands.

"You did the right thing to tell me," he says. "You're safe now. You're safe." He draws me to him. I put my head on his chest and I'm crying; he wraps his arms around me.

He hasn't found me disgusting. He assures me I did nothing wrong. He makes me *believe* it for the first time.

In the days following, it's as if all the poison I've been harboring has flowed out of me. I feel clean, pure. I have a recurring dream that I'm in a meadow of wildflowers on a lovely spring day, whirling round and round, gazing up at the faded blue sky and fluffy clouds, until I'm crazy with dizziness.

11. Miguel

MARCH 1975

I'M CLEANING OUT THE INSIDE OF A FURNACE with an air gun. It's like standing in the middle of a dust storm, my goggles and coveralls coated with the stuff. All I can think about is Duncan; I'm beside myself with hatred for that bastard. I'd like to bash his head in with a shovel. To punch him so hard he'd crash through that playhouse window into the stratosphere. I aim the air gun at some cement fragments and watch them crackle and dance and pulverize in the powerful stream of air.

To force yourself on someone like that! It's vile, abominable, diabolic! And on a little girl! How old was she? Eight? Children are sacred. Not to be touched. That was Pure Evil!

Before, when Yenny refused to have sex with me, it was tough. How I craved her. She drove me over a cliff.

But now that I understand what's behind her terror, I see the other side. She's like an injured bird in my palm, one that I can nurse back to health. She needs me; I can show her how to trust men again.

When I consider the courage it took for her to tell me her secret, I'm awestruck. From this day forth I vow never to betray her. I feel closer to her than I have to any other woman. Waiting to have sex has let me get to know her. Much better than if we'd jumped in the sack right away.

That's why I'm turning over a new leaf.

And that's not easy. Not with such temptations everywhere. In the past I've vowed to remain faithful to girlfriends, but other women come on to me. Aggressively!

And then there are those *irresistible situations*, as I call them. The woman who sits across from me on the subway with her bare ankle showing just below the hem of her jeans and the delicate silver chain on that ankle that just lures me into letting my glance slide up her body...and if she happens to be smiling, then I'm obliged to engage her in a little conversation, especially if the subway is almost empty and it's only natural to pass the time on the long ride to wherever I'm heading. Always with the utmost respect—because I *do* respect women, but that ankle burning a hole in my brain as I cast my eyes respectfully down to the floor and let them brush that ankle again, that sculpted fragile ankle of a diameter just large enough to encircle with your hand, the burnished silver chain resting against the tawny, silken skin.

Or standing in line at the supermarket, I find myself behind a woman with soft wavy hair that smells of jasmine, and when she turns a little and I catch her eye—just to be polite and say hello— the sultriness in her voice is almost more than I can bear. How can I not offer to carry her groceries to her apartment?

Yes, I've played around too much.

Then too, I've grown up around men like that. My dad, my uncles. As I got older—when are you old enough?—my dad confided in me. I became his partner-in-crime. An unwilling accomplice, a Guardian of Secrets.

All those times my dad took me to visit my uncle and cousins in Baní while my mom stayed home taking care of the house and the younger kids! While my father would carry on with some woman, I'd avert my eyes and half resent, half admire his prowess. "This is what it means to be a man," my father would say, puffing out his chest. And then, as if he sensed my discomfort and confusion, he'd clap me on the back and say, "What your mother don't know won't hurt her, right, *m'hijo?*"

Once I asked him, "Don't you love *Mamá* anymore?"

He glared at me. "*Es mi* vieja." She's my *wife*. He gave me a sharp cuff on the arm. "What's the matter with you?"

So I learned early on that men are expected to wander, and women are expected to *wonder*. And to have a hot meal waiting when their men return from the hunt.

The last woman I went with, before Yenny but during Angélica, was a Puerto Rican waitress from Brooklyn named Sandra. *Coño*, she was sexy with her petite body, push-up breasts, and dark curls that hung down to her shoulders. Her brown eyes so provocative. And the way she danced with me, all close and tight, our bodies glued together. The thought of it still makes me hot.

When I broke it off with her, when I told her about Yenny, she snarled, "*Una gringa!*" I could almost see fangs emerge from under the soft fullness of her upper lip, and I experienced a sudden fear for Yenny. I didn't tell Sandra that being a *gringa* only made Yenny more tempting.

"She's probably *un desastre* (disaster) in bed," Sandra continued. I didn't tell her that I'd never slept with Yenny. She would have said, *Dios mio, what is she, una monja?* A nun?

What she did say was, "What does she have that I don't?", her face fragmenting like a shattered mirror before she composed herself. I didn't tell her what it was that Yenny had.

When I think about what Yenny has gone through, my resolve hardens. This time I *will* withstand all such snares and focus on one person. And that one person will be Yenny. My love for her is huge—like a homerun with all bases loaded.

12. Jenny
APRIL – MAY 1975

EVER SINCE THE SMELTER ACCIDENT two months ago, rumors of a layoff circulate through the plant. Every Friday when I receive my paycheck, I breathe a sigh of relief. The axe could fall any day, and the union leadership is lying low. *What can we do,* they say with a shrug. No need for them to sweat, with all their years of seniority.

On Friday, April 18, I receive my paycheck in an ominously thick envelope. As I rip it open, a paper drifts to the floor. I pick it up. The fearful pink slip. "Notice of Reduction in Force," it reads. Two weeks' notice. I glance at Miguel, who's looking glum. Felicia will probably be laid off too. Hopefully not Roger, our day shift comrade. Numbly, I exit the building. Gloomy workers mill around in the brisk morning air.

"Gotta go down to unemployment," a man with whiskers says. "Let Uncle Sam pay my meal ticket for a while." Grunts from others.

"They'll call us back soon," says a tall man with rounded shoulders. His husky voice lets slip that he's on the verge of tears. As for the women—all recently hired—they'll probably never be called back. It's not fair, I think, my throat constricting. The plant will revert to an all-male bastion, as it has been since World War II when women were let go to make room for the men returning home from war. But the plant is less a bastion than a house of cards. We've watched helplessly as the company dismantled one section after another, sending furnaces and copper molds and machinery to Taiwan and Ceylon (Sri Lanka, that is), to Mexico and Pakistan. The plant is disappearing like the Cheshire cat.

Miguel and I shake hands with our brother and sister workers. I want to weep; two weeks from now, will I ever see them again?

On the ride home I shed tears of frustration. The injustice, the futility of it all. At times like this a hot coal of hatred against the system burns deep inside me. Global recession, inflation at 11 per cent. How are people supposed to survive? Gas is now up to 44 cents a gallon. Rents $200 a month. And to buy a house, well, who can afford $40,000? Thank goodness workers agitated for unemployment insurance back in the Depression. At least they have something to live on until they find other jobs. *If* they find other jobs.

"There's a machine shop in the Bronx where I used to work," Miguel says. "I'll see if they take me back." I smile, glad that he'll have a job. He's taking the layoff with a stoicism that I envy. As for me, my eyes brim with tears as I think how much I'll miss these men and women: their camaraderie, the way they stick up for one another, their language, their humor. The sense that I'm working for a higher purpose at the very site where, as a revolutionary, I'm supposed to be: heavy industry, what Marxists call the *point of production*.

This isn't the first time I've found myself unemployed. For over three years now I've worked in factories. I've hopped from job to job in search of the most strategic place to work. I've operated a pasta-making machine, tightened bolts and dropped batteries into automobiles, made suitcases, strung out slats for Venetian blinds, wound filaments for light bulbs, bottled shampoo until my hands reeked of Floral Sunshine, an odor which clung to me like death.

But between being fired or laid off, I've rarely held a job for more than a year. And now I've been laid off again! Capitalism can't seem to provide financial security for its citizens—not to mention pensions, health care, vacations. Everyone is downsizing, looking abroad for cheap labor. I read this morning that the unemployment rate is around 9%! And unions are blamed: *American workers are paid too much, they're greedy, they're driving corporations out of America.*

127

The thought of searching for yet another job exhausts me, but the straight-out truth is that in the past weeks I've found it difficult to muster the energy even for this job.

⋗ ⋗ ⋗ ⋗ ⋗

Two weeks later on a Monday my layoff begins. That night I prepare for bed at the very hour that I would usually prepare for work. What a luxury to surrender to my drowsiness. My body never did adjust to the midnight shift: about 10 p.m. the circadian rhythm would kick in and drowsiness would spread through my veins like a narcotic.

Tuesday morning I awake early from a delightful dream of flying. I lie on the sofa bed, admiring the slant of sunlight that pushes its way through the gap in the blinds and rests on the quilt. Oh, the joy of not working the *Death Shift*.

I turn on the radio to WBAI. A civil war has broken out in Lebanon, and in Chad the military has carried out a coup d'état. The world's population has now reached 4 billion.

I remind myself that only socialism will be able to lift all these people out of poverty. I congratulate myself that I'm a fighter for a better world. I turn off the radio and put on a Nina Simone album. In the kitchen I whip up a batter, dip bread in it, and enjoy a leisurely breakfast of French toast drenched in Aunt Jemima's maple syrup. Over breakfast I read some more of *All the President's Men,* a book about Watergate that I've been plowing through for months and will finally find time to finish.

Later today I'll go down to the unemployment office. Standing in lines doesn't bother me; I use the time to read or talk to other workers. It's guiltless free time, precious moments shoplifted from the frenzy of my life.

I stack the dirty dishes next to the sink, sharpen a number two pencil, and pull a tablet of lined paper off a shelf crammed with bills and notes and To-Do lists. Sitting back down at the kitchen table, I jot down things I can contribute to the collective now that

I'm laid off: attend that labor conference in Boston, write an article for *The Struggle* (the League's monthly newspaper), pass out flyers at factory gates.

In the right-hand column I jot down things for myself: buy clothes (it's been months since I've gone shopping), take yoga, learn to play the guitar I picked up in that pawn shop, record my experiences at Dynamic Metals before the memories grow cold, take evening classes in history at the local community college. Perhaps learn Swahili!

My pencil is already dull so I sharpen it again; I'm surprised at how many things flow onto the paper. Taking my own desires into consideration feels strange, slightly immoral. It sobers me that I'm suffering little remorse about losing my job in heavy metal. But I have to be honest; it feels more like a vacation than a layoff. My initial dismay has turned to relief and revealed the depth of my disillusionment. In the past, I couldn't wait to find another job, to get back to organizing. But this time I'm overcome with the futility of it all. Am I the only one who feels this way? Why is everyone else so damned optimistic? Or are they?

I have a suspicion that other collective members wouldn't approve of my doubts, but how will I know unless I express them? There are people I can talk to—Charlie, Felicia. Isn't that what friends are for?

⋖≺ ⋖≺ ⋖≺ ⋖≺ ⋖≺

On a warm May day, after leafleting, Charlie and I sit in a booth at Dotty's Café, sipping iced tea. We can hardly contain ourselves. The Vietnamese have won!

"We did it!" Charlie says gleefully, tapping his glass to mine.

"After all these years," I say.

"What a fight the Vietnamese people put up!" he says, beaming.

"They showed the world that David really can defeat Goliath."

"Exactly. Which is why the U.S. fought tooth and nail to crush them."

"When I first became political," I tell him, "my dad and I corresponded about the war. *We have to trust the government, honey. They have access to information that we don't.*"

"Ha! I guess Nixon shredded any remnants of faith in the government, didn't he?"

"As soon as I'd get a letter from him, I'd reply to it as fast as I could, then race to the post office on Canal Street to send it. Through those dialogues I fine-tuned my own convictions against the war when I was still a fledgling radical." I sigh.

"What's the matter?"

"I need to talk to you about something."

"What did I do?" He swirls his glass of tea and the ice cubes clink.

"No, it's nothing like that. It's just that I'm having second thoughts about things."

He wrinkles his forehead. "About what, babe?"

Why is this so hard? Maybe because in all the time I've leafleted with Charlie, neither of us has ever raised doubts about the underpinnings of the collective: Marxism-Leninism-Mao Tse-tung Thought." The Holy Trinity, I think, shocked at my cynicism. And if I'm shocked, how will Charlie respond?

"Do you ever wonder if...well, if all our hard work is getting us anywhere?" I ask.

He looks confused. "Hard work on what?"

"I mean, in general."

"Are you kidding? Of course we're making progress...don't you think?"

"I'm not so sure anymore."

"If you're referring to setbacks, everyone freely admits those," he says, sounding a little defensive. "No one is trying to sugarcoat the difficulties. But as Mao says, 'In time of difficulties, we must not lose sight of our achievements.'"

There have been embarrassments, yes. The collective events that no one attends. The near-empty, chilly halls that echo mournfully as a few speakers stand in an island at the front, between a projector and an old ripped screen, surrounded by a sea of empty chairs, except for the middle-aged man in a suit—possibly a spy?—in the middle of the back row, the two women with their yarn and knitting needles in the middle of the center row, and the scattering of shivering friends of the collective in the front left row who come out to show their support.

"But I'm not talking about those times. Besides, we have plenty of successful events."

"For example, those knocks on our doors," he says.

Who is it?
The FBI. We'd like to talk to you, please.

"And then there was Jim," he adds.

Oh yes, Jim. What most pained and shocked and angered us all, perhaps, was the defection of Jim, one of our favorite leaders, who joined a Trotskyist collective.

I suck on an ice cube while I consider that there's still time to backtrack, redirect the conversation into light-hearted banter: *Ha ha, just wanted to see if you were paying attention.* But like the guilty suspect who feels compelled to confess—against her own interest—I forge ahead.

"We've been doing this so long and we still haven't recruited any workers."

I watch a struggle play out in his eyes.

"What about the victory you just won—getting the safety rules changed?" he asked.

"That was great, but it was like one star in a vast universe."

"Don't disparage it. It was a solid victory." He presses on. "And what about Felicia and Miguel? You recruited *them.*"

His relentless optimism grates on me. "Felicia doesn't count," I say. Charlie looks at me the way my mother did when I said a bad word. "I mean, she's not a *factory* recruit. She just happens to live in my building, which is OK, but.... And Miguel, well...." My voice trails off.

"And all the folks we're on the cusp of recruiting?"

"*On the cusp, on the cusp.* We've been *on the cusp* forever," I say wearily.

"It takes time, Jenny. Working people's lives are hard, complicated."

"As if I'm not aware of that." I wave my hand dismissively. "I know, I know. There's always some excuse why people can't get more involved."

"*Excuse?* They're not excuses, Jenny!"

The middle-aged woman at the next table peers at us over her glasses. Charlie chews on his lip. I lean forward and lower my voice.

"Even though the collective has slaved away at Dynamic Metals for over a year, we're no closer to kicking out the old guard of the union than when we started. They're still as entrenched as...as toe-nail fungus."

"But I've heard you say lots of times that you're making progress." He looks at me resentfully. "Was that just bullshit?"

I wince. "No, it wasn't! I often convince myself we're making progress."

"Convince yourself?" Charlie has been tearing his napkin into strips, then tearing the strips into squares.

"I remember how it was at GM. Just when I thought we were getting somewhere, I got laid off—along with all the youngest, most advanced workers. When we were called back five months later, I was on a different shift and the collective had to start over from scratch." I toss up my hands. "And now the layoff at Dynamic Metals, Charlie. It seems hopeless sometimes."

"Dialectics, Jenny. Dialectics! Remember that. It's not a straight uphill course. There are zigs and zags. But the overall trend is upward, toward the revolution." He stacks sugar cubes. Upward.

"I don't know if I still believe that stuff about progress being inevitable."

He slumps back into the padded vinyl. His voice, when he finds it, is subdued. "Sounds like you're pretty discouraged."

"Yeah," I whisper. "I am." Don't let me cry.

Charlie sighs. "Well, I get discouraged too."

"You do?"

"Yeah, everyone does. But if we just hang in there, Jenny, we'll see results. Don't forget, history's on our side."

I have a headache, need an aspirin. "Oh, Charlie, what if that's just an empty slogan?"

"You're starting to worry me." He leans forward and scrutinizes me. I almost expect him to put his hand on my forehead: *Oh, if only a pill could fix her.*

So many landmines to negotiate. First, our botched sexual encounter and now this. I start to wonder uneasily about the consequences. Will he treat me differently now? Will he stop confiding in me?

Will he tell anyone?

I pull my sweater tighter around me. "Don't pay any attention to me," I say. "It's nothing. You know I love this work. I've just been tired lately."

"Yeah, it's probably fatigue, that's what it is." He points at me with his index finger. "Hey, what you need is a good night's sleep."

"Thanks, doc." We laugh but the laughter sounds hollow, and we finish our iced teas—which are no longer iced—in silence.

Charlie breaks the quiet. "What are you doing this weekend?"

"This weekend?" I ask vaguely. "Well, there's the strike support meeting Saturday morning. And the Vietnam celebration in the afternoon. I'm not sure what Miguel and I are doing in the evening. Why?"

"Oh," says Charlie. "No reason. OK. Have fun, then. See you soon." He heads down the street, turning and waving before he disappears around the corner.

13. Jenny

MAY 1975

WE SCHEDULE SEX FOR THE FOLLOWING Saturday, one week away. It's my idea. Planning gives me time to prepare myself, gives me a sense of control.

I'm at a peak of distraction. Monday morning, I forget to read "Strategies for Building the Party," a pamphlet from the leadership that we're supposed to discuss and critique that night. Tuesday, I neglect to tell the hairdresser not to cut my bangs so short. Wednesday, I discover I've forgotten to buy sardines and Special K at the A&P. And on Thursday, a presentation for the next collective meeting that should have taken two hours to prepare takes me all afternoon. But I'm amazed at how relieved I feel now that I've told Miguel about Duncan.

My fears of sex are irrational, just like Felicia's fear of lightning, like Charlie's fear of dentists. Back in my college psych class, I learned about *desensitization*: an irrational fear can be overcome by visualizing it, then gradually increasing exposure to it.

I start with visualization. Taking off my clothes: will I do it or will he? Taking off his clothes: will he do it or will I, like in the movies? Or will we each undress separately, then slide modestly between the sheets? Will he be turned off by my small breasts? How will I react to his...his penis? Will I avert my eyes? If I look, will it repulse me? Or turn me on? (It might be a good idea to browse through another anatomy book before Saturday.) Once in bed, will we talk first? Will he touch me immediately? Will I touch him? Where? How? What if I freeze as I did with Charlie? What if he's disappointed?

As for exposure, I've been increasing that for a few weeks now, letting Miguel get more *physical.*

Saturday finally comes. It's a warm May evening. We have a late dinner at a café on Grove Street. I have no appetite and eat very little of my steak dinner. We stroll home in the twilight, which slowly fades to darkness. My hand in Miguel's is sweating; the pulse in my neck is throbbing. We slowly walk up the stairs to my apartment. I unlock the door and we enter.

Night sounds drift up from the street through the open windows. Muffled radios broadcast the baseball game, cars roll by, children play tag, little dogs go *yip yip.*

With trembling hands I turn on the lamp, which emits a golden glow, then close the blinds. Together we open the sofa bed and unfold lilac-colored sheets, which release the scent of fabric softener as they float and settle calmly on the bed, mocking my trepidation.

I turn the lamp back off. Street lights filter in around the edges of the blinds and cast geometric patterns on the walls. Uncertainly, I unbuckle my sandals, looking to Miguel for direction. He takes off his sneakers and we face each other.

"*No te preoccupes!*" he whispers. Don't worry. He puts his arm around me and says, "Let's just sit and talk for a minute." We sit on the edge of the bed and he says, "It's not about performance, you know; it's about being with the person you love."

"I'm nervous," I say.

"I am too," he says, which surprises me. Then he says, "And I'm curious. And very excited. How about you?"

"I'm so nervous I don't feel anything," I say.

"That's normal the first time," he says. "So probably we should get the nervousness over with." He gently tugs at my zipper. I stand and my jeans fall to the floor. I step free of them. He sheds his pants and then draws my t-shirt over my head, unhooks my bra, gives it a brief toss. Now his hands are doing things and I hear "Rhapsody in Blue" but don't know if it's outside the apartment or somewhere in my head. I close my eyes. There's a moan, and at first I'm unaware that it's me.

He guides me down onto the bed. The sheets are cool. I'm surprised how solid and reassuring his body feels on mine, pressing me into the mattress.

Across the street in the park a woman's voice drifts across the night air. "Here Trixie, Trixie, Trixie." I open my eyes and see the silhouette of my bra hanging off the edge of a book protruding from the case. I think that book is *Das Kapital.*

I close my eyes again. His lips are everywhere and now his tongue is everywhere too. My body becomes captive to my senses. I no longer have a mind, just a body with a burning need to finish what's been set in motion. *Quickly. Quickly!*

It's about to happen, I can tell. The same sensation I have with the vibrator. It's coming, *I'm* coming. Any moment. From an apartment across the street I hear the voice of Ella Fitzgerald and "Summertime." But I don't let myself pay attention to that now; I can't get distracted. *Hurry hurry.* It's so close but still not yet, *not yet....*

A hot stream like lava flows through my body and slowly extends outwards through invisible tributaries that reach to the tips of my fingers and toes. *Yes!* I call out. *Sí!* He pulls me toward him and kisses me like I've never been kissed before. Then he guides me back on the bed, hangs poised above me, meets my eyes. His passion excites me; when he comes, it's like an explosion. He wraps me in his arms and holds me to him and says, *Te quiero, Yenny Apple! Te quiero!* I love you! We lie there breathing rapidly, our skin touching. It feels good that he's inside me.

Now our breaths are coming more slowly. He rolls to face me. Looking into his eyes, I think: how strange that I recoiled from this. I'm already forgetting what it was that I dreaded.

PART 2

1. Jenny
JUNE 1975

AFTER THE LAYOFF AT DYNAMIC METALS, Miguel does get his old job back at the machine shop in the Bronx. He's still staying with Julio and Hermalinda on their sofa. One day we're strolling down Grove Street, speaking in Spanish as usual.

"You should move in with me, Cimarrón," I say. As soon as I speak the words, I feel at home with them. I add, "After all, you don't have your own apartment anymore."

"And we spend all our time together," he adds. Which is true. On weekends we attend events or meetings, workshops or demonstrations. Sometimes we drive to the Jersey shore. On Saturday nights we head into the city.

"We live too far apart," I say.

"And you can save money on rent," he says. "Especially now that you're on unemployment." He squeezes my hand and kisses me. "Besides, I want to be with you all the time."

I love it when he talks like that. If only I could express my affection so easily. Two girls are twirling on the sidewalk in front of the pastry shop, their skirts and petticoats billowing. I want to twirl too. For the first time in my life, I'll be like everyone else. Finally living with a man. A full-fledged woman!

Miguel immediately counts out half the June rent—four twenty-dollar bills and a ten. Then he leaves to collect his stuff from Julio's apartment. While he's gone I rush around pulling winter clothes off hangers and packing them into cardboard boxes, which I label and consign to a high closet shelf. I clear out space for him in the medicine cabinet and empty two drawers in the bureau.

That evening he shows up with a worn suitcase and some A&P paper bags, and I realize I didn't need to worry about not providing enough space. I watch as he unpacks his few books, toiletries, jeans and t-shirts.

And a chess set. The pieces are made of honey rosewood, the board of walnut, he tells me later. It's a work of art.

The first two weeks are spent getting used to living together. We develop a routine. I cook; he does the dishes. In the mornings he folds up the bedding and closes up the sofa while I brew coffee. On weekends, if we're so inclined, we clean the apartment.

Mealtimes are fun, sharing what's on our minds. Sometimes we prepare *sancocho* together. Or while I make pasta, he lays out the chess board on the kitchen table and sets up the wooden pieces. The spaghetti boils, steaming up the windows, and the sauce simmers, releasing aromas of onion and garlic and tomato. We sit at the table and I continue my chess education, which began in the break room back at Dynamic Metals. I study the pieces, reflecting on possible moves. Hesitantly, I take his castle with my knight. Then in a wicked maneuver that I haven't anticipated, he captures the knight.

I bite my thumbnail, scan the field. Tentatively I venture a pawn out one square, anguishing over my poor queen: have I left her vulnerable? Miguel says, "Good, good," as if he's proud of me. On my next turn I'm sure he has let me get away with capturing his bishop, but again he beams as if I'm a precocious student. As I glance up and catch him watching me, something about the curve of his lips feels erotic.

When the timer rings, Miguel polishes off the game with a few quick strokes. I marvel at his skill and realize that he *has* been letting me capture his men. He gathers up the chess pieces and packs them into a box, then folds up the wooden board. Carefully he places the set on the top shelf of the bookcase, next to *The Wizard of Oz,* a childhood book of mine which I've saved all these years.

While Miguel does dishes after dinner, I often read aloud to him from the drafts of leaflets I've composed. We debate various positions of the collective: what does it mean for Black people to be part of a *nation* within the *Black Belt?* Is it correct to include bourgeois women in the women's struggle for equality? Why do we refuse to form alliances with the *revisionist Communist Party?* Which groups fighting for Puerto Rican independence have the correct line? What is the true nature of the Sino-Soviet split, and why have we taken the Chinese side?

I can't understand how I ever tolerated living by myself.

By week three, I do recall one or two things about living alone: you don't have to talk to someone when you're feeling moody. You can dive into a book at mealtime without feeling rude. You can skip meals altogether or just have yogurt and a carrot for lunch. (He's always so *ravenous!*) You can tie up the bathroom for hours, go to bed at any time, let your underwear lie around the apartment, and not have to leave notes about where you'll be and what time you'll be home.

There are a few annoyances too. I like the tub to be scoured after each use; he agrees to do so but then "forgets." I like to sleep with the windows cracked, but he complains that his ears get cold. He prefers one light-weight blanket and I prefer three heavy ones. He seems to be allergic to vegetables and he likes sweets after every meal. He leaves newspapers and flyers all over the living room. And does he have to make so many long distance calls to his cousins and friends in New York? The phone bill will be humongous!

I remind myself that I'm not perfect either. I probably drive him crazy agonizing so much over everything: Why did so and so snap at me at the meeting? Was my presentation OK, huh, huh, huh? Are you sure my breasts aren't too small?

And he probably wishes I wouldn't sing while I cook dinner and take showers, that I wouldn't repeat myself when I'm making a point, that I wouldn't interrupt him, and that I wouldn't play classical music so often.

It seems that living with someone requires a lot of negotiating and biting your tongue.

I discover with dismay that the collective doesn't approve of our living together. Cohabitation is considered a no-no: *It's not the proletarian way.* Hah! That's a laugh! "You're *what?*" Cindy asked. A corner of her mouth turned down, adding a decade to her age. There's something parochial about the collective. Its morals seem closer to the Fifties than to the Seventies. Is it just coincidence that most collective members are in heterosexual marriages? With children? And potted plants?

But the collective's disapproval of me goes deeper. More than once in sessions of *criticism/self-criticism*—a free-for-all period where everyone can say whatever good or bad thing about you that they wish—I've been reproached: *You've got to let go of your intellectualism.* Or: *You're too individualistic—going off on tangents all the time.* Both *intellectualism and individualism* are usually preceded by the words *petit bourgeois.* Are they thinking that Miguel is at risk? That I have an infectious disease? Yet they recently praised me for recruiting him.

But these irritants are minor compared to waking in the middle of the night and hearing Miguel's soft snoring, nestling into his body. After all these years of avoiding sex, I'm elated that it's now a vital part of my life. The horror of Duncan's rape has not disappeared but rather shrunk to the point that I can hold it between my hands, turn it over like a ball, and ponder it. I experience sadness but no longer feel that I'm unclean, deficient, or culpable.

And having a date every Saturday night isn't so bad either.

Several times I've invited Miguel to join Charlie and me in our leafleting on Thursdays, but he always declines so I stop asking him. He says he makes use of the opportunity to visit friends in New York. Instead of disappointment, I feel guilty pleasure at having this time alone with Charlie. If Miguel were there, it would be awkward; Charlie and I wouldn't interact in the easygoing way that has re-established itself, for we talk about almost everything again—except Miguel.

One Thursday Charlie and I are at Dotty's, sipping iced teas. We've been laughing about a woman who ripped up Charlie's leaflet.

Out of the blue Charlie says, "I admit it."

"Whatever you did," I say, "I'll come visit you in prison."

"You're right. 'History is on our side' is a slogan." A surge of relief makes me almost weak. But then he adds, "But the slogan does have teeth, Jen." I stare carefully at the two spoonfuls of sugar that I add to my iced tea. He talks faster and I wonder if he thinks that faster equals more convincing. "It *is* our time! Capitalism has nowhere to expand. People are sick and tired of being exploited. All over the world we see revolutions—Cuba, China, Vietnam." His eyes shine. "Look at Africa!"

I should let this go. "What about here in the U.S.?" Always vigilant, I glance at the white-haired man in the next booth, but he seems safely absorbed in conversation with the man across from him, so I continue. "Sometimes it seems as if we'll be the *last* place to have a revolution. They're shutting down factories, shipping entire departments overseas. 5000 Ford workers at Mahwah will probably be thrown into the streets." I turn my hands up and ask, "How can we make a revolution without the proletariat?"

A pink-clad baby in the booth behind Charlie fastens her eyes on me and wails, as if mourning the demise of the proletariat. Charlie raises his voice over the noise. "We can't succumb to pessimism, Jen."

"But, Charlie, what if capitalism's just too *resilient*?"

At this word, the baby falls suddenly silent, creating one of those startling, quiet interludes in the midst of a noisy room. The baby's wide eyes are still fixed on me. Does she too ponder the resilience of capitalism? In spite of everything, I almost chuckle; perhaps I'm experiencing a bit of hysteria. Charlie's look of concern brings me back. He reaches over and places his hand on mine.

"I'm really sorry you're going through this, babe. I can tell you've been thinking a lot about it."

A tiny tear wiggles its way down the side of my nose. Charlie rubs it away, and I'm surprised at how comforting his thumb feels. "I think about these things too," he says.

"You do?"

"But to me, even if the revolution doesn't occur for another 50 years instead of five, I'll still keep my spirits up."

"Really? How?" I pull a crumpled Kleenex from my pocket and wipe at my face.

"Because we have so much to do."

"Like what?" I seem to be capable of only two-word questions.

"Like pave the way for those who follow. Educate people, fight for reforms, show people what a more humane society might look like."

How can I disagree? If only I could be as dedicated as Charlie. Why can't I shake off my demoralization? I sigh. "So these issues don't really bother you?"

"I don't let them get me down. There's nothing I'd rather be doing than this political work. Every morning I wake up curious to see what will happen that day. There's always something surprising. Even when it's a bummer, it's usually a stimulating bummer. I dig it."

I give him an I-really-like-you smile. Charlie's one of the lucky ones. He's able to get deep satisfaction, even fun, out of this work. Whereas for me these days, it often seems like a chore.

I'm glad I've talked to him. He hasn't condemned me the way I feared, the way I often condemn myself: hopelessly mired in petit-bourgeois thinking, traitor to the working class. Even if he disagrees with my ideas, Charlie doesn't consider them crazy or counter-revolutionary. And as a result maybe I'll be able to accept my doubts as normal, a phase I'm going through, something I'll grow out of.

This conversation proves I can tell Charlie anything. I wish I could talk with Miguel about my reservations. But what if he should find my doubts disgusting, or at the very least, sophomoric? After all, it's different with him. He's an experienced revolutionary, forged in the urban battlefield.

It's Sunday morning when I rap on Felicia's metal door and let myself into her apartment with the key she's given me. "Hola," I call. She's in the living room looking sexy in her iridescent green tights and purple leotard, hanging from the waist in a forward bend. I kick off my thongs, sprawl across her sofa, and help myself to a Milky Way from a ceramic dish on the coffee table. Perdido jumps onto the sofa, sniffs at the candy bar, then stretches out next to me.

Felicia is now in a headstand. I watch her as she rolls out of it, *vertebra by vertebra*, and ends up in the lotus position. Her face looks drawn. She snatches perdido from the sofa and hugs him to her chest, buries her face in his fur.

"Is anything wrong?" I ask her.

"Nothing. It's just that I miss my son sometimes. It's his birthday today."

"Oh, Felicia. That must be so hard." I scoot down to the floor, put my arm around her, pull her to me. We sit like that for a few minutes.

"There. I feel better already. Thanks." She jumps up, places Perdido back on the sofa, and puts a kettle of water on the burner. After we have our tea and *pan dulce,* we talk about the plant. I lick crumbs off my fingers and say nonchalantly, "Do you ever have doubts about our work, Felicia?"

She gives me the same clueless look that Charlie did. But after my talk with him, I'm feeling more confident.

"Oh, yeah. I know what you mean," she says.

"You do?"

"Sure. I question things all the time."

"Like what?"

"Like how much to spend on the strike benefit, for example." Indignation flares in her eyes. "We should have allocated a *lot* more than we *did*. It wasn't *right* to only allow *thirty dollars*, Yenny." She thrusts out her lower lip. "The *place alone* cost us *twenty*."

"What I mean," I gently explain, "is whether we're getting anywhere with our overall political strategy. Will there be a revolution—*ever?* Are we spinning our wheels?"

Felicia doesn't reply. I do some sit-ups. Ten of them. I count. Is she struggling to conceal her dismay the way Charlie did? Then she sighs and says,

"Yeah, I wonder sometimes."

"You do?" I give her a resentful stare. "How come you never *say* anything?"

"How come *you* don't?"

I think it over. "Because I'm scared."

"Of what?"

"Criticism is tricky. There never seems to be a place to raise such general questions. Certain assumptions are sacred; they're regarded as facts almost."

"It's a question of loyalty, isn't it?"

"That's it!" I sit back down on the sofa. "And besides that, I don't want to put a damper on things."

"What's a *damper?*"

"Something that brings people down." I think of the pleasure Charlie gets out of our political work.

Felicia frowns. "I don't say anything because I've met such wonderful people—especially you, *querida*." She gives me a look of affection and continues, "Working with the collective is like having a family in this country."

I know what she means. The collective has replaced my former (limited) social network and given me a purpose in life.

I'm grateful but I shudder at the thought of the void that would result if the collective were no longer in my life. What would succeed it?

Felicia glances sidelong at me. "And the collective has opened the door for me to…to get to know *gringos*. The collective accepts me. They aren't *racistas* like some Americans. They don't hate immigrants. That means a lot. So maybe that's why I don't mention my doubts."

I'm stunned and confused. "So don't you believe…?"

She raises her arms to the ceiling and stretches from side to side. "Some of it I do; some of it I don't. I don't believe in dogma; that's why I gave up religion. Anyway, no one can see in the future. No one can know for sure there's going to be a revolution. Or that it will turn the way we want. So I wait, I listen, I keep my eyes open."

How can Felicia be so calm when this is tearing me apart? But then, she has more inside knowledge of revolution than most of us do. Even though she was working in Puerto Rico during the Dominican rebellion, she has family members and friends who lived through it. And Felicia worked in blue-collar jobs her whole adult life. So she probably has a more grounded view of revolution than the rest of us. Except for Miguel of course.

If I weren't working in heavy industry, where would I be today? I visualize myself reciting Emily Dickinson to inner-city kids on the verge of joining gangs:

> *Because I could not stop for Death,*
> *He kindly stopped for me;*
> *The carriage held but just ourselves*
> *And Immortality.*

Or would I be teaching them to diagram sentences? (Do they still do that?) I found it amusing and useful—the application of math to language.

But after I joined the collective, I relinquished any notions of becoming a teacher. For better or worse, I tied my fate to the proletariat. Being petit-bourgeois became unacceptable. It allowed me a life of ease compared to the working class, which has "nothing to lose but its chains." By rejecting my *class and race privilege*, I've gained...gained *what?*

For one thing, I've gained the satisfaction of being an instrument of revolution. I can sleep well at night knowing that I'm on the right side of history. But there's a catch. You can never entirely get rid of the *stink of your origins.* How can you erase benefits bestowed upon you by birth? Good schools, a college education, healthcare, nutritious meals.

And the most damning thing of all: you have a way out. You know that at any time, if the path gets too bumpy, you can desert the working class. You can become a professional.

Unlike Felicia. Unlike Miguel.

2. Jenny

JULY 1975

BECAUSE I'M NOT WORKING, I TAKE OVER the house cleaning. It's only fair, I argue; he doesn't protest. He takes me out to
dinner on weekends and picks up the tab because he's working. It's
only fair, he assures me; I don't protest either. Besides, he's late on
his half of the rent for July. He probably just forgot.

One night we're on the sofa watching "M*A*S*H," our shoulders and legs sticking to each other in the humidity. Not a puff of
air enters through the open windows, and the swamp cooler is less
than useless. Humidity in summer, like icy roads in winter, is just
something people put up with.

During a commercial for Tang, Miguel stands up. "Fuck Tang.
I need a beer," he says in English. He heads for the kitchen. When
he reemerges, a can of Presidente in his hand, he turns down the
sound on the TV. Leaning against the wall, he takes a swig of beer
and says,

"I have to tell you something." He pauses.

I prompt, "What? You're pregnant?"

He doesn't laugh. "Is about Angélica."

The hairs on my arms stand erect. "What about her?"

"Is difficult to explain."

"You're going back to her," I say.

His voice rises a notch. "Of course no! Where you get that
idea?"

"Sorry. I was just…I was afraid…." I stop trying to explain.
"Go on," I say.

His voice returns to normal. "No, is nothing like that."

For some reason, I don't feel reassured. In fact, I have a strong
impulse to crawl into bed and pull the covers over my head.

He continues. "But something happen, and I...."

"Please, please, *please* get this over with."

"No is big deal. I mean to tell you sooner, but...Angélica...she is...embarrass."

What's he talking about? Angélica embarrassed? Then I get it. *Embarazada! Pregnant!* My eyes blur.

"Who's the father?"

He frowns and looks at the linoleum. "She say is mine," he says. I can hardly hear him, either because he's lowered his voice or because of the pounding in my eardrums.

"Yours? How can that be?" But I know how it can be. "Have you been seeing her?"

"No! Why you keep saying things like that?"

"Then how...?

"This happen back *then*." He gestures behind him with his thumb.

"How far along is she?"

"In October she will have the baby."

I gasp. "So soon?"

He bites his lip.

Like a calculator I tick off the numbers. If Angélica's baby is due in October—only three months from now—she must be six or seven months pregnant! She must have conceived sometime in January, the same month that he moved out of her apartment. We started dating about a month after that.

"Did you...did you know she was pregnant when you moved out?" I hold my breath.

"No!" He paces the room.

"But at least you must have known for a long time now, Miguel."

"No no *no!* She no tell me before. She no tell any person."

"Oh, my God, Miguel!"

"No is big—"

"Don't keep saying that!" I snap. He looks startled, then wounded. I tell myself to calm down. "Believe me," I nod knowingly, "it's a big deal." I clear my throat, I swallow. "When *did* you find out?"

"I find out for a while, but...."

"*A while?* How long is that?"

"No much time," he says.

"And you didn't tell me?" I sound shrill, I know. "Why didn't you tell me?"

He squirms. "Please, Yenny, *cógelo suave.*" Take it easy. "I know you are angry if I tell you."

I sigh in exasperation, step over to the window, gaze out. Street lights blink on, one by one. Two boys kick around a soccer ball in the twilight. A teenage couple on the corner wait to cross the street, holding hands and leaning into each other.

Miguel crosses to the window and puts his arm around my shoulders, but I pull away and sit down in the armchair. He sits on the sofa.

"Say something," he says.

"Did Angélica consider an abortion?" I ask, trying to make sense of this.

"Latina women no do that. *She* no do that. She is *Católica.*"

I take a deep breath. Maybe he's right that it isn't such a big deal. I must be careful of my tendency to blow things out of proportion. Anyhow, it isn't my problem, is it? It's up to him to handle it as best he can. In the kitchen I pour myself a tall glass of iced tea and stick a sprig of mint in it. He retrieves another beer from the refrigerator.

Something distracts me: in spite of my own feelings of shock and hurt, I feel sorry for Angélica. But I can't allow that; I've got enough going on just to deal with myself.

"What are you planning to do?" I ask.

"I take it care. No problem. You no need worry. I just want tell you before you hear from...other person." He points to the apartment under us. "Like you know who."

Now that he's referred to Felicia, I can't wait to see her. She works at a factory in Newark making eyeglass frames and often has dinner with her cousin in East Orange. What time did she say she'd be home tonight?

"Miguel, how could this happen? I mean, didn't you use protection?" One of his shoulders shrugs. Although he's always used a condom with *me*, I wonder if that's due more to my insistence than to his inclination. "Well," I say, standing up, brushing my hands together, "no use crying over spilt milk." He looks confused. "I mean, what's done is done. We can't undo it."

"I take care of the milk," he says again. "Is my responsibility. *¡No te preocupes sobre nada!*" Don't you worry about anything.

If only it were that easy.

We go to bed early, in uncomfortable silence. I lie on my back, naked in the heat, and my eyes trace the shadows on the ceiling. It irks me—this ability of his to instantly fall asleep.

Just when I'm living under one roof with a man for the first time in my life, *this* occurs. Miguel and I need time, time to get used to living together, without problems piling up like cars in an expressway accident. It's not the first time I've felt a sense of foreboding about Miguel. It happens at certain moments when we're on a street corner, when we enter a restaurant, or when we settle into beach chairs at the shore. Suddenly I'll notice a woman's eyes watching him, danger lurking in her glance.

And what will the collective say? Being in the collective is like living in a small town: everyone knows everything. Privacy is considered slightly bourgeois. Like *private property*. It's your duty to keep the collective apprised of things. And I can see myself becoming the scapegoat for Miguel's break-up with Angélica because any behavior by a white person that negatively affects a minority or a woman is by definition racist or sexist.

Miguel snores softly and I check the luminescent hands of the clock next to the sofa bed. Almost ten-thirty. Felicia must be home from East Orange by now. Slipping out of bed, I pull a muumuu over my head, slide my feet into thongs, and make my way down the dimly lit stairway to her apartment. A strip of light appears beneath the door, and I tap lightly with my fingernails.

I see Felicia's eye peering through the peephole. The door opens and she hugs me. She's wearing a robe and bunny slippers. She wiggles her fingers, palm down (which means, *Follow me)* as she heads for the kitchen. The first thing I notice in the center of the kitchen table on the plastic tablecloth is the geranium. Even Felicia has the obligatory potted plant.

Celia Cruz's voice comes over the radio. I sit down. On the table is the *Guardian* newspaper, open to an article entitled "Ultra-leftism and the Communist Movement." Felicia folds the paper and sets it aside. She blends us a papaya smoothie. I select a *pan dulce* from a hand-painted dish and sip at the drink.

"How did Miguel and Angélica get together?"

"Their fathers were both in the *policía nacional* in Santo Domingo. Miguel and Angélica got engaged over there, but he came here a few years ahead of her. Besides, Angélica's not bad-looking. Sort of like a nun, but like—how do you call it?—like a whore too."

After I tell Felicia about Angélica's pregnancy, she tsk-tsk's.

"That guy," she says. "He has trouble keeping his *pantalones* zipped up."

My hand grips the sweet bread so tightly that it crumbles. "What do you mean?" Doesn't she understand that Miguel was *living* with Angélica when she got pregnant? Is this more of her vendetta against him? Although I love Felicia, my loyalties lie with Miguel. I resent the way she pressures him.

Felicia leans so close that I see the tiny capillaries in the whites of her eyes. "I hope I don't regret telling you this, but"—her voice drops almost to a whisper and her eyes narrow—"he got Lucía in trouble too."

"Lucía?" My eyes widen as much as Felicia's have narrowed. "Who's Lucía?"

"The sister of Yesenia, Pablo's wife."

"The woman who's sort of slow?"

"That's her. She lives with Pablo and Yesenia in the Bronx, works in a laundry. It happened when Miguel stayed with them after breaking up with Angélica."

"Oh, my God." The pieces fly together like iron filings to a magnet. Miguel did a lot more on that sofa than just sleep. Lucía! I met her once when Miguel took me to meet Pablo and Yesenia. Lucía is in her early forties, extremely shy. She sat demurely while the conversation buzzed around her. Possibly she'd never dated in her life. Putty in a man's hands.

"Was that before or after he met me?" I ask, chewing on a thumbnail.

"After," Felicia says. I eye her suspiciously. She's not enjoying this, is she? "After he met you but before he started *dating* you," she quickly reassures me.

"What happened to the baby?"

"Lucía had an abortion." Felicia taps her glass with her fingernails. "Which Miguel paid for."

"But Miguel told me that abortion for Latina women was out of the question," I say.

"That's not always true. Pablo and Yesenia insisted. They didn't want to support her baby. And *she* couldn't do it. Besides, they're Marxists, atheists. With Angélica it's different. She comes from a religious family."

"Who told you all this?" I ask. Why does she always know so much more than I do?

Felicia doesn't seem to notice the edge to my voice. "Yesenia. We go way back."

I want to put my hands over my ears but instead I ask, "What else did Yesenia tell you?"

Felicia leans across the table. "Pablo was *rabioso,* really pissed off. He even strike Miguel."

"Struck," I correct her, out of habit.

"Struck," Felicia says. "Miguel ended with a black eye."

I remember the time Miguel was out with the "flu" for three days and returned to work with a bruise under his eye. He said he'd run into the edge of a door. A feeble excuse, but it worked on *me*.

"Miguel had to move out of Pablo and Yesenia's. But Pablo got over it, I guess," Felicia continues. "They're friends again. They go way back."

"Tell me, Felicia, is there something about Dominican men that makes them more chauvinist than other men?"

"No, *chica*, all men are like that."

But I don't believe her. "Oh, Felicia, what should I do?"

"Nothing, *querida*. He's just that way. Anyway, it's water on top of the bridge."

"I'm so confused."

"He's a typical macho. But he's changing since he met you."

"Do you really think so?"

"I see the way he looks at you. If anyone will change him, you will, Yenny."

How I want to believe that. After all, Miguel loves me. And he's a revolutionary. And he supports the women's movement. How can someone with all those principles treat women so callously?

Should I talk to him about Lucia? But what if I cross over from *talking* into *nagging?* Before I do anything else, I want to check out Felicia's story. I don't think she'd lie to me, but maybe she's jealous. I'm still not sure whether Miguel and Felicia were once an *item* or not.

Anyway, if all this happened before Miguel even started dating me, why should I risk losing him over ancient history? As for Angélica, let him work things out with her. I'm going to pretend that neither Miguel nor Felicia has said a word to me about any of this.

Throwing myself into the work of the collective, I experience a fresh burst of energy. I write articles for *The Struggle* and volunteer for extra work, which results in a flurry of meetings and tasks. I wander through the streets of Lower Manhattan, trying to put

Angélica out of my mind, enjoying the ethnic vitality, the shops and restaurants. I paint the living room walls a light salmon. I read books on theory and history and then allow myself the slightly decadent thrill of reading Raymond Chandler. I buy a French cookbook and prepare *boeuf bourguignon*, French onion soup, and *tarte aux pommes*, serving them to Miguel on a red checkered tablecloth with candles. On these hot nights we sometimes carry food and wine onto the fire escape, where we watch the setting sun and the boys playing soccer in the park across the street.

I stick to my resolution: ask no questions. Some people might call it *putting your head in the sand*, but I call it *not making tsunamis*.

One hot July Saturday, after we've spent the day at Sandy Hook beach, I look forward to a relaxing evening at home, showering together, then smoothing Lanacane on each other's sunburns, lying naked on the floor as the heat slowly dissipates, dribbling ice water over our bodies, listening to Bruce Springsteen or Aretha Franklin, and later, when it's cooler, making delicious love. But after our shower, Miguel says,

"I have to go into the city tonight."

I'm running a comb through my damp hair. "Why?" I ask. He frowns. "Is something wrong?" My comb hangs suspended.

"It's nothing. Enrique asked me to come by. He's got a little problem."

"Your cousin Enrique?"

"Sí." His tone is abrupt.

"Please, Miguel, do you have to go?" I hate the pleading tone I hear in my voice—like a little girl begging her parents to stay home. "I was looking forward to spending tonight with you." My sunburned face turns even redder. "To making love with you."

"Enrique needs me," he says. "He's my cousin. I can't let him down. You understand, *guapa* (sweetie). Sorry." He pecks me on the lips. "Don't wait up for me. I may be late."

And he's gone.

The silence settles in around me; it feels as if he were never here. I study the fresh salmon paint on the door, stunned at how quickly the sweet afterglow of the day has faded.

Well, fine. I can use the time to put together the political education for tomorrow's meeting on the role of non-proletarian workers in the revolution; I'll be leading the discussion. I pour half a glass of Chardonnay and begin outlining the main points. I peruse the latest issue of *The Struggle* for an article on the subject by one of our national leaders. One of the *gurus,* as I call them— further proof of my petit-bourgeois refusal to respect authority. About ten o'clock I give up. I switch on "The Odd Couple." My thoughts meander. If I had Enrique's number, would I call him? About 11:30 I go to bed, but sleep eludes me. Eventually I fall into an uneasy slumber, filled with auto crashes and sirens, flashing police lights and deportations. I see Miguel standing on the other side of Broadway; he doesn't see me, and every time I step into the street, a taxi or bus forces me back onto the curb.

Sunday morning the phone's shrill ring wrests me from a deep sleep. Sunlight streams in through the window; I neglected to close the blinds last night. The wall mirror across from the sofa bed reflects puffy flesh around my eyes. One side of my hair is flattened; my head aches. I reach for the receiver, knock it off the cradle, retrieve it.

"Good morning," says a cheerful voice.

"Ugh," I say. "What time is it?"

"Sorry I didn't call last night."

"Are you OK?" I ask.

"Enrique's phone was out of order."

"Couldn't you have gone down to a phone booth?"

"I have to admit I had a bit too much to drink. Can you find it in your heart to ever forgive me?"

The teasing tone of his voice makes me sit straight up. I bite my lip and admonish myself not to *nag.* But try as I might, I can't hide my resentment.

"Damn it, Miguel, I was worried!"

"It was so late I didn't want to disturb you. I was afraid you'd be sleeping already."

So many excuses make me dizzy.

"Next time call anyway, no matter what," I say. "I mean it."

There's silence. Has the line gone dead? I'm about to say, *Hello?* when I hear a click.

Ever so slowly I replace the receiver and stare with glassy eyes at *Das Kapital,* which still protrudes from the bookcase. Have I been too demanding? Should I give him the benefit of the doubt? He said he was worried about disturbing my sleep. As if I could sleep while imagining him mugged or deported or, yes, with another woman.

And which was it? Was he drunk? Or was he being considerate? Was Enrique's phone really disconnected?

I brew a cup of espresso, carry it down a flight of stairs, and rap on Felicia's door again. I'm beginning to suspect it won't be the last time I make these demeaning treks down to her apartment.

3. Jenny
AUGUST 1974

I GET THE NOTICE ON TUESDAY AT 4 P.M. It's another of those unbearably muggy August days when I miss southern California weather, which may be hot enough to burn your bare feet on the sidewalk in summer but never so humid that you're sticky.

I've been reading *Wuthering Heights* and I've fallen asleep in the rocker so I'm late going downstairs for the mail. I awaken with my face flushed, sweat pooling inside my bra, despite the little floor fan blowing a warm breeze in my direction, despite wearing cutoffs and thongs, despite wide-open windows.

I drag myself down the two flights to the narrow entry hallway of the apartment building. It's cooler down here. Unlocking my mailbox I pull out circulars for pizza and coupons for the A&P. Then I see it. It contrasts with the other items—it's so thin and plain and blindingly white. The return address reads "Patriot Industries." My heart does a somersault. Patriot Industries is the parent company of Dynamic Metals. I throw the junk mail in the metal trash bin, but this letter I carry back upstairs, holding it by the corner, letting it hang like something toxic.

Once inside my apartment, I prop the envelope against the lamp on the end table and let it stand there while I prepare a tall glass of ice water with a slice of lime. I sit down on the sofa and rub the glass across my cheeks and forehead, eying the envelope.

Finally, I set down the glass and pick up the letter. I slide my fingers over it, feeling its cool and lethal smoothness. I've received letters like this before. They always cause the same doomed sensation. Sometimes the company leaves you a notice as you clock out. Sometimes they call you into the office.

Sometimes they send you a letter.

The only reason companies deign to communicate with you at all is to lay you off or fire you. Wouldn't it be nice if they would take a survey of worker satisfaction? This is the kind of letter I'd *like* to see:

> Dear Ms. Jennifer Apple:
>
> Our employee relations program is contacting you to ask if you would be willing to give us your input into improving working conditions and streamlining production. As a worker on the shop floor, you're the real expert. You're in a far better position than our efficiency staff (who, incidentally, earn ten times more than you) to enlighten us vis-à-vis items which would be of mutual benefit to us all.
>
> Sincerely,
> Mr. John Q. Industrialist

I sigh. Of course I don't believe there can be "mutual benefits" between workers and capitalists because we have nothing in common, but still I would enjoy receiving such a letter. I know that workers are as invisible to the owners as the maids in their upscale mansions. Invisible, that is, until one of them becomes a trouble-maker. Then the bosses spring into action. Rebellion must be quashed! Swiftly, methodically, like a time-motion study. Dispassionately, like the powerful clamp of a leopard's teeth sinking into the jugular.

I run a finger under the flap of the letter and extract it from the envelope. The first sentence tells it all: I'm *terminated.* As if I've ceased to exist.

The letter is short and to the point. It has been revealed (by whom?) that I have a college degree which I've failed to disclose.

It's a recurring dilemma. Companies won't hire you if you admit you're a college graduate. *You're overqualified. Why would someone like you want a job like this?* So you're forced to misrepresent yourself. You lie. And if you start to organize, your college education is a convenient way to get rid of you. My work history is a several-years-long saga of getting fired from plants for reasons that have everything to do with my political activity and nothing to do with the reasons the bosses give, like "falsification."

I bang my fist on the end table. Now I'll be penalized from collecting unemployment, and it'll be harder to find another job. I'm bursting to discuss this with Miguel—over a stiff drink. I glance at the clock. 5 p.m. He should be home soon. *If* he comes home. Recently he's spent a couple more nights in New York—or wherever it is he goes.

The late afternoon sun beats against the closed blinds and radiates into the living room. After taking a shower and washing my hair, I let the water evaporate off my naked skin as I roam the apartment. I dial Charlie's number, imagining him on the sofa reading the *Playboy Magazine* I saw in his apartment on that fateful night. I hold the receiver between my ear and shoulder while cracking ice from an ice tray into a glass and pouring myself a Coke, listening to its fizz and to the plaintive rings of the phone. Unfortunately, Felicia won't be home either; she's stopping by her cousin's again after work. Dominicans have too many damn relatives! I crave a cigarette but resist. Instead, I throw on shorts and a sleeveless top and head for the park. Outside under the trees it's cooler. Sitting on a bench, I watch kids playing on the merry-go-round, a Chihuahua yipping at their heels.

I feel stripped of identity.

At the collective meeting tomorrow I'll receive sympathy. But they'll want me to look for another factory job. I close my eyes. These jobs are getting harder to find, and the more often I get fired, the more elaborate my cover-up has to be the next time.

My old thoughts return to accuse me. I'll never be a true proletarian. I'll always have the ability to leave. No matter how grounded in the working class I become, that fundamental truth will remain, that guilt will adhere to me.

When I started working in factories, I believed I was in the working class for life. I made a pact to myself that I would never betray it, never abandon factory life for a middle-class job, never return to my roots.

But I'm not leaving the jobs; the jobs are leaving me!

The way I feel now, I may never go back to a factory job. The collective will be shocked and angry. I can hear them now: *She can't take the heat.*

But I yearn for something different. Not necessarily a petit-bourgeois job but something where I'll work directly with people, not with machines and furnaces. Maybe a gig as a waitress. I always imagined that would be interesting. Or as a cashier or a clerk. And a *part-time* job—yes, that's what I'd like right now. Something un-demanding, no pressure to organize. Something that will pay the rent, put food on the table, but give me leisure time to figure things out.

As I climb the steps to the stoop, I see Miguel coming up the block, his feet dragging, his backpack hanging halfway off his arm. My spirits lift. He raises his hand in a limp wave. As he gets closer, I see the streak of grease across the bridge of his nose. I throw my arms around him.

"*¿Qué pasa?*" he asks.

"Come have a cold beer and I'll tell you all about it," I say, tug-ging hard at his arm. "Hurry!" I run ahead of him up the stairs.

4. Miguel

AUGUST 1975

HOW GLAD SHE IS TO SEE ME! It's been a helluva long time since I've experienced that. I don't know when it started, but one day I realized that she was becoming morose. Always nagging at me, just like Angélica. Is it too much to ask for a little appreciation when I arrive home exhausted? After all, this damned heat is a killer. The machine shop sizzles on days like this; I feel like a strip of bacon in a fry pan. And Yenny? She's home all day drinking iced tea.

But today it's different.

"*¿Qué pasa?*" I ask for the second time. I'm in the bathroom, wiping my face with a cold washcloth. I strip down to my boxers and position myself at the kitchen table so that the fan blows directly on me. She's blending a piña colada. In a moment I'll take a cold shower and then I'll be a new man. But first I'll find out what's happening with her. She hands me a glass of the icy drink.

"I got fired today," she says in Spanish.

"No way!"

"Really."

"How come?"

"For lying on my application. That's what they said." She pushes the termination letter across the table and waits while I read it. I frown.

"For sure that isn't the real reason," I say.

"Of course not."

"Knocking off the radicals," I say, sliding my hand across the table, placing it over hers.

"Oh, Miguel, I'm so depressed," she says, getting up from her chair and coming around to sit on my lap.

I hold her and put up with the heat radiating from her body. This humidity is a bitch.

"Let's take a shower and then talk some more," I say, polishing off my drink.

Standing behind her in the shower, I massage her upper back and shoulders with sudsy water. I feel her muscles relax. I hug her to me, wrap my arms around her breasts, and let the lukewarm water flow over us. I sense such powerful love for her that it almost hurts.

I put my chin on her shoulder and remorse overcomes me. What is it that compels me to hang out in clubs and flirt with girls, then exhausted and wasted, flop onto a sofa at Pablo's or Enrique's or Julio's? What is this strange force that pulls me away from Yenny and into reckless situations? I know I'm playing with fire; one of these days she'll get wise to my ass. From now on I'm going to stay home, that's a promise!

After the shower—she says it's her second one that afternoon—I feel a lot better. I'm moved that she seems to need me; she's usually so damn independent. Gone is that sour look of disapproval, which always angers me and at the same time makes me feel so ashamed that I can't wait to get the hell out of here.

We sit on the sofa, fresh drinks in our hands, and put our feet up on the coffee table. I put an arm around her.

"Oh, Miguel," she says, nestling in, speaking in Spanish. "I can't stand to be fired again."

"We'll fight this, Yenny," I say.

"It's no use, Miguel. The union won't stand behind me. They hate me. I've burnt too many bridges."

"The *leadership* hates you, not the rank and file, *guapa*."

"But the rank and file are all laid off. Strewn to the far corners of New Jersey."

"Not all of them."

"The younger, more radical ones are. The ones who worked on the midnight shift with me." She shakes her head. "The workers who remain don't even know who I am."

"*Everyone* knows who you are, Yenny. You're their hero."

She waves her hand dismissively. "But Miguel, even if I should win my grievance—and that's not likely—I'd never get called back from layoff. I'm low woman on the totem pole."

"It doesn't matter. You'd be making a statement."

She ignores me. "And after three years, the company can void the seniority list," she says.

"Whether you win or lose is not the issue," I repeat.

"It is for *me.*"

"You got to take a stand."

"Why?"

"*Why?* I can't believe you're asking that!"

"It's in the contract that you can't lie on your application," she says.

I sigh. Doesn't she fucking get this? I can't comprehend her refusal to fight; it's not like her. "That's not the real reason they fired you. They fired you for union activity, for organizing. That's an illegal termination. That's *discrimination*. You've got a chance, Yenny. But only if you fight it."

It looks as if I'm finally getting through to her. I can see the struggle. I'll stand behind her. We'll give the company and those union shitheads a run for their money. We'll expose those assholes for the sellouts they are.

"They're after you because you led the walkout," I say. "They've probably had their eyes on you ever since." She's nodding; it's about time. "Say, how did they even find out that you were a college grad?"

She shrugs as if it's not a big deal. "Probably from the last job I was fired at. The Ford plant."

"And how did *they* find out?"

"The FBI must have talked to them. When they called me into employee relations to fire me, they confronted me with a whole mess of things. Things that no one there could have known. Like my work with prisoners in New York, my organizing with SDS, where I went to college—"

"You got to fight this, Yenny. For the sake of other activists. Even if you lose. Don't let them fuck you up without making their asses pay."

"I'm just so tired, Miguel. I keep getting fired or laid off. It seems so useless. You've got to give the companies credit. They manage to kill off their radical elements."

"I don't give them credit for anything!"

"Our strategy seems to have taken a nose dive." She looks at me as if waiting for a response. But it isn't a question. What the hell does she want me to say?

"Our strategy?"

"Building a revolutionary party based in the proletariat."

"What's wrong with that?"

"There *is* no proletariat. I mean, there is still a *little*, but it's disintegrating right before our eyes."

I'm shocked to hear her say that. "I know. The proletariat here is different than in Santo Domingo."

"Yeah," she says almost resentfully. "That's because *our* proletariat is now *your* proletariat. The capitalists are abandoning production over *here* for cheap labor over *there*."

She mustn't distract me, mustn't change the subject. It's absurd that she wants to roll over and play dead. I'd like to shake some sense into her. Perhaps it's just that she's under stress. In a few days, she'll be her old self again, ready to fight. She's nothing if not scrappy. That's what attracted me to her in the first place. That's why I joined the collective—because of her. Otherwise I never would have joined that band of gringos. They're nice, they

168

mean well, but…they're naïve. Without Yenny there, I'd prefer to work with my own people. I feel much more comfortable with *los Quisqueyanos*.

We go out to dinner, get drunk, come home, and have tepid sex. It must have been those final two beers that fucked it up.

5. Jenny

AUGUST 1975

SATURDAY MORNING I SHOW UP AT THE LAST possible minute at Cindy and Matt's apartment for the weekly cell meeting. In the study the comrades are drinking coffee, smoking, trading stories from the trenches.

Every member of the New Jersey cell is here. Esme and Sergio, the Puerto Rican couple who were recruited by Matt; Kate, the Rutgers student, wearing a dashiki, with silver hoops in her ears; Bonnie—the woman who recruited me and served as my early mentor; Cindy, our cell leader, and her husband Matt; Roger, who works on the day shift at Dynamic Metals and has avoided the layoff, thanks to five years of seniority; Felicia; Miguel, who has come directly from a rally on 14th Street against racism in the Boston schools; and Charlie, whose face lights up when he sees me. He points to an empty chair next to him. Miguel, frowning, catches my eye and pats the seat next to *him*.

Waving noncommittally, I elude everyone by heading for the kitchen. I crave a Winston but settle for a sugar donut from a pink box, and pour myself a cup of Cindy's strong coffee.

Back in the study it's obvious that I should sit next to Miguel, and I do, although I note with surprise that I'd prefer to sit next to Charlie. But it's important to sit *across* from Charlie so I can make eye contact with him during the coming ordeal. Miguel kisses me on the cheek, then glances smugly at Charlie.

After everyone is seated, their coffee on the floor by their feet, donuts and papers balanced on their laps, backpacks hanging over chairs or resting on the floor, the meeting begins. Cindy, our cell leader, usually chairs unless she's at one of her executive meetings in Chicago, in which case her husband Matt takes over. Cindy and Matt are the open members; the rest of us are secret.

Criticism/self-criticism always comes first on the agenda. We always start with self-criticism—something positive and something negative. Bonnie begins: she's had excellent conversations with workers this week while leafleting at the Ford plant; she's made new contacts. But she still hasn't followed up with them and she's sorry even though she *has* been busy but then again, are you ever too busy to make a few phone calls? Cindy informs us that she stayed up late writing reports but completely forgot the most important one of all—for the national board in Chicago. Now she's missed the deadline and screwed everything up; they were depending on that particular report to help chart their course for the coming period. Matt acknowledges that while talking to a worker at his shop, he got heated, raised his voice, and called the guy an asshole. On the other hand, Matt is excited about being on the cusp of recruiting several Puerto Rican workers.

So it continues.

When my turn comes, I tell them I've been fired. Sharp intakes of breath. I say that it's probably due to my own impatience, not waiting for the probationary year to end before I started organizing. But what I'm *thinking* is that the collective bears partial responsibility for my dismissal. After all, not once in all those months did they tell me to slow down. Because I was successful, they conveniently overlooked the risks and cheered me on.

I tell them that I'm not sure I want to apply for work in a factory again, "at least not for the time being." Eyebrows hit the ceiling, jaws hit the floor. "I'd rather finish some projects I'm working on and get a part-time job somewhere," I say, calmly belying the pounding of my heart.

Criticism/self-criticism continues around the circle, but the looks on their faces and the brevity of their remarks show that they're anxious to get back to me. When it comes to the part where we finalize the agenda, Cindy suggests we put my situation at the top of the list.

Bonnie casts me a kindly glance from across the circle. "You must still be very upset, Jenny. Getting fired is a blow. In a few days you'll feel more like your old self."

Everyone looks hopefully at me and I squirm. "That may be so, but I still won't want a factory job," I say stubbornly. I recall how reluctant I was to go to work in the past months—before meeting Miguel. And after that I looked forward to work only because it meant seeing him.

"You want a part-time job, then?" asks Kate, squinting as if trying to comprehend this strange notion.

Esme, who works in an auto parts plant, says, "It may be hard to find a factory job anyway, you guys. Sergio's been trying for weeks."

"Especially since I was laid off for lying," I add. "Corporations talk to each other, don't they?"

"If the FBI was involved," Cindy says, "then it may be hard, that's true. But you haven't even tried yet."

"Not yet. This just happened."

"Well, then," Cindy says with finality. "It seems premature to worry so much about not finding a job. Even a job in a smaller shop would be preferable to a part-time job somewhere. What would you do? Be a clerk at Woolworth's? Wait tables at some flea-bitten café? How many advanced workers would you come across at jobs like that?"

Not many, I admit to myself. It wouldn't be an effective strategy. But neither is the collective's, I think defiantly. "I don't know if I ever want to go back," I say in a near whisper. Esme and Sergio lean forward as if straining to hear me.

"That's not your decision," says Matt. "The cell decides where people work."

Here it comes, I think. The part where they tell me how individualistic I am. My face burns.

Charlie breaks in, glaring at Matt. "Give her a little time," he says. His eyes flit to mine. I appreciate his attempt to support me, but does he really comprehend the depths of my disillusionment? He hasn't in the past.

"Maybe after my grievance is over," I say. "Let me get through that first."

"So you're going to fight it!" Miguel says.

"Yes." My voice lacks enthusiasm.

Cindy eyes me sharply. "You mean you weren't sure?"

"I hadn't decided yet. I didn't want to rush into anything. I needed time to consider all the ramifications."

"It doesn't seem complicated enough to expend all that brainpower on 'ramifications,'" Matt says. I glare at him. "Besides, there are deadlines to filing, or did you conveniently forget about that?"

"Jenny, just remember that we need everyone to work in factories," Cindy says, feeling the need to enlighten me about the obvious. "That's the core of our strategy—recruiting advanced workers to help build a proletarian party that can—"

"...lead the revolution," I cut in. Cindy presses her lips together and makes no response, but her eyes tell me that this lack of respect will not be forgotten. "I'm sorry for cutting you off, Cindy, but I'm familiar with our strategy." One of her eyebrows rises.

"Jenny, you're so good at factory organizing," Bonnie says. My tears come so suddenly that I'm not able to hide them. On too few occasions have I earned their appreciation: a few presentations, the walkout at Dynamic Metals, recruiting Miguel. After the walkout Cindy had said, beaming, *You're turning a corner, Jenny*, and I'd basked in the rare sunshine of her approval.

Roger appeals to me. "I need the support of cadres on graveyard. The collective is starting—finally—to establish a foothold in the plant. I'm glad you're going to fight this, Jenny."

"I'll fight it but I won't win."

Again there's barely concealed shock as the room becomes silent.

"What do you mean?" Cindy finally asks.

"I have no grounds to win it."

"We don't rely on legalisms. It's the power of the people behind you," Cindy says. "And you seem to have quite a base."

"They're all laid off," I say, tapping my foot impatiently; I've already been through this argument with Miguel.

"Why don't we have a special meeting to strategize the best defense?" Cindy suggests. "It looks to me like a case of 'discrimination due to union activity.' But we'll have to look into it and see how to best present it."

Felicia has been sending sympathetic looks in my direction but for once in her life seems at a loss for words.

"If no one objects, let's move on," Cindy says. Everyone nods. "Shall we take a coffee break first?"

Sighs of relief.

6. Jenny
AUGUST 1975

THE VERY NEXT DAY I SCAN THE CLASSIFIED section of the *Jersey Journal* and find a want ad for a part-time waitress at a truck stop near the Interstate. Out of sight! I dial the number and a man answers. Right off the bat he asks, "You got any experience?" I tell him I waited tables one summer after college. There, I said it! The C-word: *college.* The man on the phone doesn't balk; he tells me to come in for an interview.

Small factories line the street to the truck stop, which consists of a brick building with a huge neon sign on a pole that broadcasts: "Jimmy's—Home Is Where You Hang Your Hat," and displays a blinking neon Stetson. I park in the lot between a green Datsun and a black pickup. Several big rigs dwarf the chain-link fence. Broken glass from a street light glitters in one corner. I can hear the roar of the Pulaski Skyway. I turn off the ignition and sit there. Then I take a deep breath and exit the car, slamming the door with a satisfying whack. The odors of French fries and barbecued pork grow stronger as I approach the entrance.

The more I think about this job, the more I covet it. Mingling with working people, the mental challenge of remembering all those orders—it'll be fun! How different from the long, dull nights at Dynamic Metals.

I push open the double doors and enter the diner. Fluorescent lights illuminate vinyl booths and a long lunch counter. At the entrance, miniature state license plates decorate the wall. A pegboard of key chains and chewing gum, candy bars and plastic doo-dads rests on the counter next to the cash register. On the other side is propped a display of cigarettes.

The man behind the register gives me the once-over, then returns his attention to the papers he's sifting through.

"Hi, my name's Jenny. I called about the part-time waitressing job."

The man grunts. He's short and his skin hangs loose on his cheek bones. He continues sorting.

I take his grunt as an affirmative. "Umm, so here I am," I prompt.

"Yup," he says, glancing briefly up at me again, as if I'm interrupting his routine. "So the hours are from eleven to three. Pay is 75 cents an hour, plus tips. Buy yourself some uniforms—two or three."

Is he the head honcho—this chunky man with hair thinly combed across his bald spot? Is this all there is to it? No questions, no application, no health forms? Hasn't he heard of Typhoid Mary?

"When would you like me to start?"

"Tomorrow. I'm short a girl for the lunch hour.

"I'll be here," I say. No response. He doesn't even look at me again. "See you tomorrow at eleven, then...." I turn to leave.

"Report to Babs when you come in. She'll show you the ropes." He thrusts some papers at me. "Here, bring these back tomorrow."

The next day I arrive at 11 a.m., wearing a white uniform and clunky white shoes that make my ankles look like toothpicks. The café is almost empty. Babs, a trim woman with a brisk, efficient air, greets me. A hair net covers her beehive. "Hi, sugar," she drawls in a Southern accent. "Let me show you 'round."

In the next few minutes I learn where the utensils and dishes are located, and how to set up tables, sign the ledger for a book of receipts, and fill out a ticket. "We get real busy between 11:30 and 2 p.m.," she says. "After that we clean up, take our break, and prepare for the dinner crowd." As she talks, she fills a catsup container and wipes the excess off the plastic with a damp rag. "Of course, you'll leave by three."

A chubby brunette approaches, water pitcher in hand. "This here is Sylvie," Babs says. "And this"—she indicates a well-endowed blond—"is Maddy."

Sylvie and Maddy give me friendly smiles. Maddy's teeth are misaligned, but I doubt if customers notice. "Welcome to the crew," Maddy says.

"We all get along here," says Babs. "If you do your job Jimmy won't bother you."

"Jimmy?"

She gestures toward the cash register. "The boss."

"Watch out for the cooks, though," Sylvie warns, casting a quick look toward the kitchen. I anxiously follow her glance.

"Come on," Babs says. "You might as well meet the devils." Sylvie giggles. Chicken sizzles on the grill. One cook leans on the counter and eyes me as we approach. The other cook scoops long loops of spaghetti onto two plates.

"This is Jenny, the new waitress," Babs says. "This here is Stefan and that's Milos."

"Hi," I say. Stefan continues gawking. His stringy hair is squashed into a hairnet. Milos, the spaghetti man, gives me a smirk. He's built like a boxer, and on each of his fingers he wears a thick ring. Grease and tomato sauce stain his white apron. Neither of them says a word. Is their silence due to insufficient English or are they just rude?

Babs assigns me only three booths to start with. I bring ice water to two truck drivers who have occupied one of my tables. "Hi, beautiful," says the first one, a burly guy with biceps the size of the Soviet Union. "You new here?" I smile and nod. "Bring me some coffee, pronto."

"Coming right up," I say, pretending I know what I'm doing.

"Make that two," says his partner, another Big Guy, with a five o'clock shadow and a t-shirt that reads *Truck Drivers Do It Better.* "And bring me an apple pie a la mode."

I feel my face flush. My first order! True, these men aren't proletarians—they don't work at the point of production. In other words, they aren't the most advanced workers, the vanguard of the revolution. But (the collective be damned!) at least they're workers—the salt of the earth—and right now that's enough.

That night I'm too exhausted to have sex, although Miguel half-heartedly pressures me. I drift off to sleep while he's still arguing about it.

In the coming days I'm surprised how much I look forward to work. I'm regaled with colorful stories about cross-country trips, I'm treated with respect, I'm tipped well. It's not so easy remembering all those orders—*one on the city (water) with lemon but no ice, a sirloin steak and make it alive, BLT hold the mayo, eggs over easy but not too easy (if you know what I mean, beautiful).* But I get good at it. Damned good.

The only annoyance is the cooks, Stefan and Milos, the *Evil Twins* whose purpose in life is to make my life hell. For the sake of keeping my job, though, I clench my teeth and put up with their off-color remarks and their tongue-thrusting. At Dynamic metals I'd talk back to sexist workers, tell them where to get off. But in this job that won't do; I've got to tone it down.

7. Jenny

SEPTEMBER 1975

THE MORNING OF MY GRIEVANCE HEARING my head pounds like a jack hammer. I'm dizzy and nauseated but manage to avoid throwing up. I'm probably coming down with the flu; maybe all this stress has lowered my resistence. Or is it my nervousness?

Lance Martin, the union rep, has a firm handshake. His smile is tight, business-like, and discloses absolutely nothing. His linen jacket stretches over his bulging biceps and sculpted chest, and his shoes are polished to a glossy sheen. He's young—perhaps five years older than I am. I don't trust Lance; he's beholden to the union leadership. But if I want to file this grievance (which I don't but the collective does), then I'll have to temporarily suspend my distaste.

Lance Martin precedes me to a conference room, empty except for eight chairs around a gleaming mahogany table. Not a speck of dust mars its surface. A vase of lilacs is strategically placed in the center of the table. Recessed lights provide illumination.

He motions me to a seat at the table and offers me coffee, which I accept. Maybe it will lessen my nausea. He departs to a side room, returns with two coffees, and seats himself at the head of the table. In front of him are a stenographer's notebook, three long, finely sharpened pencils—the erasers still virgin, a pack of Pall Malls, and an ashtray.

He extends the pack toward me; I shake my head although the cigarettes create in me that uneasy nostalgia. Lance extracts a cigarette, sets the pack down, and nudges it with his index finger so it lines up precisely parallel to the edge of the table. He takes a drag and exhales a narrow shaft of smoke, which is sucked upward into a vent in the ceiling. He flips open the cover of the notepad to the first page and scribbles something. My arms and legs are tense; I hope they don't cramp.

"Let's begin then, Miss Apple," he says, clearing his throat, pencil poised. "Why don't you tell me what happened?"

"There's not much to tell," I say. I briefly describe my activism as a shop steward, my role in the walkout after the smelter incident, my layoff, and then my unexpected termination several weeks later. I wince as another wave of nausea passes through me. Wouldn't it be humiliating to throw up all over this pristine table?

Lance Martin's pencil tip moves smoothly back and forth across the page. He switches pencils and frowns.

"Let me ask you this: *Did* you falsify your application?"

"Yes." No use denying it.

"Hmm." More notes on the pad. "How did the company find out you'd been to college?"

"It must have been the FBI."

He stops writing and fixes me with probing eyes. "The FBI? What makes you think it was the FBI?"

I shift uneasily. "Actually, I don't know for sure. But I can't think who else it could be."

"Haven't you told anyone else about your college education?"

I pause. Of course the collective knows, but as for people who work at Dynamic Metals, only Roger, Miguel, and Felicia know. A chill passes through me but I shake it off; of course they wouldn't mention it to anyone.

"Not really," I say.

"Not really?"

"Well, only a couple of close friends. But they wouldn't tell anyone."

"But you have no evidence it was the FBI."

"Not hard evidence, no."

"I'm sorry but I'm still not clear about why you mentioned the FBI." (Oh, how I wish I hadn't!)

I force a pathetic shrug. "Just an over-active imagination, I guess. It's probably not the FBI at all. Anyway, that's not the point." My head feels like a punching bag.

"And what is the point, in your estimation?"

"It seems that I was fired because of union activity."

Lance sighs. "Now that's problematic. According to the contract, the company has the right to fire you within the first year of employment if they discover that you falsified your application." Of course I know all this; aren't we wasting time? But perhaps he's only trying to establish a common understanding of the facts. "After one year," he continues, "if you have no incidents against you, then the contract says you've proven yourself a satisfactory worker. The company may no longer use falsification as a reason for termination. Since *you've* worked here less than one year, your case will be difficult for the union to win."

"But isn't it against the contract to fire someone for union activity, no matter how little time they've worked there?"

"Ye-e-e-s, and it's also against the National Labor Relations Board. But to prove it, we'd have to have something to go on. Do you have any evidence that it isn't just a simple case of falsification? Even if you were politically active?"

That's the dilemma. I'm convinced my firing was due to my activism, but how can I prove it? The collective told me to use discrimination. "That's your strong suit," they said. As if it were a game of poker. I know that other political activists in the shop, like Roger from my collective and Sharon from a Trotskyist collective, concealed their college backgrounds too. But they had the wisdom to wait until their probationary year was up before revealing themselves as organizers. By that point they could no longer be fired without just cause, which means without a valid, work-related reason. They were safe.

"Well," I say haltingly, "there are other people who falsified their applications, and they weren't fired. Could we build a case that the company doesn't look into your application if you're not causing trouble? I'm a good worker so they had no other reason to fire me except that I helped organize to get better safety rules after the smelter explosion. And I've spoken out on several other issues too. That's discrimination due to union activity. Isn't it?"

Apparently I was holding my breath throughout this speech; I let it out now and feel so dizzy that I grab the table. What the hell did I just say anyway?

Lance Martin wiggles his nose. He sniffs. He lights up another Pall Mall. Then he leans back and closes his eyes. Is he taking a nap? Is he meditating?

He opens his eyes. "That just might work," he says, nodding. I have no idea what it is that might work. "Who are these other people?" he asks.

"What other people?"

"The ones who falsified their applications and weren't fired."

A twinge in my gut. "Why do you need that information?"

"Now really, Miss Apple, it's obvious. How can we prove discrimination if we don't know who these other people are?"

"Will they get into trouble?"

"They can't. They've been here over a year." He smiles reassuringly. "Don't worry. They're untouchable."

I consider. Lance Martin's job is to gather information like a lawyer. And the binding union-management contract obligates him to protect union members. Even if it were legal, he wouldn't be likely to use information against other union members; that could backfire and cost him his job. And he's right that the company can't touch those others anymore; their year's probation is up. It seems perfectly logical, but....

If only I could think straighter today. Such a headache! I can't wait to get home, take a hot bath, and lie down. Lance, his pencil poised, awaits my response.

I give him the names.

Lance dutifully writes them down. "That's about it," he says, closing his notebook. I stand up. "Oh, wait, there's one more thing." I sit back down. "We got a report about you." He pauses.

My muscles clench. "Report?"

"That you accepted favors from a foreman."

"What foreman?"

"Guy on nightshift, name of Danny Sugar. Black guy. Ring a bell?"

"I know him."

"Did he by any chance rearrange your schedule for you?"

The walls are closing in on me. "He does it for everyone," I say.

"So he did?" Lance asks. "Do it for you?"

My voice is very low. "Yes."

"And it occurred while you were a steward, supposedly setting an example for other workers?"

I don't respond. The muscles in my upper back desperately need a massage.

Lance Martin stands. "I think I have everything," he says. His handshake is no longer as firm.

"It didn't seem as if I was doing anything wrong," I say feebly.

"Um-hmm," Lance Martin mumbles noncommittally. He accompanies me to the reception area and holds open the glass door. "Don't worry, we'll do what we can," he says. "I'll get back to you."

A few days after I file the grievance, I return home about 10 p.m. from a meeting. The apartment is dark; Miguel must be out late again! Before I can even turn on the lights, the phone starts ringing. I pick up the receiver, hoping it's Miguel.

A woman's angry voice says, "There you are. Finally."

"Who's this?"

"I've been trying to reach you all fucking day!"

"Who *is* this?"

"Sharon Rademaker."

I sink down into a kitchen chair. Sharon is the Trotskyist who was laid off from the evening shift, Felicia's shift, after working there for almost three years. Whenever Felicia's and Sharon's paths crossed on their shift, they treated each other with cold politeness. Sharon's collective and our collective are as opposite as a New Jersey summer and winter. Yes, both groups organize the proletariat, and both groups consider themselves revolutionaries. But our collective follows Marxism-Leninism-Mao Tse-tung Thought while Sharon's organization adheres to the teachings of Leon Trotsky and dismisses communist China as a "deformed workers' state." It's one of those grave differences between radical organizations.

"At least we're on the same side," I'd once made the mistake of saying to Bonnie.

"Oh, no! The Trots are the enemy," Bonnie replied adamantly. "Their way will betray the revolution. It's a question of life and death. The very fact that Trotsky was assassinated in Mexico for his beliefs illustrates that such political differences are not trivial." And to be sure, as I was drawn deeper into the political orbit of the Anna Louise Strong League, I wondered how I could have ever considered Trotskyism and Maoism compatible.

Sharon Rademaker continues. "The company just called me in from layoff. They threatened to discipline me for falsifying my application. Said they'd gotten the information from *you!*"

With the suddenness of a hailstorm, I know that nothing will ever again be quite the same. I grip the receiver until my forearm aches. "I didn't…I thought they couldn't touch you," I say. "I thought—"

"You *didn't* think, that's the problem."

"I'm sorry," I whisper. "I was trying to prove discrimination."

"This is the kind of shit the FBI would do!"

"I thought you were past the danger period." My voice is becoming raspy. At the sink I run a glass of water, take a sip.

"I couldn't be fired, but I could be *disciplined!*" Sharon retorts. "You *idiot!*" I realize with dismay that I hadn't even considered discipline.

"But the union had an obligation not to disclose your name to the company," I say.

"How gullible can you get?" Sharon's voice drips with disgust. "You've been so-called organizing for almost a year and you trust these snakes? They'd like nothing better than to see us communists disappear from the face of the earth."

Of course she's right. How could I have trusted Lance Martin? I've betrayed the very people who are exposing him and his cronies. I've offered up the radicals like a neatly wrapped present, tied with a satin ribbon. Why am I so naïve? If only I'd been able to think straighter that day. If only I hadn't been consumed with nausea.

"I'm sorry, Sharon, I'm so sorry."

"It's too late for sorry."

"Is there anything I can do?" I beg. Anything to lessen the pain I feel. A sharp click and a dial tone are my response.

Dazed, I allow the receiver to find its way onto the cradle. Immediately, the phone rings again. I let it ring five times; I think I know who it is.

"I got called into labor relations today," the voice says. Roger's voice, our comrade on day shift, sounding annoyed. But not furious—a sign of hope?

I profusely apologize. "How does it look for you and the others, Roger? Will the company dock your pay or suspend you or anything?"

"I'm hoping we'll be OK. They gave me a warning and put it on my record. But I think that's all they're going to do."

The company probably fears a reaction from the workers if anything happens to Roger and the others. Some of them, including Roger, have built quite a base on their shifts.

My stomach muscles relax a little. Then he adds, "I already let Cindy know. She's calling a special meeting to discuss it."

My stomach muscles re-clench.

By the time Miguel arrives home at midnight, I've already consumed a Hershey's bar, half a bag of Frito-Lay's, and a pint of

185

Butter Brickle ice cream. I look up bleary-eyed and demand no information about where he's been.

"Wussup?"

I tell him.

"You did *what?*" He looms over me.

I drop my head.

"I need a beer," he says, switching to Spanish. He pops the cap on a bottle of Presidente, lights up a Marlboro, and sits down in a chair across from me. "Did I hear you right? How could you? *¡Carajo!* That's something the *Policía Nacional* would do!"

I say nothing.

"*¡Estás loca!* You know what this means?"

"I didn't do it on purpose, Miguel."

"That's no excuse."

"I'm not saying it's an excuse. But the union took advantage of the situation."

"*¡No joda!*" Miguel says. "You were stupid. You fell into their trap. How could you have trusted them?" I put my head in my hands. Miguel slaps his forehead. "It makes no sense. Why would someone as experienced as you do something like that?"

When I say nothing, he stomps across the kitchen and leaves the apartment. The door bangs behind him.

Three days later Felicia and I arrive at the extraordinary meeting at Cindy's. Since the night I received Sharon's and Roger's phone calls, sleep has hovered just out of my reach, Miguel hasn't returned home, and now there's this damned meeting. The stress is creating nausea again; stepping across the threshold into Cindy and Matt's apartment requires all my fortitude. I give Felicia a sideways hug of gratitude as we enter the study.

Charlie sends me a thumbs-up. I return it with a half-smile. Miguel is in the rocking chair avoiding my eyes. No one is missing. The comrades are drinking coffee, looking as if it were just another meeting, but they keep throwing glances my way. Bonnie engages me in small talk: have I gotten that radiator on my Rambler fixed yet? How do I like my new job so far? Where did I get those sandals?

Sergio offers me a donut; his unaccustomed solicitude embarrasses me. Roger nods noncommittally. Kate's eyes are shielded behind her shades. Esme and Cindy chat. Matt, Cindy's husband, leans against a wall, arms folded, staring at the floor and tapping his foot.

Cindy calls the meeting to order. Talk ceases as if words have been sliced in half with a sharp knife. Everyone already knows why we're here but Cindy summarizes it anyway. Then she says, "Jenny, would you like to go first?"

She means, *would you like to say anything before we sentence you?* Only her robe and gavel are missing. My eyes trace the geometrical patterns in the rug. I've rehearsed my words for the past three days so they slide off my lips and probably sound insincere: *I've been naïve, thoughtless, irresponsible, people were harmed, I'm deeply sorry.* I add, "I don't deserve to remain in the collective."

What I don't say is that the threat of being expelled doesn't have the sting that it would have had a year ago. In fact, in a small way I wish they *would* expel me. It would free me from the agonizing decision as to whether to remain in the collective.

Cindy's eyes narrow. "Expulsion seems a bit premature, doesn't it? We haven't even discussed your case yet." Then as if remembering that she was the one who invited me to speak, she softens her tone. "But thank you, Jenny, for your opinion. What do others have to say?"

Felicia speaks up. "It's mainly the union's fault. They should never have betrayed her confidence."

Charlie adds quickly, "Yeah, it's a bummer of a mistake but it's human. Anyone could have done it."

Cindy can't seem to resist rebutting that. "We're not speaking about anyone, Charlie. We're talking about Jenny. Let's not speculate about what others would have done." I notice the tension lines in her forehead that give her that harsh, don't-mess-with-me look. No one seems to have the courage to respond except Matt. At times he seems intimidated by Cindy, but not now.

"We can't blame this on the union," he says. "The inescapable truth is that Jenny ratted people out."

"How could you have done such a thing, Jenny?" Cindy asks. "I still don't get it."

All eyes turn toward me. "I…I got confused. *Discrimination, discrimination* kept going through my head. And when Lance asked me how we could prove discrimination, I just drew a blank. He kept pressuring me. He wanted evidence, evidence, *evidence.* So I tried to come up with something concrete. I didn't think anyone would be at risk."

"Her idea of discrimination is so convoluted," Matt says, "I doubt if Karl Marx himself could understand it."

"I know this is no excuse," I say, "but you all told me to use discrimination as my defense. Now it seems as if it wasn't such a good idea after all."

As soon as I say it, I regret it. Matt bristles and turns to the rest of them as if speaking to a jury, as if I'm not even in the room. "I can't believe this. Is she trying to tell us it's *our* fault?"

I hang my head. "But Lance said no one could get into trouble. He said the others were perfectly safe; the company couldn't touch them is what I think he said."

"And you trusted him?" Kate asks incredulously.

"I haven't been feeling myself lately. I've had the flu or something. I certainly didn't intend–"

"Don't let her muddy it with 'But I didn't intend,'" Matt interrupts. "Let's stick to the facts, and in this case, the facts are clear."

"But intentions count," Charlie protests. "The worst that can be said is that she's naïve. OK, I'll give you *irresponsible*, maybe. But she certainly didn't do it on purpose."

Would you all stop talking about me as if I'm not here?

"'Ratting people out,'" Esme says, "seems a little harsh, doesn't it, Matt?"

Matt glares at her. Cindy says quickly, "OK, OK. Let's hear from other people."

Bonnie raises her hand. She looks to Roger as she speaks, and he keeps nodding. "This is what the union should have said to the company: 'Look, Jenny Apple has a great record. So what if she neglected to mention her college education. It's not as though she's hiding a felony. If it doesn't affect her job, then why are you firing her?'"

Roger says, "Then they should have said, 'It looks suspiciously as if you're singling her out because of her activism here at the plant. Is there any other explanation for you to fire her?'"

Bonnie turns to me. Her eyes are sad, and she speaks as if instructing me. Yet somehow the way she speaks doesn't sound condescending; she's like a kind mother and I'm like a little girl who loves and trusts her mommy. "Jenny," she says, "I think you're confused. When Lance Martin asked you for names, that was totally unnecessary to your defense. And unfortunately you fell for it."

The enormity of what I've done finally sinks in. I realize how confused I was. Just by virtue of my being an activist, Lance could have made a strong case that I was discriminated against, especially since I had a spotless work record. But he never *intended* to do that. Why should he? I never hid my objective of getting rid of the current band of union sell-outs—the very ones Lance is employed by.

Yet I let myself be tricked by his insistence that I had no chance unless I ratted people out. For that *is* what it is: I'm a rat-fink. I have no one but myself to blame for my naïveté, for my recklessness, that put others at risk.

Sergio speaks up. "We have to consider all of Jenny's good work in the past. Her dedication to the struggle." Tears spring to my eyes.

Kate raises her index finger and says, "But we need to avoid sentimentality." My eyes dry up. "This kind of naiveté could mean life or death in a revolutionary situation."

Felicia rolls her eyes. "But we're not in a revolutionary situation, Kate."

Charlie jumps in. "That's right." (At least not for five years, right, Charlie?)

Kate glowers.

Roger says, "Let's not blow this out of proportion. Remember, all that happened to me is that the company read me the riot act. That's it! I didn't get fired—or even disciplined."

"Not yet you didn't," Kate says.

"Well, if Roger's not that upset," Felicia says, as if the matter were settled, "then why are we making a molehill out of a mountain?"

"A mountain out of a molehill," I correct, out of habit.

"A mountain out of a molehill," Felicia repeats.

Matt snorts. Cindy puts her hand on his thigh just above his knee, digs her long fingernails into his flesh, and gives him *The Look*. She turns her gaze to Miguel.

"Would *you* like to weigh in on this?" Uh-oh. But as much as I dread it, I'm curious to hear his response.

Kate removes her dark glasses. "It's obvious which side *he'll* take." Her eyes lacerate Miguel.

Esme looks at Kate. "We're all on the *same* side, Kate. We want what's best for the collective and for the struggle."

Cindy says, "Calm down. Everyone's voice is important here. He has a right to speak if he wants to."

Miguel hesitates. "No comment." He looks at me as if to say, *See? I didn't betray you. Even though you deserve it.* Roger cocks an eyebrow and looks from Miguel to me.

There's a silence. Bonnie breaks it by saying, "Although we all—Jenny included, obviously—recognize the seriousness of this error, it's clear there are mitigating circumstances." She turns to me. "Perhaps we could put you on probation for a while, Jenny."

Roger agrees. "Yeah, we should do that and move on."

"Well, there seems to be unity about the serious nature of the offense," Cindy says, "but I'm hearing most folks say that we should take into account Jenny's history in this organization. Is there anyone who disagrees?" She squeezes Matt's knee again, not a tender, I-love-you-honey squeeze. No one speaks. "Bonnie has suggested probation as a solution. How about six months? Does anyone take exception?" Again, silence. "Jenny?"

I nod, grateful for the support of over half the members. Only Miguel, Kate, Matt, and Cindy have not spoken out on my behalf. But still, my relief is tempered with something that feels like a wisp of disappointment.

I spend the following days turning over my crime. What does it tell me about myself? Can I make amends? Can I change? Allowing me to stay and try to redeem myself was generous of the collective. They cautioned me not to be so gullible, so impulsive, so careless about my impact on others, to consult before acting. Although I still have ongoing doubts about the collective's political line, I decide to put my concerns on hold and to focus on these valuable lessons.

Miguel apologizes. "It could happen to anyone," he mumbles, without meeting my eyes. Even though I know that's not true, and I think he knows it too, I appreciate his begrudging support. We maintain a precarious truce.

Miguel is now staying out at least one night a week. I try to conceal my crankiness and resentment. I suffer from frequent headaches and nausea. Fortunately, my waitressing job dulls my pain for a few hours each day.

I continue to leaflet weekly with Charlie, but we don't discuss what happened at the union hall or at the collective meeting. It's too raw, and he seems to respect my silence about it. Ever more items seem to be taboo between us. We limit our conversation to current events and light-hearted banter. I miss our former closeness.

8. Jenny

OCTOBER 1975

ONE MORNING I AWAKEN FROM A DEEP SLEEP, feeling nauseated again. The luminescent hands of the bedside clock indicate 5 a.m. I stumble into the bathroom and vomit into the toilet bowl.

As I crawl back into bed, Miguel is just waking. I tell him what happened. He says, "I take you to the emergency?"

"Are you sick too?"

"No."

"Then it can't be food poisoning."

"Maybe is the flu."

"I guess."

"I make for you a cup of tea."

I hear him fill the teakettle. He reappears and brings me another pillow, wipes my face with a warm washcloth. "How you feel now?" he asks.

"Better," I yawn. "As if I could sleep forever." I drink the cup of Lipton tea, sink back into the pillows, and drift off. I feel his hand on my shoulder.

"You want that I stay home from work today?"

"No, honey, you go ahead. I'll be all right."

I barely register the brush of his kiss on my cheek and the faint click of the door as he leaves for work.

Two hours later I wake up and, to my surprise, feel fine. Sunshine streams into the apartment. For breakfast I make poached eggs and cinnamon toast. How strange, I think, as I dress for work.

But the following day after Miguel leaves, I'm too dizzy to climb out of bed. I fall back asleep, crawl out of bed about eight, vomit into the metal waste basket, then sleep until nine-thirty. I hurry to make breakfast and get ready for work.

On Saturday, Miguel and I are on the turnpike, driving in silence after a spat—not too uncommon these days—to a rally against layoffs, which is to occur in the parking lot of the GM plant. Finally I say grimly, in English,

"My period is over two weeks late."

"Huh?"

"My period. It's late."

"Is not that normal sometimes?"

"I'm never late."

"Are you sure you no get the date wrong?"

"I think I'm pregnant," I say.

"What?" I could toss pennies into his mouth.

A pickup truck swerves into our lane directly in front of us.

"Watch out!" I shout. Miguel slams his foot on the brake pedal and my hands bang into the dashboard.

"Are you OK?" he asks.

"Yeah." My breathing slowly returns to normal. I should never have told him while he's driving.

He's frowning and concentrating on the road. "*No es posible,*" he says.

"It's not possible?"

I prefer not to talk about this in Spanish, but he continues in Spanish anyway. "How can you be pregnant?" he asks. "You always insist I use a condom." His resentful tone surprises me. I say,

"Remember that night when I went to bed early and you didn't? You came to bed after watching some movie on TV?"

An orange Hornet pulls up beside us in the left lane. Miguel steps on the gas. In the side-view mirror I watch the Hornet recede.

"And you were drunk and woke me out of a sound sleep?" I remind him. He gives me a blank look. "Well, we didn't use a rubber that night."

"Yes, we did. We always do."

"No, Miguel, we didn't. I remember it well. I was a little worried but then I forgot about it."

"But still, it doesn't seem possible."

I close my eyes. "Why doesn't it seem possible?"

"Well, I mean, it was only one time. And you never got pregnant before, you told me. And you don't have that much experience with sex."

"Maybe you need a lesson in the birds and the bees," I mutter, glaring out the window. The driver in the van next to me throws up his hand and mouths, *What?*

"The birds and the who?" Miguel exits the turnpike.

I resign myself to speaking Spanish. "Apparently you have a problem grasping how babies are made."

"What are you insinuating?"

"The things you said are ridiculous. They have nothing to do with getting pregnant."

"They sure help," Miguel says, thrusting out his lower lip, roaring into the parking lot and jamming on the brakes.

I yank open the door and hurtle myself out of the car. "Oh, for Pete's sake," I say, and put as much distance between us as possible. I yell back, "I'll get a ride home with Felicia."

He catches up to me and snatches my arm. "But Yenny, wait. What you gonna do?"

"I'm going to join the rally and try to forget this conversation ever happened."

"No, I mean about this…this thing."

I shake off his hand. "This *pregnancy*, you mean? I'm getting a test." I scurry toward Felicia and a group of people up ahead with signs and leaflets and colorful t-shirts.

A few days later Miguel and I are listening to Bob Marley in the living room after dinner. I'm about to leave for an emergency meeting to deal with a wildcat strike in one of our plants. Miguel is drinking a Presidente. We're in a tranquil mood and haven't spoken about my possible pregnancy since the demonstration last Saturday. Now I say,

"The test came back positive."

"What test?"

"The pregnancy test."

Disbelief spreads across his face. "Do those tests make mistakes?"

"Sometimes," I say. "But not this time."

"How come?"

I tick the reasons off with my fingers. "Number 1: I haven't gotten my period. Number 2: I have morning sickness. And Number 3: the test was positive. Is that enough?" I head for the bathroom.

He follows and leans against the door jamb. I run a toothbrush across my teeth.

"I just can't believe it," he says.

"Wu ettr," I say, my mouth full of toothpaste.

"Huh?"

I rinse my mouth out. "You'd better believe it." He looks dazed. I take his hand and say, "Oh, Miguel, face the facts. Now we need to discuss what to do." I skim a brush through my hair. As I leave the apartment I say, "We'll talk later."

Shivering, I start the Rambler and pull away from the curb. It wasn't just his responsibility to remember to use a condom. But still, that doesn't excuse him. Why, I was half asleep when he initiated the sex that night; this is his doing, all right.

I drive up Jersey Avenue and turn onto Newark Avenue.

But there's a much bigger question that I need to deal with, so I mustn't get distracted by whose fault it is: how do I feel about the pregnancy?

Now that I'm pregnant, no one can tell me I'm not fit to be a mother, as the adoption agency had suggested back then. And if I don't want the baby, I can get an abortion. Just the knowledge of that right feels reassuring. I raise an imaginary glass to the long, hard years of struggle by the feminist movement as well as by all those weary, ordinary women who brought about the victory scarcely two years ago of Roe v. Wade.

Miguel will have a say either way, of course, but it's *my body*. The final decision is mine and mine alone. I shiver. The responsibility is staggering.

By mid-October my morning sickness has somewhat subsided. The doctor has put me on vitamins and ordered me to stop drinking. For some reason the pregnancy makes me feel dependent upon Miguel and even more disturbed by his evening jaunts.

Stripping off my jeans and t-shirt, I look at my naked body in the bathroom mirror, running my hands across my flat stomach. No sign at all of the life within. It's too soon, the doctor has said, but the fetus—no, he called it an *embryo*—is fine.

I didn't mean to ask him about abortion. The question just popped out without warning. He said I had a couple of months yet to decide whether to "terminate the pregnancy." *Terminate!* That word again. I've been terminated from my job, and now I'm to terminate my baby? Of course not!

Miguel keeps up his intermittent vanishing acts, returning home late on some nights if at all. Not once has he suggested I accompany him. But then, I've never asked, have I?

The next night I force nonchalance into my voice. "How about if I string along with you?" *String along?* I revise it. "I mean, I'll come with you. It'll be fun."

He casts me the same look of shocked disbelief as when I told him I was pregnant. "Uh, I don't...that would...it's not gonna work tonight. I told Rique I'd help him with a problem."

Another *problem*. "What kind of problem?"

"Plumbing. A plumbing problem. His kitchen sink. His kitchen sink is all backed up. It'll probably take us all evening."

I don't trust my ability to conceal my disbelief so I withdraw into the bathroom. Soon I hear him yell, "See you later." He sounds so cheerful.

I sit down on the toilet. How different I am now from a year ago. Living with a man, yes, but a man who's probably *getting some on the side, in the middle, and on top.* His every trip to the Bronx inflates my inferiority complex.

My problems with Miguel, combined with my political doubts, stand in the way of my recent resolve to reform. And no matter how hard I try to avoid them, doubts still plague me. I question policies that I've held gospel for years. *Gospel.* A strange word. My political beliefs aren't a religious doctrine, are they? *Doctrine. Doctrinaire.* I play with the words. The collective's views aren't doctrinaire, I remind myself, they're *correct.* There's a difference, you know. Correctness to some people might sound rigid or sectarian, but when the stakes are so high, when suffering is so great, and when you know how to fix it....then so what if others don't understand. This is not a popularity contest.

From the medicine chest I remove a razor blade. What would it feel like to slit one's wrist, I wonder. For the first time I understand why someone might be driven to do that. I sigh. Not me, though. I insert the blade into a razor, draw warm water, and put one leg onto the edge of the bathtub. I soap my legs and run the razor up and around my calf and shin.

The glow of the early days with Miguel has extinguished itself like the embers of an abandoned campfire. For some time now I've regarded him through a filter of caution and mistrust. Yet I hate clingy women; two mature people should be able to allow each other some leg room. But how much? And whose legs?

I still don't confront him. The shadow of a doubt remains; I don't want to accuse him unjustly. Is it obvious to everyone but me?

As I shower and wash my hair, I recall last night in bed. As soon as we slid between the sheets, he turned away from me. I rubbed his back, then curled my arm around his body and pressed up against him. "I'm so tired," he mumbled as he pulled away from me a little. Doesn't he enjoy snuggling anymore? I released him and lay on my back. I realized I couldn't remember the last time we had sex. I'd have to look at the kitchen calendar: I mark the nights we do it with tiny red hearts.

After my shower I look at the calendar. It's been three weeks! He used to want sex nightly; then once or twice a week. I've heard that sexual desire is strongest when romance is fresh, but should it drop so precipitously?

And the embracing and closeness seems to have hit the skids as well. I miss the warmth and security of his arms around me, the drowsy pillow talk, the intertwining of our legs. But to be honest, the desire on my part has waned too, perhaps due to the pregnancy but more likely due to my simmering resentment.

I towel-dry my straight hair and scrunch it, hoping to coax it into curls. Do I still love him? And if I don't, then what ties me (although with a very frayed rope) to the relationship? A series of images plays across my mind. Isolation, feeling unloved. Weekends alone, trying to read a cheap novel and distracted by blasts of salsa and laughter coming through the windows from large families with lots of relatives. Eating TV dinners by myself. Lying in bed with no one next to me. Having no special person to confide in, to gossip with, no one who cares just for me, whose mind is filled with *me*, who loves *me* more than anyone else in the world. This was the barrenness of my life pre-Miguel. And will it be like that again, post-Miguel?

Is it like that *now?*

I dump some popcorn into an aluminum kettle and let it pop while I dish up a bowl of chocolate fudge ice cream. I know that Miguel is hopelessly flawed, but I still can't stand the thought of losing him. Perhaps I'm not in love with him, I think, taking a guilty bite of ice cream—the doctor has told me to watch my weight—but I'm definitely in love with being in a relationship. Have I become one of those women I despise? One who will do anything to avoid being alone?

I remove the popcorn from the stove and mix it with butter and salt in a large bowl. Sometimes Miguel treats me with such warmth and love (even though not quite as intense as before) that I'm lulled into believing everything's fine. His absences decrease and I think, what if I completely misinterpreted him? What if my suspicions are due to my own insecurities? I don't want to botch what I have unless there's a damn good reason. But then doubts consume me again.

About five o'clock on Friday night I get a phone call. His voice is sprightly. "Hi."

My voice is as bleak as an overcast sky and as blunt as a dull jack hammer. "Where are you?"

"At a pay phone. In the Bronx."

I'm silent; I've heard this before.

"I'll be here for the night with Rique. His girlfriend dumped him. He's pretty down about it." Poor Rique. So many "problems."

"What's the number?" Now *he's* the one who's silent. I add, "In case something comes up. I *am* pregnant, you know."

"His phone's disconnected. He didn't pay the bill. I'm down at the pay phone on the corner. But I'll call you again later to see if you're all right."

I hang up, immediately pick up the receiver again, and dial Julio's wife Hermalinda.

"Hola, guapa," she says.

"Hermalinda, can you give me Enrique's number, please?" She does. I call and it rings twice.

"*Dímelo,*" Enrique's deep voice responds.

"Hey, Rique," I say casually. "It's Jenny."

"*Qué honda, bella?*" Enrique says, pleasure in his voice. What's happening, beautiful? He sounds not at all depressed about a girl-friend leaving him or about anything else.

"Miguel said he might stop by your place after work. Is he there, by any chance?"

"No, *bella,* I ain't seen him."

"If he calls, would you have him call me?"

199

"Everything OK?"

"Yeah. Just wanted to ask him something."

"Claro, Yenny, cómo no." No problem.

After a few exchanges of small talk, I hang up. My cheeks burn and my heart pounds. That was so easy that I'm almost embarrassed for Miguel; he hasn't even dignified me with a solid alibi, not even asked Enrique to cover for him. Does he think I'm too trusting to check out his story, too naive to figure things out?

Well, he's right, isn't he? It's taken me a long time. And even now, I catch myself wondering if maybe he's just visiting some *other* cousin somewhere.

I make a grilled cheese sandwich and salad for supper but eat only a corner of the sandwich and a few bites of salad. The stale bread sticks in my throat, the lettuce is wilted. I toss it all into the trash.

My mind churns. Miguel has made me believe that I'm lovable—for that I'm truly grateful. But all these weeks of lies, disrespect, abandonment—especially while I'm pregnant—all that has crumbled my newly won self-confidence.

I turn on the TV. Walter Cronkite is saying, "And that's the way it is. Thursday, October 16, 1975." I turn it off; focusing on the news is impossible. I pace up and down the small living room, looking out the window, hoping Miguel will appear. But the only men I see are *other* men coming home to *other* women. Back in the kitchen, I notice a moldy orange on the counter. I drop it into the trash, where it joins the cheese sandwich and wilted lettuce. The contents of the trash look the way I feel. I collapse onto the sofa. I'm pathetic, can't keep a man. Sounds like a bad country-western song. I'm going to march downstairs and spill everything to Felicia.

The phone rings. I hate myself for hoping it's Miguel. *How un-feminist of me.* I let it ring three and a half times so he won't have the satisfaction of knowing I'm sitting by the phone.

"Hello?" I say.

"Carlos?"

I close my eyes. "Sorry, wrong number."

I dial Felicia to see if she's home, and listen to the phone ring and ring. Where is that woman?

It's too early to go to bed, yet that's all I want to do. Seek comfort under the comforter. I decide to bake some brownies instead. I get out a pan, a Betty Crocker brownie mix, butter, eggs, and milk. I mix it all together and bake it at 350 degrees. I listen to Beethoven's Fifth while I wash the baking utensils and the bowl. The rich aroma of brownies gradually permeates the apartment.

9. Miguel

OCTOBER 1975

ON A RAINY AFTERNOON SO OVERCAST it feels like night, me and Nico nurse our second Cuba Libre out of green plastic glasses at Nico's apartment in the Bronx. It feels like back home—salsa on the stereo and all.

Nico is short and lean, muscular from his job in the auto shop. Laugh lines frame his mouth, and his eyes are gentle, serious. His skin is lighter than mine, like baked beans. He's wearing ragged cutoffs and sneakers with no laces.

His wife and son, Elena and Nicolito, are in Chicago, where Elena's sister has one in the oven. When Nico invited me for a visit, he said this would be a good time for us to hook up again—*de hombre a hombre*, he said. Nico and I were best friends in high school and *compadres* in arms during the revolution in Santo Domingo, but we haven't seen much of each other since we came to the U.S. and he married Elena and moved up to the Bronx.

I sink deep into the spongy orange sofa between two over-stuffed pillows. It occurs to me to wonder (due to the fact that by now I'm a little stinko) how I'll ever fight my way back up to the surface when I need to take a piss. Nico drops into a beanbag chair. Posters of Che and Juan Bosch are taped to the peeling paint on the wall. Nico kicks off his sneakers, shoves aside some votive candles on the coffee table, and stretches out his legs. The candles are probably Elena's doing, as is the large print in a gilt frame of Jesus standing on a cobblestone road with flowers strewn at his feet and little children clinging to his robe. Me and Nico have been atheists since high school. We used to discuss the existence of God and came to the conclusion that Marx was right: religion *is* "the opiate of the masses."

I skim the wooden bookcase with the Bible, a book of hymns, and a biography of St. Francis of Assisi next to Nico's books—*Das Kapital*, the biography of Che, several novels by Juan Bosch, and a Chilton repair manual. Through the door into the bedroom, baby clothes hang on lines strung across the room, over a bed with a pink spread. A crib stands next to the bed. Packages of Pampers are stacked on the bureau.

Nico hands me a bamboo-framed photo. "This is Elena and little Nico at Jones Beach," he says. The out-of-focus snapshot shows a smiling woman with a green tank top holding a toddler, who's straining against her arms at a 45-degree angle. The ocean is in the background.

"*Chévere*," I say. Great. "You're lucky, *muchacho*."

I pull a snapshot from my wallet. "Here's Yenny and me on 42nd Street." In the picture my arm is around her waist and we're laughing. We're all bundled up, and the ties of her scarf are blowing in the wind.

"How *is* Yenny?" Nico asks.

"*Tá bién.*" She's fine. I take a drink of my Cuba Libre and offer a Marlboro to Nico. I grimace. "Well, to tell the truth, things are kind of fucked-up right now."

Nico scrunches his forehead. "What do you mean?"

"She's bitchy, pissed off. Sometimes I don't even want to come home from work."

"Hmmm."

"At first things were great, but…."

"But?"

"I'm not sure what happened. I think she suspects I'm running around on her."

Nico looks serious. He takes a swig and belches. "I've sure been tempted myself. *Gracias a Dios* I never did it."

"You never did? *¿De veras?*" Really?

"Maybe it's because of *Papá*; he's not a *mujeriego.*" A woman-izer. "At least, I'm pretty sure he's not."

"¡Bomba!" Wow!

"Both my parents are *socialistas.*"

"Ah, that doesn't mean much," I say. "I know plenty of *social-istas* who get a little on the side, *hombre.*"

"That's true. But he's no *palomo* (he doesn't fuck around). *Quién sabe por qué?* Who knows why? I'm proud of them both, *muchacho.* My dad told me about one time he suspected my mom was carrying on with her boss, *un lindo* (a good-looking guy) who used to give her rides home from work in his Cadillac so she didn't have to take the *guagua* (bus). But when my dad confronted her, she told him, 'Why would I settle for plantains when at home I can enjoy the whole *sancocho* (stew)?' My dad said it was moments like that that made him '*borracho de amor*' (drunk with love) for Mamá."

I'm silent, thinking about my own parents, wishing they were more like Nico's. "I tried to cut all that out when I met Yenny," I say. "It worked for a while."

"And then?"

"*Es complicado.* I tell myself that this is the last time I'll go after another woman. But then I do it again, and each time I say, 'This is the last time. Just this one more time.'"

"Sounds like you're addicted, *hombre.*"

"Then too, I miss Latina women sometimes. Not that Yenny's Spanish isn't good; it's excellent. But it's *college* Spanish. She doesn't get my jokes and my offhand remarks unless I explain them." I take a sip of my drink. "When I talk with Sandra, it's so easy."

"Sandra?"

"The girl I'm seeing. And she's flirtatious too."

"Yenny's not?"

"Not really." I scratch my crotch. "It's not that we don't have fun. We can spend all day in the city just hanging out. And she likes my friends too. That's *bien chévere.* But she's so serious about things. Don't get me wrong, I like that about her. But sometimes I just have to get away for a while, to be with someone…well, sillier, crazier, wilder."

Nico motions to me, palm down, fingers wagging, to follow him into the kitchen. "I'm going to mix up another batch of Cuba Libres," he says.

I struggle up and out of the sofa. In the kitchen I lean against a cabinet. Remnants of torn plastic still cover some of the dining chairs. "And also—"

"There's more?" Nico interrupts, smiling. "*¡Basta!, hombre, ¡basta!*" He holds up his arm as if warding off a blow.

I look at the fogged up window and trace "Yenny + Miguel" on the glass with my index finger. Nico pours a generous amount of rum into the scratched green plastic pitcher and fills the rest of the pitcher with Coca-Cola.

"Go on," Nico says. "I'm just messing with you."

I rub out the words on the window with the butt of my hand. "She sees me as some kind of fucking hero," I say.

Nico slices a lime and squeezes both halves into the pitcher. He looks sideways at me. "Did you say *hero*? How dare she call you that?" He laughs. "Don't let her get away with it." He drops ice cubes into our glasses and hands me my drink.

I follow him back into the living room. "I admit it was flattering at first, but later it felt like a cat crouching on my shoulders and digging its claws into me, impossible to shake off. I have to be a goddamned saint, watch everything I say, be on guard not to disillusion her."

"¡Caramba!"

"If I tell her the truth about how scared I was back then, or how doubtful I am about a revolution—anywhere in the world—"

"Hang on a minute," Nico says. "I gotta take a whiz." Through the open door he calls, "So what would happen if you told her these things?"

I can hear him pissing. I raise my voice. "I'm afraid, *hombre*."

"Of what?"

"That she might stop loving me."

Nico comes back into the living room, zipping up his pants. He looks skeptical. "You really think so?"

"You don't know Yenny." I roll my eyes and take another drink. "I'm so fucked. She's got me terrified of losing her!"

"In that case, aren't you worried about screwing around with this Sandra chick?"

I sigh and adjust a pillow behind my back. "I know it's risky. I did cut Sandra loose once. But she was so hurt that I felt like a *pendejo* (jerk). I don't want to do that to her again." I hoist myself up and walk unsteadily into the bathroom.

Nico calls after me. "Do you love Yenny?"

"I thought I did, but now I don't know any more," I call back. "Let's just say I'm hooked. And the hook cuts deep into the flesh." I return and drain my glass. Nico pours me another. I'm starting to feel loose all over. "*Coño, hombre*, how much rum did you put in here? I'm getting hammered!"

Nico snaps his fingers. "Wait. I'll get us a snack. That'll help."

When he sets a plate of Saltines and Velveeta cheese onto the coffee table, I ask him, "How about you?"

"Me and Elena?" Nico grins and his eyes turn dreamy. "*Hombre*, she's so *guapa*," he says. Pretty. His words are slightly slurred and I strain to understand him. "And the sex! Oooooo. She'll do it anywhere, any time." He hiccups and pours another glass for himself, leaving me to imagine them making love on the back seat of Nico's Chevy, on the sofa (which might be impossible, it's so soft), or at a drive-in movie theater. He pulls a chair from the dining table and sits backwards on it. I'm on the floor now, leaning against the sofa.

I sigh. "Yenny is shy about sex." My body lists to the right, and I put out my hand to balance myself. "When we first met, she was terrified of sex. She had a hell of a good reason, though. Now she can really get into it. I've seen her have ten orgasms in a row!"

"¡*Coño!*" Nico says.

"Yeah, I'm not kidding," I say, enjoying Nico's response.

We've almost finished the second pitcher, and we each take another leak.

Nico says, "I love it when Elena wears a tight red dress and matching heels and pins her hair on top of her head."

I say, "I love Yenny's body, especially her *nalgas* (butt). You should see her do the *merengue!* She doesn't seem too happy about her body, but *hombre,* she turns me on."

Nico says, "I talk to Elena about anything, even though she's *Católica.* And it's *increíble* how she finishes my sentences for me."

I say, "Yenny listens so well when I tell her something that I can almost see through her eyes into her mind."

Nico says, "I love the way Elena rubs my back when I come home sore all over. And she bakes *pasteles* (cakes) just the way I like them—with brandy and raisins."

I add, "Yenny and me, we share the same politics too. She's a *socialista*—although this collective she got me to join is a little *loco.*"

"Loco?"

"They think the revolution's going to happen *mañana,* and they think they're the only ones capable of leading it." I grab a pillow from the sofa, put it under my butt.

"Sounds like some of the crazy groups back home," Nico says.

"Yeah," I say. "Sort of. Anyway, I like how excited she gets about the revolution." I stop. "But maybe she's been less excited lately. I hope my pessimism isn't rubbing off on her."

"I'd like to meet her," Nico says. He reaches down and slaps me on the thigh. "You're such a stranger these days, *hombre.* Now that Elena and I are back from Santo Domingo, you'll have to come for dinner, both of you—to see the *nene* (baby)." His eyes get teary. "Elena's a great mom. You should have seen her when she was pregnant, *hombre*; she was radiant!"

He raises his glass. A little of his drink slops onto the floor. "Here's a toast to the *mujeres* in our lives," he says. "To Elena and Yenny."

Rain is coming down hard now. It bounces like drum beats off the tin patch on the roof across the alley. Nico closes the window; I spread some Velveeta on a cracker.

He raises his plastic glass. "And speaking of toasts, here's one to Castro! *¡Qué hombre!* What a man! The revolution's lasted almost two decades, *compai* (friend)! Who would have thought it—what with the Bay of Pigs, the Missile Crisis, the embargo—"

"It won't last much longer, you'll see," I cut in. "No chance. That tiny little country against the U.S.? *¡Carajo!*" Hell!

"Don't be so sure," Nico says. "History's full of twists and turns. *Es la dialéctica.*" It's dialectics.

"But look what happened to *us*," I say bitterly. "And then there's Haiti, Iran, Cambodia, Guatemala, Panama, Indonesia, Chile—"

"*¡Basta, basta!* That's what makes Cuba so exciting, *hombre!*" Nico interrupts. "If it can hold out against U.S. imperialism, it'll encourage poor countries everywhere to kick ass. And look at Vietnam!"

There's silence except for the clinking of ice cubes and the muffled beating of the rain against the window. "By the way," Nico says. "My sister asked about you."

"Serena! How is she?"

"*Tá muy bién.* She married an intern who works at Hospital Morgan. You remember when she volunteered there during the invasion? They didn't marry until five years after that. You were the one she was hot for at the time, remember?"

"She was the first girl I really liked."

"She has three kids and one in the oven."

"*¡Bomba!*" I remember Los Muchachos lying in a row on mattresses on the floor of Nico's living room, and Serena lying beside me. All night I lay awake listening to her soft breathing, waiting for the invasion of the *Loyalistas* over the Duarte Bridge.

I bite my lip. "Do you ever think much about what happened back then, Nico?" I ask, holding my breath, hoping I'm not too fucked up.

"Not much. Why? Do you?"

"Lately I've been having nightmares again."

"What kind of nightmares?"

"Certain things. Those children shot by the tanks that came over the Ozama bridge into your neighborhood, that soldier in the tank looking out at me through the gunner's slit, his eyes filled with terror at what he was about to do. And the conditions at the hospital where Serena volunteered.

"And then there's the anger," I continue. "At LBJ. At having to come to the U.S. Sometimes the fury rises up in me. Then I can't sleep. But even that's better than what happens when I *do* sleep. The worst nightmare of all is when I see that cop strung up and all those glassy-eyed people surrounding him, chanting "Kill, kill, kill.""

"*Carajo,* muchacho."

"You never get nightmares?" I ask.

"Not really. I keep busy. I try not to dwell on those things."

"I wake up sweating and can't get my bearings. I look over and see Yenny; I put my arm around her and go back to sleep."

"*¡Bomba!*"

"I didn't talk about the rebellion with anyone for years, and the nightmares almost faded away. When I first met Yenny, she pushed me—*hard*—to tell her about it. So against my will I did. As I talked, something weird happened. I felt a burden lifting; I felt lighter. So I kept on talking—even though I was terrified. When I saw how turned on Yenny was, I thought I could milk it. I soon realized *that* wasn't going to happen anytime soon, but meanwhile it was too late to turn back. I'd unlocked the cage and set the demons loose."

Nico shakes his head. "*Oye, hombre,* try not to think so much about those things. That's the past. *Olvídalo, compai.* (Forget about it, friend.) The demons will gradually crawl back into their cage again." Nico puts another LP on. *Merengue.* Johnny Ventura. "*Oye,* Miguel, how is Felicia doing?"

I roll my eyes. "Still a *cotorra.*" Chatterbox.

"Something happened between you two, didn't it?"

"Yeah." I put two cigarettes in my mouth, light them, and hand one to Nico. "She ratted me out to Marco. Told him I put the moves on her."

"That happened back when she was still with him?"

"Yeah, but I don't see why he got so pissed off. He's an anarchist, isn't he? Believes in free love and all that. Or so he says."

"People don't always put their money where their dick is," Nico says. "Where women are concerned, men come unhinged."

"Anyway, I've never trusted her since," I say. "She didn't have to tell him. She knew it would fuck up our friendship. And it has. When I see him now, he acts polite, but that's it. *Nada más.*" Nothing else.

I can't sit still. I stand, swaying, and steady myself by putting my hand on the poster of Che Guevara. "And another thing that pisses me off. There's this guy who hangs around Yenny. Well, actually, they hang around each other. They go leafleting together every week. It's fucked up, the way they look at each other. She swears he's just a friend, but she always seems so cheerful after seeing him. Her eyes shine. The way she used to be with *me.*"

"Maybe she enjoys being with a *gringo* sometimes just like you want to be with a Latina."

"Well, I guess—"

Nico adds quickly, "I don't mean she's fooling around."

"No. But I have a feeling something's going on."

"Has she said anything?"

"When I ask her, she says they're just friends. She keeps repeating that. 'We're just friends, we're just friends.'" I pick up a framed picture of Nico's mom and dad and study it. "She says it so often I get suspicious. Now she never mentions him, but I can tell. It drives me *loco*."

"How about a *sancocho* down at the corner, *hombre?*" Nico asks. "Get our minds off these women and sober us up."

"Yeah, I am kind of hungry," I say. "Sorry, *compai*. Guess I'm just in a foul mood." I glance out the window. "You got an umbrella?"

10. Jenny

OCTOBER 1975

I STRETCH OUT ON FELICIA'S SOFA; Perdido positions himself across my stomach. Can he sense the life just a few inches beneath him? Felicia presses an ice-cold papaya milkshake into my hands.

"I'm pregnant," I say.

"*Ay, bien chévere!*" Felicia squeals, throwing her arms around me. Cool! I smile wanly. Felicia holds me by the shoulders with outstretched arms. "What's the matter?"

"I guess it's cool."

"You *guess?*" Felicia looks puzzled. Then she gets a knowing look. "It's Miguel, isn't it? He doesn't want the baby."

I try to sound calm. "Well, he's taking the news kind of hard."

"I figured. He probably doesn't want the responsibility, especially now that Angélica's pregnant."

"No, I mean, he's acting *wacko.*"

"He'll have to support two kids now," Felicia says.

"Felicia, stop! Just listen. He says he doesn't believe I'm pregnant."

Felicia chokes on her smoothie. "You're kidding."

"He says it's a phantom pregnancy."

"A what pregnancy?"

"Like a ghost pregnancy. When your belly swells because you imagine you're pregnant. It's your body playing a trick on you. It's not real." I hold the cold drink against my forehead. "Miguel said that the wife of this guy at work had a phantom pregnancy. I didn't even know such a thing existed."

Felicia jams her straw into her milkshake. "*Ese cabrón!*" she says. "Those ghost things *don't* exist. That's ridiculous."

"He'll come around after a while, I guess."

Felicia rolls her eyes and snaps, "Why do you always make excuses for him?"

Is her irritation directed at Miguel or at me? Stunned by the bite in her tone, I shoot back, "Why do you always attack him?"

Felicia opens her mouth, then closes it. She bites her lip.

I twist my straw into a figure eight. "Sorry." I evade her eyes, then sneak a glance at her. Her arms are crossed and her shoulders are hunched.

"There's more," I say in a small voice.

"*Ay yai yai.*" She slaps her forehead.

"He's spending a lot of time in New York."

"What do you mean, a lot?" She leans in close, her eyes wide.

"Once a week, usually."

"*Coño!* Does he stay overnight?"

"Well, he says he'll be just a few hours, but he usually ends up staying away all night."

"What's he supposed to be doing?"

"He's says he's visiting Enrique or one of his abundant cousins."

Felicia snorts. "*¡Que tontería!*" What nonsense!

"He says it's too late to come home or he's too drunk or...." My words swell in my throat.

Felicia paces, fire in her eyes. "You're pregnant and you let him treat you like this? You can't put that up, *muchacha.*"

I sigh. "I don't 'let him treat me like this,' Felicia. He's free to do what he wants."

"Then you're free to kick him out!" she says. "Why don't you stand him up?" she persists, close to yelling now.

"Stand *up* to him," I correct.

"*Eso es.*" That's right.

But I can't do that, at least not yet.

"I want to be fair to him, Felicia. I want to be sure."

"Ay, Yenny, that's your problem. You're too gullible. You let people walk on you."

My face heats up. "Sometimes maybe I do, Felicia, but still, *you're* the one who told me he was changing since he met me. *If anyone will change him, you will.* That's what you said."

"Yes, I *hoped* he'd change," Felicia says. "But it's obvious to everyone he hasn't." To everyone? "To everyone but you, that is. Haven't you learned anything from your problem with the union? Look what happened to your fellow workers because you trusted Lance Martin."

I bounce up from the couch, dumping Perdido on the floor, where he lands on his feet. "That's a low blow, Felicia!" For a moment I want to hit her. "Is that how you really feel? You spoke differently at the collective meeting." Even though I know she's right, I can't forgive her. How *does* she really feel about me?

"*Disculpa.* I'm sorry," Felicia says. "I just meant, you should be careful. For your own sake, *querida* (sweetheart). I'm worried about you."

"I need a little more time, that's all."

"Yenny, you don't deserve this. You know what it is? You let your inferior complex get the best of you."

"Don't play psychologist with me," I say, glaring at her.

Felicia stands up and strides across the room to the phone in the bookcase. "You need the proof?" She waves the receiver at me. "I give you the proof. This is for your own goodness."

"Felicia! What are you doing?" My breathing quickens.

She dials. "I'm going to ask Hermalinda to find out from Julio what's going on."

"But wait!" Felicia keeps dialing. "Felicia, wait! That won't work. Julio will just cover for him."

"Don't worry. Hermalinda and I, we go way back. She knows how to handle Julio—*Aló*, Hermalinda. *¿Cómo estás?*" I shrink back into the sofa. Something momentous is about to occur, something that can't be reversed, something I know I'm not prepared for. "Um-hmm," Felicia says. "Um-hmm. Sí. *Está bién. Entiendo.*" Felicia is nodding; her face is neutral. Maybe the news isn't so bad. Maybe Hermalinda has provided an explanation. My breathing slows to almost normal.

Felicia hangs up the phone. She looks at me. "Just what I thought," she says with an air of grim satisfaction. "He's been screwing a Puerto Rican waitress named Sandra." The air whooshes out of me. "Rique saw them at the bar," Felicia continues. "They were practically *doing it* right there on the dance floor. Apparently it started when he was living with Angélica."

Living with Angélica? For months he's been playing me for a fool? A series of telltale signs, all of which I ignored or denied or made excuses for, flash across my memory: a long curly hair on his white t-shirt, the scent of magnolia clinging to his denim jacket, his diminishing desire for sex. I stand up, squeeze my eyelids shut, clench my fists at my sides, and growl.

"What are you going to do?" Felicia asks.

I stumble to the door. "I don't know."

"You're not going to let him get away with this, are you?"

I open the door. "I don't know."

"You don't know? Wait!"

"I'll talk to you later."

"But—"

"*Stop bugging me!*" I race up the stairs. The pain in my gut shoots through me. In the bathroom I bend over, vomit into the toilet. I clean myself up and look in the mirror.

My cheeks are gaunt, my eyes rimmed with red, my hair stringy and ill-kempt. For weeks I've been living on canned spaghetti, peanut butter and jelly sandwiches, and Butter Brickle ice cream. Every morning I've been pining away in bed until almost time for work, listening to Haydn's "Farewell" Symphony on the stereo. I've worn the same baggy sweat pants, smelly t-shirt, and frayed terrycloth slippers around the house for days. I've thought

215

of nothing except Miguel—where he is, when he'll return, whether he still loves me.

It's time to put a halt to this. My priorities are warped. I need to take care of myself for the baby's sake, if not for my own.

Pulling Miguel's photo from the bookcase, I pry it out of its little frame and tear it to pieces. I fling the pieces into the toilet, regurgitate on them, and flush it all down. The clean toilet water gives me a momentary feeling of relief, as if I've cleansed myself.

In the kitchen, I fill a tall glass with water and add ice cubes. He's double-crossed me, but the strange thing is that I'm pretty sure he loves me. Why do I think that and what difference does it make, I ask myself. All that counts is his behavior.

I sip some ice water and watch the cubes dance, like my life, without direction. I have a hunch that Miguel will resist breaking up. After all, he's got a good thing going here. With the exception of the first month, he's paid less than his share of the rent. Now and then he contributes some groceries—a pizza, a dozen eggs, a package of Fig Newtons. Not nearly as much as he consumes. Of course, he's the one who buys—and drinks—the bottomless six-packs of Presidente. Oh, and sometimes he lays some knickknack before me like a cat offering up a dead mouse. In exchange, I contribute most of the rent, the home-cooked meals (when I'm not too depressed), and yes, the sex on (diminished) demand.

How will he respond if I kick him out? I undress for bed, my mind racing. My cousin Duncan, after he raped me, turned livid with rage, squeezing my arm, thrusting his fist into my tear-stained face, squashing my nose. I'll never forget the pain of those fingers digging into my skinny arm, leaving red welts, stark keepsakes of the horror that he'd wreaked upon me.

There's something worrisome about Miguel, something opaque. Will he turn on me as Duncan did? I pull freshly laundered flannel pajamas from a dresser drawer. Shivering, I turn up the dial on the gas wall heater.

I recall the time Miguel challenged another activist at the plant to a fight when the man "insulted" the Anna Louise Strong League. Who knows where it might have led if I hadn't stepped in? And of course, in Santo Domingo he shot at people. Who knows, maybe he even killed someone. Before, I admired that, but now it has me worried. Has such violence brutalized him, like a murderer who becomes inured to killing? I once read an interview with a serial killer: *The first one was the hardest,* he said. Of course, Miguel's not a murderer, but still…he may have *killed.*

I eat a bowl of Frosted Flakes, then brush my teeth and gargle with hydrogen peroxide. Felicia has accused me of gullibility. I'm glad she can't know that even after the revelation of scarcely an hour ago in her apartment, I'm still plagued with uncertainty. Not about whether Miguel is guilty. No, that's impossible to deny anymore—even for me. What I'm still hesitating about is whether to confront him.

Yet what are my options? All these weeks of pleading with him—*please stay home tonight, please call me if you'll be delayed*—fruitless! It's crazy to keep hoping he'll change for me. Or for the baby.

I know I'll have trouble sleeping so I try to wear myself out by doing pushups. Before Miguel and I lived together, he impressed me with his talk about the importance of monogamy in building trust, about his respect for women. One time he said, a sad look in his eyes, "My poor mother, she's a saint."

But now I think, Like father, like son.

Do Dominican men—even political ones—just find it de rigueur to default on their marriage vows? Rage burns its way through my body. I do five more pushups. He's betrayed me at my most vulnerable, while I'm pregnant. A condition he still denies.

I sit on the floor, my body spent, breathing hard. Terrible uncertainties force their way into my thoughts. What will happen after the baby is born? Will Miguel and I share custody? Will I have to make joint decisions with him about how to raise it: whether to let it cry or to pick it up, which daycare center to put it in, spanking vs. scolding. Will the baby become an alcoholic like its father? (For I've come to the conclusion that Miguel *is* an alcoholic.)

I shut out these thoughts. I won't let what happens between me and Miguel dissuade me from having this baby; I *am* going to have it, no matter what. But now that the evidence against him is undeniable, I have to confront him. I'll be brave; I'll tell him to leave.

And I'll become another of the thousands of Angélicas out there. Single. Alone. With child.

11. Jenny

OCTOBER 1975

I'VE CHOSEN A LOCALE THAT PROVIDES both the anonymity and the sanctuary of a public place. Last night he went missing again—this time to his "cousin Adán's." When he returned home at nine this morning, I suggested breakfast at McDonald's.

He orders eggs and sausage with a side of pancakes, topped with butter and a sugary syrup misnamed *maple*. Hot chocolate to wash it all down. I order an English muffin and coffee. We sit on plastic benches at a small orange table. The buzz of parents and children out for Sunday breakfast provides a welcome drone that camouflages our conversation.

Miguel is keyed-up, talkative. "Why are Americans so racist?" he asks, after commenting on the violence that has followed court-ordered busing in Boston. And what's my opinion about Leonard Matlovich, the Air Force sergeant who's challenging the ban on homosexuals in the military? The collective will probably side with the military on that one. Hah! Isn't that ironic. Patty Hearst arrested? Don't worry, her filthy-rich parents will pull the strings to get her acquitted.

I resist the impulse to engage with any of these confrontational opinions of his, even though one of the things we've enjoyed the most during our brief months together is arguing over current events, even shouting at each other, and then sometimes making love afterward.

I pick at my muffin and nod, biding my time until he finishes eating. Finally he lights up the inevitable Marlboro.

I speak in Spanish. "I'm not happy, Miguel," I say. He looks startled.

"Are we talking about Patty Hearst?"

"I don't like to be left alone on weekends. I don't like having no idea where you are. I've had it up to here." I draw a finger across my neck.

He doesn't respond; he's heard this before. How ineffectual to say the same thing over and over, and do nothing about it. *Nagging,* that's what he called it when Angélica did it. Did she *nag* for the same reason that I do? Well, never again will I nag him nor have to hear his tired alibis. This time is different.

"I want out," I say.

The flicker of surprise on his face quickly turns. He narrows his eyes and tightens his jaw. Anger? Awareness that a critical line has been crossed?

"Why are you saying this?" he asks, glaring. The baby at the table behind him throws a plastic spoon into the air. I watch it arc and land on the orange and white linoleum tiles.

"It's not working out."

"Yes, it is," he says.

"Maybe for you."

The piped-in Puerto Rican love song sounds tinny through the speakers. Miguel looks at his hot chocolate, then at me. "But I love you," he says plaintively. He reaches across the table and traces a heart on the back of my hand.

I let my hand lie there—like road kill. "You have a strange way of showing it," I say.

A wounded look crosses his face. He lets go of my hand. The baby squeals; a young boy and girl chase each other down the aisles and around the tables. In the midst of all that chaos, it seems miraculous that people find the resilience to gaze into each other's eyes and smile.

"You win," he says, bitterly. "I won't go see my cousins anymore. Are you satisfied now?" Then he adds, "You're not so perfect either, you know."

I regard his brown eyes and thick eyelashes, his oak brown skin. I want to interlace my cold fingers with his warm ones; I know they'll be warm, they always are. My voice is jagged.

"You've been cheating, Miguel."

"What?!" He slams down his cup, and the remains of his now cold chocolate drink slosh onto the table and into his lap. "*Carajo!*" he says, springing to his feet and pressing napkins to his damp jeans.

I wait patiently. After he sits back down, I say, "I know about it."

His eyes smolder. He thrusts his syrupy Styrofoam plate to the side and leans forward, putting his elbows on the table. "What the fuck are you talking about?"

"I know about Sandra."

He flinches. "Who told you that?"

I jut out my chin. "What does it matter?" I hardly get the words out before tears well up. I reach for some napkins, struggle to pull them from the container; they flake off in pieces but I manage to wipe my eyes. "You betrayed me, Miguel. Why? Wasn't I good enough for you? Didn't you love me?"

He shifts in his seat. "No, no, I did...I do...."

I continue, the hurt turning now to anger. "You violated my trust."

"I bet it was Felicia who told you about Sandra. That nosy bitch. She poisons everything."

I close my eyes and shake my head. "It's not important how I found out, Miguel. Don't you think I'm capable of finding out on my own?" A tear rolls down my cheek. "I care about you, Miguel, and I believe you care about me. But I can't go on like this. It's ripping me apart." I dab at the tear with a shred of napkin. Then I say, "It's over, Miguel. I want you to move out. *Today.*"

He hesitates, then sighs as if accepting the inevitable. "Are you sure?"

"I'm sorry," I say gently.

We trudge home in silence. He hangs back, following a few steps behind me. I was prepared to bolster my argument with a list of other grievances, including his denial of my pregnancy and his failure to pay his full share of expenses. But it wasn't necessary.

He showed no remorse. I'm glad. If he had, I might have relented. I hope not, but I might have.

I sit on the splintery stoop while Miguel clears his stuff out of my apartment. The day seems to mock my dismal mood: the morning is balmy, the sun warms my toes in my thongs. The leaves are turning, and a faint smell of smoke tickles my nostrils. Preschoolers play in the park across the street. Dogs on leashes deposit their marks on the trees. Chinese opera wafts from an upstairs window. But my life has just turned a giant corner, with nothing promising in the blocks ahead.

I offer to help him, but he says, "*No es necessario*; I don't need help from you." I feel rebuffed.

Three trips up and down stairs is all it takes. Did he realize from the start that he wouldn't be putting down roots?

Papa was a rolling stone.

It seems so final, his work boots clunking as he brushes past me, going up and down stairs, carrying in one arm a few books on Marxism, his suitcase in the other hand, a pants leg hanging out of it and dragging through the pigeon droppings. His denim jacket is slung over his shoulder. When he emerges with his chess set, I feel a sharp jab of pain. He flings his possessions into the trunk of the Valiant, which is already crowded with a spare tire, a jack, stacks of old leaflets, the *Communist Manifesto* in Spanish, empty potato chip bags, a box of chocolate chip cookies, and of course, guarding the contents like sentries: the inevitable six-packs of Presidente.

Will he be living out of his car? No, his "cousins" will take him in.

He casts a dour look in my direction. "*Pues, ya me voy,*" he says. I'm out of here. When I don't reply, he adds, "I hope you're happy." I force my shoulders into a shrug. He isn't going to see me break down.

I watch him start the motor of the Valiant, then turn it off. He gets out and strides back to me, his body taut as a guitar string. Did he forget something? I hope the engine hasn't stalled. Does he have to take a leak? Is he going to make a last-ditch effort to change my mind? He stops at the stairs, looking up at me. I'm still sitting on the stoop.

"I meant to tell you," he says. His face is harsh. "You should get an abortion. *If* this baby really exists." He stalks away, then shouts over his shoulder, "Think about it."

As he pulls out of the parking space, his tires screech. I watch the car weave down the block and still see it long after it's no longer there. My fingers push deep into the flesh of my belly. Summer is over, and I fear the coming winter will be long and chill.

Over the following weeks, the pain of being without Miguel is intense, and at unexpected moments I recall with a sharp sense of loss the fun we used to have, the intimacies we shared—playing chess, dancing the merengue, exchanging backrubs, propping ourselves up in bed to take turns reading aloud, he in Spanish and I in English, from Norberto James, a Dominican poet. The way he looked at me that made me feel so special.

Being with Miguel taught me how to fall in love, how to navigate a relationship, how to enjoy sex. Although I still resent him and know that I had no choice but to break up with him, I never find myself regretting our intimacy, only its absence.

I tell Charlie about my breakup with Miguel. He listens sympathetically but then the conversation flags. What is there to say? It happened, it's over. I have to go through this myself; recovering from a breakup is a lonely affair.

Although I keep busy with leafleting, demonstrations, and meetings, I spend private moments assessing my past political work and questioning my future. What are my goals? Do I want to return to factory work, to stay in New Jersey, to move to

Manhattan, to go into teaching? Do I want to keep working with the Anna Louise Strong League? If I left the collective, what would replace it? I know I want to remain an activist but what area of activism? I know I'm still a socialist, but what kind? I would have enjoyed discussing these things with Charlie. But I doubt that he'd approve of my train of thought. Others might judge me harshly too. It's better to remain silent.

Nevertheless, in spite of missing Miguel, I feel a trace of eagerness—like a seedling poking up through the dirt—to create a future that I, rather than the collective, will shape.

12. Jenny

NOVEMBER 1975

ONE DAY AT WORK, I CLIP AN ORDER to the spindle and tell Stefan: "Dressing on the side." A long strand of hair escapes from Stefan's hairnet as he flaps his tongue at me in reply. The cooks' snickers follow me as I leave the kitchen. *Fuck* them!

Later when I turn in an order for French fries, Stefan says, "You wanna come home with me?" Despite his thick Slavic accent I understand the words; I've heard them before. I ignore him. When I check if the fries are ready, Stefan leers and says, "I got what you lookin' for right here, baby." He points toward his crotch.

I reach for the fries but Stefan's skinny arm grips the other side of the plate. "You ficken me?" he says. Startled, I release my hold on the plate. French fries land on the counter and the floor. "*Sheet sheet sheet,*" Stefan says, glaring at me.

My face burns. I pick up the fries from the counter, slap them back on the plate, and hand the plate to Stefan.

He pushes it back towards me. "What you *do?*" His face is flushed and blotchy. "You want to waste? You want the boss to pay?"

I carry the plate out of the kitchen and dump the fries into the trash.

"The deep fat fryer's out of order," I tell my customer, a beefy driver with ruddy skin. "Can I get you something else?" His eyes flit to the chubby woman eating French fries at the next table. I never see that guy again.

When I tell Babs that the cooks are giving me a hard time, she says, "Aw, shucks, honey, don't pay them no never mind. Just tell them you don't do it with little boys."

Well, maybe that sounds tough and convincing when Babs says it, but I'm younger than she is, younger than the cooks themselves, and I'm not at all comfortable alluding to copulation in their presence. I wonder why the cooks treat me with more antagonism than they do the other waitresses. Is it my age? Or do they take my disgust for arrogance? I laugh. If they only knew how much I respect the working class and what kind of jobs I've held for the past four years.

Maybe it's one of the few pleasures they have in their bleak lives—getting a rise out of the waitresses. They probably paid a big fee to come to this country, left their families behind, only to end up in this greasy spoon.

Putting myself into their shoes calms me. But showing sympathy would only infuriate them. And I'm still disgusted at their crudeness. What can I do but bite my tongue and refuse to let them draw a reaction from me?

The following day as I clip a ticket for a grilled cheese sandwich to the spindle, Milos clutches my arm. I stand motionless, waiting for him to release me. His rings cut into my flesh; his hand is like a vice. I wipe my face clean of emotion and study the pinup calendar on the wall. Milos mumbles something in his language and pulls me closer until my body is pressed up against the counter. I silently rehearse the lyrics to Linda Ronstadt's "You're No Good."

Finally Milos drops my arm, a guttural protest deep in his throat. I turn and calmly make my way back out to the customers, resisting the impulse to look back: would I turn into a pillar of salt?

From that point on the cooks ignore me, but they take their acrimonious time preparing my orders. My tips decline. A few days later when the rush hour is almost over and only a few customers linger over coffee at my station, Babs gestures with a thumb toward the cash register. "The boss wants you."

Jimmy's clipping a fingernail. "Some guys are complaining," he says. "They say you're taking too long to get their orders out."

Snip, snip. He turns up his palms and bends his fingers, scrutinizing the nails.

"As soon as the food's on the counter, I pick it up," I say. "I like to serve it hot."

Jimmy looks at me, eyebrows raised. Let him draw his own conclusions; I've been fired before, and it isn't that bad (I lie). It irks me to admit that it's probably better for *me* to be fired than for Stefan and Milos, who have nothing going for them. Next job, I'll be sure not to let things get so out of hand. My incompetence in handling the cooks may have fueled their aggressive behavior. (On the other hand, maybe they're just assholes; there is such a thing as too much consideration.)

Jimmy sighs, "Well, watch it," and dismisses me with a wave.

The cooks stop delaying my orders. Has Jimmy said something to them? I'm gratified that I didn't succumb to the urge to complain about them; I've ratted out enough people. I hope I've learned *that* lesson. Maybe I'm becoming less impulsive.

13. Jenny

DECEMBER 1975

THE NEXT TIME I SEE MIGUEL is two months after our break-up—at the collective's Christmas party. Felicia's working so I take the train alone to the Park Slope neighborhood of Brooklyn. The party is held at a brownstone near Prospect Park, owned by affluent supporters of the collective. As I open the door into the hallway, the sound of "Norwegian Wood" escapes into the chill night air. People are chatting and munching Camembert on gourmet crackers, standing in small clusters around the dining room table, which is covered with festive desserts and adorned with twinkling lights. The chandelier over the table and the lights from the Christmas tree provide the only illumination for the shadowy figures dancing in the adjacent room.

Cindy catches sight of me and raises plucked eyebrows in greeting—or is it disapproval? I wave but don't approach, instead escaping toward the beverages in the far corner. As my eyes adjust to the dim lighting, I spot Charlie in a loveseat on the far end of the living room, his eyes fixed on a blond woman sitting next to him. I maneuver myself behind a chunky man with a Santa hat, and peek around him for a view of Charlie and the woman. Plucking some ice cubes from a bowl with tongs, I put them in a glass and add a double shot of vodka with a little orange juice. I take a sip and then remember that I'm pregnant so I water the potted rubber tree in the corner and refill my glass with soda water and orange juice. Closing my eyes, I pretend that it's vodka.

Leaving the beverage table, I join a group of folks over by the aquarium, which provides shelter for various kinds of tropical fish. Oh, to have nothing to worry about but food! The group greets me and returns to their conversation. Wavy reflections from the aquarium drift across their faces and hair, tinting them green. The group is excited about a new television show called "Saturday Night Live."

As I feign interest in the conversation, I scan the room. There's Miguel in a clench with a woman who must be Sandra—unless Miguel's cheating on *her* too. I avert my eyes, but curiosity overcomes my humiliation. Her skirt over her fishnet tights barely covers her tush. Unlike me, she's amply endowed, as her clinging angora sweater confirms. Locks of curls escape onto her cheeks from the mass of hair provocatively clipped atop her head. Is that the kind of girl that attracts Miguel? I could never compete with *that*. I admonish myself: did I attend all those women's consciousness-raising groups only to be jealous of this woman? I thought I'd learned indifference toward *male-defined* standards of beauty. What disturbs me more than her looks is that he's with someone—*anyone*—and I'm not. It's only slight solace that I'm the one who broke it off with *him*.

After the dance ends, Miguel extracts himself from Sandra and sets out across the room in my direction. I glance around and watch with growing alarm as he draws closer. I want to flee yet feel pinned to the spot. My comrades' gazes flit from Miguel to me. Miguel ignores them all. He touches my arm and I feel the hairs stand on end; I hope no one notices.

"We need to talk," he says insistently, in Spanish. I excuse myself from the group and follow him, even though I want to say: *Who do you think you are?*

He leads me through a long hallway to a glass-enclosed rear porch. Spotlights illuminate the terrace and foliage outside. He closes the door behind us and motions to one of the wicker chairs. We sit down. I watch him warily.

"How you doing?" His eyes drop to my stomach.

My pregnancy is the last thing I wish to discuss with him. "Fine."

"How's your new job?"

"OK."

"Uh-huh." He looks down at his lap and says nothing. I wait. He clears his throat. "Yenny, I want to ask you something." He shifts uneasily. "Don't get mad, OK?"

"What is it?" I can feel my heart banging.

"After the baby is born…." He hesitates and looks away.

"After the baby is born?"

The words burst from his lips. "After the baby is born, I want you to give it to me." I tell myself I haven't heard him correctly and ask him to repeat it. His words tumble out, hitting me like blows to the stomach. "You don't really want this baby. Admit it. Give it to me. I'll take good care of it."

It's like a nightmare that makes no sense. "But I thought…I thought you wanted me to abort the baby."

He waves his hand dismissively. "I was angry, that's all. Of course I didn't mean that."

My mouth is dry. It's imperative to hide the alarm that's choking me. "You already have a baby with Angélica," I say. "Let's see, it must have been born by now." He frowns and says nothing. I press him. "When was it born?"

"Any day now, I think," he says curtly.

Any day now? He told me the due date was October—two months ago.

The door opens and the woman he was dancing with appears, a Daiquiri in her hand. "Sandra," he says, looking startled.

"Here you are," Sandra says. Her earrings cast round shadows on her cheeks. She flips a lock of curls back from her face. Then she notices me. "Oh." Her eyes narrow. She comes forward, looks down at Miguel, and tugs at his sleeve like a petulant toddler. In English she says, "Miguel, I wanna dance."

He speaks sharply, sloughing off her hand. "OK, *OK.*" Then his voice softens and he squeezes her shoulder. "*Ya voy, querida.*"

I'll be right there. As she leaves the room, Sandra casts a suspicious glance back at me.

Miguel returns to the topic. "You can always have another baby," he says.

Am I just a goddamn baby vending machine? My mind sharpens as if a cold wind has swept through it and whisked away everything but the instinct to survive. I warn myself: show no fear! An eerie calm descends over me, and a voice in my head tells me exactly what to do.

Disabuse him of any misconceptions: "I do want this baby," I say firmly. "If I didn't want it, I'd have an abortion."

Disarm him: "But I told you that I'm willing to share it with you. I want you to be part of its life, no strings attached, if you want to."

Papa was a rolling stone—and a cheating son of a bitch too.

No response from Miguel. I *don't* want him involved in raising my baby but I'm scared of what he might do if I shut him out. "Hey," I say with enthusiasm, "why don't you come to Lamaze classes with me?"

"*What* classes?"

"The classes that couples attend where the man learns how to coach the woman through the childbirth process."

Light suddenly drains from his eyes. He responds in English. "Let me think over it," he says. He gets up so swiftly that he almost knocks over his wicker chair. "I call you." He disappears.

Whatever frightened him, I'm glad. What next, I wonder. I look down at my stomach and rub it in slow circles. Will this baby ever come to fruition? The solitude of the porch feels comforting but after a few minutes I return, dazed, to the party. Miguel and Sandra are again pressed together in a body lock on the dance floor. I need to find Charlie.

"Hey, Jenny!" calls a woman from the Brooklyn collective. With relief I approach her and the man she's with. We chat for a while, although my contribution consists mainly of *uh huh*'s. After a suitable length of time, I excuse myself. Just then a hand slides across the back of my waist.

Charlie laughs and pulls me into a warm hug; he's a refuge in a sea of sharks. But then he draws forth a woman—the one he was sitting with earlier. "I want you to meet someone," he says eagerly. "This is Samantha; you can call her Sam." He looks at Sam adoringly. She's willowy, with long, silky blond hair. She takes my hand. "You're Charlie's leafleting friend," she says. "He's told me all about you."

Charlie puts his arm around Samantha and says, "And I told Jenny all about *you*." But of course he hasn't.

I'm startled at the stabbing pains just above my eyebrows. Before I leave the party, I've got to check the medicine cabinet for some aspirin. I find myself resenting Samantha, but her warm smile soon disarms me.

Charlie guides me onto the dance floor. It's a slow dance—Johnny Mathis: "I'm Stone in Love with You." He pulls me close. I glance at Samantha but she's animated, engrossed in talk with a group of auto workers; I envy the open, trusting relationship she has with Charlie, who is swaying gently to the music with me. I start crying.

"What is it?" Charlie asks, his voice husky and full of concern.

Miguel and Sandra are on the other side of the room. I speak softly into Charlie's ear.

"I'm pregnant," I tell him.

There's a pause and then he says, "Are congratulations in order then?"

"Yeah…. It'll be hard going it alone, though."

He pulls away a little and looks me in the face, concerned. "I'm here for you, babe," he says.

"I'm scared," I say, sniffing.

He pulls me to him again and says in my ear, "You'll get through it just fine."

I guess he means the childbirth. If only that were all there was to be scared of. I tell him what transpired on the back porch. He squeezes me tighter and tells me he'll accompany me home.

"No, you stay with Samantha. I'll be fine. I'm just going to slip away. Thank you for listening, Charlie. I knew I could tell you. I feel better already."

The subway station is two blocks away. A draft of cold air assails me as I descend into the station. It occurs to me that I forgot to raid the medicine cabinet for aspirin. The kiosks are closed, their metal roller-doors rendering them anonymous and identical, and the station smells of urine. I sit on a bench and wait for the train to Manhattan.

The clammy terror that seized me when Miguel demanded I give up the baby returns. Is he trying to get revenge? It isn't the baby, I'm sure; he's never shown any interest in babies. If he had to care for a baby, he'd whisk it off to his mom's in Santo Domingo quicker than he could say *ga ga goo goo*. His mother, the "saint," would add it to her collection of Miguel's bastard siblings.

A man sits on a bench playing the saxophone: "What a Beautiful World." I scoop a few quarters from my backpack and drop them into the basket at his feet. The concrete is speckled with petrified gum. The man says thank you and looks right past me; I realize he's blind. The silky notes echo down the length of the station and into the shadows. This song would usually enchant me but not tonight.

If Miguel sends the baby to Santo Domingo, I'll never get it back. It would be me, a foreign woman, against a male citizen who knows the ins and outs, and whose father has clout. The full import of Miguel's words finally takes effect: he wants to *kidnap* my baby! I tremble. *Never* will I leave him alone with the baby, not even for a second.

As I wait for the train, the image of Charlie with his arm draped across Samantha's shoulders keeps intruding into my thoughts like a misplaced slide. But why?

The train roars into the station, tossing my hair with a gust of hot wind. I enter and sit in a corner. The only other person in the car is a hippy, stretched out on the bench, head on his bedroll, snoring.

The C-train arrives, clattering into the 14th Street station. I exit and proceed down a couple of long passageways to the PATH. The train's waiting and I get on. A couple of teenage boys sit at the other end of the car, their laughter coming in abrasive honks. A middle-aged couple sits across from me, not touching each other, staring fixedly at the ads on the walls. I furtively observe them; would that be Miguel and me in 20 years?

Miguel must have engaged in sex with Angélica as late as last March. But he and I started dating in February! He must have been screwing her at the same time that he was pressuring me to have sex.

Yes, it's true that I didn't *put out*. But I was dating him, for God's sake! Didn't he have a responsibility not to sleep with another woman? Is his sex drive so intense he couldn't wait even a month or two? (Well, maybe three or four, but still....)

The next day I'm home eating a bologna sandwich for lunch when I get a call. "I'm sorry about what I said about the baby."

"Miguel?" A bite of half-chewed bread lurks in my cheek.

"I was out of line to talk to you the way I did at the party."

I force down the bite of sandwich and follow it with a swift gulp of milk.

"I can't believe I said that," he says. "I guess I had too much to drink."

I take a deep breath. "Well, I'm relieved," I say. "I don't want to fight with you over this."

"Of course I'd never want you to give it up. I was just pissed. I should never have said that."

"It's OK," I say, lying. "I understand."

"Really?" He sounds hopeful.

"I've heard worse." What could be worse than threatening to take away someone's baby?

"So you're not angry with me?"

"I *was*. But I'm glad you apologized. That means a lot."

Then he says, "And I'd like to attend that class. The one where you learn about how the birth works."

I shut my eyes.

"Hello?" he says.

"The Lamaze class," I say.

"Eso es." That's it.

Attending Lamaze class will give him a more robust claim on the baby. But the baby is partly his; I can't deny the iron-clad truth of that. As the father, he has rights. And the class will serve as a litmus test. If he takes on some responsibility, then maybe joint custody will work. Wouldn't that be better than going it alone? Do I even want a baby that I have to raise with no support? I rest my hand on my belly, although of course I detect no movement yet, not even the jab of a tiny elbow or knee.

And if he doesn't come through, then I'll feel justified in demanding full custody. "OK," I tell him. "See you at Lamaze."

My life has lost its punch. The Christmas season brings no cheer. Perhaps it's the hormonal havoc of pregnancy. Perhaps it's my cold feet about the specter of raising the baby by myself. But I suspect it has more to do with the loss of intimacy and connection that has followed the breakup.

Do I miss him?

The thought disgusts me. After what he's put me through? After what he said at the party (even though he did apologize)? What's wrong with me?

The next time I leaflet with Charlie, I ask, "How's Samantha?" I'm surprised how the mention of her name unsettles me.

"She's fine," he says. I force a smile. "Well, not really," he adds, handing a leaflet to a stocky man with galoshes. "She's in the middle of finals, her dog got run over, and she's getting obscene phone calls." He laughs. "Other than that, she's OK."

I give what I hope is a sympathetic look but ask for no details. From now on I decide to avoid the subject of Samantha. I recognize what's going on with me; I've experienced it with Miguel as well. *Jealousy.* But why would I feel jealous of Samantha? Am I so lonely that any male friend looks desirable?

I tighten my wool scarf around my neck and reach into my backpack for more leaflets.

"How's it going with Miguel?" Charlie asks.

"He called the next day to apologize."

"That's good."

"Yeah, it was a relief." I hesitate. "But he wants to attend Lamaze classes with me."

"You don't sound too happy about it."

"I'm not sure he'll come through."

"It'll be a good test, though, won't it?"

"That's what I was thinking."

After a moment I say in a burst of warmth, "I'm so thankful for your friendship, Charlie. Whatever happens." Saying something so emotional is uncharacteristic of me; it must be my hormones going crazy.

Charlie's eyes crinkle as he smiles. "Me too, Jenny." He gives me a hug. "We have so much in common, it's too bad...." His voice trails off. I blush: is he thinking about *that night?* What does he mean "it's too bad"? I wish I had the nerve to ask him, but I can't bear the thought of being disappointed.

Disappointed? About what?

One day just before Christmas I try yet another strategy to put Miguel out of my mind: reorganizing the living room. I heave all the furniture to one end of the room, vacuum the walls and ceiling, scrub the floors.

But it doesn't work. After a few minutes the image of Miguel and Sandra, pressed up against each other, comes flooding back, as it has every day since the party. I remember when *I* was the woman locked in his arms. If only he would look at me again with the same pride that he did in the refinery when I led the walkout. I want to struggle shoulder to shoulder with him for socialism. I want to have this baby with him.

I extend the broom behind the sofa and fish out cobwebs, a hairclip, a turquoise earring Miguel gave me for my birthday. It's my loneliness. And being pregnant. It makes for fuzzy thinking. *Desperate* thinking.

Why can't I get him off my mind? I know that intimacy isn't enough; physical attraction, sex—those things only go so far. They aren't worth the sacrifice of my peace of mind and my self-respect. I *know* that!

I focus on the devastation of those weekends when Miguel deserted me for his "friends" and "cousins" in New York City. Yet my life stretches before me like an endless desert. Should I have tried harder to make it work?

I thrust my hands into a bucket of hot sudsy water. A rap at the door startles me. It's probably Felicia. "Coming," I call, and rinse my soapy hands in the sink. I put my eye to the peephole, then step back and suck in my breath.

On the other side of the door, in his denim jacket, stands Miguel. Will my heart never stop turning cartwheels when I see him? I slide back the chain, unlock the deadbolt, open the door.

"Hi," he says.

"Hi." The word comes out as a whisper.

We stand there awkwardly.

"I just came by to see if you want to take a walk or something," he finally says.

"I'm in the middle of a project." His body sags. "But it's nothing," I say quickly. "Just give me a minute. Do you mind sitting in the kitchen?"

"No problem."

I escape into the bathroom, close the door, lean over the toilet, and heave. The porcelain rim of the toilet bowl feels cool and comforting. I curse myself for my nervousness and my exhilaration. I rinse out my mouth, brush my teeth, gargle with mouthwash, and run a comb through my hair. As an afterthought, I apply a touch of violet eye shadow.

In the kitchen, Miguel is reading an article in the *Jersey Journal*. I glance at the headline: "Lynette Fromme gets life sentence for attack on President Ford."

We leave the apartment building and head down the avenue toward the Hudson River. I hunch forward against the wind.

"I broke up with Sandra."

"You did?"

"Yeah. The day after the party. I haven't seen her since then. I wanted to tell you, I've been trying to get the guts."

I say nothing.

He stops and faces me. "I want to be in this baby's life, Yenny." Tears appear in his eyes. He takes my hand. "I want to be in your life too."

His tears bring on mine. We continue on down Grove Street, holding hands and crying. An elderly woman looks at us curiously. Two teenage boys nudge each other and snicker. The wind dries our tears.

"A peso for your thoughts," he says.

We've stopped in front of a café. "I'm thinking I'd like to get out of the cold," I say.

He chooses a booth near the back. After we order he says, "I'm going to change, Yenny. I don't understand why I play around, but I'm going to change."

"I want to believe that, Miguel. I've missed you so much." Have I missed him or have I just been lonely? Is it him or the intimacy I've missed? Are they the same?

He reaches across the table for my hand. "I want to be with you. For life."

I pause. It's one of those pivotal moments. My intellect tells me *no!* But all the loneliness in me cries out *yes!*

"Yes," I say before I can think. My voice seems to have a will of its own. But suddenly I feel so euphoric.

"I'm so happy, Yenny." He's crying again.

"But, Miguel"—I make a final attempt at sanity—"I can't go through this shit again."

"Don't worry, I understand. I don't want to lose you. I'm over all that; I know what I want now. I know what's important, and that's *you*, Yenny."

I love it when he talks like that.

That night he helps me move back the furniture, and we make sweeter, more poignant love than ever before.

Afterward I lie awake while he sleeps, his body snuggled into me. How I've missed nights like this. How I love being part of a couple, no longer alone in the world. Someone to share intimate secrets with. I listen to his deep breathing which will soon turn into soft snores. Will things be better this time? Has he learned his lesson? And I—have I learned mine? I'm throwing myself back into the same situation with no proof that he's changed. Just faith, that's all, like that of the most devout Jehovah's Witness on a street corner pressing the *Watchtower* into my hand. Blind faith.

I press closer against him. The problem is, I love him. I love the color of his skin. I love how he makes love. I love the way he looks at me. I love feeling special and having someone who loves me more than he loves anyone else. I love the political history he embodies. I love that he's a real proletarian as opposed to me and all the other *pretend-proletarians* in the collective. I love that he's from a third-world country.

Love love love. Love is like an iceberg; you can't see the treachery underneath until it's too late.

14. Jenny

DECEMBER 1975

I ARRIVE AT THE CLINIC AND CHOOSE an upholstered chair in the softly illuminated and empty lobby. Miguel has agreed to meet me at seven, half an hour before class starts. By 7:15 the lobby is filling up. By 7:20 he still hasn't arrived. His tardiness does nothing to bolster my confidence.

I've persuaded the Lamaze instructor to let me start classes in my first trimester although she warned me this was "highly irregular." But I'm impatient to find out where Miguel stands. In the two weeks since we've reunited, we've seen each other nearly every evening. Often he stays over, but I haven't invited him to move back in, and he doesn't pressure me, for which I'm thankful. I'm waiting. Waiting for a sign.

I bite my lip. This is supposed to be a positive experience. I direct my thoughts to the pleasure of a few hours earlier. Leafleting with Charlie; coming home under the drifting snowflakes, backlit by moonlight; listening to "Midnight Train to Georgia" on the way to the clinic. I focus on the pregnancy. Since the decline of the morning sickness, I've suffered no further discomfort. Perhaps later I'll be groaning as I puff my way up a flight of stairs, one hand on the small of my back, but for now I'm fine.

Carrying this baby has connected me to life in a way I've never experienced before. This is as close to magic as I'll ever come. Every day I feel as if I'm communing with my child-to-be.

By 7:30 there's still no sign of Miguel. *Damn him.* I mouth the words to myself. Most chairs in the waiting room are occupied by now. I'm the only one whose belly isn't puffed out like an overstuffed cushion. I'm the only one who doesn't have a fawning husband. And, as far as I can judge by the way the others dress and carry themselves, I'm the only one with a working-class job. The men seem to be professionals; they wear sports shirts and slacks. Some wear suits and ties, as if they haven't had time to change out of their work clothes before coming here. The women are probably housewives; they wear maternity tops and wool pants, or maternity dresses with long sweater coats. As for me, I've abandoned my jeans and t-shirt for slacks and a red blouse that I discovered tucked away on a high shelf of my closet. Some couples hold hands across the gap between chairs. No one speaks, but they smile shyly at each other and at me. Everyone here is Caucasian. If I feel different among these people, how will Miguel feel?

A woman appears from inside the community room and holds open the door. The five couples and I file in past her. "Hello. Welcome," she says to each of us. The soft lighting is probably meant to sooth jittery nerves. An easel stands at the front. Colorful posters of women's anatomy line the wall. The prospective parents sit in armchairs and sofas arranged in a semi-circle. My feet sink into the thick carpet as I approach the rear and take a seat in one of two empty chairs.

The instructor sits down near the easel and introduces herself. Rachel. She's probably in her late thirties, with sleek bobbed hair and stylish, large-framed glasses.

"Welcome, everyone. I'm so glad to see you here tonight," Rachel says. "You're about to undertake an incredible journey. It's a special time in your lives." Her eyes glow. "First let's get acquainted." She turns to the petite woman on her left. "Hello. Tell us your name and when your baby's due."

"I'm Molly," the woman says, slightly breathless. Her belly is almost as big as she is. She squeals, "Only eight more weeks!" Her husband bestows a look of adoration on her and squeezes her hand.

"Hi, Molly. Welcome. And tell us what brings you here."

"I read that pain-killers aren't good for the baby," Molly says. "I want to do this right."

Rachel comments on each person's words, affirming them, adding bits of information. The women seem nice enough. They want the same things I do, to give their babies a healthy start in life, to be fully present at the birth, not drugged and groggy.

I consider the husbands. They gaze tenderly at their wives. The couples seem deeply in love, stable, punctual, responsible. I'm the odd one out. I'm the one that has no spouse or companion whom I can rely on. The collective has always touted proletarian marriage values but right now these petit-bourgeois marriages look pretty good. I fear more than ever that I'm fighting a losing battle with Miguel.

But how deceptive appearances are, I remind myself. What seems idyllic about these couples may paper over all kinds of dirty secrets: resentment, infidelity, incompatibility, mental illness, abuse, addiction, and just plain falling out of love. As far as I know, five years from now they may all be divorced.

It's my turn. Rachel asks, "And your partner?" I say that my *husband* is delayed. "Well, let's get started then," says Rachel, betraying no dismay at the delay of my partner. I relax a little. "Tonight we're going to cover women's anatomy and the six preliminary signs of labor. But first, let me ask you a couple of questions. How many of you have held a baby in the last year?" Most hands go up. Mine stays down. Then she asks, "Who's changed a diaper?" Fewer arms rise. I'm eager to see how these questions relate to Lamaze. Rachel picks up a pointer and turns toward a whiteboard.

There's a noise. Rachel stops talking, pointer raised, and everyone looks at the doorway. In the threshold stands Miguel. He's wearing his work clothes—jeans denim jacket, and felt beret. He searches the room. Rachel asks, "Can I help you?" Her expression implies that he's stumbled into the wrong room.

"I…I…," Miguel says, and gestures toward me. Rachel's concern changes to relief. "Ah, you're Jenny's husband. Welcome." I glance at Miguel. How will he react to the word *husband?*

All eyes watch him make his way to the back of the room. And just then something disturbing happens: I see Miguel through *their* eyes—these well-off, white middle-class couples. I become *them*. Miguel is no longer the man I love. I see only a stranger, a dark immigrant with a strong accent. I see a manual laborer who seems not to be in sync with the rest of us. Including me. For a brief moment, I'm ashamed of Miguel and ashamed of myself for being with him.

He sits down stiffly in the chair next to me. I reach over, squeeze his hand, and give him a look of reassurance, while struggling to regain my connection to him. Suddenly a deluge of tenderness flows over me. How much more alienated am I from these couples. Look at how self-absorbed they are, oblivious to suffering in the world. And they probably look down on the working class, probably hate communists.

But I shudder at how easily I identified with them, how easily I sacrificed Miguel to their standards.

After Lamaze class we meet back at my apartment. I offer him a beer. He doesn't reply but sinks into a chair at the kitchen table. "I just don't think I can do this, Yenny." He speaks in Spanish and puts his elbows on the table, resting his forehead in his hands.

I feel a twinge in my belly. "Do what?"

"It's not just the classes," he says.

I stand motionless, a container of orange juice in my hand. His face is a lighter shade of brown than usual. "It's the birth," he says. "The baby coming…coming *out*. I don't think I can handle it."

Another contraction in my stomach, this time accompanied by pain. Carefully I set the orange juice on the counter and sit down.

"Are you all right?" he asks, alarm in his voice.

"It's just a contraction." I sit up and breathe deeply. "Go on."

"It's the blood, the mess. It makes me faint. When my sisters used to get their…their…you know…."

My voice is hard now. "Their periods?"

"Yeah. They used to leave their…their—"

"Sanitary napkins?"

"Yeah. They used to leave them in the wastebasket. When I was little it made me want to puke. I never got over it."

My eyes blur! I want to shake him, to tear at his clothes, to scream: *You phony! You stick your dick in any vagina but you can't stand the idea of what that vagina is for!* A wave of nausea passes through me.

Quickly I stand up. "I'm feeling a little dizzy," I tell Miguel. "And exhausted. It's been a big day. I need some rest." I hurry into the bathroom, lock the door, and turn the tap in the bathtub, waiting for the water to get hot. Miguel raps lightly on the door.

"Go home, Miguel," I yell over the running water.

I take a long, hot bath, soothed by the water sloshing over my body. When I emerge, I wrap myself in a large body towel. He's left a note on the table, written on a sheet of my stationery, scrawled diagonally with a black marker. *"¡Disculpa!,"* it reads. Sorry. I tear up the note and let it drift into the garbage amidst orange peels, egg shells, and an empty jar of Skippy's.

I throw sheets and blankets onto the sofa bed, and cocoon myself in the down quilt. Dreams plague me. Dreams of giving birth all alone on a bunk bed in a large barracks, which echoes with my screams. No one is there for me. No one at all.

The phone awakens me. The alarm clock reads 9 a.m. I reach groggily for the receiver, sweeping books and magazines off the bedside table onto the floor.

"Yenny? It's Hermalinda." Julio's wife. "Just wanted to let you know, *querida*, that Angélica gave birth to a seven-pound girl last night." The room seems to slant; I grasp the edge of the bed. While Angélica was going through labor, Miguel was with me at Lamaze class?

Murmuring thanks, I place the receiver carefully back on the hook and sit motionless. I spread my fingers across my belly. Our children will be half-siblings. Will they ever meet? How will Angélica manage? Her job, whatever it is, probably pays next to

nothing. Will Miguel help support their baby? Will he help support our baby? Can he afford to support two babies?

Are there only two babies?

For the second time I feel sorry for Angélica, and I equally
pity myself. Angélica and me, we have so much in common. Both
screwed—literally and figuratively—by Miguel. Both abandoned
while pregnant. Again the question arises: do I want this baby
enough to raise it on my own? I slam the door on these terrible
and depressing doubts, on this treachery to the little person-to-be
in my womb.

The worst part is having no one to talk to. I can't face the sympathy and judgment in Felicia's eyes. I shrink from the censure of
the collective. I need someone who will listen—just listen.

Suddenly I know just who that someone is. I rummage through
scraps of paper in my desk drawer, pick up the receiver, and dial
what I hope is a current number.

15. Jenny

DECEMBER 1975

IT'S ALREADY DARK ON TREE-LINED WEST 91ˢᵗ Street when I stand on the stoop of Amber's red brick apartment building and ring the bell. A buzzer lets me enter the hallway. Rather than taking the elevator, I hike up the three flights. The climb is a challenge but I need the exercise. As I near the top, I see Amber leaning over the railing.

"It's been *soooo* long," she squeals, her dangly earrings shimmering in the dim light of the stairwell.

We haven't seen each other since we roomed together at Columbia. As I hug her I take in the lavender scent of her thick black hair. Arm in arm we float into the warmth of her apartment. Full-length, unadorned windows display the Manhattan skyline, and large abstract canvasses hang on rust-colored walls. Her apartment looks like an art gallery.

I take a good look at her. She's wearing a leotard and a gauzy skirt. "You're so beautiful!" I say. My eyes drift to the canvasses with their bold slashes of color. "And these—they're yours, aren't they?" From our phone call, I learned that she's part of the Manhattan art scene and has an exhibit in a gallery near her apartment.

"My breakthrough, I hope," she says, crossing her fingers and squeezing her eyes shut.

I admire the energy and color of her canvasses: the thick brushstrokes of magenta, beige, and orange that make me imagine a hurricane, the angular shapes in chalky white and lava black, the aggressive diagonals of egg-yolk yellow crisscrossed by unruly circles of deep burgundy.

"This one was inspired by a dream I had."

"Was it a nightmare?"

She laughs and gives me a squeeze.

While Amber gets the tea, I move around the spacious living room. Albums are stacked next to the stereo: Emmylou Harris, Ella Fitzgerald, the Grateful Dead. Helen Reddy plays softly on the turntable. Orange crates form bookshelves, containing dog-eared copies of *Fear of Flying, Zen and the Art of Motorcycle Maintenance, The Happy Hooker,* and *Sexual Politics.*

I wonder how my own living room would look if I weren't a political activist. On *my* walls are posters of revolutionaries, and in *my* bookcase are books on political theory. To me they're precious, but sometimes I crave a trashy novel.

Amber enters, bearing a tray with coconut macaroons and a pot of oolong tea. She sets the tray amidst incense and candles on a trunk that serves as a coffee table. She motions for me to sit on the sofa, which is draped with a purple tapestry. Amber pours the tea, then hitches up her floor-length skirt and curls into an armchair. As I take a bite of macaroon, Amber reaches across and taps my knee. "Now let's catch up."

It's strange talking to someone who isn't part of any of the movements that have shaped my recent years. At Columbia Amber was on the periphery of the peace movement. She showed up at demonstrations waving colorful, hand-lettered signs painted with flowers and peace symbols. She hung out with what I called the *artsy* crowd; she called me a *peacenik.* Although we were close, I was frustrated at what I labeled her *obsession* with painting and her indifference toward politics. Later, after I joined the collective, I became even less tolerant of anyone who wasn't a political activist so I let our friendship lapse, like an unused library card.

But now I have no stomach for judgment. I need a friend, one who *goes way back,* as Felicia would put it.

I summarize for Amber my work with the collective, vigilant for any signs of disapproval. But she just murmurs noncommittal *uh-huh*'s.

When I finish she says, "I had no idea! But I'm not surprised. You always were into the protest scene."

"And then there's Miguel."

"Your boyfriend?"

"I guess that's what you'd call him."

"What's he like?"

"I'm pregnant."

"You are?"

"About three months," I say.

"You don't show."

"He came to Lamaze class with me."

"That's a good sign." She scrutinizes me. "What's the matter?"

"It turned out to be a fiasco. Afterward he told me that being present for the birth was more than he could handle."

"Oh, sweetie." She pours us more tea and her eyes take on a distant look. "I think a lot of men are like that. In my biology class some guys actually fainted while watching a film about natural childbirth. I think men are just built that way. I'd rather have a good female friend with me any day."

"Well, maybe I'm too hard on him."

"What's he like? Do you love him?"

"Love him? I thought I did, but now I'm not sure." I pause, then laugh and say, "He's attractive."

"That's a plus," Amber says, smiling. "Is he good in bed?"

"Yeah." I grin. "That's not the problem. Oh, hell, why am I mincing words? I just can't seem to trust him."

"And you're still with him because…?" When I don't respond, Amber stretches her upper body. "I don't know if this is relevant but you know the expression: 'A woman without a man is like a fish without a bicycle.'"

But I *don't* know. The only fish quote I know is one by Mao: "The guerilla must move amongst the people as a fish swims in the sea." I sip some oolong tea and think about Elsa's quote. Despite the women's movement, the concept of not needing a man has never taken hold with me. For years I've assumed that *single* equals *defective*, like a bird with one wing. That this assumption might be false, that someone as confident as Amber might believe otherwise, intrigues me.

"But I'm one to talk," she continues. "I can't seem to live without men."

I try to hide my disappointment. "So you don't believe what you said? About the bicycle and the fish?"

"I do," she says. "But for me it's not about the emotional ties to men."

"What *is* it about then?"

"It's about sex."

"You mean that's all you care about?"

"Right now I have *zero* time for an emotional relationship." She winks. "But I do manage to get sex."

"But not with a boyfriend?"

"No."

"How do you do it then? With women?"

"I meet men."

"Where?"

"In bars. There's one a half block up the street."

I suck in my breath. "You mean...you pick up...strangers?" I shiver, imagining her lying brutally murdered on this very same sofa, like the protagonist of *Looking for Mr. Goodbar*, who brought men home from a neighborhood bar. But at the same time, although I'd never go cruising myself, I admire Amber's boldness; it's men who usually behave this way.

Which doesn't take away from the foolhardiness of it. "You scare me," I say. She tosses me an enigmatic grin. "For me," I add, "it's the intimacy that I enjoy even more than the sex. I'll miss that."

"Why? Are you breaking up?"

I sigh. "I think so. I don't know. I admire him—what he went through in the Dominican Republic."

"Which was?"

"He fought in a revolution there in 1965. It was almost successful until LBJ sent in the Marines to quash it."

"Wow! That's deep."

"To me he's still this revolutionary hero with lofty principles and respect for women. Even though he's proven otherwise."

"What did he do?"

"The usual. Played around."

"Mmmm," Amber murmurs. She swirls the tea in her cup as if studying the tea leaves.

"I know I should be stronger, shouldn't let it hurt me so much, but...."

"There's nothing wrong with wanting love and support and trust," Amber reassures me.

"But somehow I feel I'm too weak, too...un-liberated. As if I'm betraying my feminist self."

"It's confusing," Amber says. "We're trying to grapple with all these ideas floating around out there. We're the *transition generation*. I sure hope future women appreciate what we went through for their sake. I hope mothers teach their daughters how hard it was for us. We paved the way. It's not easy—all these new expectations we have to fulfill, without any models to show us how to navigate."

"But it doesn't seem hard for *you*," I say.

"That's not true. I'm just like you. As I said, it's a generational thing."

Amber reaches for a ceramic bowl on the bookcase and extracts cigarette paper and marijuana leaves. I watch her roll a joint. She lights it, sucks smoke into her lungs and holds it there, then hands it over to me. I shake my head. I haven't been offered pot for years. Not that I wouldn't like a hit, but pot is taboo: it could provide a pretext for arrest.

After taking another drag, Amber reaches for the sketchbook on the coffee table. "What do you really want out of life, Jen?" she asks. The smoke in her lungs makes the words sound squeaky. She exhales with a swoosh. "I mean, if you could do anything you wanted, without duty getting in the way, without taking Miguel into account."

I'm not used to talking about personal goals. When your life is prescribed for you like mine is, goals seem irrelevant. No one asks me what I want out of life because they know my future as I know theirs: working in a factory and organizing for the next 30 years, until we're worn out and ready for the retirement heap.

When I was five, I made the decision to be a kindergarten teacher—influenced by my teacher Miss Tennyson, who wore colorful silk scarves twisted in fascinating loops about her neck. I held on to the diminishing goal of teaching until I became a communist, but then I buried it once and for all like a dead pet in the back yard.

"There's so much I'd like to do," I say. "I want to travel. To visit Nelson Mandela in prison, go to Cuba with the Venceremos Brigade, learn the flamenco in Spain. I could go on," I say as she looks at me with amused attention. "Visit the haunts of the expatriates in Paris, climb Machu Pichu.

"There's a 60-year-old autoworker I know; I'd like to write a biography of his life. Or maybe enter the Peace Corps." I laugh. "And I've always secretly wanted to run away and join a circus, learn to walk a tightrope." Amber has returned to her sketching and only smiles.

"But what I really want to do is be a teacher." I imagine myself the protagonist of *Up the Down Staircase,* standing before a blackboard, chalk in hand, expounding on Robert Frost's "The Road Not Taken." Or reading *To Kill a Mockingbird* to 30 fascinated boys and girls.

My practice teaching at Columbia didn't quite go the way I'd envisioned it. Instead of paying attention to me, students sat off to the side and snapped rubber bands, applied makeup, gossiped, or exchanged comic books. Once when my master teacher thought I wasn't looking, I saw her shake her head and cluck.

But still…there was magic in those moments when a class discussion would take off like a rocket, when eyes shone with comprehension, when students got drawn into learning despite themselves.

Amber is still sketching. "Teaching." she says. "I couldn't do that."

"Why not?"

"I'm too scrambled."

"I'm super-organized," I say. "I think it's one of my few strengths."

"You've got *lots* of strengths," Amber says. "You're calm, for one thing. You're willing to put up with things." If she only knew what I've put up with. "I'd be too impatient," she continues, "dealing with all those run-away hormones."

"I confess, the thought scares me, but I'd like to give it a shot," I say wistfully.

"Wouldn't the baby get in the way of a teaching career?"

"The baby?" I ask blankly.

"Your baby." She gestures to my belly. "Wouldn't it be an obstacle?"

"Oh…I don't see why."

"Well," she says, "the logistics seem a bit daunting." She takes a drag of her joint.

It suddenly hits me—how crazy it is to think that my dreams could come alive. Any of them. How would I care for an infant while traveling, how could I get a master's degree and teach at the same time? No, from now on my life will be circumscribed, I remind myself. And I'd better get used to it.

"Excuse me if this is too personal," Amber says, leaning forward, looking concerned, "but are you ready for this baby?"

"I'm not sure," I reply, and quickly backtrack. "I mean, of course I want the baby." My hand flies to my stomach and I direct a silent apology to my unborn daughter or son for my initial hesitance. Words somersault from my mouth. "When I look into my future, I see this baby. It will love me unconditionally. I won't be lonely anymore."

"Oh, yes, *unconditional love*." Amber raises both hands to the ceiling as if beseeching the heavens. "Is it out there somewhere?"

"You don't believe in unconditional love?" My tea cup hovers halfway to my mouth.

"Not really. I'm over that."

"What do you mean?"

Amber sighs. "Parents are supposed to love their babies no matter what, right? Well, maybe parents do, I'll give you that. Even if her kid turns out to be a monster like a murderer or rapist, maybe a mother can still see the wounded child hidden in there, can trace what went wrong, can see the blows the kid suffered. I guess I believe in that."

"But?"

"But I don't believe in unconditional love between adults, and I sure as hell don't believe in the unconditional love of a child for its parents."

"But at least I'll no longer be lonely," I protest.

"Who knows how it will shake out?" she says. "The baby may isolate you even more."

I can't refute that. It'll be more difficult to attend events, pass out leaflets with Charlie, go to parties. "But...but...the baby will give me the love I'm missing. It'll give me a family."

"So you're lonely and want more human connection, and you've decided that a baby will provide it. Is that right?"

"Pretty much."

But when stated like that, something is amiss, like a piece of a jigsaw puzzle that seems to fit—but doesn't.

As I leave, Amber hands me a card on which something is written in calligraphy with a purple marker. "It's the name and number of an abortion clinic that I used once," she says. "If you should decide to do it—and I know that's a big *if*—I'll be glad to go with you." Then she tears a page off her sketchpad and hands it to me. "Here's something else."

I stare at a portrait of me, signed "With love always, Amber."

"It's a wonderful present," I say. We cling to each other.

16. Miguel
DECEMBER 1975

WHY DOES SHE ALWAYS DUMP ME IN PUBLIC places? She's asked me to meet her here at our café in Washington Heights— *Quisqueya* Heights, as we Dominicans call it. Doesn't she know that it's uncomfortable for me to meet her here, given what we'll be talking about? That's why I choose a table in the rear, where I hope no one will notice us.

She enters and looks around but I don't wave; for one more minute I want to con myself into believing this will be an ordinary meal. But the way her voice sounded on the phone—lifeless, polite, neutral—tipped me off. I'm not stupid.

Her hair is getting long. Remembering the scent when I wrap my arms around her from behind and bury my face in it makes me dizzy. I shake my head *hard.*

She sees me now.

Ever since that night at the Lamaze class and our conversation afterward, I've had a sense of doom, like waiting for the *Loyalistas* to cross the bridge across the Ozama River to invade us. It started the night I told her I didn't want to be there at the hospital. When I saw the look in her eyes, the hurt and disappointment that swiftly turned to anger, I knew something had snapped shut.

But what should I have done? Don't I deserve credit for being honest? She always said she wanted the truth, and this is what I get! Was I supposed to fake it and then fall apart while she was in labor? What if I got sick at the very moment when the baby was slithering out (in all that slime and goo)? I shudder. When I was a teenager, a guy showed me a book with graphic color photographs of the baby at various stages of development in the womb. One picture showed the baby being lifted from the vagina, all bloody, with blue splotches and mucous, and the cord still attached. I gagged back then; what would I do today?.

No, I wouldn't have been any help to her. Why won't she accept that?

She slides into the seat across from me and smiles so briefly that if I'd blinked, I'd have missed it. I reach for her hand. She lets me hold it for a moment and then gently pulls it away and opens the menu. Doesn't she want to hold my hand? Or does she just need both hands for the menu?

The Dominican waitress brings water. A new girl. I've never noticed her there before. I order *una fría* (a beer) to start; Yenny, an iced tea.

She looks pretty good, considering. A little pale, perhaps, her green eye shadow slightly smudged, her mouth a little tight at the corners. But she looks healthy. Probably because she no longer smokes. I really ought to give up that habit myself.

I light up a Marlboro.

We talk about nothing. I'm impatient to get through all this *buzz buzz buzz* to the crux. I resent her keeping me in suspense. The waitress brings my Presidente and Yenny's tea.

"I don't know any easy way to say it," she says. Finally! "So I'll just say it." She's speaking in Spanish. "I'm sorry to hurt you because I know that you care for me." Her face contorts. Oh, God, don't let her cry. "I tried," she continues, "but...it's just not working. I didn't mean to lead you on." Her words have jagged edges.

"It's the Lamaze class, isn't it? Because of what I said that night?"

"It's not that." She's lying. "I dig it that a lot of men can't handle watching a woman give birth."

"Well, what is it, then? Please! You owe me an explanation."

She sighs. "Maybe it's cultural differences."

"Like what?"

"I don't know. Differences in how women are treated in your country."

"American men don't fool around?"

She hesitates. *Aha!* Just let her deny that one. "Maybe not so openly anyway," she says.

"That's racism, pure and simple." The volume of my voice surprises me. I've never heard her talk this chauvinist shit before. Has it been lurking in her thoughts all along? But she's always defended other cultures, always opposed chauvinism.

"Well, of course American men do cheat. You're right."

"You better believe it!" I should lower my voice, but I can't seem to. I wonder if people are looking. Well, fuck *them!*

"You should have seen the guys in the student movement," she adds, her words coming fast now. "Some guys interpreted the sexual revolution as a blank check to sleep around. Even when they had girlfriends. Of course, it was a different story if their *girlfriends* slept around."

I blink. Is she taking my side now? "I hate these stereotypes," I say.

"You're right. Dominican men aren't any worse than other men."

"Worse than other men? There you go again with the men-this, men-that thing. Do you hate men? Is that why you're dumping me?"

"No, Miguel, it's not about hating men. It's about finding myself as a woman. I wonder if you can understand that. You're a feminist yourself. Or so you always said…." Her voice fades as though maybe she doesn't believe I meant what I said.

I *am* a feminist, but she carries it to an extreme! Always talking about discrimination against women. What about discrimination against the working class?

"And the men in my country? The men in the copper refinery? Aren't they oppressed too?"

"You're right. *You're right.*" She waves her hand in front of her face, brushing away my comments as if whisking away a fly. "That's why I worked in factories all those years…. Look, can we change the subject, Miguel? It feels as if you're haranguing me."

I shut up. After I order another Presidente and take a slug, I say, "OK, I'm listening." I sit back in the booth, cross my arms.

Yenny slowly unwraps her straw, sticks it in her iced tea, and sips. "Well, I need to understand, Miguel. Why did you do it? Weren't you happy in the relationship?"

"That wasn't it."

"So?"

"You want to know why? I'll tell you why," I say. This is too much. I told her I'm not going to run around on her anymore and I meant it. Yet she won't give me a chance to prove myself. OK, if she wants to know, then I'll tell her. "I was curious," I say. I look her straight in the eyes, as if challenging her. But as soon as I say the word *curious*, I wish I could take it back. *Curious* doesn't do it justice; it's far more complex than that.

"Curious?"

"Sometimes when I meet women I have this desire to find out what they're like," I try to explain. "I know it's wrong, but—" I stop short because I sound just like my father.

"That's what it was all about? *Curiosity?*" Her eyes are fixed wide, in horror or disbelief or something else.

"You don't get it—"

"Oh, I think I do."

"No, you don't!" I say sharply. "Let me finish, damn it!" She takes a breath as if about to retort but curbs herself. "This desire, it's so strong, this desire to find out. I don't expect you to understand, but—"

Her face collapses. "It hurts, Miguel. It hurts so much."

"I told you I'm not going to do it anymore. Ever since we got together this last time, Yenny, it's only been you. I swear."

"I just don't buy it."

"Buy what?"

"I don't trust you. Not *enough*. I can't get past all those weeks you lied to me about another woman. Or *women.*" She puts her elbows on the table, her head in her hands. "God, I don't even know how many women. I can't let it go. I've tried, but-"

"You won't give me another chance? Just one more chance? Please!"

"I don't believe people can change that fast. Maybe it's related to the way I feel about revolution."

"Revolution?" What the hell is she talking about?

"I think change takes a long time. I have doubts that there'll be a revolution. At least, in the near future."

I stare at her. This is something I never expected. Is she serious? *I've* never bought into the collective's line about the revolution being right around the corner, all that stuff about the working class being so advanced. Maybe in *my* country, but certainly not the U.S. working class, which is so racist and so bribed by high wages. But I was convinced that Yenny swallowed everything the collective preached—hook, line, and Little Red Book.

"You're dumping me because you don't think there'll be a *revolution?*"

She shakes her head. "The point is that this is not just about you, Miguel. It's other things too that have nothing to do with you personally."

Not personal? Is she fucking with me? "What other things?"

"I need to figure out what I want to do with myself right now." Not that sorry line again. "It takes time. I've always desperately wanted to be with a man because I thought it would fill a void in me. Then I *was* with a man. With you. And I was still miserable. Either way, I've let my life be driven by *men*—whether wanting a man, or having one that made me unhappy. Do you understand?" Her voice tapers off as if she's talking to herself. "Either way."

I slump back against the booth. She won't give me another chance? After the huge changes I've gone through for her—giving up Sandra, spending entire weekends with her when I was longing to kick back with my friends for a little while.

And we also had so much fun together. Making out in all-night movies on 42nd Street; lying next to each other, half naked, in the sun at the shore; dancing salsa and merengue; playing chess. And the sex! *Coño*, how she turns me on!

Then too, I like seeing things through the eyes of a *gringa,* even a confused one. Through her I found out that revolutionaries in the U.S. revere the 1965 revolution in my country. And when we talked politics, it was exciting; like me, she's an intellectual. Even if I don't have a higher education, I've read the classics: Marx, Mao, Lenin, Trotsky; and also Frantz Fanon, Herbert Marcuse, Paulo Freire. And Yenny keeps up with me. Even her anti-male rhetoric is kind of fascinating sometimes. (And yes, I *am* a feminist. Just not a rabid one like her.)

Something is squeezing me so hard I can't breathe.

The trips I've looked forward to with Yenny will never happen now. I wanted her to show me California. I wanted to take her to Santo Domingo to meet my family; they would adore her.

Suddenly it dawns on me: we haven't talked about the baby yet. There's still the baby! We can raise it together; we *must* raise it together. Because a baby needs a father. Everyone knows that.

With renewed vigor, I wave to the waitress, raise my empty glass. She sets another Presidente before me and clears away the old bottle. Yenny is still only halfway through her iced tea.

"What about the baby?" I say. "You have to consider the baby. I'll be a good father, Yenny. I won't do all the things *my* father did."

"It's too late, Miguel."

"But I'll help you raise it. You can't do it all alone."

"I...I don't...I don't have it anymore."

"Don't have it?"

"I…I had…I had an abortion."

The room grows hushed. Neither time nor space exists. The only sound is the blood roaring in my temples. The next words I speak sound like sandpaper.

"You *what?*" Her face is drained of color and she looks almost scared. "You're kidding, right?" I say when my normal breath returns. She gives a fleeting shake of her head. "You got rid of the baby without asking me?" She lowers her eyes. I bang my fist on the table and raise my voice. Her head jerks up. "Without even asking me?" Customers turn toward us and gape. "I hate you for that."

She sits up straight and defiance glitters in her eyes. "First you tell me it's a phantom pregnancy, next you tell me to get an abortion," she says. She juts out her chin. "Then you tell me to give you the baby, then you apologize. How am I supposed to figure out what you want? I feel like a damn punching bag."

"It wasn't just your baby!" I'm shouting now. I want to seize her by the shoulders and shake some sense into her. *How dare she?* "It was mine too," I say.

"But it's my body!"

That feminist shit again! I speak between gritted teeth. "It takes two to make a baby. No matter what the fucking feminists say."

She gasps so loud I'm sure the whole café can hear her. Her eyes burn. "Sure it takes two," she says. "But for you it's sperm squirting into the vagina in a moment of ecstasy." She's speaking way too loudly in her gringo Spanish, drawing attention to us, butchering the words—*sperm, squirting, ecstasy.* I know everyone's listening; I don't dare look around. *Dios mío,* she's going to say more! "Speak English!" I yell.

She does, and she lowers her voice, speaks precisely. "For me, Miguel, it's nine months of pregnancy, 30 hours of labor, and 18 years of care-giving. I have no decent job and no prospects. I'd really be dependent on you if I had a baby. And I can't count on you to be there."

"Of course I am there. I help you...." My voice diminishes and comes to a halt. She's already won. Raising the baby together was my last hope of getting her back. Now that hope has dissipated like the smoke from my cigarette.

She's speaking but it sounds like gibberish. "...have to rely on any man," she's saying. "I'm afraid you're still thinking this is about you. I want to be my own person. I want to figure out who I am, what I want, before I have a kid."

"You should have thought of that before you got pregnant," I blurt out in Spanish. My words sound constricted, as if my throat were clamped off, but words are futile anyway. I sink back in the booth and hope I won't barf onto the tattered plastic seat.

She looks at me from across the table with such concern that tears well up. I feel my face growing hot. I swallow hard. She waits. My voice cracks as I say, "How did it go? The abortion."

"No complications. Felicia was with me."

Felicia! Once again that meddling bitch.

"*I* would have come with you," I say.

"You would?"

"Claro que sí." Of course.

"Thank you for saying that, Miguel." She reaches for my hand and squeezes it. But something in the way she doesn't meet my eyes makes me suspect she doubts me.

"I mean it," I say, but do I doubt it too? I pick at the label on my bottle. "So this is it then?" I ask feebly.

"I guess so," she says. She lays a bill on the table. "I got this."

"It's OK." I push the money back at her.

"Can we still be friends?" she asks.

"No es posible."

She closes her eyes; she looks so frail. But I harden myself.

263

"Well, goodbye then," she says, looking at me hesitantly, as if she hopes I might say something else. At least I have the satisfaction of refusing her pathetic wish to remain friends. After she's just dumped me!

She stands and pulls on her duffle coat with difficulty, forcing her arms into the sleeves over a thick sweater. She bends and kisses me on the cheek; I pull my face away. I watch as she goes through the door. A gust of wind blows in behind her. I shiver, light another Marlboro, order another Presidente. Anger rises in me like a river overflowing its banks. I'll never forgive her for this! Never! I can't remember when I've been treated so unfairly. The pain of losing the baby is bitter. The waitress brings my beer. I wrap my fingers around the bottle and squeeze; veins bulge in my forearm.

I shouldn't have carried on with Sandra that way at the party while Yenny was pregnant. I just wanted to show her that I was cool, despite what she'd done to me. I suck furiously on my Marlboro and light a new one with the stub. By demanding the baby, I just wanted to get back at her a little. Tit for goddamn tat.

I chug half the bottle.

I always intended to make up with her. When it occurred to me how I'd probably scared her that night at the party, I called her the next day to apologize. For I cared for her more than for the Ozama River, more than for my country even.

And now she's killed our baby! It doesn't matter what I did, she had no right. Conceiving a baby takes a woman *and* a man. No matter what los *pinche feministas* say. "A woman's right to choose"—that's a crock! Does she think that just because I didn't carry it around in my belly, I'm not involved? What's all this rot about sperm—how did she put it?—"squirting into the vagina"? That's so gross. And that shit about "ecstasy"? The least she could have done was tell me ahead of time, not just spring it on me. That's so heartless.

I take another swig of beer.

A fact protrudes into my thoughts like a splinter under my thumbnail. It's me who told her to get an abortion. That day when she booted me out of her apartment. Of course I hadn't meant it. Could she have believed me?

Actually, I can't remember exactly what I did mean. I was angry, I know that much. But I'm certain I never wanted her to abort. Even if I did, I never thought she'd do it. Why, she told me she'd even tried to *adopt* a baby once.

I look out the window. Street lights are on; how has it gotten dark so fast? The café is filling up with Dominican families coming in for supper. I should leave, free up a table.

That Lamaze thing—that was the final straw for her. But from the time I was a boy, whenever someone in the family got sick even, I would stumble around just getting in the way. I learned to lie low until things got back to normal.

But I should have just popped a lude and gone through with the birth. That seems important to American women; it seemed important to Yenny. In my country, women wouldn't even *want* their husbands there. How would a man know what to do? A girlfriend, a sister—now *that* makes sense. I've even overheard Yenny and Felicia saying that women are better than men at "nurturing"—wasn't that the word they used?

And now she's dumped me just when I'm forcing myself to toe the line. She doesn't give me credit. She expects me to change just like that. It isn't reasonable! But I did it anyway! Stopped! Cold turkey!

Except, I remind myself, for the few times recently that I've seen Sandra. But just for coffee and just to comfort her. She keeps calling the machine shop where I work. My boss summons me to the phone, grunting about *too many personal calls.* I have to remove my goggles and my gloves, wipe the sweat from around my eyes, and go to the office to talk on the grimy black phone that sits on his desk. He probably listens to every fucking word. Sandra's sobs come over the line. *She's so depressed, she must see me, she'll do* algo desesperado. *Something desperate.* It alarms me. It's my fault that she feels this way; it's my duty to comfort her.

An image swims into my head of that clerk I see at the bakery where I buy coffee and pastry. Sarah, that's her name—a Jewish girl. I'm sure she's flirting with me, and I have to admit that in the past the idea would have crossed my mind that something might come of it. But I'm proud that I'm resisting the temptation. (Although I do look forward to stopping in there every morning. *Is that cheating?*) I try to clear my head of these thoughts. It's all so complicated.

I order another Presidente. The waitress asks me in Spanish if I'm doing OK. "*Estoy bién,*" I say. As she flounces away, my eyes follow her butt, which wiggles beneath her tight uniform. Was there a deeper meaning to her words?

17. Jenny
DECEMBER 1975

I ASK FOR THE REST OF THE WEEK OFF, which will give me four full days to recover. Rattling over potholes in Felicia's old sedan, we drive into Newark. I told my boss there was "a death in the family." He pursed his lips but said nothing. I've been a model worker—conscientious, punctual. I've shown restraint, organized no one, smuggled in no leaflets. I've simply done my job. Everyone—except for the cooks—seems to like me, customers and waitresses alike.

Absorbed in my thoughts, I scarcely notice when Felicia pulls to the curb and locates a map under some papers and make-up in the glove compartment. Frowning, she lays the map across the steering wheel and opens it up.

I feel uncomfortable about lying to Miguel, and I understand that he feels betrayed. But this will be harrowing enough without his resistance. And it's my decision. Although I wonder what rights fathers do have in such situations.

Felicia eases back into traffic. "Almost there," she says. She swings the car around a corner and swerves into the oncoming lane to avoid a large pothole. A male driver gives her the finger.

From the beginning my pregnancy has been fraught with distress—Miguel's denial, his demand that I abort, the threat that he'd kidnap the baby. My relationship with Miguel himself was turbulent. When he told me he hated me a few days ago, I thought to myself, *You know what? I don't care anymore.* And I didn't.

The car sputters and Felicia looks worried. Spark plugs probably. I hope we'll make it without being towed. If something happens to the car, I'll have to reschedule, take additional time off work, and chew off more fingernails. Now that I've made the decision, I'm impatient to get it over.

I thought a baby would take away my loneliness; that's a laugh. Too much to ask of a baby. I have to learn to be satisfied with my own company. And I wanted someone to love me. But a baby can't provide the intimacy that I long for. Thank God for the talk with Amber; it made me see reality. No, the kind of closeness I seek can only be met by a loving relationship with an adult. And I can't hope for love to take root if I don't first love myself, can I?

The engine seems to have smoothed out; in fact, it's almost purring now. I glance at Felicia's profile; she looks over at me and smiles. Felicia is the one I've chosen to accompany me on this ordeal. My closest friend. We've stood in the icy rain in front of factory gates at 5 a.m. distributing leaflets together, broken bread—*pan dulce*—every morning. We've dissected current events, gossiped about collective members. It's Felicia who has laughed and cried with me about Miguel. (Mostly cried.)

She switches on the radio to a Johnny Mathis song. Soothing. Felicia supports my decision unconditionally, I think, but then I realize that Amber is right—few things in life are unconditional. Felicia expressed discomfort with my decision and would never do it herself, but she understands what *Roe v. Wade* means to women.

She down-shifts into first and slips the sedan into a parking space on a tree-shaded street. Narrow wooden houses, sub-divided into apartments, line the block; one street further is the clinic. It looks very busy there; people seem to be lined up outside. Are they doing that many abortions today?

As if I were disabled, Felicia holds the car door open for me. I pull my overcoat more tightly around my body. She links her arm in mine and we amble up the block. Just a morning stroll, I say to myself, suddenly wanting to turn around and rush back to the car.

I've read about the procedure. It may involve some bleeding and cramping, but within a few days I should be *back to normal.*

268

I can't remember the last time I've felt *normal.*

What if I experience guilt or regret for the rest of my life? The problem is that abortion is so irreversible. Like the way I broke up with Miguel. Irreversible. Did I do it that way on purpose so I'll never be able, in a fragile moment, to reconcile with him again? But in the three days that have passed since I met him at that little restaurant, I continue to believe I've made the right decision.

We're half a block away now, and the crowd grows noisier as we approach. I realize in horror who they are. About twenty people carry signs and chant "Choose life, choose life!" A young girl with blond curls holds up a sign that says, "Thank you, Mommy and Daddy." She locks eyes with me. A man brandishes a Bible at us. His sign says, "Love thy unborn neighbor." His t-shirt reads: "Stop American Genocide." Too bad he hasn't tattooed his forehead as well. A woman blocks our way to the steps, wagging her index finger, a tragic expression on her face. Her t-shirt displays a picture of a baby and reads, "Please let me live." Felicia and I wait until the woman grudgingly lets us pass.

As we start up the steps to the entrance, a man in his twenties with wild-looking eyes thrusts a plastic doll in my face. "This is what a 10-week fetus looks like," he growls, spraying saliva. There's something unsettling about the man. I pale. Felicia, grim and determined, steers me past him and through the metal door into the clinic.

Once inside, the contrast is marked. We find ourselves in a softly lit lobby with peach-colored walls. Soothing classical music—Vivaldi—plays in the background. Three other women in various stages of pregnancy look up from armchairs covered in flowered slipcovers.

A woman with scarlet lipstick and auburn hair comes toward us, carrying a clipboard.

"Hi, there," she says in a motherly tone. "Which one of you is Jenny?"

"I'm Jenny. This is Felicia."

"Glad to meet you both. I'm Gladys." She puts her hand on my shoulder. Her voice drops a decibel. "I hope those idiots outside didn't unnerve you." Lines appear between her eyes. "We're trying to get an injunction against them. But in the meantime...." Her voice grows cheery again and she turns to Felicia. "When it's over, you can pull up to the back door to get Jenny. No one will bother you there; it's private property." Why didn't the clinic mention the rear entrance when I called for the appointment?

Gladys gestures to some empty armchairs. "You make yourselves at home." She turns to me. "We'll call you soon, honey. The first thing is, you'll speak to Ramona Rivera. She's our social worker." Gladys melts away.

Felicia and I sit on adjoining chairs. I cross and re-cross my legs and bite a thumbnail. Felicia picks up *Glamour* magazine.

"How do you feel?" she asks, flipping pages, perusing the ads.

"Nervous."

"Those demonstrators are revolting."

"Free speech, I guess," I say. I'm breathing deeply, trying to calm myself. "Demonstrations do have an impact—as you and I well know." There's a pamphlet in Felicia's hand. "What's that?"

"Oh, nothing," says Felicia.

"No, let me see it."

"It's garbage. It'll just upset you."

"Really, I want to see it."

Felicia reluctantly hands me the pamphlet. It's folded into three sections. "ABORTION IS MURDER!!!" shouts from the first section. Below the heading is a drawing of an almost fully developed baby in someone's hand. The baby looks sad and a teardrop glistens on its cheek.

"Ugh," I say. I pass the flyer back to Felicia.

"I told you," she says.

I'm silent. Then I say, "I don't believe it's murder." I lower my head and speak softly. "But I'm not sure what it *is*." I twist my hands. "I keep remembering all the weeks that I communed with this baby, or should I say, with the baby it would *become.* I feel as if I'm killing something. But not something that exists. Something…potential. A dream, maybe."

Gladys appears. "Jenny, sweetie, come this way."

Felicia squeezes my hand. I follow Gladys down a short hallway to an office with a plate on the door that says, "Ramona Rivera, Social Worker." Gladys knocks softly and opens the door. "This is Jenny," she says. She retreats.

The office is neat. No piles of messy papers on the desk's surface. An upholstered armchair for her clients, a tilting office chair for Ramona herself. "Hello, Jenny, please have a seat," Ramona Rivera says. Her voice sounds professional, skilled, confident. But in contrast to the orderliness of her office and the confidence of her voice, Ramona herself looks disheveled, dowdy. Her navy blue suit has wrinkles. I have the urge to take a comb to her hair.

Ramona gives me an everything-will-be-OK smile, and we chat for a minute about how I'm feeling. *Fine, thank you,* I lie. "Before we can proceed," she says, "I need to make sure that you're fully aware of all your options. Things like adoption or having a relative raise the baby."

"I've already thought about these things for days," I tell her.

"So you have no need to further explore these alternatives?"

"Not really."

"All right. Now it's my job to ask you a few more questions, just to make absolutely sure that you're at ease with your decision. I'm not trying to sway you in any way. Only you can know what is the best decision for yourself." Now she gives me another comforting smile. Her lipstick is crooked. "Do you have any lingering doubts you'd like to talk about?"

"Uh…."

Ramona Rivera waits, relaxed. "You may be feeling conflicted," she prompts. "Such doubts are natural, by the way."

"I suppose."

"After all, it's a difficult decision," she emphasizes. "There is no perfect answer. People choose the path that best fits their needs and values."

"I've been so connected to this baby," I say. "I've talked to it. I told it that I'm looking forward to its birth." Ramona looks confused. "I mean, before I decided to...to abort, I thought a baby would solve my problems."

"Problems?"

"I thought it would take away my loneliness."

"And you no longer feel that way?"

"Now I think a baby would create more problems."

"What kinds of problems?"

"I want to find out more about what I want, what I'm capable of. I think a baby might tie me down." Then I add, "And I don't want to raise a baby alone. If I had support, it might be different."

Ramona nods. "The baby's father? He's not in the picture?"

"He's unreliable."

"Does he know about the abortion?"

"He's not too pleased, to put it mildly, but I can't be concerned about that now."

"Um-hmm," Ramona says, looking thoughtful. The eye shadow on her right eye is smudged.

"I mean, if I did what he wanted, I wouldn't have the abortion. But if we can't see eye to eye on this, then I get to decide, don't I?"

"That's right," she says. "Roe v. Wade." Then she looks pensive. "While we're talking about options, have you considered letting the baby be adopted?"

"I can't bear getting more and more attached to it...to her, him, only to give it up. Once it's born, I could never let it go." Ruby waits. She seems to want to understand me. "It's different at this stage of my pregnancy; I don't really consider the embryo a person yet. Just a potential person, you know?"

"It sounds as if you've given this a lot of thought, Jenny."

272

"I have. I really have."

"And you're convinced that abortion is what you want." I nod. Ramona folds her hands on the desktop. A strand of hair pokes up at an odd angle. "So. Let's move on. I need to tell you what to expect afterward."

I may experience sadness, even post-partum depression. I should pamper myself for a few days, take a break from my routine, gather friends around me. Allow myself to grieve. She peers at me from behind smeared eyeglasses.

"Does that sound doable?"

⋘ ⋘ ⋘ ⋘ ⋘

Back in the waiting room, Felicia is still leafing through *Glamour*. She looks up quizzically. I make a circle with my thumb and forefinger and try to look perky. But as I sit back into the chair, I put my hand on my stomach in a spasm of anxiety.

Only one woman remains in the lobby. She sits by herself on the sofa, smoking a cigarette, biting her lips. I'm tempted to warn her that smoking might harm the fetus, but I remember that it no longer matters to the fetus whether the woman smokes, does drugs, or sniffs glue. I smile at this girl/woman. Is she old enough to have an abortion without parental consent? A strand of limp brown hair falls over the girl's eye. Perhaps my smile encourages her, because her unobstructed eye looks at me and she smiles back weakly. "No one knows I'm doing this," she volunteers, as if in answer to my unspoken question. She twists the strand of hair around her finger.

"Oh?" I say. "I bet that's lonely."

"Yeah," the girl admits. Her name is Tess, and she's thin, almost scrawny. She doesn't look pregnant at all, but then, neither do I.

"It must take courage to do this, Tess," Felicia says.

A tear rolls down Tess's cheek and she pulls a wad of tissues from a box on the end table. The back of her hand bears a tattoo. A heart pierced by an arrow.

"My Dad would kill me if he found out that I'd been having sex," Tess says. "Even though I'm 18. He told me if he ever caught me with a boy *that way*, he'd get his rifle, shoot the boy first, then come after me. I'd end up 'like a deer in hunting season,' he said."

My mouth falls open. "He said that?" Tess nods.

"*Dios mío!*" Felicia says.

Gladys appears. "They're ready for you, hon."

Felicia hugs me. "Don't worry, you'll be fine." I follow Gladys down the hall. It still isn't too late to back out, I say over and over under my breath.

In an examination room, a gray-haired nurse silently sticks a thermometer in my mouth, monitors my pulse, checks my blood pressure. She thrusts a hospital gown at me. "Undress and put this on, open to the front," she says. I'm relieved she can speak. I put on the gray-blue gown, open to the front, tie the strap, and wait, hunched over, on the examining table. The gown gapes, but I don't notice. I use the time to clear my mind, but pictures of the various stages of the embryo keep intruding.

The evening before in my living room, I turned off the lights, lit candles, and put on soft music. I sat cross-legged on the floor and meditated on the creature inside me, on the child that will never be. I told it I loved it but wasn't prepared to be a mother yet. I bade it goodbye. Afterward, calmness descended upon me.

But today I feel edgy and unresolved.

According to the large, round clock on the wall, twenty minutes have elapsed. A light knock and a doctor enters the room. Why do doctors bother to knock when they never wait for a response? He's young, in his early thirties, probably just a few years my senior. He even has an impish face.

Is this his first abortion?

He introduces himself—Dr. Colson—asks how I'm feeling— *fine, thank you*—and informs me, "Everything should go fine. The vacuum procedure at this stage has even lower risk than a regular delivery." He pauses, then breezily proceeds. "Of course, like all procedures, there is some risk." He leaves and Ms. Taciturn re-enters, as if through a revolving door.

She leads me down the hall into the procedure room, where Dr. Colson has materialized and is pulling on plastic gloves. "I'm going to give you a brief pelvic exam, just to verify the stage of the fetus," he says. I lie back, my feet in stirrups, and wince as his gloved hand reaches inside me. I console myself—this is nothing compared to a full-term delivery—and focus on the sprinkler head in the ceiling.

The nurse straps me onto an operating table and gives me an injection. "A local anesthetic combined with a little amnesiac," she says. I quickly grow light-headed. The doctor and nurse hover over me, almost floating.

The next thing I hear is the nurse saying, "Everything went fine." The clock on the wall indicates that forty-five minutes have passed.

"I don't remember anything," I say, amazed.

"That's the amnesiac," the nurse says. "How do you feel?"

"A few cramps." I place my hand on my stomach.

"That's normal. No problem. Can you walk into the recovery room?"

"I think so."

In my hospital gown, I hold onto the nurse's arm and proceed slowly down the hallway. My groin aches. We enter a large room with curtains over the windows. The other two women from the lobby sit in dark brown recliners and drink from Dixie cups. A skinny young nurse's assistant in a yellow uniform helps me into a recliner, covers me with an afghan, and drapes a heating pad over my stomach. The assistant unscrews the top of a large bottle of Canada Dry ginger ale, pours the fizzing liquid into a cup, and arranges two Oreo cookies on a paper plate. She puts the refreshments on a little table next to me.

"How do you feel?" she asks.

"Not ready for Mount Everest or anything, but OK." A joke of sorts! Am I already adjusting? Or am I just callous? And how will I react in a few hours, a few days?

The assistant chuckles. "We'll save Mount Everest for next week." She tucks the coverlet around my legs and pats them. "You just rest a while."

I must have dozed off. I gradually become aware of the conversation across from me. "This is my third abortion," a woman says. My eyes open. The speaker is slim, with long, sleek black hair and eyebrows that are penciled in an arch. The second woman, chunky with stringy brown hair and a gentle expression, says she has four other children, and her husband demanded she abort this one.

"'Five is over the limit,' my husband kept telling me, even though I insisted I could handle another." She crushes tissues to her eyes. "I wanted this baby."

Why don't people use birth control? I wonder. But I'm a fine one to talk.

"This your first?" the three-abortion woman asks, nodding in my direction.

"Yeah. My first." *And my last.*

"Don't worry, it's not so bad," the woman says. "You may pass a few clots, which are unpleasant, but that's about it. I know I should be more careful but it's a drag to always remember. I'm going to try harder, though. Maybe it's not so good to keep doing this to my body...."

The other woman sobs bitterly.

About an hour later, after receiving instructions on stretching and uterine massage to relieve cramping, and after removing the gown and putting on my baggy corduroy pants and t-shirt, I ease my way into Felicia's car and we proceed down the alley. Although I can't see the demonstrators, I can hear them, still chanting. "Choose life. Choose life."

I roll up the window.

For days afterward upon waking up in the mornings I experience the shock of bereavement. While doing dishes I dry the same glass for ten minutes or stand absent-mindedly in front of the bathroom mirror, forgetting why I'm there. Maybe it's the vestiges of hormones, as the clinic has suggested. I decide to take their advice and pamper myself. I stock up on Butter Brickle ice cream, read every novel by Raymond Chandler that I can get my hands on from the public library, buy a low-cut gown that shows off what little cleavage I have—but then have nowhere to go in it. I roller-skate with Felicia at an indoor rink in Secaucus and take yoga classes in Greenwich Village. As usual, I share breakfasts with Felicia and leaflet with Charlie. I make long phone calls to Amber.

Slowly I get used to being un-pregnant. I awaken in the morning without immediately grieving. I stop resting my hand on my belly. My life settles back into a hesitant routine. Little by little, as my grief grows less raw, a new confidence arises in me, unlike any I've experienced before. No longer can I recall why I hated living alone. I find the solitude restful. I love the luxury of silence—to daydream, read, or listen to music.

18. Jenny

DECEMBER 1975

ONE AFTERNOON IN JANUARY, I MAKE my way down Grove Street to meet Charlie. The sun is warm on my face; it's one of those rare winter days that tricks you into believing spring is not far off. I look in a bodega window, pull down my hood, and run my fingers through my new perm. Behind my image, a man materializes and smiles through the glass; I smile back and walk on.

These days the image of Miguel is often edged out by the image of Charlie. I see him passing out leaflets, young co-eds clustered around him. I hear him saying, "I win" or "*Ten years?*" or "You're the only woman for me, babe." I think of our many conversations at Dotty's.

Why do I feel such a pinch when I think of him with Samantha? I'm wondering if Charlie means more to me than just a close buddy. But anyway, it's too late; I let him slip away. First, there was that embarrassing fiasco in his bedroom, then I was with Miguel, then I was getting *over* Miguel, then I was with Miguel again. Besides, as far as I can tell, Charlie has never shown any sexual attraction toward me. Except for that one night—which was nothing more than alcohol plus lust. It was obvious that our romp in the sack was just another fuck to him. The next morning he was nonchalant, even agreed that it was a mistake to jeopardize our friendship.

Have I missed something?

Checking my watch, I hurry on, stepping over some dog droppings and around a buckle in the sidewalk.

I'm glad—or should be—that Charlie has found happiness with someone. I have to accept the way things are or I'll have to renounce our friendship. And I need friends. But I keep feeling the heat from Charlie's body when he danced with me that fateful night.

For the first time something about that encounter makes me chuckle. How panicked I was. If I hadn't been so paralyzed with anxiety…, if we weren't so drunk…, if he were ever to hold me like that again…. Now that sex is one of the great pleasures in my life, I'd like to relive that night with him. Only this time we'd be sober, I'd see to that. This time I'd tell him exactly what I wanted.

After we finish leafleting, we relax over coffee at Dotty's. "How's Samantha?" I ask. "Still having problems with those obscene phone calls?" See? I can be mature about this.

"No more calls, the last I heard."

"Haven't you seen her lately, then?"

"Her husband just got a raise, so they're celebrating. Skiing in Maine."

I choke on my coffee. Her *husband?* Is Samantha cheating on her husband with Charlie? Aren't there any honorable men—or women—left?

"So Samantha's married?" I ask, trying to keep my voice calm.

"Yep."

"The woman you were with at the party in Brooklyn?"

"Yeah."

"But how can that be, Charlie?"

"How can what be?"

I try to think what to say.

"How can what be?" he repeats.

"Nothing."

It's all ruined. He's not who I thought he was. He's betrayed everything he says he stands for. If he's just like Miguel, then who can I trust?

"No, tell me, Jenny. What's wrong?"

"How could you do that?"

"Do what?"

"Be with Samantha. If she's married. I mean, Charlie, everything we profess: honesty, integrity, respect for marriage—"

"For Christ sake, Jenny, she's my cousin!"

I can't speak. This makes no sense at all.

"Your cousin?"

"Yes."

"Samantha?"

"Yes."

"She's your cousin?"

He laughs. "I'm getting dizzy on this merry-go-round."

"You're having an affair with your cousin?"

"No! You think I'd get it on with my cousin?" He looks shocked, annoyed, but then apparently decides it's funny.

I laugh too—a laugh that I hope conceals my relief. "I thought she was your girlfriend."

"You did?" He cocks his head. "But I introduced you at the party."

"Yeah, but just by name."

"Oh," he says, as if trying to remember. "No, she's my cousin. My *favorite* cousin. We practically grew up together in Park Slope."

"Oh…*Oh!*" I raise my coffee cup to my lips with unsteady hands and regard him over the rim.

"There's just one person I'm attracted to, babe," he says, grinning, wiggling his eyebrows, reaching across the table and tapping me lightly on the arm with his fist. "And that's the one sitting across from me right this minute."

Always the jokester. "Ditto," I say, winking, just to let him know I can kid around too.

But why *doesn't* Charlie have a girlfriend, I wonder.

It's Saturday. Felicia's sitting in my kitchen and we're drinking steaming cups of cocoa. I tell her about my misunderstanding regarding Samantha and Charlie's relationship. I expect her to laugh, but instead she looks smug and says,

"I'm not surprised."

"You're not?"

"No, I always knew he liked *you.*"

"What are you talking about?"

"Don't you see the way he looks at you at meetings?"

"He doesn't look at me."

"You're blind, Yenny. Everyone sees it but you."

"But Charlie and I are good friends, Felicia. Of course he looks at me with affection."

"Hah! This is more than affection or I'm an idiot."

A feeling of wild hope flutters inside me. But what evidence does she have? Just a few glances, a few smiles.

"Look how he brought you soup that time when you were sick. And read poetry to you. Now really! You think he'd do that for just a friend?"

"Yes, Felicia, I do. Maybe you don't understand the way friendship works here in the U.S. between men and women."

"That's a blow low," she laughs. "Don't believe me if you don't want to, but I think you're *scared.* I think you like him too and you don't want to get hurt."

"Sorry, Felicia, but I just can't believe that bringing someone soup, someone you've been leafleting with for so long, signifies anything special."

"You mean in all those months, before you met Miguel, you guys never even kissed?"

I blush. "No, we didn't."

"Then he's as big a fool as you are," she says.

"I never felt attracted to him that way."

Could that have deterred him? I suddenly recall Charlie telling me that he hoped that I too was curious about what sex with him would be like.

"Sometimes you're so focused on things," Felicia says, "that you don't see the jungle, only the trees."

"It's true," I say. "I'm in my head a lot. But still…."

Later I can't get Felicia's interpretation out of my mind. What if she's right? But what if she's not? I don't have the courage to approach Charlie about this. What if he gives me a blank look? A puzzled look? And what would that do to our friendship? One bad night a year ago made us self-conscious for weeks. I can't risk scaring him away. I wish I knew how to flirt, but I'd probably embarrass us both. Isn't it tragic that I can't talk to him about something this important when in the past we've talked about almost everything else?

I wait on a cold bench in Washington Square Park near the Arch, watching the people. A man on a unicycle, chess players, school girls with lunch pails. At the fountain, a guy with long hair and a windbreaker plays guitar; a few people throw coins into his guitar case.

Chances are slim that Sandra will show up. I wince at the memory of her at that party in Brooklyn. The spit-fire glare, the dismissive toss of her hair. When I phoned her last week, she said, "What's the point?"

As for Angélica, why should she appear? After all, I was the trigger for Miguel's leaving her. When I first called her, the phone rang and rang. It took three tries before I finally reached her. She appeared confused at first about who I was. When she finally figured it out, she responded simply, "*No sé.*" I don't know.

So even though there's not much chance they'll appear, I'm determined to enjoy the outing anyway. The crisp air on my cheeks, the stroll through the streets, the sparkle of the city. I gaze at NYU in the distance, but my attention is diverted by mothers with baby carriages, chatting in the nippy cold. If things were different, I might have been one of them. I search their faces, their gestures, their posture. Are they content with their lot or are they chafing at their restraints?

When I first came up with the idea, this bizarre gathering of Miguel's ex-lovers seemed like a good one. We've all suffered because of Miguel, and if we could just meet each other, maybe some of the bitterness would go away. But now, sharing confidences seems ridiculous. More likely it will result in resentment. Once again, I acted impulsively. I suppress the urge to bolt.

A Latina woman, appealing in her innocence, approaches timidly, wearing a white wool coat, pushing a baby carriage. A delicate gold cross hangs on a chain at her throat.

"You are Yenny?" she asks.

"Angélica?" I hope my voice doesn't betray my astonishment that she showed up.

Angélica stands awkwardly in front of me. "I come only to see how you look." Bending over, she adjusts the blanket that covers the baby in the carriage.

"That makes sense. I was curious too."

"So here are we," Angélica says.

"May I see the baby?"

She hesitates—does she think I'm going to steal her infant?—then turns the carriage and gently uncovers the blanket to expose a miniature face. I peer in. The baby is asleep. The little hair she has is fine and brown. Her plump lips are Miguel's, and she has Angélica's olive skin. One tiny hand is in her mouth. From her throat emerge tiny squeaks.

"How beautiful," I say, tears filling my eyes. Through my blurred vision, I see Angélica smile tentatively and readjust the blanket loosely over the baby's face.

Suddenly, Sandra stands there, looking sensual in a black silk jacket, patent leather boots, a red beret, and gold hoop earrings. Her eyes flash and I think how in the past I would have tried to recruit this working-class woman who exudes so much spunk.

"Let me see the baby" are Sandra's first words. Again, Angélica peels back the blanket. Sandra's hand flies to her mouth. "Oh," she says. Just "Oh." She looks at Angélica and holds out her hand. "I'm Sandra."

"Hola."

"Hi, Sandra." I motion to the bench. "Do you guys want to sit down?" Angélica balances on the edge of the bench as though ready for flight, one arm clutching the carriage. Sandra sits stiffly on the other side of Angélica.

We all stare straight ahead as if watching a movie. All that's missing is the popcorn. I bite my lip. Angélica rocks the carriage back and forth. Sandra plucks a Kool from her patent leather purse and lights it. Then she says to me in Spanish, "So. What are we doing here?"

I respond in Spanish. It's easier for Angélica that way, with her obviously limited English. "I'm not sure why I asked you to come. I wanted to get to know you. I...I didn't want us to end up with hard feelings."

"A little late for that, isn't it?" Sandra says, tossing back her hair.

Angélica pulls at the chain around her neck and looks across the park as if wishing she were over there with the other mothers and babies.

"I know this is a strange gathering," I say. "I just wanted to say that I'm sorry."

Angélica starts crying. If I dared, I'd put my arm around her. Sandra ignores Angélica. "Why do you care?"

"Because we've all been hurt and I don't want us to remain bitter toward each other. That will make the healing harder."

"*Healing?* Sounds like a hippy thing to say," Sandra snaps. "Miguel told me you're a college girl. You think you can undo what happened by talk talk talk. Well, it won't work. And anyway, speak for yourself. *I* haven't been hurt."

Bringing us all together was a stupid idea. I want to cut and run across the park and never see either of them again. But Sandra isn't finished.

She glares at me. "You can never know how hard it's been."

"I guess I can't," I say, and I want to say, *It hasn't been a joyride for me either, you know.* But earlier I counseled myself to listen more than I talk, no matter what.

"No, you can't." Sandra raises her chin. "I was with him first. You didn't respect that."

"Um-hmm." How much more of this can I sit through?

"It wasn't fair," Sandra continues. "He lied to me. He led me on. He told me he loved me." Tears come to her eyes. I nod.

Angélica, who's been intently listening, speaks up. "At the time I believed that he loved me too, but he never did." She gestures to the baby with a tenderness that makes me wonder whether the abortion was a mistake. "At least he's been coming around to see *her.* I named her after him. Miguela."

Sandra and I look at her as if she's named Miguela after the devil. I shudder.

Angélica's voice rises slightly. "Sí," she says. "I figured if I named her after him, he'd be more apt to help with the cost of raising her. I did it for *her,* for little Miguelita Josefina." She slides the backs of her fingers along the baby's cheeks. "When he's not around I call her Josefina," Angélica adds. Do I detect a trace of slyness in her last words?

"How are you managing?" I ask her. "Does Miguel support you?"

"Oh no. Sometimes he slips me a little something. But mainly I clean houses, and my aunt takes care of the baby. My brothers help me too; they both work, *gracias a Díos.* "

"And you, Sandra? Are you still waiting tables?"

"I got laid off but I found another job as a maid at the Hotel St. George. In Brooklyn." She rubs her fingers to her thumb. "The tips are better."

"How about you, Yenny?" asks Angélica. She looks up from the baby and nods at my stomach. "How are you feeling these days?"

I pause, swallow, clear the lump from my throat. Both women are looking at me with curiosity.

"I don't have the baby anymore."

They look confused. "What does *that* mean?" Sandra asks.

"I had an abortion."

In unison they suck in their breath. "An abortion?" repeats Angélica. "You're kidding, *verdad?*"

"I know it's hard to understand, but—"

"That's not right," Sandra interrupts. She sets her jaw.

"I could never do that," Angélica says, grasping the carriage with one hand and reaching into it to touch Josefina.

No one speaks. Angélica adjusts the blanket over the baby. Sandra bites her lower lip and frowns. I cast down my eyes and brace myself for further criticism.

Finally Angélica says, "My cousin had an abortion last year."

"Yeah?" I say.

"Our whole family was crushed."

"I'm sorry."

"She's in medical school now."

"Oh…, that's good…, isn't it?"

"*Solo Díos sabe,*" Angélica says. "It's not for me to judge."

Sandra sighs. "And how you doing otherwise, Yenny?"

"I'm getting along. I miss Miguel but I'm glad we're not together anymore. I couldn't take all the lies."

I tell them about my dream of becoming a teacher, moving to Manhattan. We chat about schools, babies, jobs, housing. As we part, Angélica invites us to come visit the baby. To hide the tears springing to my eyes again, I bend to look at little Josefina, who is yawning and stretching, emitting tiny kitten mews. Angélica pulls a bottle from her cloth bag, sets it on the bench, picks up the baby, coos at her. Then she places the nipple in Josefina's mouth. Sandra and I watch, fascinated.

So in the end it turns out to be this baby, the product of Miguel and Angélica, that melts the last bit of ice between the three of us.

19. Jenny

JANUARY 1976

I'M TAKING ORDERS AT A TABLE of four truck drivers—clam chowder, onion rings, fried chicken, fish and chips, Buffalo wings, cheddar bacon burger, cherry malts, double hot fudge sundaes. I imagine their hearts collapsing, their trucks careening off the highway.

Ten minutes later I approach their table with three plates fanned out on one arm, a fourth plate in my other hand. The wiry man wearing the Yankees cap reaches out to help me, but as he does, his hand strikes the edge of a plate, which crashes to the floor, scattering fried chicken, mashed potatoes, peas and carrots across the linoleum.

"Well, if that don't beat all," says the tough-looking guy, staring dumbly at the mess.

"That was faster than a knife fight in a phone booth," says the slim guy with the Southern drawl, shaking his head.

The man with the cowlick helps me scoop the food back onto the plate, and I return it to the kitchen.

"I need another fried chicken dinner," I tell Milos. "This one hit the floor. Sorry about that."

Milos grunts. I go to the rear corner of the kitchen to get a mop. I glance at Milos, who's watching me, his lips curled in disdain. I wring out the mop, then hurry back to clean up the mess.

"Hope you're not so clumsy in bed," I overhear Cowlick say to Yankee as I approach.

Seeing me, Tough says, "Shhh. Have some respect."

"Your mama shoulda named you Grace," Cowlick says. He smacks Yankee on the back of the head.

"That's what you get for supporting the Yanks," says Slim.

I return the mop to the kitchen and notice a chicken order sitting on the counter. It can't be mine already. I check the slip: it's mine all right. An uneasy feeling comes over me. "This isn't the same chicken that fell on the floor, is it?" I ask Milos.

He actually blushes. "Is OK. They never know."

"But...that's not sanitary...."

"I wash it and put it on the grill again. Is OK, I say."

"But still...aren't there regulations about this?"

His face turns a shade of purple. "*Just take it*," he snarls, and resumes slicing garlic.

I'm shaken. I hope the heat from the grill has cooked off any harmful bacteria. I carry the plate back out to Yankee.

"Already?" he asks. I nod, my face growing warm. If I say nothing, am I lying? His eyes seem glued to the plate as if trying to figure things out. Then the whites of his eyes grow enormous. "Hey! This is the same chicken, ain't it?"

"The cook tells me it's been washed and re-grilled...," I say.

They seem dumbstruck. Cowlick's eyes cling to mine, and his mouth hangs open so far I can see his tonsils. I stand there, unable to move. Finally Slim says, in wonder, "Well, that's a goddamn shame!"

"I'm sorry," I manage to say.

A man wearing a hat with a feather in the brim is summoning me. "Oh, Miss!...*Miss!*" I gratefully excuse myself.

Yankee doesn't touch the chicken dinner. I keep an eye on him as he carries the plate over to the cash register and stands in line to talk to Jimmy. But just before he gets to the front of the line, a woman in a bright yellow muumuu whines that her ribs aren't cooked enough. At the same time, exhausted grandparents order a banana split for their granddaughter, who's pounding her fists on the table to accompany her rhythmic shrieking. After I ask Stefan to redo the ribs and after I nearly sprain my wrist digging out ice cream for the banana split, Milos slams a fresh plate of chicken on the counter and shoots me a vicious look.

"For your boyfriend," he says.

I rush it out to Yankee. "I'm really sorry," I say again.

"It ain't your fault," he says. "But management needs to clean up their act."

After the men leave, I pocket a five-dollar bill that they left folded under a corner of the sugar dispenser. Quite a generous tip, and one I hardly deserve!

I hope this is the end of the incident. Throughout my shift I cast apprehensive glances at Jimmy. Focused on his accounting, as usual, he pays no attention to me or anyone else. But at three o'clock, as I'm leaving, he motions me over to the counter. I approach with trepidation. Without looking up, he hands me an envelope.

"What's this?" I ask. Payday isn't until Friday.

"It's all there," he says. "Your wages."

"I'm being paid early?"

"Yep. Don't bother coming back tomorrow."

"Am I being fired?"

"Too many waitresses."

"Is it the chicken?" I ask.

"You shouldn't have told him it was the same chicken," he says, still not looking at me.

Fighting back tears of anger, I slip out the door. This very morning when I arrived at work, everything was fine. And suddenly just one unanticipated incident, like a blow from nowhere, changes everything. I expected a dressing down, perhaps. But termination?

Now that I'm fired, I'll be ineligible to draw unemployment. I'll have to go job-hunting again. And obviously, I can't use this job as a reference.

An all too familiar dilemma.

The next morning, Felicia urges me to register for unemployment. I remind her that I've been fired. She stops whisking eggs and asks, "Did Jimmy say that?" As I slice *pan dulce* I try to remember if he used that word. "He may be afraid to fire you for fear you'll rat on him to the health authorities," Felicia says. I wince at the word *rat*. "Oops! Sorry. You know what I mean."

"It's OK," I say. And it is. I'm over my shame about ratting out my fellow workers. I understand my confusion during my grievance hearing, even though I wish I'd thought it through ahead of time and consulted with people first.

Even though I think it's a waste of time, I go down to the unemployment office. But Felicia's advice turns out to be correct: Jimmy has reported a layoff. I qualify for unemployment.

After the first week, as required by the government, I call three companies to see if they have any work. *Currently not hiring*, they tell me. I'm not surprised; this capitalist recession is stubborn. Meanwhile I check the want ads for another part-time waitressing job but again nothing. For the time being, however, my unemployment check is more than enough to live on. My rent is cheap, my lifestyle modest.

Now more than ever, I'm convinced I want to make a change. Jersey City isn't the place for me to sink roots. Except with Felicia and Charlie, I have tenuous emotional ties here, and, besides, Jersey City bores me. Although New York City is close on the map, the barrier of the Hudson River makes it seem far away.

I've been saving money for months and almost have enough to make the move. Should I rent a place on the Lower East Side where apartments are cheaper or look for a rent-controlled lease on the Upper West Side to be closer to Amber and to Columbia? Or should I leave the United States and live in Europe for a while? That idea fascinates me. Then there's always the Peace Corps.

Teaching still has a hold on me. New York City finally needs instructors. "Desperately," the papers say. Especially English-as-a-Second-Language teachers who can speak Spanish. That job has my name on it in capital letters. I would have to get a Master's degree in education while I'm teaching, which would be stressful, but I could do it. I call the school district and leave a message. A man with a slight Puerto Rican accent calls me back and sets up an interview for the following month.

Without informing anyone except Felicia and Charlie, I get rid of excess possessions and finalize my plans to leave Jersey City. Amber has offered to let me stay with her in New York for a few weeks until I get a job. Now it's time to break the news to Cindy. On a sunny Saturday morning I ring the bell to her apartment. Even in jeans and a cable-knit sweater, she looks composed. Does she iron her jeans?

We sit in the study, my chair butted up against her desk—the same desk that Charlie and I used as a backdrop to our hanky-panky at the party over a year ago. Neat piles of leaflets are lined up in rows on the desktop next to an electric typewriter. The study's window looks out on the brick wall of the apartment house next door. To my relief Cindy tells me that Matt's not home; he's in Manhattan at a meeting of the regional collective.

After fixing us some tea, Cindy sits down beneath a Rosa Luxemburg poster, picks up three skeins of different colored yarn and a partially finished sweater, and starts knitting. I sip tea and relate my plans for the future; she listens without expression and then asks, "Will you be working with the Manhattan branch then?" Click, click go the knitting needles.

"I'm not sure," I say.

Her icy blue eyes regard me as she continues to knit without looking at the needles. "I'm not surprised to hear it."

"What's that supposed to mean?" My voice is sharp but I don't care. Little by little they've been shutting me out. I've sensed the undercurrent of disapproval in their lack of enthusiasm toward me. *Oh, hi, Jenny,* they'll say, as if I'm an afterthought. My disciplinary period for *naming names* is drawing to an end, but from what Cindy just said, I'm guessing they've come up with fresh grievances against me. One thorn in their Marxist-Leninist side may be that I haven't yet applied for another job at the *point of production.* And then there's the Miguel thing....

"It means that I expected you'd be leaving us," Cindy says.

"But I didn't say I was leaving."

"I thought—"

"I notice that you've been rather cool toward me," I interrupt. "It's because of Miguel, isn't it?"

A siren passes by in the street below. The sky is overcast now. Snowflakes strike the window in futile blows.

"It's just...well...after the criticisms you had of us...."

I feel the color drain from my face. My eyes trace the red banner and Rosa's white blouse in the poster above Cindy's head. "Criticisms?"

Cindy leans forward, reaches out an arm, then retracts it. "I'm sorry, I thought you knew...."

My voice is lost somewhere in my throat. "Charlie...?" I croak.

"Frankly, I'm surprised you stuck it out with us this long."

A dog barks somewhere. Cindy has resumed her knitting. I'm trying to get this all straight. Charlie wouldn't have told Cindy about our political conversations—but who else could it be?

"How long have you known about my...my *second thoughts?*"

"It's been quite a while since Charlie talked to me."

"But why would he do that?"

"He was worried about you, Jenny. Quite worried."

"If he was worried, then I'm sure he wanted you to explain things to me," I say.

Her eyes narrow and fine lines appear between them. "It didn't seem worth the effort; you'd made up your mind already."

"But I hadn't," I protest. "I just had doubts. There's a difference, you know."

A neighbor's door bangs. Cindy's face sets, like a parent bracing herself against her child's entreaties. "Would it have changed anything, Jenny, if I'd talked to you back then? Wouldn't you still be leaving us?"

Tears cluster in my eyes. "How can you know that?"

She finally stops knitting. "Well, from what Charlie said," she continues with just a slight waver in her voice, "it seemed like you had so many criticisms of our fundamental political line that…." She shifts in her chair and asks with less conviction, "*Would* it have done any good?"

I sigh, feeling defeated. "Probably not in the long run," I concede. After all, if I can't even trust Charlie….

Cindy looks relieved and picks up her knitting again. It strikes me how fearful we are of wrong-doing. Always vigilant. I recall the weekly criticism/self-criticism sessions—everyone on the hot seat—and the faint uneasiness that used to accompany me between meetings. Yet, other members manage to relax and have fun. Look at Charlie! So why do I feel as if I'm in a straitjacket so much of the time?

Cindy changes tack. "But perhaps you'd like to reconsider," she says in a softer tone. "Perhaps I didn't give you the benefit of the doubt. If you've overcome those reservations, the collective embraces you. There's so much to do. We need everyone who agrees with our line."

Even you, Jenny.

Without waiting for my response, Cindy begins to organize my transfer to the New York branch, as if ticking off a checklist. "Of course, the first thing we'll have to do is iron out any remaining differences." *Iron out.* Smooth it all over: no wrinkles, no tension, no contradictions. No meandering off on a diagonal, running wild: unmanageable, fractious, feral. I always reproach myself for my *impulsivity* but now it seems more like *spontaneity*.

The notion of joining the collective in New York fills me with distress. It's inane to think that the revolution will occur within five or even ten years, as I've previously thought. Maybe even *fifty* years won't be enough. And if a socialist society isn't on the near horizon—or even the far one, then why does there need to be such secrecy, strict discipline, and total dedication to the cause? But whenever I've raised even slight doubts about these matters, I've been met with uneasy stares.

My comrades are right about this, though: I am going to desert the proletariat. Some will consider me a turncoat. And I admit it, I'm on the road back to the petite bourgeoisie, where I probably belong. (Whether I ever left is arguable.) I'll be a *professional,* not a proletarian.

"Teaching and night school may take all my time," I mumble, but I realize how feeble that sounds; many comrades hold jobs, go to school, and do collective work, all at once.

Cindy glosses over my remark. "It's possible that the New York branch may determine that teaching is not the best utilization of your skills…." Her voice tapers off as my face probably reflects my revulsion at her words.

I leave Cindy's and walk down Grove Street, considering. Nothing she said could have more effectively driven me away. I'm fed up with a democratic-centralist organization—with its *correct analyses,* its *ideological uniformity,* its promise of a democratic future but its authoritarian present. I don't want my life prescribed anymore. Mao has said, "We think too small, like the frog at the bottom of the well. He thinks the sky is only as big as the top of the well. If he surfaced, he would have an entirely different view."

The mere thought of returning to a factory depresses me: the mind-numbing essence of it, the pretense of being someone I'm not. And Charlie's betrayal is the final nail in the *termination* of my work with the collective.

That doesn't mean I won't continue to fight for a more humane society. I will. Socialism is the only way to block the rampaging hurricane of capitalism, which wounds or destroys everything in its path. And I'll always be grateful for meeting men and women from so many cultures in the factories. The Dominicans who shared their history with me will remain in my heart—and hopefully in my life.

But lately I've also looked back with appreciation on the liberal arts education I received at that little college in Oregon. I wish every factory worker had the opportunity for a higher education. Not just for the job prospects it provides but for how it expands and enriches your mind.

The move to New York will be an unobtrusive way to exit the collective's stage. I don't need a top-down organization. Manhattan offers lots of ways to get engaged: teachers are involved in union and anti-racism campaigns, the Puerto Rican independence struggle is thriving, and low-income housing is a huge issue. As Mao says, "Let a hundred flowers bloom, let a hundred schools of thought contend."

As I leave Cindy's apartment and walk down Grove Street, I suddenly feel—despite Charlie's betrayal and despite the grayness of January—like a fish without a bicycle, a fish who knows how to swim.

I place a Beatles album on the stereo—"Sgt. Pepper's Lonely Hearts Club Band—tie back my hair, and slip a gingham apron over my shirt and jeans. From a bottom cabinet, I extract a cast-iron skillet, then slice onions and add them to the skillet with a splash of oil. Just as I'm about to crush garlic, the doorbell rings. I wipe my hands on my apron and peer through the peephole. My legs suddenly feel shaky. The peephole reveals the fisheye face and foreshortened body of... *Charlie!*

"Please, Jenny, I need to talk to you," Charlie calls. I slide the deadbolt aside and open the squeaky steel door. Snow melts off Charlie's boots onto the floor as he stands in the hall, hands in his parka. His eyes, usually so mischievous, are flat.

"Can I come in?"

Shrugging, I turn my back on him and return to the kitchen.

He closes the door and follows me, halting awkwardly in the threshold.

"Oh, for Pete's sake, sit down," I say, motioning to a chair. At the table, he observes as I crush garlic, toss it into the skillet, and ignite the burner with a match. To escape his gaze and gain time, I duck into the living room and lift the needle from the album, turn off the stereo. "With a Little Help from My Friends" seems maddeningly inappropriate. Back in the kitchen, I avoid his eyes.

"What are you doing here?"

"You didn't show up for leafleting tonight."

"Did you expect me to?" My voice is acidic.

"I was hoping."

I cut some green peppers into long strips, set them aside, pare an eggplant.

"What are you making?" he asks.

"Ratatouille Provencale."

"Oh." Silence. I wait, curious in spite of myself, to see how he'll try to weasel out of this one. Finally he stammers, "Just wanted to say, I hope you don't hold it against me that I talked to Cindy."

I laugh bitterly. "So she told you that she told me that you told her what I told you?" He opens his mouth to respond but I cut him off. "Oh, no, I don't give a damn." I dice the eggplant.

"I knew you'd be pissed," he says.

"Come on, Charlie. Did you think I'd be ecstatic?" I say, looking up from the cutting board, raising my hand for emphasis—the hand with the knife in it. "You thought I needed *fixing?*" Charlie looks at the knife. "You thought Cindy could *set me straight?*" I wave the knife. He looks from the knife to me. "How could you do that to me, Charlie?" I return to chopping eggplant.

"Cindy shouldn't have mentioned it to you. If she hadn't—"

"*If she hadn't?*" My voice shakes with outrage. I wave the knife again. He shrinks back into his chair. "If she hadn't, then what? Would that have justified what you did?"

The knife bangs against the cutting board as I slice zucchini. It occurs to me I could cut off a finger. I open the silverware drawer, take out a mismatched fork and knife, and place them with a thwack on a vinyl placemat. *One* placemat.

"Well," he says, "since she never brought it up with you back then, I don't see why she had to do it now."

"And get you into hot water?"

He hesitates, then mutters, "She did betray my confidence."

"Like you betrayed mine?"

He turns as red as the two tomatoes I'm peeling and quartering. I remove the garlic and onions, and layer them with the other chopped ingredients back into the skillet, adding salt and pepper to each layer. "At least you could have let me know that you'd talked to her, Charlie."

"I was afraid you wouldn't understand."

"That was a good guess. How would you feel if I'd done that to you?"

He seems to consider it. "I was worried about you. I hoped Cindy would clear up some of your confusion. I did it because I love you, Jenny."

That stops me. What does he mean by "love"? As a friend? As a comrade? Romantically? Whatever it is, it's too late for all that. I'll never get past this double-cross.

"When I told you those things, I was thinking out loud, Charlie," I say, leaning against the counter, facing him. "I wanted your opinion. What I said wasn't meant for anyone else's ears. That was obvious." I turn back to the counter, wipe the knife and board, and hang them on the wall.

"But I had an *obligation* to tell Cindy. You know we don't keep secrets from the collective."

I sigh. "That explains it all, doesn't it?" Wiping the counter furiously, I say, "We don't have private lives and for damn sure we never dissent." The next-door neighbor's kid bangs into the wall and wails.

"You make it sound so harsh," he says. "There are reasons for not having secrets, you know."

"But, Charlie," I say, facing him. "When you told Cindy those things, what did you suppose she'd think? She'd think I was attacking the collective."

"No!" he says forcefully. "I'm sure she didn't think that." There's silence. I wait for him to explain what she *did* think. The gas heater hums. "She probably thought you were confused," he says. He raises his chin defensively. "Which you were."

"If she thought I was confused, why didn't she try to help me?"

"I don't know." He throws up his hands. "I don't get it."

"It's not so difficult to grasp, Charlie."

"What do you mean?"

"She thought I was violating *democratic centralism*."

"How?"

"Because everyone's supposed to follow the line that's agreed upon," I say. "Criticism debilitates, they think; it undermines."

"But we criticize things all the time."

"That's true, we do. But only *afterward.*"

"But you know there's a good reason for that, Jenny. If we're always sniping at everything we disagree with, how will we ever know if it's working or not? That's why we wait until we've given it the best chance to succeed before we evaluate it."

"Exactly! It makes sense, doesn't it? But I don't want that anymore. I need to discuss issues while they're red-hot. I don't want to be muzzled."

He looks stricken. "Oh."

I take a carton of lemonade from the refrigerator, pour myself a glass, and sit down across from him. He's staring at the table and his face is red, but I hardly notice.

"I wasn't confused, Charlie," I say, my voice grim. "I just had a different opinion and a different way of approaching it."

"All I wanted to do was help," he says plaintively. His eyes look past me and out the window. "Oh, my God," he mumbles.

"What have I done?" I watch layers of emotion like a light show cross his face.

I don't care what he's going through; *I'm* the one who's wronged. "Please leave," I say.

He stands up. The melted snow from his boots has dripped onto the linoleum. He regards the wet spots. "Sorry about that," he says. He tears off a paper towel, bends and reaches toward the puddles.

"Oh, don't," I say, snatching the towel from his hand. "Just go."

He leaves the apartment as if in a trance, and I hear his footsteps slogging down the steps. I close the door and stand there, observing the puddles on the floor.

20. Jenny
MARCH 1976

I'VE GRADUALLY CURTAILED MY WORK WITH the collective. After I give notice to my landlord, I have to be out in less than a month. By April Fool's Day. I hope it's not a bad omen, I say laughingly to Felicia. I realize how much I'll miss living in the same building, our breakfasts, the *chisme* (gossip), even the hysterical midnight crises.

Thoughts of Charlie keep crowding out other thoughts. I can't rid myself of our last conversation. The more I put myself into his snow boots, the less righteous I feel. After all, what he did is not as bad as my ratting out my fellow workers at my grievance hearing. I didn't intend to harm anyone, but neither did he.

I decide to believe that he meant what he said: he wanted to help me. It's just that his view of the collective is so different from mine; he accepts things I can't. I think he's bought the collective's line in its totality. As I did for many years.

But I've changed.

If I can change, why can't he? After all, he's even younger than I am. But *will* he change? And will he change in the direction of thinking more critically? That's the question. I recall the look on his face—stricken—as if he realized something terrible.

What was it that he realized?

At the very least I need to talk to him again.

On Saturday afternoon the New Jersey collective throws a farewell party for me at Felicia's. There are sugar cookies with red stars on them, and popcorn, and a sloping chocolate cake that Bonnie made, with purple frosting and the words *Buena Suerte, Yenny Manzana!*—Good luck, Jenny Apple—in white letters that are melting on the edges. There's even grape Kool-Aid, which some-one has spiked with vodka. Apparently the collective has loosened up for the occasion.

Everyone shows up except Miguel. After we broke up, Miguel went AWOL from the collective, as he went AWOL from me so many times. Felicia, who's kept tabs on him through mutual friends, informed me that he isn't involved in anything political. Whether he's involved in anything personal, though, I don't ask nor does she reveal.

There's chatting, laughing, teasing. I realize with surprise that I'll miss them all. Perhaps it's like an amicable divorce: we realize we can't stay together but we still like each other. Charlie is con-versing with Sergio on the sofa. A bust of Juan Bosch on the coffee table partially obscures my view of him. I feel anxious; before the party ends, I need to talk to him, yet I fear his reaction.

After a while, I see Charlie head toward the bathroom so I wait in the hallway until he emerges. "We need to talk," I say, and before he can react, I grab his arm and steer him into Felicia's bedroom.

I push aside a red purse and sit on the bed, which almost fills the room. "Please, sit down," I say, patting the bedspread. "This will just take a minute." Charlie perches on the edge of the bed. Perdido jumps up, his tail arched, and steps gingerly onto Charlie's lap. Charlie strokes him, and Perdido circles twice and stretches out across Charlie's legs.

I sit on the other end of the bed so as not to give any false impressions. "I'm sorry, Charlie," I say. "I was so angry the other night that I couldn't really think this through. I know you had good intentions."

"It's OK. You don't need to apologize. I'm the one who's to blame."

"No, Charlie, no one's to blame. You were trying to help me. You're a good friend. I appreciate that."

There's a knock at the door and Sergio pokes his nose in. "Oh! Sorry," he says and leaves, pulling the door shut behind him. I slide the bolt in the lock.

"I feel so rotten about what I did to you," Charlie says. "And you know what's weird? I can't even remember anymore how I thought I could help you by talking to Cindy. I mean, what was I hoping for? How could I be so stupid?"

Perdido jumps off Charlie's lap and onto mine. I gently place him on the floor. Bonnie shouts from the hallway, "Where's the guest of honor?" She rattles the doorknob. "Yummy yummy! Cake and ice cream! Don't be left out!"

"Just a minute," I call. "I'll be right there." I turn back to Charlie. "It's OK," I say. "I *was* violating democratic centralism just by talking to you."

"But that's no excuse," he says. "I was violating your trust. I'll never forgive myself."

Another knock. "Hey, you two." It's Roger's voice. "What's going on in there?"

"Coming!" I yell. I stand up and take Charlie's hand. "You're too hard on yourself, Charlie. Look, we each did what we were convinced was best." I pull him up. "We should get back out there." He nods.

I look at him, then hug him. He returns my hug, so I hug him harder as if to squeeze out any lingering resentment. I find it difficult to let go.

As I open the door, a blast of music confronts us, along with exuberant conversation, inspired by wine, beer, and purple vodka-Kool-Aid. Charlie wipes the back of his hand across his eyes.

"There you are," someone shouts. Applause and cheers.

"Shame on you, Charlie, for keeping her away from the party," Sergio says. Uproarious laughter, whistles, hoots.

After cake and ice cream, one by one they approach me.

Bonnie, wearing a Mao t-shirt, says, "Let's get together in New York for sure, go see a play."

Esme and Sergio promise to invite me over for dinner "real soon."

Roger, who looks more like a blue-collar worker than all the rest of us put together, gives me a hug and says, "Don't be a stranger." He laughs. "And fuck the bosses!"

I laugh back. "You give 'em hell, Roger."

Matt stands stiffly by the coffee table and says nothing, but he sends me a sidelong glance, nods, and gives me a thumbs-up. Quite an offering from Matt, I think, smiling and feeling a burst of warmth for even him.

Kate says, "Sometimes you got to listen to your own drummer" and gives me a fist bump. At least there's *that* from Kate.

Even Cynthia allots me a stiff hug with a few pats on the back, then firmly grips my shoulders and says, "Remember, you can still change your mind and join the Brooklyn collective, you hear?"

I want to cry but Felicia has put "No Woman No Cry" on the stereo. "I won't cry, then, I'll laugh instead," I tell them. And I do, and so do they. As Sergio hugs me, my eyes seek out Charlie. He's leaning against the wall across the room under the Che poster, studying me, on his lips a cryptic smile. I can't escape the notion that after the party something very intriguing is going to happen.

Kitty Kroger is a retired English as a Second Language teacher who lives in Los Angeles. This is her debut novel.